CHAPTER 1

A presence at the top of the world

Jed flitted in and out of perceptive reasoning, conversing with his alter ego in a faint and emotional soliloquy.

"Why couldn't any of you make it this far? You were so close!"

He sighed quietly but with some volume, sending jets of breath into an icy atmosphere, simultaneously stamping about, in frustration...

"After all that effort we put in, you don't even get to see this amazing view and I end up talking to myself about it!"

He continued to express his exasperation and mostly everything else to the cosmos in wheezing gasps, whilst sliding about on loose summit rubble and indiscriminate slopes. It was as though he could communicate with his absent party somehow, through the ethers. There was comfort provided by vocalising as such, as well as a sort of pride expressed via his commentary, regarding such an achievement. Euphoria was certainly significant amongst his emotions. Nevertheless, a personal dialogue was now his only sense of contact with the world, so far below, and he continued to fashion it, whilst fighting to stay fully alert in a weak and wearying atmosphere.

"Feels like it's 'here I am' but I'm actually not! If that makes any sense? If this is real though, I'll need to book a confession with Father Murphy for leaving you all and the camera. All we'll ever have to take from this mammoth crusade, is my recollections and rubbish powers of description. Even my phone's frozen-up and given up the ghost!"

Jed had found that his smart phone was not so smart in cold temperatures and had shut itself down. Now he had no device to record anything of the culmination of months of preparation. He was babbling fairly randomly now...

"Am I in heaven or, as Fr Murphy described something the other day, Dante's Hell? Either way bruv, Father Smurph, Miguel and that special girl with the palindromic Christian name... I really wish you could all be here, sharing this. All those efforts to get each other here in five pieces, but it's only me at the end of it. Crazy! Gutted for what you're all missing. It's like granddad's favourite poem about that rare desert flower... so amazing, and betraying the laws of nature, to grow anything like near where it did, in a dry desert, never seen by anyone and wasted all its beauty out there, where no-one ever saw it. How often might that have happened? So here I am today, right now, seven kilometres up in the sky, seeing this on my own. You'll never know! I suppose I must sound emotional, but I guess it's not just the sights and sounds. It's also all those times we talked about this in the pub and at home around the dinner table with Father Murphy, and the fact that, with all the build-up to get here, I'm out here on my own. It feels kind of ironic. So amazing, but pretty sad. Hope you're all OK back there."

Dazzling wisps of crystal cirrus, blazed over a wash of deeply shaded sapphire. So close to the troposphere's ceiling, their vivid, streaking edges caught crimson fire from a glorious, golden star. Feathered orange and pink streamers merged into rainbows before deep-shaded sky. Jed pondered numbly; his breath continuing to launch into a freeze, heading upwards, as though from a steaming kettle. The atmosphere, rendered so painfully thin, left even his strong heart pounding and muscles limply throbbing. He wavered and swayed uncharacteristically. Candid brilliance spared nothing for his narrowing eyes, whilst merciless vents of noxious gas billowed thickly across his countenance, afflicting tear ducts, and depriving further his struggling inhalations, amidst sulphurous odours reminiscent of school days in a chemistry lab. At the mouths of fumaroles, millennia of sulphurous discharge had drenched and tainted icy igneous rocks with putrid, greeny-turquoise taints. Icing-sugar flecked sharp edges of the crater rim. Once a powerful volcano ventured so far above any merits of breathable reason, that cold-blooded crystals had advanced, in insipid hues, like a mottled coat of chemical armour over a table-top of human limits.

Jed had arrived, excessively fit, for one who had come so far through so much adversity, though he was still nowhere near acclimatised. His live commentary continued, but now he addressed himself...

2

A CLOSENESS OF PLACE

MARTIN POWER

authorHOUSE®

AuthorHouse™ UK
1663 Liberty Drive
Bloomington, IN 47403 USA
www.authorhouse.co.uk
Phone: UK TFN: 0800 0148641 (Toll Free inside the UK)
        UK Local: (02) 0369 56322 (+44 20 3695 6322 from outside the UK)

Published by AuthorHouse 06/29/2022

ISBN: 978-1-6655-9974-0 (sc)
ISBN: 978-1-6655-9976-4 (hc)
ISBN: 978-1-6655-9975-7 (e)

PROLOGUE QUOTE

'One who hunts everywhere for that which is hidden should also search time'

Martin Power 2021

CONTENTS

"I have to stop imagining I have a recording device. If my phone hadn't frozen to an ice-block, there'd still be no signal up here. Maybe some aliens will hear me first? Feels like all of space and time could intercept my airwaves up here before anyone else below. Hope you all get them on a rebound somewhere, somehow."

He paused for a moment, distracted.

"Hang on!"

Jed felt something unusual, behind him, in the space and shadow of his peripheral vision.

"What's happening?"

"Oh G...!"

Gasping for breath and swallowing, still vocalising his thoughts and feelings, whilst dazed and bedazzled with altitude and brilliance, he mused...

"I definitely thought I was alone. Actually, I really wish you *were* all here right now. I don't know what the hell's going on."

He emitted a fairly lame but troubled exclamation of...

"HELP!"

...then made as rapid a 'three-sixty' as he could manage amongst precarious conditions, but detected nothing of note; only perhaps, a slight blur, which might have been something from a fumarole or part of a mirage...

"This isn't just the effects of altitude is it? There's someone else here. I don't get it."

Jed sensed something, seemingly like a whisper, inside him. It was utterly inexplicable. Uncharted facts, fresh memories and concepts seemed to be pouring into his mind. He reasoned in ways he had never known. There were no means to interpret his experience. None of his wits could explain what was happening. He fell into a fearful silence and stood, confused, with limpness in his body; his feet involuntarily crunching small stones against a bed of larger rocks. Something powerful was manifesting itself inside him. It was an astonishing infringement of unknown process and immeasurable emotion. He stood still, receiving what felt like far more than just a psychic communication. Nothing inside him could put this into perspective.

CHAPTER 2

Roots in sleepy flatlands

The Carvey family's household, which was frankly named *'Carveys' Cottage'* sat dwarfed between two hefty English trees; so large, they occasionally seemed to enjoy their own weather. Its estates existed somewhere amidst a colossal cabbage patch in The Far East of The Midlands. It was a place of sky, as much as land, flat beyond all of its horizons, gifting whosoever ventured upon its fertile farmland, a magnificent spread of pastoral heaven. Although it was labelled a 'cottage', the Carvey residence was ample, with two floors and a reasonably roomy cellar. At over two hundred years old, it was something of a historic building.

Jed's slanting, thick-glassed bedroom window, which yielded a view to the rear of Carvey's Cottage, framed quite a panorama, when one glanced out from a low height within his room. As a typical bumpkin, appreciative of his own rural surroundings, Jed used to love lying on his bed, gazing up through an ancient, but fairly large, blotchy-glazed window, which, with its approximate forty-five degree slope, was both a look-out and a skylight. Through it, he was a witness to a brand-new skyscape every morning upon awakening, and every evening when he returned home from college, where he had recently commenced his second year of a Business Degree course. Mental exhaustion resulting from extensive periods of inactivity and intensive note-taking would generally render him useless for a while upon his return, until an appropriate action was usually to flop down upon his soft quilted bed and gaze up adoringly, towards whatever sky might be currently imposing itself though his bedroom portal. The atmosphere could sometimes resemble an ocean of islands with misty peaks, distant shores and pretty much, themed-clouds, slowly progressing across everything else. They might all look like sheep, tee-shirts, jumpers on a line, or something else a mind might conceive as some sort of personification. Also, those giant trees, could sometimes seem to have a life of their own, around twilight, performing scary, swaying dances or inexplicable, dark shapes which could spook Jed into burying himself under safer covers, before his natural bedtime. Gawping at the firmament, though, generally fuelled young Jed with dreams, although they did not tend to be ones of escapism, involving world travel. He was, perhaps oddly, for one at such an age when discovery might have rated high in a list of personal ambition, rather comfortable inside what was certainly a somewhat remote and restricted community. It was, when all was declared and weighed-up, all he had ever known. His thoughts tended to angle more towards outer limits of the mind, rather than directions pursuing what might be, to him, terrestrial extremities such as Australia or Hawaii. He would often fantasize about possibilities beyond those parameters of his working life, which he regularly expressed and regarded as something of a monotonous ordeal, than of adventures abroad or swimming with dolphins.

After a fun-filled day, as Jed would often describe it, with a very high level of sarcasm, he would recover first, eat second, then thirdly, depending upon the time of year and another possible option, do what many students of his age do so well... turn up for a pint or two, but seldom three, at The White Rabbit, about half a mile down the road. Such proximity meant that no-one had to battle with regard to whose turn it might have been to drive. In fairness, the third, optional exploit happened at all times of year. It was just that, during the longer summer days, it may, occasionally, have been pushed into fourth place, behind a walk in his local outback. This would very often involve getting bitten by tiny insects (once or twice by a *large* one), being scarred for the next few days by a few rogue thorns in the thicket, getting waterlogged feet, whilst trying to cross a slopping, wet ditch, developing burning rashes and stings from the local flora, and falling headlong, on occasion, as a result of a hidden bramble shoot ('nature's trip-wires' as Jed called them) into even more of the same things that had tripped him. However, all of this would certainly confirm to Jed that he had been for a walk in a *real*, and not *virtual* world; something which was very important to him in all aspects of life.

Despite having never dwelt in suburbia, Jed was always somewhat satisfied by the thought that nature had caressed him with its *friendliness*, and was very used to the scars. His slightly elder brother, Joe, was never keen to accompany him. The endurance factor was too great. It also held-up going to the pub, and disturbed his continual efforts to reach a certain top score on his phone, to which he was invisibly glued, so Jed would keep himself company on these walks (or *scrambles*) by conversing with himself, embarrassingly loudly. True it was only the birds and field creatures who would hear him, but it was a spectacle to behold, as Jed took on a full debate about anything that had traversed his path, that day. He would often unleash some of this discussion at the pub. He was also fairly open with his family, about talking to himself, although they never seemed convinced that this wasn't a distinguishing trait of madness, despite the fact that Jed had, distinctly heard all of them, on a reasonable amount of occasions, conversing with their own alter egos.

The subject of chatting to one's own persona, became a discussion at the local, more than once. It might have seemed as though Jed was needing to convince himself that he wasn't heading round a bend. He would argue that addressing oneself or sounding out one's thoughts, as he put it poshly, was perfectly rational and acceptable as long as one *was* alone. It was only when *one* self-indulged in front of *other* people that *one* might be regarded as being a few notches below a locally accepted level of sanity. He would then proceed to back this up, using song lyrics which recommended freedom of personal expression. Whether he had written this libretto himself, no one was quite sure. The band name was also very suspect. However, all of this provided Jed with some soundness of mind and a reassurance that he might continue these individual, vocal debates in future.

To behold, Jed was, in ungenerous fairness, a skinny youth. He would often be witnessed, preparing himself a liberally-filled marmalade or banana butty, and appeared to consume rather a large amount of what could not be regarded purely as sustenance due to its significant regularity, which deeply irritated his tight-fisted banker parents. It was, in truth, an obsession with marmalade and banana sandwiches, coupled with the fact that Jed had far too much time, on an evening or weekend, to think about food. However, the fact that he consumed as much as a young gorilla, seemed to add little to his physique, unless, as his father had conjectured, the food was going straight down to his large feet.

Jed had the trademark Carvey nose, which was slightly like a beak. His mousy, brown hair seemed to will itself to wrap around the sides of his face despite its straightness. His parents had threatened him, on many occasions with a short back and sides, but Jed had stood strong and allowed it to reach his shoulders on several occasions. He had been weaned on rock music from the nineteen seventies and eighties and had formed a physical appearance with regards to the type of people associated with it. It seemed that everything in his wardrobe was black. A few of his tee-shirts bore names and logos of satanic bands, such as 'Dead People' and 'Skeleton Skratch'.

Mr and Mrs Carvey, whose first names, Adam and Edie, almost rang a biblical bell, had lived in the same home now, together, for over thirty years. Their cottage had been a Carvey residence since before Victorian times, when it was built. Mr Carvey, himself, had lived there with his family twenty-one years before he invited Edie to co-inhabit, whilst working alongside her as a clerk at the same bank. They had drawn-up a cunning plan to move in with Adam's mother, who had been, rather unfortunately and prematurely, widowed nearly two decades before that. They mused that she would be more than grateful to enjoy their company, out there in the sticks. Should Adam have left home to reside with his new spouse, he would have plunged her into a desolate life as a hermit. If only their intentions had been so completely unselfish and not tainted with the notion that they would be saving money on what would otherwise be a free house to live in, whilst also hoping to inherit it! It was a blessing for Adam's mother, however, that their financial motives were always obvious. She had brought him up well, or so she thought, as a single parent, and saw right through these intentions. Despite this, she was more than happy to enjoy the company of her son and his wife instead of a bitter alternative, and was proud of the fact that he had remembered to keep his financial thinking cap on, as far as important matters of housing were concerned. Not only this, but she would also benefit from their affluence as bankers, as well as being comforted too, that their precious family cottage would remain the property of a Carvey, for a bit longer. Wretchedly, she developed an unfortunate illness and passed away within a year of her son and spouse moving in. Mr Carvey liked to think that the spirit of his mother, as well as all the Carvey's, were at peace and close-by in their house which had seen a century and a half of his family's historical evolution.

Mr Carvey had attained a medium height and was fairly stocky, with a little excess around the midriff and slightly balding head. His son, Joe, seemed to have inherited something of his physique and would, surely, go on to abuse biscuits and cake, as he had done, and fall foul of the same middle-aged developments. Jed, on the other hand was more like his mother to behold, with a slender physique and, pretty much mostly, an ability to avoid the compulsions that his father had, apparently, passed on to Joe, apart from those banana and marmalade butties, of course, which he did often succumb to. In the grand scheme of things, he did seem to eat a lot more of the right things, as well as add that magic counteraction into his habitual movements; exercise! It may well have been the absence of such a discipline within the rest of his family's lifestyles which, possibly largely unrealised, caused them to marvel at his uncanny slenderness. Jed's mother, however, though similarly slighter and also fair in complexion, had a secret penchant for crisps and tried to keep it a secret. This was very difficult with a husband who kept a count on absolutely everything and frequently accused one or another of his family members of nicking items of food. He had a set way of wording many things. For this he used language such as...

"Someone has been partaking of unofficial sustenance".

There would then follow a short but firm investigation, during which he would enjoy the practicing of, what he regarded as, very useful detective skills upon his hapless family, interrogating them each in turn with some measure of aggression and precision. To be found guilty, would mean the suffering of a harsh penalty from which he, himself, would usually benefit. Mr Carvey was calculated and utterly self-motivated in his administering of discipline. Of course, he would never have pilfered any items of unregistered food himself! These callous enquiries were delivered with a dry sense of humour yet not always appreciated by his family in that respect. He would, first, dress in an old school robe from his grammar school days and place a wig on his head, which had once served a rather less fortunate purpose. Now, in Mr Carvey's perception, was the view that it may as well be put to a more affable employment. He would adorn himself in secret, upstairs, before descending down the plain, grey, stone staircase towards an unsuspecting family, who tended to congregate in the living room, most often generating very little sound. It was a good job he had stealth on his side. He would enter completely silently in his high court judge costume and deliver a single, stern phrase such as...

"Obviously the fact that I'm once again inside this disguise, means that another transgression has occurred and someone must pay the price".

Whatever the introduction, it would always be met with a mighty wave of disapproval. It may, sometimes, disturb a television program. More often than not though, it would be two peoples' novels and one person's phone-gaming activities being interrupted. One way or another, they would all be unsympathetically informed that none of their activities were important enough to defer the enquiry. Thus they had obvious reasons for not being enthused. Mr Carvey, on the other hand, would lap up every minute of his cavorting. Within the emptiness of a highly humdrum life, this roleplay was one of the few bits of fun, he ever enjoyed. During the investigations, Mrs Carvey would often fall silent and let her husband 'get on with it' whilst musing upon something more useful. In her estimation, this was part of his effort, to nurture discipline within the boys via, what he considered to be, humorous masquerades. She ignored the jibes and concentrated on other things.

Mrs Carvey was, above all, a fairly gentle soul. This was not down to any weakness or submissiveness, rather a cool and calculating brain, suited to dealing with numbers, but also mundane situations. There were many of both in her life. Indeed, her marriage to Adam seemed a match made in heaven, though perhaps more realistically, a bank. Their private conversations were most often material and practical. If a dream life was like running or flying over rich, exotic landscapes, or through impressive, stimulating cities, theirs was a pedestrian walk through a dull, sanitised, inner city area of recreation. They dreamed of wealth and status, never travel and discovery. They talked of financial possibilities and parallels between themselves and esteemed people. They filled their final, precious daily bedtime moments with thoughts of alternative mortgages, favourable interest rates and cleverly-tweaked tax rebates. If they had ever needed contraception, their conversations might have provided it. As it was, however, they had two wonderful sons in the forms of Joe and Jed. Unlike many couples in their situation, they had not striven for a girl. According to bankers, fifty-fifty odds were not good ones and unworthy of a bet. They had also been advised by Edie's mother, who along with her father, had passed away in the same year just a handful of years before, that the second son, upon the birth of a daughter, would often reason, whether accurately or incorrectly that their parents had been hoping for a girl. To add to this legacy of family nurture, Adam's mother had once stated, some time ago in the history before he was even married, that to have more than two children would inadvisably bump-up the population of the world and, one day, cause everyone to begin to struggle. It may just have been a cloudy awareness of these past thoughts which had terminated their attempts at procreation, long ago.

The Carveys' two sons were now pretty much grown-up, although Jed, who was almost unnaturally wise for one of just nineteen years of age and certainly a lot wiser than his elder brother, had once exclaimed that...

"One does not actually grow up. Rather, one is born into a single journey which ends at death. We are always developing"

... or words to that effect. Adam and Edie had never looked back and were most proud of their boys. Who to worry about the most was a quandary. Joe was currently *in between* girlfriends, as he liked to put it, but Jed had never found a soul mate of any description, whatever his leaning in life. Jed had his head in the air but was upwardly mobile and heading in the right direction, in their respective opinions, at a college of economics. Joe had his feet on the ground but was travelling nowhere fast. He was content to be where he was in life, hold down a simple job, sprint home each evening as fast as possible and put his feet up for as long as he could. At completely the opposite end of the human profile, Jed was never happy to experience any aspect of his life without questioning it, and learning something new. He would not rest until all stones were unturned and all new paths made clear. He and Joe were blood brothers yet, mentally, as about as unrelated as chalk and cheese. As the science goes, like poles attract. Perhaps this was some of the reason why the two youths got on pretty well, most of the time. Perhaps also, despite the broad, creative universe that was Jed's mind, the rest of his family could still relate to him, *almost* as well as one another. They would commune together at the pub, ride a bus out to the nearest town in the same vehicle to shop, and attend their local church every Sunday as a family unit. Jed would relish his family's company and tag along, as long as it wasn't Joe's turn to drive.

Their polished shoes squelched through rotting November leaves as they approached a large, glass door, in the side of St Joseph's Roman Catholic Church, on one particular Sunday morning. Weak sunshine barely permeated a watery, grey firmament and did little to improve the sight of what was, realistically, a pretty ghastly edifice. St Joseph's was an eyesore, even on the most generously, sparkling, summer's day. It was a modern building, possibly thrown-up in a rush, from a giant flatpack, and resembled something between a modern council house and a prefabricated classroom. After pausing for a few moments to allow an elderly lady with a Zimmer frame to enter, they blessed themselves with holy water and progressed towards some hardwood benches, about which people sometimes proclaimed, it was usually a relief to kneel down at the appropriate time after enduring them for long enough. Today however, they were greeted en route by a close family friend, Father Murphy, a fairly hearty-looking, gracefully greying, late middle-aged gentleman, who seemed to possess more energy and zest for life, than most men of his age.

He shook each of their hands with a simultaneous, self-humbling nod of the head and a calming, quiet, Southern Irish voice, repeating...

"Hello Mrs Carvey. Lovely to see you... Hello Mr Carvey..."

and so on.

"I take it you're not on the altar this morning?"

...inquired Mrs Carvey

"No not I... oh no... indeed..."

He employed a sort of nervous laugh as though what he was saying was funny...

"It's Father John this morning"

Jed and Joe eyeballed one another with grimaces. Father John was a very serious and often uptight individual who would find fault with his congregation for talking in the church before a service. He had quoted a passage from The Bible about Jesus knocking over stalls which had been set-up for commerce, in a place of worship, numerous times, cheesing people off before he'd even started. His aim was simply to appeal to their better natures to enter the church quietly and respectfully, not as though they were in a Persian market. However, his provocative efforts did not seem to match his good intentions. He also, always made the same, single joke at the end about not praying for the outcome of football. It was clear *he* never had, as his favourite team sucked. Always the same handful of individuals laughed at this repeated effort, though perhaps, out of charity. Whilst Fr Murphy himself had once preached that the word of God was not entertainment, he had always made services interesting, via careful and impassioned use of vocal expression and humour. He would explain meanings of texts, which might, otherwise, be mindlessly repeated, week after week. How often would one simply be thinking about what they were having for dinner or how funny someone's hair looked, instead of pondering on what they were uttering, supposedly as a prayer? He certainly managed to make his flock smile. There were snide comments about being tight-fisted with the collection, funny stories about what some people had actually put in their envelopes as a donation, anecdotes about drunken Catholics, jokes about going to hell or heaven and teasing St Peter on the way up. One way or lots of others, Father Murphy had truly won the hearts of his congregation through warmth and character. He had also put his money where his mouth was, practicing what he preached, in that he would urge people to follow good examples from the scripture and emulate Jesus by treating one another as one might like to be treated, themselves. He would visit elderly and sick people, in his parish, pop round to their houses to check everything was fine; even help them with their shopping. Fr Murphy's life was an example to everybody.

In truth, Fr Murphy did not usually meet and greet his parishioners when conducting the service himself. Part of this was a result of personal nerves before the delivery. After years of experience, he had concluded, perhaps unconsciously within himself, that *no nerves* meant one had possibly not put enough effort into their program and was not amply anxious about its success. On his Sundays off, however, he felt there was a need to subtly calm-down those who might be, simultaneously, entering and socialising. Anything to save them from the wrath of his compatriot. Fr Murphy was 'The Parish Priest', higher up a chain of office than his colleague, John, yet was often his victim, at times. Calming the church was, therefore, also a personal defence mechanism, helping to maintain peaceful relations with Fr John.

Services seldom passed without incident. Those who chose to enjoy the ironies of humour amidst stern mishap would not be likely to forget the time that Fr Murphy had struggled to release the ciborium lid, but persevered, until it shot off and smacked into an unfortunate family on the front row. Through the clattering, complaining and jostling, Jed had heard Fr Murphy say 'sorry' fourteen times amidst his embarrassment at a point in the mass which was supposed to be particularly spiritual. Most incidents were not this profound but it did seem that there was always something to talk about at the pub, afterwards, though it was largely Jed or his brother who would bring it up. Their parents would politely ignore anything untoward and would seldom be interested in what their sons had dragged-up.

That particular morning however, it might have seemed that the Carveys themselves, were a talking point. It was not just the Blessed Trinity that came in triplicate. According to Jed there were three reasons, that morning, why he might be ashamed to be a Carvey. The first was his brother, Joe. It might have seemed understandable for him to play on his phone during what was a particularly dreary and harshly-driven sermon by Fr John; all about how heaven was not actually in the sky and how people shouldn't keep looking up when they prayed to God as he wasn't up there. Jed whispered anxiously to his brother...

"You can't pray with that, you know. Put it away, bruv."

...Joe was playing some game with pink dragons floating about and trying to shoot them. Whilst this all took place inside his coat, the physical lurches were causing immense embarrassment to Jed who knew that people behind weren't stupid.

A second cause of Jed's discomfort, was his mother, who mistimed the Responsorial Psalm, which on that day was 'God goes up with shouts of joy. The Lord goes up with trumpet blast'. She had always attempted to place extra expression into the dialogues of a service. Perhaps it made her feel as though she was being more holy. One way or another, she expressed for a bit longer than she ought, placing the final word, 'blast' some moments after everyone else. inevitably, some heads turned to judge what might have sounded like a spot of blasphemy.

There was more. This time it concerned the sense of smell. Mr Carvey was a country man who liked his vegetables. He had a fairly unusual penchant for spring onions and would demolish several at breakfast time. This might well have been one of the reasons that the Carveys all ate separately in a morning. He devoured them like chocolates. Edie was fairly understanding. She had frequent cravings for beetroot. This morning, during the hymn, 'Bind us together Lord', he suffered a deep bout of indigestion, which was stifled fairly competently under his breath. He may have suffered minor distress during this flurry, though not as much as a handful of other people around him! By the end of the hymn, his family had subtly shunted themselves, closer to the ends of the pew, leaving him somewhat isolated in the middle. Heaven knows what the poor people in front, most who were unable to move, were experiencing. The final 'Thanks be to God' was a most heartfelt occasion. Jed was outside before the priest had finished processing. The final hymn, 'Go the mass is ended,' was a message too late.

It would be untrue to say that Jed did not see the value or appreciate the meanings of ceremonies like these, although he saw beyond dogma, repetition, and the strange, almost forced behaviour of some who attended his church. He believed that the universe could not be an accident and didn't understand why scientists often ruled out the possibility of God. How could everything he saw, have arrived by itself? To Jed, it seemed that the human race would always fall short of understanding the limits of the cosmos, the depths of time or the existence of a supreme being. The big questions would probably always remain as questions. A scientific hypothesis would always rely on proof and begin with an idea or assertion based on experiences, gut reactions, the mind or the heart. Faith would always be an element until everything, everywhere was understood. Jed had a very deeply inquisitive mind and could also be very scientific. Maths, Physics, Chemistry and Philosophy had assisted him at school, helping to spark his thinking into eternal propulsion, but as far as he delved, he could always, somehow, maintain a reasoning for God, and took it on faith.

Jed was a complex young man, almost a fish out of water in his simple, rural life, and largely undervalued. His parents could not possibly understand, in their strivings towards conventional, material goals, the depths to which their son was mining, within his everyday reasoning. There was but one individual who might have been beginning to appreciate him more fully. Fr Murphy would have to be the one who recognised the true being within, and lead him along a more suitable path.

CHAPTER 3

The Ss'iyn

An age-old river etched deeper into its rocky bed, far below resistant structures that now towered a huge distance above it. It was a frothing torrent; a silver ribbon, way down, inside the history it had carved. Once there had been a broad and sluggish body of water meandering in ample, patient curves about the plains. Now it raged like an unstoppable, snaking spirit upon an impetuous line through the rocks it had engraved.

Across plains, to the east, rose a range of dry, dusty mountains, worn and cracked over eons and left to bake in desert heat. To the west, a wall of fresh, alpine peaks, much greater in stature, faded into the troposphere, jagged, and painted aloft with winter glass. From these younger moulds came raging torrents that poured relentlessly into the canyon side via a series of spectacular cascades. From some angles, they created an impressive system of rainbows arching fabulously from voluminous clouds of spray.

Out on the plains, heat was usually unremitting. All was dusty and arid. Fleshy shrubs and coarse grasses survived, however, storing moisture within their, sometimes, gargantuan bulk. Withering conditions brought much of life's spectrum to the water supply. Herds of leathery, titan beasts with protracted, snake-like necks, bathed in safe numbers en route to distant forests. Monster flies with hard-beating wings and powerful, grasping jaws sought larvae, smaller insects and even tiny, glinting fish in life-giving, yet bloodthirsty waters, and thunderous, mammoth birds cooled their mighty frames through repeated plunges into mists of spray rising from the ravine.

Colossal precipices formed the canyon walls, thematically decorated with multiple pigments, ranging from red, sandy rock to cream and black strata. All was coated in a varnish of eternally permeating moisture and mottled with dark patches and shadowed lines. If one looked more closely, they might have observed that some of the patches were caves, formed from lava tubes, where molten streams had forged underground through soft clay, emerging into the canyon. This had left a labyrinth of passageways and holes in the walls of the ravine. Those shadowy lines were ledges which, by geological coincidence, connected many of the cave mouths externally. These were created by the sheering of vast slabs of rock falling away from cliffs, and by eons of erosion, brought about by extremes of heating and cooling or soaking and drying. This grand tale of history was visible from the plains, above, all the way down to the torrents at the curvaceous base of the ravine. If you looked even more closely, and exactly in the right place, you might just spot a Ss'iyn.

They were an exceedingly small race of sophisticated individuals; primarily reptilian and dominantly viridescent, though their green shades were subtly variegated. In the mouths of caves and dark ledges, their bodies seemed to graduate through jade and emerald. When caught in a bright sunray, an oily-looking, turquoise stripe could, sometimes, splash across their scales. Extra luminance might also reveal vermillion tints around their feet. Their scaly exteriors were highly glossy and reflective. In certain light conditions, a Ss'iyn might appear virtually invisible, or at least fool the eye into believing they were witnessing some kind of apparition. They stood upon two slender limbs but had used their upper extenders for so long, within a hugely lengthy evolution, that these were well-developed with thoroughly independent digits on sensitive-looking palms; great for climbing and clutching. Multiple bones in the skull had, long since, melded without a need to expand jaw size. Meals were small, as opposed to barbarous feasts devoured by many of their creature relatives. Unlike locally related species, who often consumed a kill in one singular, frenzied monster snack, consisting of an entire, wretched creature, swallowed within one continuous sequence, the Ss'iyn never appeared to sense any particular motivation to obliterate their resident fauna, nor persecute other animate life forms for the sake of attaining supremacy. They found moments to ingest miniscule amounts of vegetation which grew around their canyon; picking and grazing at regular intervals.

Contrary to those predators that terrified their more diminutive neighbours, the Ss'iyn had existed for great periods of time, within a peaceful balance, inside their canyon labyrinth, covertly hidden from most of their surroundings. Effectively, they lived in a bubble. It seemed that nature had long since begun to lead them away from any lines of development which might have ensued with greater interaction amidst their surroundings. As time progressed, any reintroduction into the wider world, seemed to be increasingly dangerous. Their ecosystem appeared to have become a separate and safe universe of evolution. All of this had continued for a profound amount of cycles. Now, physically, within their own reptilian fellowship, they were minnows. Cognitively, they were giants.

This diminutive and select species had always lived in situations similar to their current one. Travel around their limited ecosystem had always consisted of sheer drops, slim ledges or awkward connections within dark caves. This had come about, historically, via a need to hide from the dangers of fearsome beasts and threats posed by open spaces, but also a need to keep cool. Their canyon and its caves provided all the shade and moisture they needed. Also, as a result of continual vertical challenges within their local environment, they had been first-class leapers and climbers for much of their history, with perfect heads for heights. Now, it seemed, by flaps, which had started to develop, between upper limbs and torso, that they might even be developing wings, via the intelligent psyche of nature, perhaps as a result of a continual, evolutionary need to negotiate such obstacles quickly. In fact, many other signs had arrived, recently in the history of Ss'iyn that significant changes might be afoot. Great metamorphoses, whether affecting an individual, a race or an ecosystem, can often occur, seemingly and metaphorically, overnight compared with those vast tracts of evolution within the great river of time. This particular species was on a move into unmapped territory. Unusual aptitudes had, clearly and fairly abruptly, emerged in certain individuals, which had been received with discomfort by some; particularly those who had not been blessed. This was not jealousy, merely feelings of disquiet. The Ss'iyn were not at all partial to change. They were, largely, a creature by nature, that liked to stay still and, depending upon current climatic conditions, 'sun itself' or else, 'cool down'. This primal trait had now become a part of a mantra; to seek perfect contentment, for self and all. Physical stasis was a part of achieving that. Yet this alone would not yield karma. Personal satisfaction could only be accomplished with a knowledge and sensation that all around were content too. They were a race who survived and even thrived by looking-out for one another.

The Ss'iyn were a misplacement in their time. They had lived the same way for countless millennia. The wider world had evolved around them whilst they had, in many ways, changed very little. In such a competitive world, size seemed to be everything, yet they were diminutive and successful. Everything moved about, hunted or migrated, whilst they stayed put. Few but the Ss'iyn could be truly regarded as happy, despite their juxtaposition within a mutually murderous world. Although so many beasts upon their planet were endowed with superior physical attributes, it was none but the Ss'iyn who had really mastered their own environment. Control of their surroundings had ensured there was little need to move on or change. Why alter something that's already as good as one might ever want it to be? The Ss'iyn were certainly at peace, although much of that tranquility was down to their ability to hide both themselves and their environment, which could, perhaps, be regarded as an isolated utopia. Within that ideal existence, it was their collective objective to maintain each other's personal contentment.

To any lifeform capable of such discernment, all Ss'iyn would, most likely seem identical. They also looked practically the same as their local geology, decorated with mosses and lichens, mainly amounting in a resultant appearance of green. They were somewhat camouflaged, but also literally as old as the rocks. They and the landscape which sheltered them had developed analogous colours, simultaneously. Their physical disguise was a shield against their greatest threat; giant birds which could, in theory, attack them, yet, in reality, seldom noticed them. A Ss'iyn being caught was extremely rare as they were, by nature's gifts, highly adept in invisibility. It was a unity of spirit that seemed to keep them communally aware, but also their lack of material need or any necessity to travel or migrate which kept them so happily and so safely rooted to a spot. All of this seemed to have preserved them more carefully than the chopped-up landscape around them. Who else could possibly maintain such peace and happiness inside what most other intelligent genera, about the universe, may even regard as a prison? Yet how could anyone imagine the depths the Ss'iyn might have travelled within their own intellects, via strengthened links of such a small number of fluidly-linked minds, for so many precious millennia of their planet's history? So much time. So little disturbance. So much chance for nature, the intelligence of the cosmos itself, to meld them, by now, virtually as a single communal mind.

Most of today's backward world was too busy, cumbersome or ill-coordinated to venture down to the Ss'iyn 's layer, even if they could possibly find it. There were several small entrances upon the plains, leading to their labyrinth below, which were relatively concealed by growth. Larger beasts would find no way in, though these outlets had occasionally been escape-routes for slighter creatures being identified as dinner. However, there was always a risk from more aggressive lifeforms, perhaps possessing speed or agility rather than super-size, who preyed upon those who were still smaller than themselves. The Ss'iyn had learned to be aware of a particularly fearsome reptile which hunted in packs, also a breathtakingly, elongated serpent which could arrive before it was sensed. There was also an ominous multiped, longer than the Ss'iyn was tall, which sometimes scuttled through their tunnels in search of food that, fortunately, wasn't them. The whole process would, however, be most unsettling and preferable to avoid. There were memories, from some, of waking to find they were being crawled upon. Happily, however, this was not a common occurrence. Despite these threats from the carnage above, there was a need to allow a movement of air through the tunnels, which would cease if one or another end of the labyrinth were blocked. However, in their favour, was the fact that, even in the event of a deadly predator entering their quarters, the Ss'iyn were still devilishly difficult to detect.

The only normal disturbances to the Ss'iyn 's silent existence were the grumbles and groans of vulcanicity and occasional planetary tremors. There would also be infrequent showers of giant beasts from above, as dumb and interdependent creatures fell to their demise through badly controlled, mass migration. On these occasions, a stupendous rumbling and shaking would be followed by disturbingly large rock falls, followed by the flailing of stubby limbs and stunted arms, thrashing at uncooperative air. Alas, nature continued its 'survival of the fittest' whilst the Ss'iyn maintained a personal evolution inside their own limits. When all stampedes and avalanches had ceased and the Ss'iyn world had become silent once more, new carcasses would have found their resting place amongst the innumerable bones of others to become forage for the only life forms that could venture as deep as the canyon bed. That would be the giant birds. Apart from obnoxious swathes of dust that were usually associated with falling monsters, something of a blessing would be provided too, as the birds would now be diverted to the base of the ravine for some days, and thus, the levels of happiness of the Ss'iyn might rise, at least for a while, to a modest degree.

As far as the Ss'iyn were concerned, they had no names for one another, nor their race. All Ss'iyn recognised individual traits. There was no need to remind anyone, verbally or otherwise, as to any aspect of an individual's identity, so communication was immediate without an address. It also went a long way beyond audible utterance. One particular expression, shared by most, however, was a commonly repeated diphthong in the form of a hissing blast of breath, which might have sounded as though they were relating to one another as Ss'iyn. In truth however, the miniscule, audible part of their communication, if it could have been observed by an intelligent and thorough observer, may well have revealed a wealth of utterances, some seemingly repetitive. To one who persevered, an evolving pattern might have surfaced, adapting new stresses and trends during separate periods of interaction, sometimes over excessive periods of time. Each of the Ss'iyn expressed individual articulation and assertion. In that context, a discerning observer might have chosen to use some approximations of those utterances as handles for each individual. By that token, they may have been awarded distinguishing names such as Ki'iss, Gauk, Kekadae, Soryss or Pep.

Vocal utterances were, it might have seemed, just the tip of an iceberg. The Ss'iyn demonstrated very expressive eyes and precise facial nuances. In between what might, generally, be a subtle dialogue of croaks, clicks and gurgles, was a lightning-quick sequence of head movements and eye gestures. Limbs were mostly still during conversation. All was focus and concentration. Who knows what was communicated between vibrations of air or their visible gestures? It might have appeared that whatever world existed, within the inner landscape of the Ss'iyn, was possibly a vast network of aspiration, discovery and empathy; maybe even telepathy. Between them, they seemed to nurse and nurture something secret and undetectable to anyone or anything outside their fellowship. One might even have conjectured that there was some network of knowledge and memory, known mutually and precisely in all its facets and depth by each of the Ss'iyn.

In the world of the Ss'iyn, there was only them. For huge lengths of history, they had accumulated nothing physical. If one was to question their intelligence, they might begin by defining the word and asking some questions. Is it the ability to construct dwellings and transport links, control other creatures via enclosures and farming methods, evolve advanced technology and so forth? the Ss'iyn had none of these things. There were no material possessions, no personal, physical adornments. In fact, for millennia, there had been nothing but mutual dialogue, meditation and natural feeding on lichen, shrubs and pure water, all of which was always in abundance around their network. If, however, intelligence has something to do with an ability to learn from experience and duly progress, this would surely be attributed to the Ss'iyn. There may have been few physical or material signs visible for their world to discern, yet it seemed that a citadel of thoughts and experience might have existed, somehow, between them. If one was to observe their visual communications and interactions amongst an environment of zero physical possession, it might have led to a feeling that they harboured all that was dear to them elsewhere. They may even conjecture that the Ss'iyn had created something of a neural universe amongst the connectivity of their biological brains; a communal memory bank like a library of learning, perhaps contained within each of their minds and shared via whatever communication was possible for them. They certainly appeared to relate intensely, seeming to communicate in-depth concepts with obvious affirmations, reactions and exclamations, though little was audible. More was visible, but who could tell by what other means they may have been conveying their thoughts? In truth, for eons, within them and between them this vastly complex, virtual, communal bank of memory, knowledge and ideas might have been nurtured and developed with an un-dwindling enthusiasm and appetite for knowledge. Perhaps a favourable truth for the Ss'iyn was that whatever they were doing was, perhaps, easier within a culture who were so content to sit still, meditate and centralise their thinking.

Perhaps a major reason for the success of the Ss'iyn, as a species, was their numbers. Procreation was measured and infrequent. Most Ss'iyn could generally look forward to a very healthy lifespan, although inevitably, there would come a time when their physical forms began to remind them that they were not immortal. At such a juncture, an elderly member of the community might feel compelled to discuss a need for their compatriots to perhaps arrange a way to fill the hole they may be leaving, at some point in the future. A sensitive dialogue between community members, might culminate in a decision, between two Ss'iyn of opposing sexes, who may have found something of a more special connection, to add a new, miniature lifeform to their miniscule ecosystem. This was not a regular occurrence. Due to such spectacular longevity, there were few children, and due to such limited numbers, in a species that endeavoured to maintain the size of its population, their attempts to procreate had become somewhat incestuous. In the eyes of Ss'iyn, however, this was merely thoughtful, genetic engineering, designed not just to balance their numbers, but also to maintain resilient offspring from the healthy heart of their stock.

The needs of the Ss'iyn appeared to be internal and spiritual. By evidence of observation, theirs seemed to be a race of potentially, powerful brains made so by eons of reasoning and experience, undistracted by all that springs from a pursuit of material possession, but also assisted by what could ensue when an entire community cooperates and supports one another mutually. It seemed that all they might possess was untouchable inside the vaults of the mind. In amongst cool, reptilian calmness, was a composed and controlled coordination of life's progression and an unruffled ability to memorize and store what might be real, what once existed or what might be created.

Nature had willed the SS'iyn into existence and brought them thus far. In congruency with that, they had, for an inconceivably long line of existence, progressed themselves along a suitable path amongst nature. They appeared to revisit ideas together and consolidate alone. They seemed to recount stories. They looked to be making plans, based upon their vast experience and potentially, expansive intelligence. They seemed to juggle powerful concepts, conjecture, hypothesise and conclude conversation with affirmation and approval. Now, it appeared, after an eon of almost utopian existence, which predated much of their physical surroundings, that nature was already rewarding *some* of their individuals with *gifts* that seemed to have appeared, relatively abruptly, at this advanced stage of Ss'iyn evolution, far beyond the general, communal aspirations of their species. Perhaps, at long last, some evidence of nature's generosity, within their solitary and virtually undetectable evolution, was about to become apparent. Some swift, surprising and distinctive changes had already occurred, in the Canyon of the Great Rainbow.

CHAPTER 4

Jed's routine avoidance of routine

A biting breeze persisted early, on an uninspiring, late November morning, unchecked without the shelter of hills, buildings or trees. A compound of farmyard scents dominated, with cabbage in first-place, followed by a skirmish of reasonably nasty whiffs such as silage and compost. Beyond some swishing and rustling caused by wind in the vast oaks that stood either side of Jed's cottage, which were so large that they had become worlds of their own normally supporting a great diversity of bird and squirrel-life, and the highly-active wind chimes suspended above his dark green front door, there was little other sound to record as most local fauna had retreated now at the onset of winter.

Greenbank College, which Jed called 'Brownbank' on account of the fact that everything there *was* brown, stood a long way from Jed's home, *out in the sticks*. To make matters tougher, he was completely reliant on public transport. Getting there, five days a week, provided a gruelling marathon, which was also very time-consuming. Jed would often deliberate, en route, about other such processes, which might be regarded as a complete waste of life. This was a bus journey of some ninety minutes each way, when things were smooth with the traffic. Hiking to and from bus stops ate-up vast tracts of time, too. A very early start was required to reach the college on time. Even tougher, for Jed, was the fact that Greenbank was a place of strict time-keeping and liked to honour schedules. Punctuality would become a necessary observation, in the world of business, for all of its students.

Wasting too much time in a bus, continued to be one of Jed's greatest moans. What could he otherwise be achieving instead of being in transit? His commuting amounted to more than a day and night each week. Too much time to spend, trapped within an inescapable, moronic routine!

Jed's slightly elder, stockier and rougher-looking brother, Joe, generally took pleasure from a simpler existence and working role, in which he managed his own transport, delivering mail to isolated hamlets and farms. He had learned to drive typically unsafely, like many of his colleagues. This arose from an urge to complete his rounds as quickly as possible, with hopes of gaining 'quality time', spent browsing news and sport in some country lane, or else playing a game on his phone, such as one involving weird jellyfish. Joe's stress in life often derived from his own rushing and desperation to reach more preferred parts of his life. Sadly, this anxiety was sometimes passed on to others, such as when he stopped abruptly at a postal address, smacked on the brakes, so as to achieve forty miles per hour to zero in less than a second, whacked open the van door and left motorists gibbering from jolts, suffered from having to engineer abrupt swerves or sequences of emergency braking. However, this, for Joe, was all part of being a postman, and part of his job description. He lived his life as though he was an action figure in a film or computer game. Much to his parents' chagrin, he was chaos personified, and in his time-off, a layabout.

Jed was utterly different to Joe; far more careful and calculated. He reasoned and imagined, to create the world he wanted, or looked to solve enigmas he encountered within everyday existence. He explored boundaries of his mind and sought, not just, to explain things he saw, but also reason about other things that *could* occur or exist. Yet his life was still reliant upon a lot of other factors and quite a few other people, including his parents, who had great banking plans for him, and had somewhat directed his life, against his own, better instincts, towards that particular direction. He now had twenty years behind him but was still, largely, a dependent, living at home. His habitat and lifestyle, there, as opposed to his less desirable college life, were all he had ever known or wished for. It seemed that, even with prospects of a degree qualification, just around the corner, Jed would not be aspiring to a life elsewhere. He was simply content to remain in his family residence. To Jed, there was no particular excitement attached to moving elsewhere, particularly halls of residence. However, even if he were offered a plush flat somewhere reasonably desirable, it would not necessarily have appealed. Home was home; always a place of peace and calm. There was space to meditate and reflect. In Jed's opinion, journeys of the mind were often of greater value than those in physical space.

Mr and Mrs Carvey, generally left home at the same time as Jed. They worked at the same establishment which had brought them together over two decades ago. Sadly, the high street bank, where they were both clerks, was seventeen miles distant, in exactly the opposite direction to Greenbank. They had reasoned that a round trip of more than 80 miles a day was too much for anyone, but, especially, for their aging automobile which might, anyway, soon be on its last wheels. This was, in no way, a reflection of what they could afford. They were merely tight-fisted individuals who's strong wishes to have money in the bank, far surpassed their will to use any of it. They had also reasoned that Jed would benefit from the independence of getting to college by himself. He certainly *was* by himself for great periods of time!

Each Carvey generally helped themselves to breakfast on a weekday morning, and cleared up their own mess. Even Joe had recently begun to achieve that part of the process. It was a fussy family whose diverse tastes and preferences made it too impractical for any one person to cater for all of them. Yet, somehow, they usually managed to chat, during their personal food preparations, from different corners of their kitchen and even leave home at approximately the same time. Despite understanding his parents' logic, however, Jed would still question why it was that they couldn't take him to college, even just once or twice in a week; even just to the bus stop! He would make his feelings known by calling them a 'couple of bankers'. They certainly reasoned like them. Life was all about cutting cost, economising and fobbing-off your poor, downtrodden son with arguments such as…

"You'd still have to get the bus to come back"

And…

"The exercise you get, walking to the bus stop is beneficial".

Jed had not yet asked his parents why it was that *they* never did any.

Jed's bus stop was about one and a half miles from Carveys' Cottage. There were no hills to climb, but for half of the walk, there was no path either! He was often forced to walk on soggy grass or mud. Sometimes there was a need to straddle extensive puddles; relatively tricky when one is wearing a suit and polished shoes. His college principals insisted on a strict dress code, in attempts to instil a business-like awareness within all students in any way possible. Out there, in flatter regions of Eastern England, there was often little or no shelter. Jed would sometimes be subject to severe weather, and might arrive at his bus stop with a red face, glossed by rainfall, and even prickles of sweat from his endurances. He had ruled that a hood spoilt his hairstyle and a brolly would only have turned itself inside-out or else made him do a 'Mary Poppins' into the road. Wind and rain would often sort his hair out for the day, anyway, and on superlative occasions, a lorry might blast its tonnage through surface water, nearby, and finish the job completely.

Jed's bus was, gratefully, hardly ever late, reaching *his* stop at least, yet it had sometimes caused him further problems by being early. He had learned, by humiliations caused when arriving at lectures, long-time in full swing, to arrive prematurely at the bus stop himself. This meant that he nearly always had an annoying wait, further adding to the amount of wasted time in his life. Things were never quite so easy for his bus driver, either. Their route was reasonably complex, demanding a few excursions from the main road. They would also have to wait, graciously for people emerging from farm complexes, or even look out for others, standing some way from their bus stops, under trees, for the purpose of shelter, which was lacking at a number of them. There was no protection for Jed, at all, at his stop, thus he frequently suffered consequences. In such a dispersed, rural community, where people were scattered about in random locations and dead ends, any form of inter-connecting public transport would have to tie itself in knots. Jed's journey was a tedious assault, visiting almost every single settlement within a vast area. He often dreamed of helicopters, and, when the bus got stuck in suburbia, a tank.

Regardless of Jed's feelings, it was certainly fortunate, that a bus *did* serve the college, from his awkward location. His commute was not all that grim, either. He took mild pleasure in sitting atop the usually meagrely-populated, dark-blue double decker, right at the front. This sometimes provided a sense of flying, high above the road with a commanding view of flat, extensive lowlands all around. Each journey brought different lighting, fresh happenings; even new people, although he was often able to measure his progress via certain familiar characters, along the way. Each of them would surface, amidst time-honoured routines, in transit towards whatever it was that granted their lives a purpose each day. However, there was usually something Jed had never seen before, such as a 'one-off-wonder'. This was an umbrella term for many things, such as anyone boarding his bus on an isolated occasion. It could also be used for unfortunate events, occurring on the roadside, or for people arguing within the bus itself. Once, the bus approached a stop, where a lady was sporting a hat with tassels dangling from it. From an upstairs window, it might have seemed that she was having trouble with an octopus. There were also things the bus passed every day which Jed had never noticed before, such as a large historic-looking building with a monkey-puzzle tree in front of it, far away behind a humdrum estate at the beginnings of suburbia, or a woman who wore an unrealistically decorated, lycra suit for an even more unrealistic and bouncy-looking workout she seemed to do every morning within her drably-lit front room.

Jed's morning commute was something of a perk after most things preceding his arrival at the bus stop. Most exertion was over. He could gather his thoughts with a degree of comfort. If the top deck was empty he could do this out loud, and often did. After that, he could even switch off and dream. This had to be done with care. On one, isolated occasion, he had achieved a bit more than that, and missed his stop with hazardous consequences. Yet another silver lining, connected with Jed's journey, was that he could look down through a viewer, intended for the driver's upper-deck monitoring, and see his balding head. It was always the same driver; a grumpy one, who never had a word to offer to anyone boarding his bus, even when they offered a pleasantry. Any attempt to provoke a positive retort would be significantly less successful than Napoleon invading Russia in winter, yet still people tried, such as an elderly lady who always boarded the bus at Linden Farm. Perhaps she was deaf or something, but it was as though she never noticed that this bus driver seldom responded, when she expressed her surface comments about weather. Perhaps she did actually succeed in mustering the odd muted grumble, as she continued to her seat with a cheery and unmoving sunshine face, whilst he drove impetuously forward, as usual, making her passage seem slightly drunken. This morning's comment was…

"The sun feels miles away today" …

"That's because it is!"

…muttered Jed silently to himself, within earshot, just up the steps, before training his ears for another almost inaudible grunt. It was moments like this which provided Jed with continual amusement on his otherwise lonely journey to college.

Amongst many other surface comments, made by the elderly lady, on previous days, the most memorable ones for Jed were…

"It's hot in the sun, isn't it?"

…about which he'd had to agree, it *must* be! Also…

"Oh dear, the sun doesn't want to come out today, does it?"

…to which Jed could only reason that the sun *really* didn't have any cognitive skills of its own. Maybe it was just that there *were* no answers to these frivolous, old-school weather comments. One way or another, he judged that his bus driver's personality was frostier than any weather, out in this unprotected, broad, eastern cabbage patch. Maybe he didn't even have one!?

Today's final pick-ups were done. A score of people now inhabited the bus, all dotted about in separate zones. There was no interaction or sound other than a somewhat aggressive engine drone, mixed with continually ascending and descending pitch, following each change of speed. This was a crew of individuals who lived highly independent and isolated lives. Each would interact to some degree, today, within their professions or alternative daily schedules, but would return to silence, later, somewhere amongst fields, inside a human wilderness. This scenario spoke volumes about the community in which Jed resided. He was not blatantly extroverted, but was certainly not uncomfortable within himself.

Into the town, there were those, boarding the bus, whose social discomforts provided Jed with silent amusement. One gentleman had a gammy leg and would drag it with him, generating a sweeping sound as he went. It was most unfortunate, but difficult not to grin. There was also a very elderly gentleman whose bowels would often let him down, whilst standing to dismount the bus. A combination of aggressive deceleration and heavy braking, often caused him to lurch, whilst defending his grip on a slender metal bar, on the back of someone's seat, and he'd let one go, much to the disapproval of a few traditional characters, sitting close to where he stood. With no intent to be malicious, Jed was compulsively drawn to the funny side of life; in particular, those things which happened as a result of unfortunate circumstances. Life provided its own humour, yet he often wondered if he was the only one who ever seemed to appreciate it.

At college, Jed made his way from a small bus & car park, adjacent to the campus entrance, taking a shortcut over a grassy bank that gave the college its name, and a sign saying PLEASE DO NOT WALK ON THE GRASS, through a cluster of fine English trees (he could never remember the difference between cedar and ewe), then to a further green area, with picnic benches and a forbidding-looking black, metallic statue of some economist, known to those who founded the college for some reason he had not yet discovered. Beyond this was the front entrance to a rather fine Georgian building, in which all of Jed's lectures took place. He entered via an arched, sandstone porch, just inside of which, on the left, was a small inset, shielded with glass, labelled 'Reception'. A barely perceptible voice mumbled from inside, with only vowels emanating, informing him that the usual electronic sign-in machine was out-of-order and all students would have to sign-in manually for the foreseeable future. Obviously her external communication device was broken, too!

Reception always smelt strongly of polish. Today, like a lot of days, it induced a few sneezes. This did not just involve Jed, either. Beyond Reception, was a large, heavy and thickly polished brown door, which was kept open during the day. It led to a central corridor. Jed walked briskly. There was no sign of students, which was a *bad* sign. His first lecture should now be commencing. His arrival time could so easily be affected by slight differences in the average speed of his bus, even regardless of any hold-ups. Obviously, this morning's journey had been a little bit slower than Jed might have appreciated.

It was a dull, brown corridor, looking like something from World War II, and appeared all the more sinister, combined with an anticipation of being slightly tardy for a situation of strict time observation. From this point to the lecture room, in which Jed suffered three, two-hour-long business and economics sessions, five days a week, it was as though anything attractive, comforting or energising had been sucked into some inhumane extractor, leaving only clinical emptiness, artistic deprivation and a resultant brownness. The dullness of Jed's college venue, certainly added to an endurance factor within his daily routine. Now though, he would have to face a little metaphorical music.

There are many time-honoured excuses which teachers and lecturers will often find too unoriginal to accept. 'The bus was late' is one which has been tried and tested too often, and can sometimes also be quite difficult to prove. It was certainly the fault of a bus journey today. Jed had been blissfully unaware of its effects upon his schedule, as he gazed beyond horizons and clouds, without a care in the world. Nor did he wear a watch or use a phone, unless absolutely necessary. In this way, he was utterly different to most of his peers. There had been an obstruction of traffic cones in a street. As usual there was *nobody* working there and *no* holes in the road. In typical British fashion within a modern world, where a cause of much inefficiency was often safeguarding, a restriction had been set up to protect workers, when they finally arrived at their contracted time, which might have been several days. At least though, the area had been rendered *safe*. Also, as Jed had discovered only a few days back in time, when he had been rendered horizontal on a wet floor, thanks to a safety sign in the college *Gents*, safeguarding could sometimes even be dangerous. Today it was possibly going to cost him more than a few brownie points for reaching his first seminar of the day, a few minutes late.

Jed dusted around his shoulders for the presence of any dandruff. He straightened his tie and lanyard, polished his shoes on the back of his trouser legs, without taking them off, then drew a sizable breath, and slowly pushed open the weighty, brown door. His plan was to enter unnoticed at the rear of the class. If he had dressed in brown there might have been a good chance of him remaining relatively invisible. However, his entry was betrayed by the door, which emitted a weak groan followed by something similar to a glissando on a small trumpet. It was partly for this reason that, Jed's lecturer, Doctor Alexander, had decided it was better to arrive before his students. His balding head rose slowly upwards, as far as it needed to, for him to be able to peer over his audience and also the top of his half-moon spectacles. He had perfected this withering look over many years, finding it to be most effective. Any recipient would feel as though they were being bombarded with silent radiation and suffer serious social burns. Jed stood motionless for a moment like a rabbit in headlights, enduring noiseless but powerful rays of denigration. Then, in an initial sentence, uttered with measured control and sternness, honouring a sizable gap between each superfluously emphasised word, Doctor Alexander addressed the crowd...

"A... PROFESSIONAL... BUSINESS... PERSON... IS... ALWAYS..."

During a lengthier and well-timed gap, he dimmed to a whisper, like calm before a storm, before unleashing a carefully-controlled explosion...

"PUNCTUAL!!!"

He revolved his head slightly and subtly, towards Jed, maintaining a bright-enough pitch for all to hear and note...

"Those of us just entering this room will most likely be demonstrating to us *all* that they do *not* have the credentials required, to step into such esteemed roles as those in the higher and more respected levels of our business world."

Jed wilted throughout a desperately uncomfortable twenty or so seconds of silence that followed, during which, all eyes incinerated what was left of his pulverised ego. There was no need for further punishment. Such a reception was castigation enough for anyone. He remained internally wounded throughout the session, missing vital information due to feelings of revulsion and urges of retribution.

"Professional business people might never be late but the blinking bus often is!"

...thought Jed, silently, within the chaos of his own personal storm.

In the lecture room, its brown, plastic chairs were comfortable for perhaps fifteen minutes, after which it would normally become obvious that a significant number of people had begun to struggle with posture. This was evident if one observed the way that legs were continuously crossed and uncrossed at reducing intervals throughout the progression of a seminar. Some individuals would also rock back and forth on occasion, or even stretch carefully and subtly without raising arms above the head. However, one rather distinctive character, who was cursed with restless leg syndrome and didn't seem to possess much awareness of his personal impact on an environment, often produced fairly startling frenzies of rapidly repeated chaffing sounds, as his right trouser leg brushed up and down, violently, against the flanks of his chair, plus a polyester raincoat which was usually hanging over each side of his seat. These repetitive distractions, which he created during each spasmodic sequence, might sometimes have caused individuals to question what someone was doing behind them, before they learned of his involuntary habits. Fortunately, all were now familiar and accepting of this fairly uncomfortable condition; even sympathetic within the context of these awkward, lengthy lectures. Jed worried that he, himself, would suffer DVT or some other physical trauma if his routine did not change soon. But there was an up-side to all of this, in the form of a very large person who, realistically, could have used two seats to host his profoundly giant buttocks. Jed would usually hover before the start of a lecture until the hapless individual was seated, then position himself in his slipstream in the knowledge that he would get away with a momentary rest of the eyes when emergencies arose; even a quick glance at his latest lecture-accompanying volume, 'A little book of big economist jokes'.

As per usual, today's lectures contained lots of statistics, jargon, graphs, videos of good practice, even more statistics, lists of procedures, tips for success, evaluation, analysis and everything else you might want to throw into six hours of pitiless punishment. Jed had come to realise that this stuff would be even more useful than a bedtime, if it were used for the purpose of putting people to sleep. It even worked on him during the *day*.

At breaks and lunchtime, Jed would wonder where everybody had gone. It was as though they'd been vaporised or perhaps beamed up to a secret space ship. It certainly felt like a certain sci-fi story he'd read where one person had been rendered alone on the Earth. One exception to the rule was a man who often remained in the lecture room. How on God's Earth, could anyone actually want to sit there any longer and turn three, two-hour stints into a personal shocker of eight hours or more?

Silence and solitude at break times was not, in the least, a problem for Jed, who was usually more than comfortable with meditating on the energy of any calm surroundings, for fairly lengthy periods of time. It was one of the traits of being a country dweller. Peace and quiet had rendered itself within him. Unlike most of the students with whom he shared a class, Jed had no need of games, apps, or any other artificial means of entertainment. There was a boundless world all around him, but, even more fascinating for Jed, a fathomless one inside his head. He would frequently sit and travel around his mind, relating to memories and surmising about possibilities. It seemed to Jed that there was so much to discover without even travelling an inch. His own mind was a source of self-perpetuating entertainment.

There was no 'as usual' in Jed's life, even if his routine tried its absolute best to create repetition. Today at lunchtime, he found what was, in his own descriptive accuracy, a 'south-west passage'. This new route through the college, to whatever would be today's picnic spot, would require a spot of trespassing; something Jed enjoyed fairly regularly. The fact that he had already been in trouble today, only heightened the buzz. Jed's plan was always to find new territory, new aspects, fresh ideas, different views and breaks to what would otherwise be possibly a very humdrum routine.

Without hesitation he left through a door labelled USE IN EMERGENCY ONLY and was compelled to progress in a forward direction as it slammed shut behind him, leaving him dangerously exposed on an external patch of turf, with windows all around him. He quickly noted that it was the college kitchens standing before him across a small, overgrown space. He could deduce this very easily, as all of his senses informed him simultaneously. His ears caught the percussion of large pots, pans and mass-catering machinery, coupled with rustic accents and hearty laughter as chefs prepared the college lunch that he'd not be consuming. His eyes found their off-white overalls and blue *hair protection nets* through the smeared and steamed-up windows, but also, he couldn't miss the vertical plume of white steam belching from a short silver pipe on the flat roof. This signified *serious* boiling and frying! His nose picked-up a distinctive aroma of cottage pie, which seemed to be mass-produced almost every day, regardless of what appeared on the menu. It was, it seemed, somehow, always the resultant bouquet of everything that was ever being prepared in this particular catering establishment.

Jed progressed eastwards from his southerly direction, departing calmly through an old brown door. Experience had told him that, when you're somewhere you shouldn't be, it's always best to act 'official' and even learn a few useful bits of terminology to ensure that you sound as though you know what you're talking about when interrogated inside a restricted area. In this case, as Jed was just about to enter an annex of the kitchen, he had created in his mind, a situation in which he was going to inquire for the future, which was whether or not the college could cater for pesca-vegans. He had simply put his limited knowledge of dietary description into this idea, which he hoped he would never have to use. At least it was *almost* accurate.

Jed found himself in a room where machinery seemed to have come to die. He glanced around its musty environs at what were relics of the past forty or so years, standing in the shadows of a dark, temporary building. So temporary, was the building, that it had stood for even *more* than those four decades. It had been mostly ignored; even forgotten, obsolete or awaiting repair. From here, there was only one door and that, unfortunately, led to the kitchens.

Much like a scenario in which one is considering jumping from a high rock, Jed had reasoned that it is often just best to get on with it. He reasoned like this, much of the time, and much of what he had reasoned here, was proving to be most useful, in pursuit of this highly forbidden shortcut. In he went, without hesitation, forcing a slightly stubborn, steel-coated fire door forwards, with his stronger, right arm and sliding inside. This was, indeed, the main kitchen. Espying a safe exit across to the east (Jed *owned* the points of the compass) in the form of an open door, he pressed on forwards, in a confident-looking manner with a short, measured cough and headed out, visually composed and official-looking, into the kitchen towards a doorway that led to his safety. There was a concentration of cooks, all about their business, across a sizeable space to his north. They were mostly situated immediately behind or in front of a serving hatch, which opened out into a large refectory beyond. All were about their business and oblivious to Jed, it seemed. He negotiated a multitudinous assault of hazards, including a large tub of potatoes, a fire bucket nearly halfway out in the aisle, a mat next to a cooker which had a peeled-up tripping edge, and his favourite, from recent luckless experiences, a yellow warning sign advising of slipping dangers due to a wet floor. There were also a few instruments of food torture, such as sharp knives, spoons with short, radiating blades, and a spikey implement for skewering something. All were sticking out a little further than the edges of worktops. Clearly, thought Jed, these kitchens were exempt from safeguarding.

For the second time in the same day, Jed had made it to a door of pivotal importance. The first had let him down with betraying groans. This one gave away his position for visual reasons, before he could celebrate a smooth traverse of a new passage and exit to freedom. As soon as he yanked the door open, an intense flood of light poured into the kitchens, alerting a lady, who was preparing some purple-sprouting broccoli, not too far across the kitchen. In momentary shock, Jed abandoned his idea of a fish-loving, vegan student role play and improvised. Arching his back somewhat and raising his head position slightly in an attempt to adopt, what he envisaged might be body language appropriate for an esteemed food hygiene specialist, he informed the room, with a minimal but stern proclamation, that this had been a student walkthrough inspection. After a short pause for effect and a totally confused silence, he departed resolutely through the welcoming exit to flustered mutters, into joyous sunlight, and a more attractive part of the college, with well-kempt grounds and historic stone-work within the walls he was about to leave behind.

With distinct awareness of a need to lay low for a while, Jed avoided an obvious route, which was a wide, paved walkway, leading past rows of staring windows. He also chose to avoid a smaller trail which led gracefully around a series of circular herbaceous borders to another path, leading along a short, topiarised laurel hedge, punctuated with benches, upon which, one could rest and drink-in a very pleasant environment. Instead, Jed planned to break away, across the grass, to a clump of rhododendron bushes, north of where he had exited the kitchens. From a distance, it appeared that there was an aperture, leading inside the bushes, which might offer a prospect of hiding himself, possibly, within a sort of tree cave. In such a covert situation, he may be able to enjoy a quiet lunch. Leaving the official inspector persona behind, at the kitchen door, Jed resumed his stealth-work mode and legged-it across the lawn. With a casual, peripheral glance through his metaphorical wing mirrors, he executed a rapid change of direction into the gap, he had observed, between the rhododendrons.

Jed was pleased to find a narrow passageway, leading into the heart of the bushes. He squeezed through, with excitement and anticipation. It was a bit like venturing through a maze, but with the added interest of possibly finding something secret. The cutting led into a small, circular clearing; obviously deliberately designed by the creators of these grounds as a concealed hidey-hole meant for who-knows-what? Jed was surprised to find that he was not alone. Strikingly contrasted against the dark, natural shades of the clearing, with shocking, long, pink and purple hair draped over a flowing, black skull-infested dress, was a girl, of about Jed's age, standing facing him with her back against a dead-end, leaning against thick shrubbery with hands behind her back. Without shock or movement, she turned-up a smile. A bombardment of unrelated thoughts sprang through Jed's head, virtually simultaneously. Here was one of the many students who always disappeared at lunchtime. Where were all the rest? Where they in similar places, like this? What a shame he, definitely, couldn't spend his lunchtime here; it might intimidate her somewhat to be invading her in such a situation. What was she studying exactly? Why had he never seen her before? She stood out more than the large cerise flowers on the outside of the bushes that surrounded them both. He guessed, in an instant, that her name was Celia. It wasn't. Jed, gratefully, managed to preserve his poise, and, with a comfortable smile, turned and calmly retraced his steps, out to the mouth of the living cave and proceeded to continue north towards some more distant benches. Each one was dedicated to a founder member or influential figure, associated with the college, via a small bronze engraving, inlayed into the wood at the back of each seat. He chose a bench, commemorating someone called Alfred Scheidt, with a view of open space, and fields beyond the campus, which were for Jed, beyond the far side of town with respect to where he lived. He had never ventured this side of the institution, until now. There was no distraction from the human race, nor much, out there, that could remind him of his daily schedule, so he perched in the centre of the fittingly placed pew, with purple rucksack to his south, and ransacked his lunchbox.

Jed's packed lunch was a typical reflection of his parents' money-saving obsession. What else might one expect from a couple of bank clerks? An account with the college canteen would not have incurred much more cost. Instead, Jed's daily mid-day diet was at the mercy of his mother's conservative planning, which was not necessarily such an attractive prospect. His round of two sandwiches, cut diagonally into triangles, always consisted of a statutory single slice of whatever 'filling of the day' happened to be. That was it! He prayed each day, that it wouldn't be ham. Mrs Carvey's sandwich ham was wafer-thin, purchased from a 'basics' selection, like most other items in his lunch box. Sometimes, a singular slice, would depart the rest of a sandwich during the first bite, like a flap of elastic, and smack him in the chops, leaving him with just bread. There seemed to be no pattern to the lunches he was given and therefore no chance of predicting any odds. The only sure thing was an un-thrilling yoghurt which seemed to smuggle itself in amongst his sandwiches, every day; always bottom of the range, and either raspberry or strawberry (except you'd be hard-pressed to find any). Jed was sentenced to these two flavours, forever, simply because his mother refused to buy anything else less economical. And his traditionally sexist father would not even conceive making lunches for the family. It was interesting how *his* lunch often seemed to contain an extra item, which Jed and his brother would identify through transparent plastic each morning and heckle a bit. But it was fruitless to complain, and boring to keep hearing the same old stock replies connected with family hierarchy, a lifetime of effort, and privileges which had to be earned.

At last, and for at least forty minutes, there was peace. The tempest had eased inside Jed, after that disgraceful and, for him, unavoidable incident, earlier, which had unfairly caused him a spot of verbal bullying from none less than a college professor. By now he was beyond it all, and somewhat distracted by the girl in the tree cave, with whom he felt he'd perhaps shared some sort of favourable connection. He contemplated his encounter with her at length. Had he turned away from a meant-to-be moment? Was Celia thinking about him? July energy warmed him, and his thoughts even more. He grinned with a gentle surge of adrenaline which felt like a summer breeze.

Heavy-laden, English trees rippled lightly, betraying the path of a placid squall, across a meadow of lengthy, swaying grass and wild flowers, that had been left, for now, to lie fallow until next year's tractors rumbled at the boundaries of the college once more. Soon, there was idyllic calm and a soothing silence.

Jed had recognised that a whole new sense of a place or situation could be gained by blocking one of the senses. He would, sometimes cover his ears, finding that he noticed a lot more detail in a view than he did when distracted by anything audible. Today, he closed his eyes, and explored an experience of sound and scent. Most prominently, he observed a distant and dispersed flock of sheep. As usual, with a group of such creatures, one of them was angrier than the rest and was, unmistakably, making itself heard, shouting at the others. Amongst other, more subtle resonance was a light rustling of leaves, also his tie flapping against jacket buttons, and one or two flypasts from bees, possibly doing important business amongst a wealth of blooms, all about his immediate environs, within this outrageously beautiful flower garden. Indeed, these grounds were a bright, welcome contrast to the interior of the institution. Jed also sensed a light fragrance from nearby flowers; especially those on trellises either side of his park bench. This was blended with a slight scent of must from an ancient stone wall and the earth round about. More prominently though, was a strong stench of cow muck and fertiliser, being employed, somewhere, by a local farmer. One way or another, as was routine for Jed during each day at college, through an intelligent choice of setting for lunch, an interesting, refreshing and adrenaline-provoking route to get there, and an ability to release all stress, via a unique and personal means of meditation, he had once again, achieved some sort of karma *before* lunchtime.

Jed had reasoned that, for so much of their lives, people seemed to venture up and down similar routes, in both a physical and social sense. They seemed to be constantly retracing their own steps within time-honoured routines, even outside their working lives, and were mainly, in Jed's opinion, only comfortable with familiarity and conformity. He believed that people were often unhappy concerning change, questions they couldn't answer, departures from their norms, or the loss of something belonging to their daily world. Yet, he thought, so very often, it is those times when a change is forced by circumstance that they, at last, have something to talk about. He had also noticed that, often, some fairly interesting things were created by chance, including quirky inventions. Jed always strived, sometimes through boredom, rather than deliberate venturing, to keep discovering new pastures and evolve his routine. However, he had also found that the mind was a fathomless cosmos, and that travelling around physically was not always necessary for unearthing fresh inspiration. Simply meditating upon experience, feelings, memories and aspirations often yielded ideas and innovation. Jed's mind was unusually developed for one of his age, particularly in terms of all those things which cannot be stated in words or even explained in pictures. It was also his belief, that intelligence could not be measured by any particular test alone. Too many people, he thought, seemed content to accept that it could be quantized via a simple sequence of puzzles. Perhaps, he conjectured, it is all those things that a being observes and interprets through expressions, body language, gesturing, use of vocal pitch, and sometimes, whatever it is that goes on in the back of a person's mind, behind all of their expressions and communication. Perhaps, he considered, intelligence is also partly one's ability to express all of that, as well as what one chooses to communicate or judge important to convey. To add to that, he had read about divergent thinking; the sort of processing which creates invention or leads to concepts never before envisaged. Creativity like that, seemed to be boundless and immeasurable as an intelligence, yet he had reasoned that it might take some sort of cleverness to know how to direct that sort of thinking. When one is thinking outside the box, what facts are there to go on?

Jed had developed a habitual routine of searching for new things. One of his favourite pastimes was to reach into his mind for something completely random, such as a 'yellow being, standing on a stage in a garden of red trees and flowers that radiated their own light'. Within the process of attempting to explain how any of this might be possible, he would sometimes turn-up an idea which was fresh and interesting. Sometimes the whole procedure would fall flat on its face and seem like a complete waste of time, yet Jed would persevere with the conviction that there was so much to discover, so much of the brain unused and so much that was never sensed, enjoyed or marvelled at. If he persisted, he might uncover some of these things. That was potentially exciting and fuelled his continuing efforts. Jed had decided that divergent thinking should always accompany his reasoning. That way, he might begin to learn how to walk right round everything he encountered and view it in all contexts. He had once heard somebody say...

"Intelligence is a spaceship, discovering a cosmos."

This had led him to envisage his own thinking processes as something similar. He liked to imagine that he sat at a hub within his own internal network, looking out from a complex, which was *him*, into eternal space. He could launch himself outwards, in an infinite number of directions, in search of absolutely anything he fancied. Periodically, whenever something in life particularly inspired him, it would seem as though he had travelled through the universe and encountered something ground-breaking. He would check each new 'find' against everything he knew or sensed. Then, musing over facts, feelings, experience and imaginings, he would commit new knowledge to his network of thinking, deduce new facts and concepts, or even dream up something completely innovative. He had simply learned, via fairly high-powered reading, plus the assistance of a life that gifted time, peace and quiet, to entertain himself with his own mind. A further reason for continuing to muse like this, had been a powerful quote in a sci-fi novel he'd relished, which proclaimed that...

"The mind is the greatest toy anyone will ever be gifted".

He had translated things he'd read into a means of thinking. Now he could sit and ponder, for great tracts of time, independent of material stimulants. There was more than enough in his own intellect to keep him eternally amused; a whole universe, in fact.

Jed had also reasoned a lot about, what he believed, was a slimy incline, down which, he thought society seemed to be heading, with its facts, figures, testing, inspecting, scrutinizing of one another, safeguarding extremes, and virtual reality. Technology was now a constant accessory in people's lives and movements, even a prop, to which they appeared to be becoming too dependent. There seemed, to him, to be too much, in life, leading humanity away from nature. He had read a story, in which the human race had become reliant upon a great machine, which provided for their every need. They had ceased to produce or prepare anything for themselves, as their technology had long-since taken care of everything. There was no longer a need to travel, nor visit one another in person, nor exercise, nor even own a pet. A list of what they had lost would have been profound. Their humanity was largely gone. Not that Jed felt people were at this stage yet, nor would certain individuals, he knew, ever dream of being governed by machinery.

Despite a slight resentment of routine, there were still a few things which Jed had not yet wished to alter. These were generally, parts of life which one looked forward to. Repetition of enjoyable things might be desirable. For instance, he could quote some words he spoke to his mother-in-law, who always cooked a casserole when his family visited their bite-size cottage in the Fens. She would apologise for always doing the same thing for them, and not trying to branch-out as she didn't believe she could muster up all those *clever* things some people on the telly seemed to produce. But Jed would generally retort with words to the effect of...

"Don't you see, after coming all the way down here to see you, we're all dying to have exactly what you always do for us? Your casseroles are a family institution. Why change them?"

Despite Jed's constant and overwhelming urges to change his daily routines, there was still a place for those things in life which were beacons of hope. There would always be something familiar to generate hope or excitement. Perhaps a life without any repetition at all would be devoid of structure and anticipation. Even Jed embraced this reality, and acknowledged certain loopholes of repetition in his life that were still welcome, although there were a few daily scourges too, such as endless bus journeys and dross lectures, from which he could not, presently, easily escape.

If one was to attempt to coin the character of this discerning and rather individual young man, they would need to observe that he was a very rare exception within such a world, in that his life was largely devoid of personal interaction with technology. In his own estimations, he was more 'wired to the Earth' than most individuals of his age. He possessed, but seldom used, a mobile phone, and a laptop computer. Throughout his college course, he had needed to become fully savvy with the workings of such devices, yet he seldom used them outside necessity. The only technological adornment visible on his persona, was an ancient, analogue wrist watch, relinquished to him by an uncle in Norfolk. The mobile phone usually remained inside his college case, with his laptop, for such eventualities as a bus breaking-down or aliens invading Greenbank. He used them *that* often.

It was not just negative aspects of technology, which were constantly repelling Jed from a life bound to machinery, such as damage to posture and eyesight, addiction to games, or an under-exposure to the natural energies of Earth, outside cars and buildings. It was also the draw of feelings of wellbeing, when he walked, talked, read real books, or played music on such archaic devices as a record player, or via his ancient and battered, acoustic guitar. His family dined together, in the evenings at least, around a table, which they had christened, fairly tritely, the *round table*. He enjoyed the sound of the wind, moaning through cracks and crevices in his old house. He mused over stars for very long periods of time, when the sight was gifted him. Out in the *sticks*, there was little light pollution, nor much atmospheric contamination. On a summer night, when night temperatures were affectionate, Jed could lay a good distance from his abode on, what was always a perfectly mowed lawn (on account of his own or else his brother's efforts... never his father who always delegated the job!) looking aloft. It could sometimes seem as though he were in space. He could identify planets, moving independently to fixed stars. He could name some of those angular shapes that spoke, silent as mime, with their, almost deliberately organised forms, in patterns and pivotal positions, as though it were some sort of code for humans to decipher. Jed mused about this, though was not, at all, taken by the art of astrology, connected with constellations. He preferred to base his conjecture upon facts he knew to be evidential, or conclusions which resulted from his own direct experience.

Simply via avid reading, Jed was aware of such things as recent theories regarding the shape of the Milky Way, which is difficult to perceive from a side-on viewpoint. He knew that Planet Earth was rather a long way out, towards the edges of his galaxy, and the faint, creamy strand of light, seen as a blurry ribbon, on a clear night, was its centre, thick with myriads of suns and worlds, seen through arms that spiralled towards him, and far beyond the centre, of an impossibly big swirl that would never be fully appreciated until humans managed to travel to a point where it could be viewed properly. Jed often wondered why so many people did not seem that interested in the cosmos. Maybe they were scared by its infinite size, and our insignificance in comparison, but how could anyone not be aching to find out what was out there? Who would not want to discover it, if they were gifted a chance to travel safely through it?

Jed could also locate the nearest galaxy to his own, within the constellation of Andromeda. He could trace it via a line of stars leading from the great square of Pegasus. Transporting his gaze upwards from a bright star, named Mirach, he found a fainter one. Above that, the same distance again until a weak smudge was visible. This was the most distant object visible from Earth with the naked eye, and could be seen, more easily, if one looked at a space immediately next to it, viewing it with peripheral vision. It filled Jed with awe, that there might be trillions of stars in a galaxy, but also that there might be a similar number of galaxies, in the cosmos. Just how far out into space did all this universal material stretch?

Jed had also deliberated over the overall shape of the universe. He had once seen a documentary, at someone else's house. He watched little TV in his own home. There had been a forum of scientific reasoning, regarding this particular subject, somewhere in California. Jed had been amazed that a collection of the world's foremost astronomers had each concluded completely different hypotheses regarding its shape. If they were so smart, why had they not come up with more similar ideas? One had decided it was a cigar shape, another, a large membrane and one of them a humongous doughnut! The group of six individuals watching this program, which included Jed's parents and brother, and a couple of family friends, had been in much closer agreement with each other, than the scientists, in concluding that they must all have been on something *very* strong. Jed, himself was keeping his theory simple. He had reasoned that, in every direction, was infinity, thus he was always at the centre of an infinitely large sphere. Mind you, if this was true, so was everyone else! This led him to wonder if there were more dimensions, people didn't know about. Infinity always seemed impossible to understand. It was daft how a third of an apple was, mathematically, nought-point-three-three, recurring-up-to-infinity, of a whole one, yet he could *see* the third of an apple, and it certainly wasn't infinite! Maybe no-one would ever be able to explain infinity. Recently, Jed had entertained a possibility that all universal beings, humans included, had been born into a cosmos with naturally limited understandings of dimension; perhaps to keep a few facets of reality, a secret.

Jed also believed, most emphatically, that there must be life on other planets. He felt that it was mathematically inevitable. Amongst centrillions of worlds, there *must* be life, all about, in many forms and stages of evolution. How much of it was intelligent, and why had none of it arrived on our doorstep, yet... or had it?Jed was passionate about such debates. His fascination concerning boundless skies and worlds beyond his own, was reflected in what he read, and his favoured topics of conversation. Once, he had attended a Grantham pub, on New Year's Eve, dressed as a well-loved star ship officer, with his brother Jo posing as a very specific alien. Strange, perhaps, that he was not the type to integrate such TV shows into his living, nor attend their spin-off conventions.

Whatever inspired Jed was subsequently incorporated into his thinking and experience, though he always seemed to keep one foot in the existent world, whilst exploring his speculations and fantasies. These conjectures formed much of the direction of his personal life, and fuelled his movements. Why should a person who always keeps one foot on the ground, still not be able to dream?

Jed was fairly convinced, at this stage of personal experience, that the universe could not be an accident. Whether it had always been around, in one shape or another, or else suddenly arrived via a giant explosion, he found it harder to believe that everything round about him could be an accident. On several occasions, with Father Murphy, at the local pub, he had deluged impassioned strings of thoughts, which might have been delivered with a health warning. One such download had been this one...

"How can all of this possibly have been an accident? How could it all have just arrived here from nothing? If there's nothing to start with, how can there ever be something? And... if there never was a giant fire-cracker at the beginning, and everything has always been here in one shape or form, as either matter or energy, why does that mean it couldn't have been created, maybe by a greater power who created 'time' too? This world seems all too amazing to have arrived here by itself. There could, also, have been nothing at all from forever in the past, but it *is* all here. Given the fact that there might have been nothing, but there isn't, isn't it likely that this has all arrived and evolved here through some more intelligent power than us?"

Upon receipt of such blinding flurries, Fr Murphy would sometimes have lost so much energy, during his attempts to follow such intense logic, that he would sit, staring at Jed for a while, hoping his heart rate would return to its standard level. His delayed responses were often minimal, too. They might have included something like the following...

"Do you feel better, now? For what it's worth, you've been preaching to the converted!"

Or...

"Me too!"

As far as Jed was concerned, after much personal pondering, the universe was deliberately designed, though he was unsure as to how some people, within religious circles, seemed to accept all of this on faith, without even attempting to reason. Father Murphy was most happy for him to muse about existence, creation and all else that could be dissected within his own professional field, despite the fact that Jed's family were a part of his local flock, and perhaps ideally, ought to conform to their faith without questioning convictions. Despite a duty to sell his religious politics to Jed, he would often throw up arguments himself, unreflective of his own beliefs, simply to challenge and charge Jed's viewpoints, perhaps considering that exploring one's mind towards outreaching possibilities, was a healthy pastime. Certainly, Jed seemed to be arriving, anyway, at similar conclusions to his own. Fr Murphy had spent some time, when a youth of Jed's current age, studying the philosophies of St Thomas Aquinas, which had stimulated his brain processes, when training to be a priest. He did, however, believe that the existence of a higher power, whom he referred to as God, should be accepted with faith. If people knew God for certain, surely they would be as good as gold for the rest of their lives, knowing for sure, that they would transcend from their lives on Earth, to an eternal paradise, by doing so. Perhaps the Divine Creator he believed in, had hidden himself in nature, so that faith would always be necessary, if one was to live the sort of existence, he perhaps wished them to aspire to. As far as Fr Murphy was concerned, one of the essential messages of Christianity was that its followers should be prepared to accept suffering within a world where anything could happen, as Jesus had demonstrated with a life of self-denial and an agonizing death. It was all those things which people created and sacrificed for other purposes than themselves, which were deemed to be important. But to perform those acts without ever being certain of God or an afterlife, made them all the stronger, as far as Fr Murphy was concerned. Thus he strived to take what he believed on faith. However, it was still very stimulating to discuss life's big questions with Jed; a very promising young gentleman, who exchanged convention and routine for individuality and employed his experience to deduce further possibilities, and live a more informed life. Still, he seemed to arrive at conclusions which did not, generally, undermine Fr Murphy's principles. One way or another, however they played-out in the field of morality, Jed's ardent philosophical outbursts were a huge source of entertainment for a man like Fr Murphy. After the fire of each outpouring had cooled to a degree which could be handled, and all jokes were out of the way, he would join the discussion.

During these, ostensibly harmless but fierce debates, which became more animated after the first pint, Joe would wilt into his phone and become lost in a cesspool of cyber addiction, only occasionally surfacing to verify a banality or prove, by way of his enthusiastic reactions and retorts, that his motivations were rather more material than spiritual. Until each deliberation was concluded, he would immerse himself in back-to-back games of 'Dirt-bike Drongos' or 'Brian's Bad-feel Bakery'. To hear from Joe, at the pub, when these spirited discussions were taking place, meant that he was either beating his top score, or else being knocked-off his dirt bike by a drongo. Either way, his imagination seldom ventured from the Earth or down a road through history. His life was *here* and *now*; a total contrast to that of his brother. Joe kept *both* feet securely on terra firma. Or did he? His brother had arguments on that theme...

"What is actually real?"

...he would ask Joe, who seldom had answers, and knew that his brother had them all anyway.

"Is all that virtual reality real, or does its name give the game away?"

Joe sometimes retorted with a simple answer such as...

"No, but it's a lot of fun!"

Jed would, generally continue his verbal punishment, rounding proceedings off with something like...

"The things we see in space might be a long way off, and the past a long time ago, but they're more real than the things people do on phones and computers. Life's in the real world and the future's out there, mate. Get real!"

This was only verbal punishment in that it bored Joe to bits. He was not devoid of clever reasoning but preferred to experience more obvious stimuli, such as a shocking headline, a challenge or dare, or a pint of beer. He also drew comfort from the fact that most other people were probably fairly similar to him and might compare more simple and universally accepted things with one another, such as football scores, food and fuel prices or how much they tended to drink. Joe was comfortable in his skin, in his surroundings, and in his pursuit of a relatively simple life. Jed's philosophies were lost on him. Jed recognised his feelings and perceptions, yet continued, as often, there was no-one else to continue with. He also relished the fact that he had a weapon, in his ability to bore Joe to bits, that was more powerful than a machine gun. However, he was also aware that these same outbursts of wisdom and philosophy would most likely frighten other people away, if he unleashed them in conversation. Thankfully, he was usually discerning enough, not to do so. Even so, considering his personal interests, his destiny seemed to be a distant and lonesome one. Nevertheless, he was inspired. He was independent and generally robust in the face of personal isolation. He would probably be able re-enter a busy world, a confident person, after several years as a hermit.

Jed's keenness to discover more about cosmological truths, was a flame that could never be extinguished. His college course would surely satisfy his parents but send his life in the wrong direction. To survive it at all, he would need to nurture resilience and maintain a strong sense of humour. A sense of humour, he certainly had! Armed with crude and cutting sarcasm, dry wit and an acute perception of the absurd, he was equipped for a boringness record-breaking course of Business and Economics with some particularly plastic people. He would revel in those feelings he received, as his humour bounced off unimpressed entities, who were often attempting to grow up, leaving their most endearing features behind, as he believed adults so often seem to do. At the close of college, Jed would see clusters of students, young and mature, accumulating around a great brown door, leading to the Bus Park and front entrance. Often, they would all be checking their technology, for messages missed during lectures, or for a reply to their previous turn in an online game. Social interaction was rare. Jed was proud to breeze through them; technology-free and poke fun with such sarcastic comments as...

"Hi guys. Anyone managed to download a social life yet?"

Or...

"Hey, can you teleport out of lectures with those things?"

Today, the day he had taken the kitchens by storm and discovered Celia, he decided to target a spruce-looking, greasy haired guy, who was posing with discreet head movements to externally, inaudible music in his headphones. Jed mimed words, intending to appear as though he were conversing with him, guessing that the youth with phones would not be able to hear, and would think Jed was trying to say something important to him. Off came the headset, with an utterance of...

"Sorry... what?"

…which Jed followed seamlessly, walking off, uttering a single word…
"…hijacked."

…thus creating the impression for the young, trendy youth, that he had just missed a bit of salient spiel about someone or something; maybe his bus, being hijacked.

Jed loved to shake-up his college associates, though he was never close enough to any of them to call them friends. In fairness though, neither were they! During brief opportunities at break, lunch or the end of the day, when they might have built bridges towards one another, it seemed that technology was keeping them apart. This fact, by itself, might have appeared more heart-rending than humorous, but, from Jed's point of view, there was definitely a net outcome of hilarity. Many incidences had reinforced this. As most people will have witnessed in today's wired-up world, Jed had observed students falling into holes, tripping or walking into parked cars, whilst looking down at their mobile phones, or embarrassing themselves in lectures with ringtones, revealing poor musical taste. There was also a youth, who held up many a delivery lorry as he sauntered up the main drive each morning, lost in his headphones. In Jed's opinion, there was lots to laugh at, but nobody laughing.

Jed had, himself, unconsciously amalgamated the parts he had loved about himself as a child into his adult persona. Jed had perceived that one never grows up. The process of aging and developing is a continuous journey; a part of evolution. There was no instinct to be sensible. Jed's father had seen to this, leading by example, even in public, reciting Shakespeare once, in the middle of a busy Norwich shopping street, playing opera in the car, extremely loudly, with the window down, when dropping his sons off at primary school, solely to embarrass them. He had also performed a square dance in a restaurant, where there had been little atmosphere, at least until he had finished expressing himself. The memory had always been recounted with Joe's comment...

"At least it wasn't a pole dance!"

Indeed, Jed had been trained by the best and was proud to be banal, quirky, philosophical and *different*.

To escape the conventions, routines and schedules of humans, might have seemed appealing enough to Jed, but he was congruently aware that it might be damaging for him, to deviate too far from the schedules of nature. Night and day, for instance were far more noticeable to one who lived, for so much time in near isolation, out in the flatlands of the east. Like many of his liberally scattered, country neighbours, Jed would often experience a burning wish to rise at the crack of dawn. Saturday morning was clearly the superlative. There was no college, no marathon bus journey, and seldom a deadline of any description. Jed would, normally, have completed most of his assignments during dead time, including during the prison-sentence-length, return bus journeys he endured each day. This would be carried-out via a laptop, which went straight back into his college bag, for the rest of the evening or even *weekend*, proceeding his efforts. College and home would never be combined, as long as he could help it. Always work *then* play.

From the moment Jed arrived back at his quarters, he would begin to continue his *real* life; not the *virtual* one he had perceived so many others were now leading, in their developing estrangement from Planet Earth. In so many ways, it was possible he was correct. People had appeared to be becoming domesticated for some time now, driving to nearby shops, communicating through wires, sitting apart at work and during school or college classes, glued to separate monitors. They spent so much time, boxed indoors, whether a building of some sort, or else virtually airtight transport, upon a commute. In Jed's opinion, they spent far too long, shielded from the natural rays of the world which had given them life. Many businesses and institutions had their assets stored entirely online, with many of their operations being electronic. The internet was becoming a vast, global metropolis of virtual institutions, libraries, bank vaults and warehouses, or any implicit money and space-saving structure required and designed by society. Everyone was becoming increasingly pressurised and scrutinized. Raising the bar to aspirational levels, in attempts to increase peoples' achievements, was providing more stress, than in more relaxed times, that Jed related to via accounts from his parents. Humanity also seemed to be interacting less, in person, due to the glamour and demand of online socialising. Even those gaps of dining or vegetating between home and work, were so often accompanied by technology and personal detachment. Some even dined as they walked along. It seemed as though these virtual bubbles, now containing so much of the human race, were depriving them of terrestrial awareness, such as an ability to judge distance or be conscious of the positions of other people or objects. People backed out from cash points without looking, they stormed out of shopping aisles with no thought as to whether someone might be about to cross their path at the end of it. Some stood in the middle of an aisle, taking-up all of it, with both themselves and their trolley, spending copious amounts of time choosing an item. Some would feel every tomato to assess its ripeness, keeping a chain of people waiting, but also daunted that every tomato had been grappled by someone else! Some drove onto mini roundabouts, obscured by buildings or walls without slowing in an assumption that it was likely that another car was coming. And so the list of symptoms continued to worsen. To Jed, even within his shortened perspective of the flow of life on Earth, people seemed to be losing touch with the natural world. He had already entertained a possibility that, one day, people might become virtual beings themselves.

There was so much space, at home. Jed often perched himself on the 'Carveys' Garden Seat'. It was much like those benches in the college gardens, with memorial plaques. Theirs had one, commemorating Mr Carvey's parent, at the rear of the house, overlooking a short and fairly wild garden with typically, English-looking woodland obscuring any further horizon. Sometimes it could feel as though nothing had changed for centuries. Apart from a simple, untreated, wooden fence either side of the garden, all was nature. Jed would sit there most often after college, unwinding from an arduous day, listening to birds and the breeze; cogitating at great length. Such deep thinking could never be classed as doing *nothing*, and was certainly a routine habit. Perhaps it would lead somewhere he could not predict.

CHAPTER 5

Annual holiday plans

This year, once again, the usual and expected holiday plan went as follows...

"Are you guys getting excited about going on holiday?"

Clearly a question inviting a shower of juvenile shrapnel! Jed had replied initially with a rhetorical question, but with a touch more reservation than in previous years...

"And where might that be?"

"Thetford, of course!"

... retorted dad, looking surprisingly alarmed, as if after all these years, he'd never picked up a single sign of cynicism or sarcasm...

"I'd assumed I didn't need to mention that bit".

Joe dived in, before breathing...

"But we *always* go to Thetford!"

Dad continued...

"It's got all we need as a family! It's got your favourite bike trails. It's got your..."

"Can't we go to Tenerife or something?"

pressed Joe again, relatively rudely.

"Why travel so far when what we all need is so near?"

Mr Carvey's words slowed down somewhat dramatically; a bit like a voice-over for a rail company advert, boasting unrealistically, about efficiency and comfort. Then, without Joe calling for reinforcements, Jed arrived to his rescue, in a calm, slightly over-sincere, but un-confrontational manner...

"Perhaps a holiday could be a bit more than just 'what we need'? Maybe a vacation could be more about something..."

...he searched for lost words...

"...something we've never experienced before. Know what I mean? Something fresh or invigorating, that a trip some place new could give us all?"

Unfortunately his father was far too easily invigorated in terms of his own plans and continually skirted any issue, likely to undermine them. He had been well educated in the art of filibustering, as a member of a school debating team, within his most impressionable teenage years, at Appleby Chillingham Grammar School, and certainly still practiced the art, when not wishing to listen to the views of others, particularly his family. This same plan had succeeded for many years, whilst the boys were infantile and easier to fleece. For Mr Carvey, sometimes known to his wife as Adam of Appleby, this was simply about swindling his wife and sons, at least one last time. He would somehow win his annual trip to Thetford Forest; a land where milk, honey, and even more regularly, Scotch whisky, flowed in abundance, and seldom threatened his personal bubble, inside which he would do little more than eat and read. Inevitably, he continued his one-sided campaign...

"There's *always* something new in Thetford Forest!"

"Like other trees?"

...mocked Joe with acid sarcasm and irritated body language. Unfortunately, as would have been predictable, dad was relentless in his quest to defend the Carveys' annual holiday, for at least one more time, and continued in a blinkered, forward motion, proceeding with a verbal 'coup de grace'...

"And it's a *family* holiday! We all get bonding time with the Carveys."

"Things just get better!"

...mocked Joe, with a scorning smile on his face.

After these ungenerous, and pretty negative altercations, Jed was fairly well moved to defend his father, as in actual truth, he really did enjoy his time-outs, camping in Thetford Forest. When all was set up, it was pretty much a great stage-set for his own personal needs and happiness.

"Err... end of round two? I have to declare... sorry bruv! I know this is a kind of back-stab but I kind of look forward to all that out there down south in Thetford. I'll get you a hol somewhere exotic. Promise! Maybe when I get famous?"

Joe had now departed life and was pretty unreachable. Mr Carvey sported a blissful smile, seemingly unfeeling towards the wishes of others, as things played into his hands. Jed continued...

"But Thetford Forest is somewhere in my life I like to go, away from all *that* stuff. You know... the things we're all subjected to in society these days... all that pressure. There's so much peace when I'm being like 'Aquarius' at night, fetching water from a tap in the twilight. I kind of enjoy all that space and time, in a wild forest. It's all I need, really."

Joe arrived back momentarily with the living, but with wilting body language...

"Pretty much lots of space and time here too. What's different?"

Jed was aware that he'd just rather let his brother down. There would be relationship renovation work to do. He arose to make some tea.

It didn't seem to matter to Adam that he'd, once again, been a brick wall. His was very much a traditional and thoroughly sexist attitude, upholding that a father would always be 'Head of the House'. He'd tried this title with his wife. She'd bravely informed him many times that he should not regard himself in that manner, but kindly managed to endow him with an alternate title of 'Head of the Shed'. As the father of a family, he was positive that certain powers were granted with status, including the right to decide where everyone went on vacation. He also felt that modern holidays had become misinterpreted as ventures in which people constantly partied, drank away their money, fornicated, slept at the wrong time of day, saw nothing of their faraway destinations and returned to work with giant hangovers and lots of shame. In all of this he may have had more than one fair point, yet sadly, his main, true underlying reasoning was that foreign holidays were expensive, and of course, there would certainly be no-one in the Carvey family who could not see this amongst everything he said. As Joe removed himself wearily from the sofa, covered with an attractive throw, bearing currencies of the world, he aimed a muted, sour comment at his father...

"I know you. You're a banker!"

He sauntered off to find some undeclared sustenance.

CHAPTER 6

An angry world

The planet itself was aggressive now. Always dynamic displays of fire, fury, tremor and trauma. Each event would trigger another. New vents appeared in the ground, anywhere and everywhere. Fumes poured from fresh craters, cracks and fissures, from the sides of hillslopes; even under trees. This new, ferocious temperament had compromised, too often, those species whose conditions of existence were narrow. More sensitive specimens had perished already in this newly corrupt version of nature. Amongst such volatile dynamics, *surviving* might have been a more suitable term than *living*.

The Ss'iyn were no strangers to quakes and eruptions, currently animating their planet, but they were, themselves, a delicate cluster of lifeforms who had dwelt, since ancient times, in an utterly ideal but precarious balance with nature. It had taken millennia to hone such an exclusive environment of extraordinary harmony in that unforgiving world of cut-throat survival. They had, for an immense age, confined themselves to a diminutive but self-controlled utopia. Was it possible that their very precise and limited existence could render an ironic price? They were creatures of a distinct and isolated ecosystem, yet somehow, very much a part of universal nature. Their awareness of the movements of their world was deep and instinctive. For some of them, now, a deep-rooted discomfort had permeated their collective consciousness. They were becoming ill.

An eerie half-light infiltrated the labyrinth, on yet another sickly morning. For some cycles, now, laborious dawns had disconcerted the posse of reptilian troglodytes, who normally caressed early brilliance with enthusiastic expressions and purposeful meditation. Now they stood, each daybreak, as a forlorn assembly of Ss'iyn, pining for that energy they desired to absorb, for greater wellbeing. They seemed to console one another with sensitive strokes and tilts of the head and face, but skies had become dark and tainted, polluted by gases from sequences of volcanic eruptions, triggered around the planet. Many fauna and flora had already suffered symptoms resulting from poisoned shadows, where the great star's rays could not reach them, through dense and bitter clouds. Some would never be seen again. The world of the Ss'iyn was also intimidated to a significant degree. Once more, on an inhospitable morning, the light of the great star had largely failed to penetrate thick gloom. A nauseating ambience replaced verve, in the canyon environment. Ss'iyn caves and passageways were filled with poisonous breath from the planet's crust. A once bubbling torrent of ether and freshness, that had been their lifeline, hydrating their bodies, cooling their skin; even carving-out their home, was now a course of noxious chemical.

The contentment level of Ss'iyn was less than diminished. Not only were they a race of, fundamentally, cold-blooded creatures whose internal energy mirrored that of their environment, but they also seemed to thrive, even rely under normal circumstances, on the cheerfulness of one another. It was certainly true to say that they were beings of mutual empathy and could only attain a truly contented state in the knowledge that all of them felt the same. Today, like so many days recently, they could not generate that wellbeing. A deeper reason for their dwindling serenity, predated the darkness and was difficult to conceive. It was as though each of their kind had sensed that they were on the brink of something far worse than a tarnished environment.

A Ss'iyn female, Kekadae, squatted motionless, like a statue, above the great precipice, traumatised by disturbingly, discoloured waters far below. Her deep, fiery-red eyes had become transfixed in a gaze that could not be severed. Her posture would have spoken volumes to any remotely cognitive being. In a slump, with head down, she rocked herself gently back and forth, as though regressing to childhood roots, when her mother cradled her, gently swinging her in a comforting motion with soothing murmurs and smiling eyes. There was little comfort now, in chilling gloom. She struggled for breath and energy in the poisoned air, yet it was her heart that was more afflicted. A combination of senses had suggested something she could not know precisely. A bleak future seemed to present itself as part of a vague, instinctive vision. To her species, the planet was a giant, living and reasoning organism. They absorbed its voice in the nature around them. Now it was sick, as was she. There was much wrong with her world.

Outside the canyon, and mostly everywhere else, it was strength and aggression that survived the longest. The most dominant beasts were ruthless killers. Even after countless cycles, the world was barbaric and heartless. There was no other direction; no creation. Only the Ss'iyn, a virtually imperceptible collective, inhabiting a singular, specific point on the planet's surface, had employed the strength of their minds to understand and develop a universe within, without altering the world outside their bubble. Though mentally advanced, they had made no real changes to a planet that knew nothing of their existence. The nature of their world was purely physical and aggressive. Could it be possible that a planet could crave a new equilibrium? Was it possible that the world itself had a conscious urge to alter its own balance? To the Ss'iyn, their living world was a lot more than physical material.

The rocks supporting Kekadae were trembling. Water sources that had maintained most of her form were poisoned. The flora that sustained her existence was choking. The planet which gave her life was fuming. As she struggled and gasped in the arduous air, was the voice of the world so hard to hear? Aggression, that seemed like intent, was all about her in raging outbursts and fitful tremors. Was it so incredible to imagine that her vision of doom might manifest itself in reality? Her heart ached for all of her kind. Her sadness was as charged with empathy as though she were a part of everyone else. Yet she, herself had something unspoken which had grown inside for most of her life. Never wishing to provide questions or apprehension within her kind, she had not yet used that which had been given until now as a mark of respect. Now, as she had often done, she attempted to assess its meaning.

On occasion and for quite some time now, some of her community had witnessed events relating to other Ss'iyn, who had alarmingly appeared to alter, wholly or partially, their own physical structure. Usually this had been a fleeting transformation, and had, by those recounting their witnessing of events, usually been something of a surprise even to the individual undergoing changes. It was as though they had conceived, within an impulse, a need for something that might have otherwise been unattainable, but nature had provided them somehow, with necessary bodily alterations to access it, within the space of that single thought. One individual, who may be called Pep, on account of an utterance he sometimes made, had slipped close to the canyon's edge and had saved himself by instantaneously but temporarily developing extra bulk, in order to balance himself away from danger. Another, who may have been christened 'Gauk', had seemed to be suddenly, somewhat translucent, when attacked by a ferocious airborne predator, which was unable to latch on to any meaningful mass and gave up its assault. To add to the list, one who could be called 'Soriss', had encountered a fierce, angry lizard, larger than himself, with the head of a bird and powerful jaws. This threatening creature had slithered through damp, slimy rocks from the world above, in search of prey that might be hiding inside the sheltering tunnels below its own hunting grounds, amongst the jungle that thrived on the lusher edge of the plain. Soriss was fortunate to identify the threat before becoming a victim. In an instant of shock and unconscious instinct, he transmuted into the same creature as his attacker. It was possibly the surprise and fear of the transformation itself, that terrified and confused the predator, which then turned and fled towards the distant light from which it had emerged. And so, these incidents had continued, seemingly becoming more regular through unrealistically, short lengths of time, in terms of evolution. A Ss'iyn's account is the mirror of truth. All was believed, and conflabs would ensue as to any explanations or meanings of these phenomena.

The Ss'iyn drank from a small pool along one of the ledges upon which they resided. It was more of a large puddle, created by continual spray from the falls that plunged from plains above. Now the cascades were tainted with venom from the planet's belly. What had been the source of purity and hydration was now clouded with contamination. Kekadae approached the pool but feared to drink. Nature's voice spoke inside her without words or any certain meaning. Sure, as an airborne object falls towards a world with a clear direction, her new-found gifts stirred something inside her to recoil, via distress then instinct, and lead her to drink. She gulped the soup of hurtful fluid without consequence, then paused. As ripples in the shallow, ashen pool cleared, she was gifted with a vision. It was the face of a new future. Through an odd, grey, shimmering countenance staring back at her from the pool, she glimpsed a means of hope; not just for herself, but for all of her kind. Surely now she could carry their identity; all they had been, thought or felt, long into a new future. Their spirits would be with her. This was a fleeting hope for the legacy of her brethren but not for their lives. As her true face returned, she disturbed the waters once more with her tears.

It seemed that the very world which had, long ago, given life to the Ss'iyn might now be taking it away. Yet, even in the depths of their discomfort, they might have been keen to surmise whether or not there had been a reason for that. They would not accept that this was merely fate. Great forces of nature had given, it seemed, some special gifts to a few of their kind which could possibly assist them, not just in survival, but in continuing their heritage into a distant future. Perhaps they would not, now, be forgotten. They would share a significant joy in the knowledge that everything they had ever succeeded in thinking, feeling, willing and creating would not be lost. Perhaps their future form might dwell in an alternative environment in which it was easier to reside? They reasoned as they had always done, parallel to their uneasiness and did not despair.

There was an uncanny essence in the throbbing sky. An inner voice spoke stridently to all who were awake to nature's being. It came from far beyond the horizon; from depths of the cosmos itself. There was no dialogue, only an implanting in all souls, conscious enough, of something significant. Its nature was indefinite, but made itself apparent, as a feeling in every sentient soul. It spoke through thick shrouds that blackened the sky. It reached all souls, through the heat that agitated them and fireworks which rained from above. It spoke loudly.

CHAPTER 7

The Dinosaur Exhibition at Alderstow

R ain hammered down mercilessly on tents but bounced-off caravans. Woodlark campsite was well-drained in normal circumstances. However, today's downpours were not normal. Already, its finely-cut grass was saturated and strewn with puddles. This was serious deluging and had been doing its best to drive away those with less staying power, for some hours. Quite a few pitches had already been vacated, by the time Jed emerged, head only, through a zip, shouting to his parents about the whereabouts of food and tea whilst receiving an involuntary hair wash. According to dad, who had, as usual (it was a personal pride of his) been up since first light, and noted a weather forecast on the door of an office at reception, these miserable conditions were here for the day. Not only were campers suffering from adverse elements (some had woken to find their tents standing in pools), but also the pretty expressive bird life, which tended to announce itself at unearthly hours in the morning. Dawn's chorus was far too loud here, according to Joe who had reacted somewhat aggressively, to some unrealistically raucous birdsong. This had commenced, it seemed, even *before* dawn had been awarded a chance to break. Joe had threatened all local wildlife with unspeakable violence, consisting of specific tortures, culminating with being shot out of the trees.

From outside, Jed and Joe's tent seemed to be buffeting about. Large bulges and small points on its surface appeared, as they struggled to prepare themselves for a such a day, in quite a confined space. There were occasional shouts of...

"Will you watch that?"

And...

"For God's sakes, can't you get your flipside out of my face?"

...and so forth. Most of this however, was muted to distant vowel sounds by continuous down-pouring, which drowned everything that might have been audible, particularly inside a tent. Eventually the two young men had wrestled themselves into readiness for the most difficult challenge of their holiday... running those eighty yards, or so, to the toilet block, through sheets of water on inundated grass.

"You first!"

...yelled Joe, attempting to project his voice above serious white noise.

"One, t..."

...and Jed was gone, running like Forrest Gump in a manner affected by his heavy, yellow waterproof and cumbersome, green wellies. A faraway, shrill cry came back...

"Made it! Your turn now".

Joe prepared himself, all kitted out, if not a little over the top, in extra layers of waterproofing. Jed sometimes mused that he could be quite a wuss about physical matters such as weather, walking distance, and *yes*, lots of issues one faces when camping properly in a tent!

"Are you ready?"

Joe barked out to an invisible, admiring audience; always quite self-assured, but often unjustly full of himself...

"Here we go!"

His take-off was awkward, tripping slightly on a guy rope, before righting himself as much as might be expected, under the weight of so many layers. An uncomfortable impersonation of sprinting ensued, as he attempted to negotiate saturated grounds, defensively, with eyes half shut, through pitiless stair rods. For a brief moment, there was an inundation of heavy, squelching footfalls, sucking into waterlogged ground. Joe sensed the thumping of his own heart and rapid breathing, more laboured than at other times, perhaps when it wasn't still first thing in the morning. Then his sense of gravity became muddled. Earth was spinning rapidly in uncertain directions. All sounds became confusion. By the time Joe could register his bearings, he was slithering in an approximate direction towards the toilet block, on his back. Five upper layers quickly wrapped themselves around his head, blinding him somewhat. His late teenage-spread confessed itself to a bemused child, who was making her way back to a sodden, orange tent on the far side of the site. There was a brief muttering of something containing 'eew' and 'Oh my God!'

as Joe shot past, uncontrollably volunteering too much of himself, amidst a non-negotiable situation.

Stifled laughter from somewhere ahead rose above Joe's slithering and bumping sounds, as he cascaded, wretchedly and ungracefully, down a slight gradient, virtually as far as his brother's standing point, by the door of the gentlemen's washroom. Thankfully, he came to rest; unthankfully, in a natural vat of sludge-water. After a few scufflings and strainings, his clothes were reassigned to just about the correct regions of his body. There was no 'wiping down' or further attempts to regain presentation or composure. The chance for any of that, was past. All that lay ahead was a mild threat of mockery and sarcasm from his brother, followed possibly, by supplementary humiliation from his parents. When all was said and done, these were his clothes for the day. He would have to carry out a 'bodge-job' in the bathroom. Before that though, he would have to sort out his brother. The ridicule began immediately...

"Taken up the luge, have we?"

...began Jed, with a mild amount of cheek but a pretty big smirk. This was answered with a mild punch to the solar plexus. Jed 'regrouped' as they headed towards the washroom, both in differing types and degrees of comfort. Jed's cosiness was short-lived. Even with some intuition of the possibility of a minor beating, he still failed to resist the temptation of any further commentary to the detriment of his brother's dignity...

"That little girl must have thought you were a bit desperate for the loo?"

...japed Jed, hammering nails into his own coffin.

A few moments later, a retired bank clerk, called Alan, who had worked in a different neck of the woods to the boys' parents, arrived in the Gentlemen's washroom to find two young men, one covered in sludge, trying to drown the cleaner of the two of them, in a sink of water he had prepared for his own morning wash. Instead of enjoying his ablutions, the cleaner one seemed to be receiving some sort of baptism. Thankfully, this lasted only moments, as Alan was fairy relieved to be informed by Joe that he was just helping his brother, who had a phobia about swimming, to hold his breath. Joe continued to keep up the pretence, patting and reassuring Jed, and using the sort of terminology one might use when actually trying to assist someone in an operation like that. Even Joe was somewhat relieved to find that he had not actually drowned his brother, but might have been disappointed that he looked, almost, refreshed.

The morning wash was now over, even if one of them was dirtier than before he walked in.

"Nice day again!"

...chirped Jed, seemingly unmoved by either the events, which had just occurred, or the weather.

"Least I can't get any wetter or filthier"

...grumbled Joe.

They headed to their parents' tent which was quite a deluxe affair. Compared to their own shelter it was a mansion. They had, in fact, been offered one of the compartments, but had preferred to win their independence. A different tent meant they could talk longer at night, tell dirty jokes and slag-off their parents.

There was an overwhelming aroma of bacon as they approached. Speeds increased accordingly. Before any visual contact was made, a brash voice emerged through a partially open zip on the front of the parental tent...

"DINOSAUR EXHIBITION!"

...bellowed Mr Carvey, through some rolled-up newspaper in the shape of a cone, trying to be larger than life, for fairly trite reasons, and attempting to muster-up enthusiasm (a quality sternly lacking in his family), though perhaps forgetting that his sons weren't eleven years old anymore.

"That's pretty random"

...added Joe. Jed turned to his mother...

"Is that some sort of Tourette's, dad has?"

"I think so"

...she replied, playing along, continuing to invent some slander...

"This morning he was randomly listing the names of different cereals."

"Cereal Tourette's! Get it?"

...joked dad, well within seven seconds, bravely dissing himself. He continued with his plan...

"It's in Alderstow."

"Where the Crusoe is that?"

...inquired Joe, trying to be unusually innovative in his expressions, but mystifying everyone with this one.

"About thirty miles south west of here. Anyone game? It'll be better than staying here at 'Flood Park Farm'"

He acknowledged the adverse elements, via an ingenious corruption of the campsite's name, despite an understanding that, on the strength of today's weather, his family might be wondering why, on Earth, he didn't ever seem to want to consider a trip abroad, even despite his obsessions with money-saving. However, just as with their holiday plans, all and sundry knew that when dad *did* have a plan, that was that. So, after breakfast and tedious pot-washing via more mud, they were off to see, what had been described on a poster in the campsite office window, as 'The Greatest Show on Earth'.

A brutal downpour lashed the Carvey-mobile as it rounded a tight bend into the fairly insignificant-looking Main Street of Alderstow village.

"Look, there's nothing here!"

...taunted Joe, wishing to be anywhere else but *here* or especially, anywhere there was food.

As their fine, off-white, British retro saloon skirted the heavily eroded and uneven stone market cross, it became clear that there was not much function to this particular village. In terms of a service centre, it boasted just a single convenience store, which looked as though it had just manifested itself there, somehow, from the nineteen-forties. There was also, a very small primary school, tucked-away down a cul-de-sac. In fairness, there were some fairly impressive-looking residences with clear historic charm, including one or two Jacobean buildings and one very splendid Georgian house.

"That's where the 'cock of the village' lived!"

...suggested Mr Carvey. Unfortunately, however, as so often is the case amongst such fine British heritage, there were also some dismal-looking council dwellings which had been thrown-up just a few decades earlier, cheaply and un-cheerfully with complete disrespect to any aesthetic or architectural qualities in what might, otherwise, have been a completely attractive little settlement.

The cul-de-sac's entrance was decorated with a bright, red pillar box to the one side and a perfectly rounded, bright-green bush to the other. The bush sat plumb in the middle of one of several well-groomed grassy borders. At the end of this very short dead-end, was a large makeshift banner, rather unconvincingly strung-together with sheets, and painted, using brush strokes of red gloss, obviously intended to create an impression of blood. It bore an inscription... 'THE GREATEST SHOW ON EARTH'. Underneath that was scribed, in similarly, slightly, rough-and-ready block capitals, pretty obviously produced by a different and slightly less careful individual to that responsible for the inscription... 'ALDERSTOW DINOSAUR EXHIBITION'. The final result seemed ludicrously ironic when one considered that this was a holiday weekend when, perhaps not necessarily in whatever might constitute an average British village, a lot of people just happened to be away and no cars (certainly no coaches) were parked anywhere along the deserted cul-de-sac. Such silence and desolation would surely not convince anyone that this was not likely to be such a great show.

The Carveys approached cautiously, under brollies and hoods, with some trepidation that had nothing to do with deinophobia (fear of dinosaurs). Perhaps it had more to do with a dread of embarrassing circumstances in small spaces. However, they had travelled far enough on a cruel day and had nowhere else to shelter.

"Well..."

...began Mrs Carvey with a Dickens of a long pause, after the first word, and a lot of obvious doubt communicated within it...

"We may as well see it? It'd be a shame for the poor people who did this, if no-one turns up!"

The others nodded in ghostly silence. Her logic was acceptable. It seemed they would all be making some sort of sacrifice, in terms of suffering emotionally, by witnessing 'The Greatest Show on Earth', if the distinct whiff of awkwardness in the air was anything to go by. A spiteful flurry of mossy drips spattered Joe's wiry hair as he, ironically, attempted to shelter underneath the arched entrance of sopping, Victorian stone. This was merely a speck of discomfort, however, compared to his earlier suffering in the campsite, at the expense of nature. To add to his suffering though, it seemed he would now have to walk around an exhibition looking as though he had just rolled around with pigs.

"May the assault commence!?"

...whispered Mr Carvey in a pretentious, posh voice, pushing open the heavy, wood-stained door, and inwards they went.

Something of an internal downdraft hit them as they entered the meagre surroundings of a very petite and, seemingly itself, Jurassic-aged primary school. Their discomforts were not perfectly concealed so completely, behind humbling expressions, adopted by the Carveys, as they were greeted by two 'door-people'; all gracious and gleaming, with politeness and pride. This was *their* exhibition, along with a small team of local science hobbyists. Each Alderstonian, involved in the project, was adhering to a mutually-agreed rota, and would get their chance to host this magnificent presentation themselves, during a peppering of days throughout the entirety of August. Today's stewards were a very friendly, senior-aged couple who had already, rather quickly, disclosed that some of the exhibits on show here had been prepared by none other than themselves. The directions of their whereabouts had been made known just as quickly! Uncomfortably, humbled facial expressions and fabricated smiles had been quickly worn by all the Carveys, within a flood of necessity and social accosting at the entrance. Their embarrassment could scarcely have been made greater if one of them had accidentally unleashed a personal force of wind amidst the pressing silence of THE GREATEST SHOW ON EARTH.

Having been financially challenged, in the name of charity, with a door fee as well as an optional donation to school science, which could not easily be *considered* optional under the guilt-tripping circumstances, they proceeded further into an almost impenetrable, library atmosphere. This was an unspoken hush, requested strongly without words, from silent powers at the door. It was difficult to judge which way to proceed around the room, given the fact that so much of the show consisted of information rather than realistic exhibits. There was also an absence of signs or a system of direction in place. Mrs Carvey lurched in a general direction towards her family, looking as though she was in some sort of pain and perhaps suffering a minor spasm…

"I think we should head for the exhibits they've done, first"

…she whispered with tremendous care and excruciating enunciation, attempting to gesture towards the couple at the door with a finger pointing at them through the invisible, far side of her body. It was clear, as the family glanced back, that *all* of their movements would be monitored, especially whilst they observed those most cherished exhibits! They continued to muster-up false smiles and fake enthusiasm in an attempt to satisfy their captors and survive the experience without a conscience.

In just a few moments of intense, silent reading, it became clear, from the information, that there *was* in fact, an order to the proceedings. Everything was arranged in a timeline. However, they skipped the birth of Planet Earth to visit a future point, when dinosaurs first appeared, and so too did a model made by the couple at the entrance, whose intense gazes had finally burnt through anyone's resolve to view the exhibition in chronological order. To achieve this, the Carveys had skipped more than four billion years of history, landing in the Triassic Period, almost two hundred and fifty million years in their past. The elderly couple's model, consisted of a painted papier-mâché landscape, complete with its volcanic peak, a few miniature, living cacti and shrubs, representing jungle and a small scattering of rubber dinosaurs, all surprisingly minding their own business. Whilst cleverly emulating positive, creative facial manifestations and body language, separate to what he was actually saying, Jed managed to murmur, in words almost totally devoid of consonants…

"Shouldn't that one be eating the other?"

He was gesturing towards a tiny dinosaur, labelled as a 'compognathus', which was standing virtually right next to a nonchalant T Rex.

"Perhaps he's already had his 5-a-day?

…retorted Mr Carvey, referring to dinosaurs rather than vegetables, and using equally flamboyant gesturing to accompany his whispering. By now, the two at the door were clearly ecstatic to see their noble offering at The Greatest Show on Earth being so admired. One of them had sat down, perhaps due to over-excitement.

As time passed, their whispering died-down somewhat. All four of them returned to Earth's creation and began reading the timeline. There were two main reasons for this. Firstly, this was a family controlled by bankers. With such a price for household admissions, it would be necessary to grab their money's-worth. Secondly, however, although nobody declared it out loud, the subject matter was proving to be rather interesting, even with a lack of exhibits and a small-time village ethos. They were all avid readers and this was a highly absorbing book, scattered about a room. Even Joe, who was sometimes a bit restless and difficult to amuse, had become more than keen to ingest the grand story of his own planet's natural history.

By the end of the first row of home-crafted exhibits, upon cheap dining tables, over four billion years had passed. The dinosaurs they had first perused, began to reappear. Some way down the next row, after much detail on these great monsters, including a memorable collection of large, plaster-of-Paris bones, was a sizeable placard, with a grand amount of information, presented like the opening of a story. By now, Jed who had begun the tour in pole position, had been relegated to fourth on account of his fascination and scrupulousness with reading, plus a wish to observe as many details as possible. Now he stood transfixed by the momentous story of a planet which was once subject to an event that almost deleted its history. Jed sensed much passion from these writings. Despite a pretty embarrassing atmosphere, he saw great spirit inside the 'Rome' which people had tried to build upon their humble stage. The introductory sign read as follows…

'Almost fourteen billion years had passed beyond the birth of our cosmos. For *four* of those, this glistening jewel of a planet had subsided in peace. Its heavenly beauty, shone out into the depths of space. Upon its richly oxygenated surface were wild forests, luscious jungles, awesome, ice-capped mountain ranges, freshwater lakes and salty oceans. Freshening rain and cooling breezes soothed those creatures that thrived amongst its generous vegetation and sheltering trees. Life was barbaric. Strong preyed upon weak. The death of one creature was life for another, yet nature thrived, in full flow. All was balance and beauty. For so long this unfettered world flourished, like a giant garden floating amongst the stars. It seemed that nothing upon Earth itself could alter what had so long been a utopia, but therein lay a question!

'About sixty-five million years ago, Earth was covered in ash and noxious gas...'

At this point, Jed was distracted by his brother, pulling a demented face at him from the next row, but was unamused and continued to read about how an enormous meteorite, about seven miles across, which created a crater, reputedly ninety-three miles broad and twelve miles deep, had been the final straw, when added to so much volcanic activity in recent times. All was plunged into darkness and sickness. A precious utopia was lost forever. The author brought everything to the reader, with blinding reality and emotive language. Jed almost shed a tear at this point. Whoever had written this, possessed more than just fervour and succeeded in illustrating to him, just how stunning his world might once have been. It was vibrant, flourishing and wired to whatever forces of nature, pulsed throughout the great beyond.

Jed continued to read the latter part of the description...

'Food supplies ran out. The giant beasts' size was their own downfall. So much of their planet's vegetation was quite suddenly gone. All that remained was the rotting corpses of their neighbours, cloaked in a blackness of continual night. This was their last chance saloon, for sustenance. After that, there was nothing but themselves, needing to feast upon something equally as great. They became dead meat themselves! A monumental era had perished with them.

Only those who could fly to better grounds, or else take to safe and un-acidic or non-molten bodies of water, would survive the holocaust. Perhaps, there were species, amongst the multitudes lost, which could adapt in other ways.

When a species, like our own, has lived upon a world, for just a blink of an eye, how can they ever know of *all* that has gone before? Our planet will carry secrets into eternity. Perhaps we should ensure that we don't become a secret, ourselves!'

Jed was riveted and full of speculation. Why had he taken no notice of all this before? The great meteor had destroyed so much including, surely, lots of evidence. As usual, Jed began to cogitate upon details, events and possibilities. In his opinion, The Greatest Show on Earth had provided him with the mightiest inspiration he could ever remember.

The show closed with a joke which Mrs Carvey claimed had been stolen from the internet. It read…

Q: What do you get when a dinosaur breaks wind?

A: Out of the way.

Jed's family left the building, a little short of pocket and disenchanted with the calibre of the show, though somewhat absorbed by all they'd read. Perhaps this should simply have been a magazine or book, not a show. Jed himself, however, was an individual who required little celluloid magic to crumble his cookie. This was something spellbinding to feed his hungry mind. He thanked the people at the door with a sincerity seldom witnessed in most of his personal exchanges and raced out through the rain towards his family. There was little to cheer about outside, but Mr Carvey lightened the mood with his single utterance of…

"Food!"

A spark had been lit in Jed's mind. There was something about this experience, he could not discern. It was as though he shared a personal connection with the things he had just experienced. Something in the past had alerted his spirit, somehow. His attentions were open. A lot of things in life were still a mystery. He would keep asking questions. Jed believed that the universe had a voice, which people did not hear much in their domesticated lives. He was listening.

CHAPTER 8

Awake, asleep

Much time had passed since the charms of Thetford. Jed had long since forgotten he had ever been on holiday. It seemed, from limited experience, that a couple of days back in the grind, was all it took to provide him with this impression, though by now, a lot more water than that, had passed under his bridge. His term-time reality graduated between a quiet, mundane library atmosphere in lectures to utter silence amongst pastures around his home. A juke box in the pub was his only regular departure from that hush. In truth, Jed was fairly used to this manner of living by now, and did not require too much of a shake-up in life to be content. He had mused that, were he ever to reside in a city, he would mourn the loss of all that space and peace. Indeed, it seemed to be quite a suitable antidote for a day at Greenbank.

There's little more effective than a mind-numbing day, spent mostly in freeze-frame, suffering lacklustre business classes, amongst grim lecture room furniture, oppressive lighting and 'nodding dogs of convention' (as Jed had labelled all those who accept and adopt all those norms of society), to ensure a good night's sleep. He was sometimes convinced that all of this gruesomeness, was the course organisers' deliberate attempt to determine which hapless students would find those necessary levels of stamina, that would enable them to maintain a wholesome equilibrium, within an enormously humdrum life. Couple all of that with his marathon bus journeys and award-winning walks to bus stops, in both directions, then one might reason that a need to count sheep or employ any other techniques, for a relaxation purpose, would be superfluous to requirement. Jed was blessed with such a slumber therapy, five days a week. His mundane yet exhausting existence had certainly become a sleeping pill. Tonight was unquestionably no exemption.

Jed had not bothered to shut his curtains, since the days he was a small boy. He'd heard so much about air raids, via grandparents, who had experienced a few close calls with German doodlebugs traversing local skies, cruising menacingly aloft with deep, rumbling drones and menacing clatters. They had passed above them, terrifyingly slowly, considering their fairly monstrous stature. Jed's grandparents had recounted to him, in vivid detail, their unspeakable panic, as they waited for their disturbing rattling and rumbling to stop and a great mass to fall steeply towards the ground. This could always happen, almost anywhere, within a large radius. Where they dropped was pot-luck (or pot-*bad*-luck!). Terrifying was the lottery; indescribably petrifying. Jed's grandparents must have passed on their experiences of this, as well as some terrifying accounts of air raids. A young and tender Jed with infantile psyche, had become fearful that any light source, even a torch in his hands, might make him visible to enemy aircraft, at night. His curtains remained tightly shut, whenever his light was switched on. Every effort would be made to irradicate any gaps in them. Thankfully, the philosophy of slightly older age had now reasoned away any further need for blackouts.

Jed's skylight had become, for him, a sort of spaceship window, during the night time, which also gave him his first and last views of the day. Through this star ship portal, he perused the heavens, and marvelled about what might be out there. Sometimes the view was sharp and clear, gifted by a lack of light pollution, thanks to a quiet, rural setting. He would also *sound the ship* at the start of each new day, as he termed it, inspecting horizons and scouting for activity. He could also gaze down, if he manipulated himself, over and against his upward-slanting portal, and attempt to discern weather conditions across a very broad landscape, stretching out for miles in several directions over fields and hedgerows, from the rear of his family home. There were no roads visible, nor thankfully, any pylons or power lines; just endless pasture. The only local road was at the front of the house, at the end of a lengthy drive, lined with small, circular bushes. He saw and heard nothing of any traffic from the isolation of his room. Few vehicles used the restricted thoroughfare, which led, in one direction, to a handful of homesteads in a most widely-scattered community. In the other direction, quite some distance from Carvey's Cottage, was civilisation.

Jed knew little about other folk, who occupied smatterings of land across his local sweep of Mid-Lincolnshire farmland. Most lived from the abundant fruits of Earth and conducted their lives according to natural daylight timings, up to points when night or day became either too long or short. Now they slept. So too did the world around them. Jed's thick glass window seemed more like an opaque board, with no moon or street lights to penetrate it. Clouds blanketed the stars. Meadows were rendered in deep shadow and silence. From a lower, horizontal position, there was little more than blackness.

As nature's close-down process began to work upon Jed, all perspective and reason diffused into blankness. As he sank down into his own mind, retreating from a world of real events, recent feelings, voices he had heard, characters who had made an impact on him that day, and images which had made their mark, began to come alive. It was as though his brain was playing bizarre, random recordings of memorable elements of recent experience. Echoes of the day persisted without structure or meaning. It's ironic how, sometimes, dreams can be so mixed-up that it's possible to feel relaxed and soothed whilst terrible images flash by. On the other hand one might suffer terror or anger during the memory of something quite mundane. For a while, that night, Jed dreamed of unreal events, seeming to be based at his college, though an awful lot had changed. There were characters who would never have been at Greenbank, in reality, also peculiar happenings that would have been unlikely in such a place, and conversations which were associated with nothing at all sensible. It was as though some newly-made brain connections, from recent interaction, were sparking-off. Jed's consciousness had detached itself and was now drifting in an ocean of memory. After the curious show, there was silence.

Three or four hours of emptiness, might have passed by in a second as Jed, finally, slumbered deeply and soundly. There had been a complete shutdown as his physical being made repairs, but soon something very significant had begun to capture his attention. He grew considerably cold. An icy breeze was buffeting him, and a feeling of intense exhaustion was somehow stirring him into focus. Jed, sluggishly, opened his eyes, or so he thought. He seemed to be conscious, yet aware by some means, that he was still asleep. He repeatedly jostled himself but never seemed to reappear in his bedroom. Before him was a spectacle, completely alien to anything he had yet experienced, anywhere, in his entire verve. He was reasonably certain that he had been displaced to somewhere on the top of a pretty elevated mountain. It must have been extremely lofty as there seemed to be little else below him but sky.

Jed had travelled very little. His furthest conquests had been humble. He was coerced, annually, to receive a vacation at a campsite near Norwich. A few times he'd visited Grantham, once London and, on one occasion, long ago, somewhere in the Pennines, to visit an aunt and uncle. That was about it. His family were far too content, not to travel significant distances through physical space. For Jed, this experience was outrageously unusual and a long way indeed from any occurrence in his life so far. What he saw, now, seemed utterly real yet crazily unfamiliar. It was as though something or someone had penetrated his dreamworld and kidnapped his consciousness.

Somewhere at the back of Jeds's mind was the feeling that, although he was alone, atop an extremely elevated mountain summit, there were others of his kin around, not too far away, but then, it was clear he was not alone at all. Whilst there was no presence visible, he felt something reaching inside him, accessing his thoughts and feelings, detecting his fear and confusion. There was a very powerful force behind Jed, though he could not seem to turn around and face it. Whatever it was, had muted his ability to move or even control his own reasoning as his mind had become unstoppably engaged and deluged with improbable content. There were inexplicable emotions he had never felt, concepts he could not possibly have thought-out nor comprehend and memories of things he had never known. It was as though he were experiencing a stupefying hallucination but was too weak to shout out or react. Limply, he endured the assault until so weak that he felt he might wilt. His head was stacked with pressure, though oddly, he suffered no stress or alarm. His skin prickled with invisible electricity, yet no discomfort ensued. A resultant, reverberating cacophony, sounding something like, alien exclamations and percussive booming, screamed inside his brain but created no distress. Jed was wound-up as far as it seemed he could withstand, yet he was somehow numb. The upsurge seemed relentless but then was quickly at an end. Frothing circuits fizzled-down, speedily. Some pressures within areas of his head, he had never sensed, vented themselves, somehow, as chaos layered itself down, excessively promptly; almost with no diminuendo. Abruptly, all was calm and quiet.

Jed stood, mildly shaking and tingling, not even beginning to try to assimilate what had just happened, although it seemed that within a momentary glimpse, he might have witnessed another world; a completely different way of being. As his mind and body settled, he reached inside for answers, anxious not to forget what had been an enormously powerful experience, but as is often the case when waking from such a dream, the revelations he could have sworn he had witnessed and understood were gone. Only a basic memory of a special place and a feeling of something very dramatic occurring, remained. Everything now seemed to be just a spectacular blur. All was dark and silent. Jed's mind was clearly fatigued as though something had given him a good shaking-up. He descended into sleep once more, but it was a deep slumber without dreams.

Jed awoke to rays of sunlight forcing open his eyes. It was Saturday. He breathed a sigh of relief and lay still, half-closing them and un-focussing until he saw particles as though through a microscope. Long, interconnected, worm-type shapes floated back and forth in his near vision. While this occurred, he attempted to find meaning in the dream he had experienced. Jed was somewhat shaken but could not reason exactly why. He had stood on top of a mountain. That part seemed very real. What made it seem so plausible was the fact that he had never seen such a view, let alone with such intense detail. How could he dream about something he had never experienced? For that reason, he felt certain that there was more to all this. Fr Murphy had sometimes told him…

"Always leave the back door accessible."

In short, keep an open mind. Jed craved explanations but could not find them. Most details of his dream were gone. Whatever had been so mind-blowing had, ironically, slipped his mind. However, emotions require no words or meaning. Even if he could find no logic, he had been deeply affected and was aching to share his experiences. How this could be done, was another thing. What was there that could be put into words? He readied himself for a new day and descended for breakfast.

As it was the weekend, the Carveys would be sitting around a table to dine. In this traditionally sexist relationship, it was Mrs Carvey who prepared most of the food. Mr Carvey had now been sitting at the large, unpolished, round, oak table for some time. Adam and Edie were early risers, even on their days off. Mr Carvey had already sneaked-in a round of toast but failed to conceal all the evidence. This was normal. Jed's entry into the world this morning, for him, was not. Mr Carvey commenced the day's banter with…

"I don't wish to seem rude…"

…which *is*, ironically, often proceeded by rudeness…

"…but you look like you've had a fight with a Yeti *and* lost!"

Jed, with his head still in some very high clouds, returned the serve, somewhat gently, with…

"You don't look so radiant yourself. Too much back-up breakfast, I'm guessing. Extra muffins was it?"

"Now, now!"

retorted his father, partly offended but partially wondering how on Earth his son had deduced this.

"I won't be accused of such things. Besides, if I look at all tired, still, it's because your mother keeps nicking the covers and making me restless!"

Joe was not yet on the horizon.

"Restaurant closing down in five minutes!"

… bellowed Mr Carvey, nipping his nose and believing that he sounded like someone with a loud haler. Joe's room was a very long distance away, upstairs, at the other end of the house and down some ancient stone steps, usually accessed via one or two cobwebs.

"Are you alright, Jed?"

… inquired his mother.

"I'll take the next question, thanks."

…replied Jed, now seated and staring into his strong, builder's style tea.

"Whatever it is… will a sausage butty with brown sauce ease the suffering?"

Jed mustered a faded smile…

"It'll certainly do some of the work. Thanks mum"

Silence ruled for some time while Jed's mood somewhat dissuaded conversational contributions. Finally, a series of thuds, from upstairs, indicated that Joe was on the move. In a brief moment, the peace had been battered with a sledge-hammer, as a fairly out-of-shape figure hurled itself through the door, leaving it to slam, then marched, with aggressive purpose, towards the food zone.

"Did you miss me?"

…quipped Joe, knowing that nobody would be too quick to reply to that. His question was not followed by an answer…

"Zero marks for presentation"

… jibed his father, instead, perusing the scruffy, pulled-on clothes, spare midriff spilling out between them all, and an illegal hairstyle. All was born of the ethos…

"I don't have to wash or topiarise myself at the weekend".

Joe proceeded to tear off more than a *share* of the 'tear and share' loaf and paste it with copious amounts of peanut butter and jelly.

"You look like... well... you don't look too good today?"

... decided Joe, aiming at his brother.

"Thanks, bro"

...retorted Jed without moving a muscle; still studying his barely-touched tea.

There was a further, awkward silence. Jed's mood was certainly holding back the usual exuberance, which generally ensued like a low-key, bubbling stream at the start of a weekend. Mrs Carvey could hold her breath no longer and attempted to address the issue with above-the-norm, sympathetic tones...

"Jed... darling"

...she began, working fairly hard with expressions and body-language, then slightly altering her seating position for the next bit...

"We're your family. You can tell us if there's something troubling you"

She paused and altered her tone slightly...

"You seemed fine when we all went to bed last night?"

Jed was not upset. He was not consumed with emotion. He was inwardly shaken and not even completely certain as to why. A major part of him was convinced that something, perhaps supernatural, had somehow got into his mind in the middle of the night, but then, there was also that large fragment of him, which embraced what his family would all be thinking. What, on this planet, might there have ever been, to convince them that he might have endured more than a dream? Although he was fairly anxious to disclose his encounter, with someone, he couldn't help feeling that his family might not be the best outlet. However, he was somewhat cornered here, by people who cared for him. He opened-up.

"Take a deep breath and promise to take me seriously"

...he began. They all breathed in and out, fairly audibly and visibly...

"Last night..."

he swallowed...

"It seems as though I was transported to the top of a really high mountain and mentally invaded by an alien force"

There was a hush. It seemed, if their expressions were anything to go by, that there was actually some understanding amongst them. All three of them looked, even, slightly awe-struck, but then *one* might have thought again. Jed's family unit which was, ideally, supposed to be ready to look after him at times of need, was fighting for composure. Their intense expressions were a bit overpowering and off-putting. Fortunately, Jed had temporarily adopted a position with his head down and continued.

"It was so real. I know I was there!"

Joe's head went down too, now for different reasons. He was struggling and might not hold out much longer.

"Okay, you're still with me. Thanks! It was an amazing atmosphere. You two were back here, at home, I think..."

Jed gestured to his parents...

"...but you..."

He glanced at Joe, who was on the brink, but had managed to raise his head again

"...were somewhere not too far away, down the mountain".

Mr Carvey lifted his eyebrows in puzzlement. That was enough to defeat Joe. There was a sudden nasal snort, like the sound of a plastic ratchet and a poorly-stifled gasp. Unfortunately this released an undesirable beast from the rest, and uncontrollable laughter ensued.

Jed raised his head slowly with a blank but un-shocked expression. It was no surprise. How could they possibly have taken him seriously? Joe waltzed off with his food, tittering in detached spasms, to fill-up his tea cup. The entertainment value of Saturday morning had risen, at last. Mr Carvey was, in truth, convinced that this had been some sort of set-up. Jed had often stitched them up via similar pranks. The result here seemed to be akin to that of crocodile tears. Jed's chances of any understanding would be massively depleted.

"Very clever, son. Very, very clever! You had us all going there, for a while."

He chuckled some more before proclaiming...

"Good acting too! Have you thought about a theatre group?"

Jed's expression had not changed though Mr Carvey had not observed it. He too slithered-off; his excuse being to fetch his weekend leisure-pursuit, a financial newspaper. He had to believe this had been a wind-up. The alternative was too undesirable and would question his son's mental health. Mrs Carvey looked long at Jed. It was true his wit was usually dry. Even after making his family smile, he often tended to remain solemn. That seemed to be a regular part of his act. However, there was something here which unsettled her. Something was not normal, whatever that was for Jed. This was not acting. He would surely, at least have explained himself by now. She began searching for inroads...

"I do know that dreams can sometimes seem very real. I can think of a few I had. I once dreamed about a donkey chasing me along the lanes where I lived. When it caught me up, it talked to me about different types of flowers. I know it all sounds daft, but the feelings were so big, they stayed with me for days."

"Thanks mum"

…uttered Jed, dryly and faintly.

"It's OK. I don't expect anyone to believe me. I can't even remember exactly what it all was, myself. I'm not mad. Don't you and dad worry. There *was* something last night."

He raised his head…

"Look at me. Do I look like I'm lying or joking? Something got into my head"

Mrs Carvey was silenced. Behind it all she was concerned. As an individual who lived in the land of logic, banking with real assets and reasoning with provable facts, drawn from a fairly routine day-to-day existence, she had run out of favourable solutions. Was her son losing the plot? Notions of medical options raced through her mind. Those with paranoid schizophrenia are usually convinced that their delusions are happenings born of reality. She would have to wait and see if these delusions became more complex. Jed mustered a lame smile and stood-up. His mother skirted the table and enveloped him with a hug. It provided some release for his frustration, thankfully. He expressed further appreciation, muted of consonants through her thick cardigan, before putting on a jacket and heading outside.

The Carvey's extensive front drive, leading to civilization, was covered in soggy Autumn leaves from those voluminous trees above. As Jed squelched through them towards the main road, he encountered his brother, behind one of them, carving his name into the chunky bark. Joe looked up and smiled…

"Thanks for the laugh, this morning. Have fun, wherever you end up"

Jed felt no reason to scowl or enlighten him, and simply retorted with…

"No problem, bruv. Thanks!"

As he stepped out of the gate, some thirty yards away, he heard Joe's voice shouting against a slight breeze, rustling in his ears…

"And stay off those drugs!"

Jed humoured his brother by swivelling himself around and raising a thumb.

It was a very long way to anywhere from Carveys' Cottage. The nearest library was at college. Jed would not be visiting that, on a Saturday, and made tracks towards his usual bus stop to travel even further afield. His mission was simple. He must find an image of the volcano summit he had visited in his dream, before it disappeared from the mind. As far as Jed was concerned, he had actually been there. Such was his resilience, as an individual, that didn't matter too much, if his family thought he'd lost the plot and couldn't believe him. Making sense of it all, seemed more important. As bizarre as his experience had been and as much as he could easily have believed, in the name of reason, that it was just a powerful dream, he had a gut feeling that it *really* wasn't.

Jed's journey, to Lincoln Central Library, took several hours. Incredibly his buses were punctual and his timetable's schedule, accurate. The boulevards of Lincoln were pretty inspiring and full of history. There was a steep, cobbled street and a very fine cathedral on the hill above it. But sight-seeing would have to wait. Jed was single-minded in his quest and didn't even stop to find food en-route to the library. It was a large establishment, all very plush, modern and comfortable inside, with carpets, comfy seats, computer consoles and a very thorough filing system. Jed's family had joined the library some time ago online. He breezed in and began inspecting lists of its contents.

Exploring a selection of large, colourful travel books, Jed found some of the sort of picture he was looking for. There was a peak somewhere in the North-West Rocky Mountains whose summit view looked fairly similar to the one in his dream. He also inspected photographs taken from Kilimanjaro, Fujiyama, plus some volcanoes in South America, Java and Mexico. He read the name of the world's highest volcano whose name sounded something like a person called Jo, selling salad. There were lots of pictures with climbers, posing on top of it, but no details of its summit views. After some time, Jed began to question himself. There were no exact matches in the books he examined. Surely a mountain of such notable stature would appear in them somewhere. He left the calm and peace of the library and headed back to Lincoln's bustling streets, beginning to doubt why he had spent so much time there. His dream seemed a bit less powerful now. As he returned east through countless acres of rural England, on an even more rattly bus than the one he caught to college, his spirits flattened, somewhat like the landscape.

Jed returned to a fairly concerned family. He had disappeared without communicating to them regarding his quest to piece together a vision. As he rounded the corner into his extensive drive, he decided to keep things quiet and pretend it had all been a joke. Joe and his father were not surprised. Both thought that Mrs Carvey had been a little imperceptive in not reading her son's usual dry sense of humour. She was livid with Jed for leading her astray and making her worry, but relieved he wasn't going mad. Jed apologised, manfully hiding his true perceptions, and promised to make future jokes more obvious. As he ascended the ancient dark, wooden staircase after a fairly unusual day, he began to sense the same emotions he had felt when he last descended that way. It's often noted that people remember their previous night's dreams when they return to the actual location of their bed, yet his feelings lasted for just a moment, after which he was relieved, to begin to sense, that his room might not actually be haunted. Jed slept soundly that night in deep darkness, with no moon or stars, nor any dreams.

Sunday, supposedly a day of rest, arrived rudely, with a sharp crash upon a small gong, which Mr Carvey had acquired from a stall, on the periphery of Sleaford Farmers' Market, a year or two ago. He had chosen to obtain it, for the very reason that he would have something with which to awaken everyone if they were late to rise, which would compromise his chances of winning a decent place to sit in church. As they pulled themselves together and convened, once more at the round table, the banter resumed as indelicately as usual.

"Any more funny dreams last night... the last one was priceless?"

inquired Joe, angling himself awkwardly towards Jed, with all of his cutlery in one hand and the other searching for an overused nose tissue in his opposite pocket.

"No. You weren't in *any* of them."

...responded Jed, keeping his eyes fixed on a half-grapefruit, which had just fired itself at his father.

"Oh, that's hilarious!"

...was his brother's response...

"I've had a few, you featured in which were ...drum roll please ... nightmares"

"Boys, boys, boys!"

...objected Mr Carvey...

"It's Sunday; a day of peace and goodwill"

"Is that why you bang that ruddy gong at us?"

...moaned Joe.

"It even woke me at the other side of the house!"

His father smiled in approval.

"I was having an incredible, amazing dream."

...he declared with a lacklustre use of adjectives.

"Best keep the details of that to yourself!"

...jibed Jed.

"We should all exercise a bit of goodwill, I think, like your father says"

...added Mrs Carvey, managing to chip-in finally.

"You lead the way, mum"

...followed Jed.

"Respect, lad!"

...demanded his father, in truth enjoying the usual light-hearted chit-chat, which was normally just harmless cross-fire...

"Your mother shows enough goodwill just by getting our food ready, while you two sit there grazing on it like a couple of angry farm animals"

The conversation had arrived at its lowest ebb as Jed and Joe began to create farmyard soundscapes and were subsequently attacked by their father using a roll of tin foil. Mrs Carvey squealed from the side-lines, something about a lack of hygiene and dandruff.

Within another hour, the Carveys were paying for their sins at their local church. It was another severe homily from Fr John. They sat for a lengthy period of time, with heads all slightly bowed, suffering guilt for things they might not, necessarily, have done. During this period, he attacked everyone's scruples, took a pop at their lifestyles and criticised their approaches to life. He then placed a topping on it, with a reminder that they should all be attending evening confessions. He then added a cherry on top of that, by indicating that he was fully aware of those who attended and those who didn't! As usual, the only antidote to mass would be the pub. This would be a short, but desperate drive, to The White Rabbit, at the other side of the village. The Carveys would not be the only parishioners to be 'off like a shot', after that particular service.

A virtual, rustic fire, glinted in the varnish of mock historic beams, with a dancing, orangey glow. Horse brasses, which had never adorned a horse, were glossed with dancing splashes of light, from mock, candle chandeliers. A magnificent fake of one of the Earls of Lincoln, posing in full military regalia, atop an imposing, shiny, black steed, robbed all attention within its splendid, moulded, gilt-effect frame. Perhaps surprisingly, was the fact that a pub, bearing the name 'White Rabbit', had no picture of one. Certainly, in terms of history, this family hostelry was a counterfeit through and through. In fairness, it was more of a memorial, constructed with love, care and lots of insurance money, to a tavern which had once stood on the same patch, before being tragically levelled by an all-consuming blaze, only a few years previously. Indeed, The Carvey's visits, for the best part of a decade, had become an important part of the pub's history, within a meagre-sized but close-knit community. They had certainly come to look like part of the furniture.

Who knew how many pints Fr Murphy had consumed already, as he propped-up the bar.

"So this is why you employ a second priest?"

… teased Mr Carvey, sauntering in, with his beleaguered-looking family.

"You're not wrong."

…admitted Fr Murphy

"…but, by the looks of it, your needs are greater than mine, today!".

Mr Carvey nodded in agreement, shaking his head as he turned to the barman and ordered…

"Five pints of Best, please."

"What are you're family drinking?"

…joked Fr Murphy.

There was a slight lull, as Mr Carvey's wit seemed to dry-up; a fairly unusual occurrence. Fr Murphy sniggered inwardly before heading back into his pint and also losing the battle to resist adding…

"I realise you've all been Fr John-ed"

It was as though a fuse had been lit. All chipped-in at once, off-loading exasperation in his direction. Mrs Carvey attempted to coax him into having a word with Fr John about his sermons, though she was obviously not getting a word in edgewise. Joe was trying to make him comprehend how difficult it had been for himself not to play secret games with brightly-coloured, mythical creatures, during it. Jed was attempting to explain that his brother usually did that anyway. Mr Carvey was simply pointing towards five glasses of bitter being poured, in a single gesture, which said that their Fr John experience had driven them all to drink. In fairness, it would be the only drink Mr Carvey would enjoy at the pub, as he had the unenviable responsibility of driving back home. As for Fr Murphy, in the same boat; he would have to sit-out the remainder of his socialising with nothing more than a glass of water. Whilst he had preached the gospel of the wedding feast at Cana for years, where Jesus turned the water into wine, he was now working with a teetotal colleague, who believed it was evil. He would not wish to return, in any way, tanked-up to such an individual. For this reason, the fact that he too was sentenced to drive home, and also had recently been attempting to reduce his sugar intake, which would not be assisted by drinking juice, he would be compelled to imbibe only Adam's Ale. He readied and steadied himself for abstinence, comforted himself with the thought that the pub was where a lot of his parishioners ended-up after a Sunday service, and justified his presence there by concluding that it was therefore an extension of his church. He considered it something of a duty to drink amongst them.

The elements were shocking. Drenching rain lashed against mock-Georgian windows. A peculiar lighting ensued, with bright rays of luminescence, beaming dazzling radiance from a far horizon, breaking through an extremely dense, daytime darkness. All over the rest of the firmament was a sickly, yellow haze, with an evil dimness on the opposing horizon. Low rumbles of thunder grumbled, virtually continuously. Those mock-Georgian chandeliers, hanging from the mock-Georgian ceiling, flickered on and off at irregular intervals, adding almost biblical drama.

"Feels like a scene from a Frankenstein film"

… remarked Fr Murphy.

"All that's missing is Frankenstein!"

…added Mr Carvey, cheaply.

"Or is it?"

…quipped Joe, fixing his brother intensely.

Jed looked intense and neglected to react. Mrs Carvey became quietly concerned. She had witnessed changes in her son lately which had then turned out to be play-acting, or had she missed something? Her fears were soon dispelled as Jed looked up, slightly startled…

"Oh! Err… sorry… yes, Frankenstein… I sometimes do get mistaken for him. Don't worry. I find that a compliment"

He slid back down into his private thoughts. The others glanced around slightly bewildered. Fr Murphy piped-up…

"You're a bit muted today, Jed…"

He tailed-off and produced an inquiring smile…

"Everything alright?"

His family waited with baited breath. In truth, Jed *was* a bit quieter than usual but only because he was actually trying to recall and memorise five stages of economic growth, in case he was cornered in tomorrow's lecture by his favourite professor, Doctor Alexander. He was determined to be upheld, this time, as a developing, professional businessman.

"Err… I'm trying to memorise college stuff for tomorrow… do carry on without me…"

He produced an outrageously false smile.

As time ticked away, skies brightened, moods lifted and conversations around the room modified into a restful hum. Daytime drink soaked up most cares and, for the Carvey family, soothed the bruising of Fr John's sermons. Mr and Mrs Carvey had regressed to a conversation about stock market shares and Joe had degenerated even further onto his mobile device. After all, his brother was being a bit boring. Fr Murphy, who had been left to read the back of his crisp packet whilst drinking his water, turned to Jed, next to him, and whispered subtly...

"How are things really... you know..."

He winked, perhaps rather disturbingly but well meant...

"...the official version?"

"Thanks for asking, but I'm fine. Really! I am literally trying to memorise stuff about economics for tomorrow. Fr Murphy's face became an irony of smirk and grimace...

"If I was you, I'd be trying to forget all that instead! Is it *really* you?"

He whispered very carefully.

"...or is it what your parents want? I sense that you're not sparking on full power at the moment..."

He went on to suggest that Jed might be misplaced in life, but couldn't really discuss such matters right now without inciting a full-scale family riot, which he described in his own words as 'nothing too serious!'

Jed was quietly invited to come and talk with Fr Murphy at 'The House', as was the way he referred to his own residence, perhaps using an excuse; a lie somewhere between grey and white, that Jed would be picking-up some books on church accounts for a model economic example study. Jed was not particularly anxious about anything, in fact he tended to be highly robust and recover quickly from shame or bad news. However, a chat with his old, respected friend, Fr Murphy, was something which always seemed to bring revelations and new direction to his existence. It was always worth a visit.

Since the inclement weather, a pond had manifested itself in the car park. A now, washed blue sky, reflected itself with giant, fluffy, upside-down clouds, most attractively, in front of the cars. The Carveys arrived at their sickly, lilac-coloured and slightly rusting space waggon, via a torturous journey around the curbed edges of the car park. Their former car had recently fallen to pieces. A new bone shaker had seemed more economical than fixing the old. After attempting to traverse the waterlogged car park, their shoes were tarnished with claggy mud whilst their clothes became damp from extraneous manoeuvres, rendering them pressed against soaking cars.

They drove away having gained a substantial amount of car park surface, but having lost their younger son, who had already departed for a mental break.

Jed was always game for deep questions, though he had since learned to ask the right people, such as Fr Murphy, who also liked to philosophise beyond a general human comfort zone. As a priest he had always had to be game for a debate about life, the universe and whatever else. However, he too, had long ago learned not to open-up with such questions in everyday circles as…

"What do you think about death?"

or…

"Is God a ghost?"

Before he and Jed had driven, just three miles to the village of Calby, a discussion had taken place as to what shape the cosmos might be. Fr Murphy had long thought of it as an uneven volume which had been filled by matter and energy. Beyond that, he believed was nothing as it couldn't exist yet. Jed had argued his 'infinite sphere theory', but questioned how anything could have an unlimited number of centres, with endlessness in every direction. However, Fr Murphy felt that he'd trumped that by declaring that space, which was made of empty blackness, i.e. nothingness, did not exist until one went there. This made no sense to Jed, as he conjectured that 'nothingness' neither exists or doesn't exist and would also still be 'nothingness' if one were to go through it. Fr Murphy then argued that the nothingness would be 'something' as someone would have witnessed it! They agreed to differ, but also agreed that the nature of an infinite universe might prevent any concrete perception of its size or shape. As Fr Murphy suggested…

"Perhaps it's because we're not meant to know?"

Fr Murphy's house was far more attractive than his church and the pub. Whilst beauty is said to be in the eye of the beholder, there were surely few who would disagree. Its history alone brought fascination. Poplar House stood, proudly elevated, above a surrounding sandstone wall and yew hedge. Unlike the White Rabbit Pub, it was pure Georgian. Its central point of interest was unquestionably a large, pillar-box-red, front door, framed with ornate, white pillars. There were two grand windows at either side, and five more, balancing overall symmetry, on its upper deck. Above that was a steep, terracotta roof with two perfectly spaced attic windows and two tall chimney stalks, which had been outlets for many a proper fire, beneath them. The interior was tastefully and appropriately furnished, in keeping with the period from which it had sprung. As they approached the grand entrance via a crunchy gravel path, Jed remarked that visiting Fr Murphy at his residence was always like arriving at Buckingham Palace. He pointed this out in jest, as he was well aware of Fr Murphy's distaste at inheriting a priest's residence, which was so obviously a fortress of boastfulness and wealth; quite inappropriate for a humble individual who wanted and needed to live by example.

Even though each room was adequately furnished, there was a distinct resonance, as Fr Murphy and Jed entered the house. This was, no doubt, some result of the fact that extra space had been created, via excessively high ceilings, but also due to the fact that there was so much bare stone, around, and no carpets. Fr Murphy's most favoured space, when accommodating a guest, was the kitchen, not just because there were facilities such as tea-making, but because it was small and felt less like being in a large cave than an impression given by most of the other rooms of Poplar house. Indeed, its rooms were so lofty, they'd probably be able to accommodate small poplar trees! It had been modernised and minimized fairly recently when one large room was converted into two. The kitchen now had another diminutive space through an arch which contained just a large, brown leather sofa, a small drinks table, an electric heater and a TV. Fr Murphy had applied Feng Shui to this area himself, having been told that such minimalism might provide focus and space. In truth, he rarely frequented the other rooms. All he needed, was situated around the kitchen. Besides, the other side of Poplar house, accommodated Fr John, who came and went via a door at the side of the property. They rarely coincided at home. They had little need or opportunity. Besides, they were both men who enjoyed their privacy.

There was a clank of cups, a tinkle of teaspoons, the roaring of a quick-boil kettle, and finally, a welcome rustle, which had to be a packet of biscuits. Fr Murphy was inadvertently making the latter sound as though they were being ripped apart by a frenzied, foraging animal. These soon appeared in an inviting huddle on a small Lake District tray upon the drinks table, by a sofa, which was now accommodating Jed. Fr Murphy descended upon it, somewhat quicker than gravity was supposed to have dictated, as his knees were certainly approaching their sell-by date and had failed him somewhat upon his attempt to sit down. The net result was an effect similar to that of a large sack of flour impacting upon an air-filled cushion, but with an added interest of also nearly knocking over his coffee table. Jed sat unmoved. For Fr Murphy, this was par for the course. Without a pause, he began to address Jed, with some authority in his tone...

"Now, young man, you must tell me what you think it is you should be doing in this life. Heaven forbid that it's not what you're *actually* doing at the moment!"

In truth, Jed had not been totally certain what this visit was all about. It was, by now, fairly obvious though, that Fr Murphy had concerns about his directions in life. He stuttered, not really having much idea about other career possibilities. Greenbank College was all he had known for some time. He had adjusted to most hardships being suffered, both at the college and in transit, and was largely content with his life, despite a drabness which stretched all the way from Monday mornings to the very end of each week.

"Err... I'm not really certain"

...offered Jed in a fairly bewildered tone.

"That's because you don't know what else there is! You've been forced into this channel by your well-meaning parents... Jed, could we please keep this between you and I?"

"Sure"

...whispered Jed, without any need to whisper.

"Thanks for that"

...smiled Fr Murphy, continuing...

"Your parents are financial people who have made you think along their lines. I see in you, a lot more than that. You have imagination, for God's sake!"

...blasphemed Fr Murphy...

"You have creativity and intelligence which thinks a long way outside most boxes; inside them too! You can't just restrict yourself to the kind of thing *they're* feeding you."

For that, he wrinkled his features to look disapproving, and gestured somewhere outwards, towards civilization...

"Sure, there's a person suited to every career, just this one's *not* yours. Sorry to come on a bit strong and sorry to undermine your parents a bit."

Jed was not wholly surprised about the points Fr Murphy was making, but was riveted that he cared so passionately. It was certainly true to say that his life was often humdrum and a lot of time was spent meditating upon concepts he never used in life. He simply uttered a time-worn cliché...

"I didn't know you cared!"

"I could show you things that would change your life."

...continued Fr Murphy, with zero acknowledgement of Jed's frivolous sentiment...

"I've shared a banquet with locals on a remote Pacific Island. I've watched a sunrise from the Roof of Africa. I've seen great poverty; people who have nothing but still remain smiling and spirited. I've built missions abroad and witnessed unbelievable hardship, cruelty, inequality, prejudice; even terrible violence. I've walked through jungles and deserts. How far do I need to go? When was the last time you were really excited about something? When did you last laugh like a chimp in the jungle or see or feel something that rocked you to the roots?"

Fr Murphy writhed around with excessive waving and gestures as he painted his questioning. He was trying to wake Jed up somehow from what seemed to him to be a dull, grey dream. His answer, however was somewhat unexpected.

"You might well be right about this. I guess my life has been a bit shabby, lately, particularly at Brownbank."

… Fr Murphy nodded and sniggered softly, not so much at the humorous tag, Brownbank, but because he was pleased to see his concerns being accepted and faced constructively. However, there was more…

"I did experience some pretty big emotions the other day, or should I say, the other night"

This merited a change in position from Fr Murphy and an exclamation…

"Oh! Right! …Go on…"

Jed continued…

"A few nights ago, I had an unusual dream. It was unusual because it didn't feel like a dream"

…He paused for effect…

"It felt *real*!"

Fr Murphy was most interested, despite wishing that they could remain on the topic of reality. He really was most anxious to change the course of this particular member of his flock, but he listened with the patience of a priest.

"It was as though I was conscious but didn't wake up. Either that or it *was* actually real. I know it sounds daft but the whole thing really shook me."

"Keep going"

…urged Fr Murphy, by now quite keen to hear the rest.

"I was on a very high mountain. There was so much detail but I've never seen anything like that before. How could I have been dreaming it?"

"Oh, the mind's a powerful thing, Jed. So much we don't know yet. So many skills we might pick up."

Fr Murphy's body language apologised for the interruption as he slid back down into his former position with a slightly bowed head, obviously resuming a listening stance.

"I can still see every detail of the view, but I can feel it as well. It still seems as though I've actually been there; the freezing air, amazing colours in the sky, stinky gas coming out of some of the rocks."

"Hmm!"

...pondered Fr Murphy...

"Sounds like a very big volcano".

"That's just the setting, too"

...continued Jed...

"It's what happened after that!"

Fr Murphy was intrigued and glued to the spot. Although, as open-minded as he had always been, he assumed this had to be just a powerful dream, and trusted in Jed to convey things as they really happened. This was becoming quite interesting. Jed began to describe the action.

"I was struck dumb by the scenery; just taking it in, trying to stand up straight. I was really tired and couldn't breathe all that well, because the air was too thin"

...To Fr Murphy it was as though Jed was relaying something he might have read about or seen in a film, but he persevered with his faith in Jed's account. The saga unfolded further...

"I became aware that someone or something was behind me or somewhere round about that I couldn't see. I felt a sort of numbness and couldn't move properly or think clearly. It was as though I was being taken over by whatever it was. I just stood there with my eyes shut while a load of stuff just poured into my head. By the morning I couldn't remember any of what I had received from this being or thing. All I know is that I had seen unbelievable things, felt stuff I didn't know I was capable of feeling and known other stuff that I don't believe anyone else could know about, either. All the details were gone by the morning but the emotions were big. I tried to tell my folks but they laughed and thought it was one of my practical jokes, so I went along with that. I suppose it was just a dream but it shook me for a bit, and I still can't help wondering if there's a chance there's a bit more to this world than I knew about before."

Quite a few seconds passed. The silence of the countryside was a sound like a soothing hum. Fr Murphy's eyes had been fixed on a distant copse, through the only window in his living room. Its trees swayed with a high degree of synchronicity in a fairly hypnotic waving motion. He retracted his gaze from the distant landscape back into his sitting room and fixed upon Jed, gently patting him on the shoulder and relinquishing his thoughts…

"Quite remarkable! Quite remarkable…"

Jed turned his head slightly to one side, looking quizzically at Fr Murphy, with raised eyebrows, wondering if he'd actually go for the 'repetition of three'. He did…

"Quite remarkable!"

Another pause of silent rurality ensued before Fr Murphy conceded…

"Well, you've certainly out-dreamed me!"

Jed was glad to have been able to share at least one impactful experience after all the situations he knew Fr Murphy had encountered in his own substantial life. He went on to explain to Jed, that he believed dreams were merely an individual switching-off and swimming through one's own memory banks. He attempted to explain his thoughts…

"We encounter strong childhood memories, also recent experience, and its incorporated emotions. Somehow, they all get interpreted as a totally different and often bizarre experience. I've had a few very strong and memorable dreams myself! Once I was flying over my old school and became, I thought, conscious within the dream. I was able to look closely at every detail, feel the cold breeze on my face, smell the soggy, weedy area around the school gate and see steam coming from the school kitchens before the place opened to the kids… I was almost sure I'd been there when I woke up, at home".

Fr Murphy began to conclude that it was probably *just* a dream, Jed had experienced, but it was possible, somehow, that his psyche was craving more interaction and telling him that these concerns over Jed's current path through life were well-founded.

"Leave it with me… I'll do some thinking and try to be your careers advisor. Please don't talk to the parents. I promise to do that if we find what we think is your calling. I may try to unleash a surprise on you. Is that okay?

…He didn't wait for Jed to answer, and simply wrapped-up proceedings with…

"Watch this space!"

Fr Murphy was very keen to redirect his young parishioner along a better channel. He continued with a suggestion…

"How about climbing a real volcano? I *can* arrange it".

Jed shook his head from side to side slowly, staggering his words alternately with each shake of the head...

"I-don't-think-so"

Fr Murphy was having none of it and insisted...

"This is the defeatist attitude of someone who has never experienced anything like that and also never enjoyed any experience which told him he could achieve it. You'd get training, you know"

Jed inquired about health risks...

"What if it blows-off or I fall down a crater?"

"Worthy risks, my boy! Live on the edge of life. Take risks! When have you ever done that before? Life has black and white, rough and smooth, pleasure and pain, easy and tough. That's what makes us live. Without all that, what would we be?"

"Safe!"

...insisted Jed

It was now time for bribery. Fr Murphy was determined to, as *he* saw things, wake Jed up and began to rise from his seat and prepare a potion of hot chocolate with extra chocolate bits. However, he was startled by an off-course bird which hit the window suddenly with quite a crack. He rocketed back down onto the sofa for a second time, uttering...

"Jesus!"

"That's most of the Holy Trinity you've blasphemed at, today"

... pointed-out Jed with a smirk.

"I'll not to follow your example on this occasion"

"Good lad"

... said Fr Murphy, recovering... and became quite animated.

"You see, that's what I'm talking about! You have wit and intelligence. You also have an inquiring mind and little to inquire about. Time you discovered the rest of the world."

Once more, Jed sat alone on a comfy couch with nothing but his brain and the chaos of Fr Murphy's scuffling, coming from the kitchen. In a few moments, he returned with two fine-looking mugs of hot chocolate, topped with foamy cream. Chocolate sprinkles were melting on top that.

"There's a trick I learned in Chile"

...He explained with a shrewd up-beat-ness in his voice, attempting to buoy Jed up. He mustered some sincerity, knowing when he was being very kindly looked-after.

"That really is great, Fr. Just great!"

…expressed Jed, with a high degree of emotion, smiling in Fr Murphy's general direction, so as to credit him justly and unmistakably.

"Think nothing of it. However, despite the fact that someone like me is not supposed to count the cost, it could be said that one good turn deserves another. To return a favour, you could respond to the thoughts I just ran past you."

Jed had perceived a great amount of sense in what his good friend had expressed. He was also most grateful for all the understanding and consoling.

There was a lull, as they sipped their drinks simultaneously. Fortunately for both of them, neither was a 'slurper', unlike Jed's father and brother. There were few things worse for either of them, than suffering one, or both of them, eating a packet of crisps and drinking from a plastic bottle.

In his own words, Jed promised Fr Murphy he would listen to anything he had in mind and think about it for a while before accepting his ideas. Secretly he was quite excited. For once, in his mind, there was a pretty bright patch of fluorescent, evening sky on his horizon. It was warming to know that someone rather special was looking out for him and seemed to have much of the planet at his fingertips.

On the journey home, as the sun kissed goodbye for another day, through rear-view mirrors, Jed tried to envisage a few potential scenarios, Fr Murphy might come up with. He was also mindful of the wishes of his parents and the goals they had always set for him. It was difficult to imagine how they would ever be satisfied with any plan that threatened to derail the track they had set him upon, for a life they might have hoped he would aspire to. Then again, it was *his* life. Should he not take the bull by the horns and forge a way which was more suited to his ability and temperament? Jed figured that, as long as he was tactful and understanding towards his parents and there were no signs of a revolution, they might, even, accept any new way forward that could make him happy. During the same journey back to Carveys' Cottage, Father Murphy comforted Jed about possible dialogues with his parents and again, promised to help, as an extended family member, but he also reiterated that Jed was not of his family's kind! They would always be his flesh and blood but, probably never, his food for thought. They would never understand his ways. Someone who is never understood could grow mentally despondent or even insular. Jed respected the man who was driving him home. He was aware of some remarkable experience and vision, and allowed himself to be guided.

Upon arrival, through deep darkness, in the presence of nothing more than a wisp of a moon, Jed stepped out of the Murphy-Mobile. As he landed upon an uneven piece of turf, on an unkempt roadside, and struggled to balance, his ears just about absorbed the careful vocal pitch of Fr Murphy, rising above the farty rattle of his cheap car...

"Sleep soundly tonight, young sir. Keep up that healthy imagination of yours... all that jolly folly... well, not really folly! Can you even imagine what sort of dreams bankers have?"

Jed grinned as The Priest-wagon sped-on, then headed off on the lengthy trail towards his front door. It was the first time he had genuinely smiled in a couple of days, but also the first time he had ever gained a notion that the world he knew, might be about to open up for him in a stirring, new direction. To add to that, there seemed to be someone special in his life who was listening.

CHAPTER 9

Unexpected night

Not too much had changed beneath the rainforest canopy. For many horizons it stretched out; the lungs of a planet, breathing in vapours from the ether sphere and exhaling overwhelming freshness and richness. So much lived under its protection, on the forest floor, in black, soupy pools, bubbling torrents, small caves of bark, within colossal trunks, in thick, heavy leaves, larger than many a forest creature, or springing from isolated treetops, emerging, victorious, from layers below.

Shade-loving shoots uncoiled into life from the deep cool of a moist forest bed, amongst spiky shrubs, gargantuan floras with monstrous foliage, and bright flowers in the forms of bells and stars. A vibrant hum pervaded the understory, emanating from robust snakeflies and humongous, hovering insects; visiting lilies on ponds then skimming their gooey surfaces. There were large, spiny creatures, feasting on regimented advances of ants and smaller beasts which clung and hung in trees. On less fortunate occasions, a fearsome, hungry tyrant with curved, external teeth, preyed silently and suddenly on all of them.

Thanks to the sheltering forest, life here had continued to thrive in eternal interaction, despite recent threats from an angry world. Maybe there would be more to come.

The Ss'iyn knew of dances of lights in the night sky. For much of their history they had noted positions and arrangements, sometimes in shapes which looked deliberately ordered, yet they had, long ago, reasoned that this was coincidence. They had also rationalised, that on a clear night, they were being witnesses to an ancient reality whose evidence had only just reached them, and had construed that these were all worlds which in their present time may now look very different or even perhaps no longer exist. During a clear night on their canyon rim, in the absence of any other lights than those from the heavens, it was easy for the Ss'iyn to sense that these were simply other worlds, perhaps even similar to their own, dancing gently through the same great void.

For many periods of their existence, the Ss'iyn had been gifted views of the cosmos, far less now, as shrouds of fumes from an angry world, wrapped around the entire planet, seldom offering a gap. This was challenging for life everywhere outside the great forest. It would be inconceivable to imagine that there might be even worse distress ahead.

Lately, there had been a more prominent light, which grew, unlike all the others. The Ss'iyn were aware that some worlds moved across those that remained in position. Some even expanded, often bearing streams of light behind them. But this one, now glowed as brightly as their smaller orbiting planetoid, and was visible, even, behind clouds. Energetic discussions ensued though even the Ss'iyn could not wholly realise the true impact this alien intruder might bestow, until it dominated the skies even beyond the intensity of their smaller satellite, whose phase had now all but reached its completed self.

The Ss'iyn were becoming most uneasy and had started to congregate atop a large, rocky protuberance at the highest point on the upper canyon rim. From there it was possible to view much of the horizon on their side of the chasm. And, on an evening of uncommon *clarity*, they witnessed a formidable reality, now perceptibly edging across their skies.

It was a simple, natural event, and a miniscule incidence measured against universal record and dimension. Yet comparisons can be subjective. To the Ss'iyn, this was a spectacle of unspeakable malevolence, even despite their ability to reason its status as a blameless, innate phenomenon. This was a rogue shard of dense and deadly matter, so outsized as to compare with a minor planet, hurtling, at hyper-speed, towards a region not so distant from their dwelling place, that an utterly catastrophic outcome would, unquestionably ensue. By reckonings of communications and affirmations between the Ss'iyn, it would, possibly, taking into account its current angle and increasingly alarming movements, which told more of its progress with each moment, impact within the lowlands of a peninsula, located in the direction of the daily rising of their great star. Yet, for a beast of such proportion, this would be no distance from their patch inside the canyon. With plain reason, the Ss'iyn had conceded that wherever this uninvited and inconceivably, immense alien bulk collided, it would provide a shattering, even cataclysmic outcome, for anyone or anything upon their planet.

After many darknesses, at first almost imperceptibly expanding, the intensifying light source had revealed something of a tail, as it angled towards the gravity of the Ss'iyn's world. Now the outer-worldly imposter was an explosive ball with a blazing train of pyrotechnic debris, streaking towards the centre of their heavens. It was a tumorous furnace, guzzling on the generous richness of the ethers and far more massive than the Ss'iyn could have predicted from distant observation. Now, as they witnessed its passing, overhead in the upper atmosphere, it was clearly immense in stature, a fragment of a planet, perhaps, and coming down very quickly.

In this world, the Ss'iyn were, by profound degrees, the only sentient beings who could, truly, be described as *awake*. They would lay testament to these events in their mental archives for whosoever of their species should succeed this seemingly devastating catastrophe. Yet they bore no means to thwart its progression, nor ease the effects of its inevitable impact. For so long they had married their movements with nature, as much as they could, within chosen isolation. They had fashioned no material possessions, including technology; not even medicines. They had lived with that continuous line of evolution, bestowed upon them by their environment, without interference. They had relied upon and developed complex memories. They had advanced their thinking, and maintained a calmness, via their meditations, which had allowed the energies of their planet to flow through them for as long as they had occupied organic lifeforms upon that world. Perhaps that was why some of them, after so long, following the natural tides of time, were now receiving special gifts, which might even be highly opportune. However, now the Ss'iyn might, ironically for the sole species in their planet's history, who had ever enjoyed a fair degree of control over their own destiny, be victims of an epic, natural disaster. They were highly advanced yet minimally protected. Their only strategy now would be to wait and witness.

Streamers of breakaway fire fluoresced with brief life, around the meteor's core. As it expanded, with proximity, and progressed, its larger details revealed more composition. In a very short time, it was overhead. Seemingly, now it had reached the Ss'iyn's world, it wasted no time in racing to inflict destruction; even its own.

The collective level of Ss'iyn morale was akin to a translation of pain in head and heart. This would be, for most of them, their doom. Yet through endless time they had grown as one, expanding a citadel of their common thoughts, knowledge and feelings. What they mourned for now was not their own, personal demise, but that far weightier loss of their dear species. What had established itself through endless rivers of time, might now be sentenced to instantaneous termination via an unfortunate rarity of nature's somewhat random drive. Or was it so arbitrary? As the Ss'iyn had debated amongst themselves, at the summit of their canyon, this astronomical intrusion could perhaps, be a result of compensatory effects of, what they deemed as *intelligent* nature, that might now cleanse their planet of *aggressive* fauna. Could it be possible that there had been an instinctual reaction within the ecosystem of the universe itself, which was now about to repel those aspects of a world, where beasts of great might and stature led the weak by terror. Might a force of cosmic, self-awareness now be reacting against their planet and, through greater necessities, be sacrificing the Ss'iyn within the process? From their viewpoint, their planet was a massive organism, which even during their history, had seemed to cleanse itself from time to time, either through storms of the ethers, fire from the world's crust, or else widespread ailments amongst creatures. They might have been forgiven for sensing that, perhaps, their planet possessed its own personal survival instinct; one which was passed to all life growing upon it. They themselves, were children of that same world who had often felt that their kind movements upon a planet, were returned in other ways; like for like. The ecosystem in which they lived would often seem to compensate for their movements, even in complex ways which might not be so obvious. Their planet provided all they needed, yet sometimes appeared to yield more richly when they perpetrated outgoing acts of generosity, or merely, lived harmoniously. For some time now, their world had seem to be sickening. Its fire was often visible. Its rivers flowed with unhealthy hues, and its dark atmosphere was heavy with poison. Yet the Ss'iyn mused that this might not be sickness as such. Perhaps it was a periodical cleansing of its own surface and all that existed upon it. However, there were gaps in their understanding, which might now be answered by this intrusion. One way or another, it seemed that nature's intents were far more complex than their creative imaginations had so far stretched, yet far less random than they once might have thought. Could it be that some effects they were undoubtedly about to suffer, were derived from a compensation of universal scale? Could the cosmos itself, possess an interstellar intelligence; even feel a need for change, within its own self? Had that listening mind, somehow sent this deadly emissary to perform its requirements?

Above the forests of distant coastlands, all sky was ablaze. The trees were not so dense that local wildlife could not be terrorised by the sights of Armageddon. This was indeed, more than a burning rock. It appeared as though an entire world was descending rapidly upon another. A tarnished skyscape, already carrying the legacy of continuous poisoning from the belly of the planet, now yielded little but fire. All life was distracted from its rhythm. An invisible sense in all that thinks and breathes, had alerted each consciousness to the possibility of personal annihilation. Those beasts in pursuit of prey called off their chase to peer upwards at an all-encompassing ceiling of flame, which slid, now very quickly across their view with increasing proximity. Great tracts of atmosphere were displaced and tortured with heat, generating a dull, but deep and disturbing reverberation. With those rumblings, came a sense of accumulating compression and heat as the lower atmosphere was squashed against its planet's surface.

A sense of panic ensued with knock-on effects. At first, the ear-splitting squawk of a giant reptilian bird, provoked concerns from myriads of small, two-legged reptiles that then emerged from every imaginable hiding place, all at once. The giant lizard, who had not moved for a great time, and who all about, had thought was a log, vanished into the sheltering darkness of nearby foliage. The great bird itself, with modest, rounded torso, but thunderous legs and long, spiny neck, hid its head in a clump of shrubs.

The gap closed very quickly now. From the invader's first dealings at the edges of the upper atmosphere, to its impact with terra firma, there were just a few brief, but unique and spectacular moments. Incessant rumblings had intensified to explosive percussion. Random flashes of lightning, streaked across the colossal surface of rock, unsystematically linking bursting spouts of flame. Some connected with the forest, sparking immediate infernos.

Hunters now fled like the hunted. Great beasts squealed, trampling undergrowth. Diminutive lifeforms were sacrificed within a reckless rush. The forest floor shook with an evolving stampede. Creatures, which never flocked before, did so now, even with their enemies. All life dashed together in an effort to escape a *greater* adversary, and reach imagined safety. Instinct had told them what they felt they should do, yet had not guided them, soon enough, towards the possibilities of their current reality. In the minds of Ss'iyn, it might have been preferred to imagine that the planet, who had given life to these hapless creatures, had sensed this invader's approach, yet perhaps purposefully, not warned their instincts. One way or another, whatever happened previously was now inconsequential. Out of all the places on the planet to be, this was the least preferrable. There were no legs or wings capable of escaping what had now thoroughly announced its arrival.

In far less time, than such an immense object might be envisaged to travel, the asteroid had contacted ground beyond the forest, where waterlogged ground was soft and penetrable. With astronomical velocity and power, a gargantuan meteor fireball, as vast as a mountain range, was driving itself deep into planetary crust, beneath the great peninsula that stretched out into boundless ocean. The effects of its impact would soon be felt everywhere, but continue for a profoundly longer period, altering the balance of everything, forever.

This event was a mark of punctuation, amongst the world's story, heralding a new eon. Evolution's path would be reset. Life would have to find a means to emerge from darkness and ashes. After eternities of progression, this planet was being asked to write a new chapter.

The Ss'iyn would deeply mourn their demise but, somehow, embrace the philosophy that this was either a wretched but simple, natural movement of nature, or else one of universal design with a higher purpose, which might not be for them to question. They would watch and wait, from a distance that was quite significant, relative to their world, but miniscule in comparison to the ensuing effects of the giant intruder. They would stand to the last, as a family who had grown together through immeasurable tracts of time. Those with the new gift might discover ways to counter the threat and progress into a new era. These fortunate individuals, now bore the hope of Ss'iyn, who could hardly help being tempted construe now, that *the gift* had been awarded by nature, not coincidentally, but intentionally, so that a part of their species might bridge the divide between this ancient world and the seeds of a future, just about to be sown. Those with the gift might bear the memory of their kind. All experience, all facets of their existence *must* survive this event. They waited in despondency, but with the smallest hidden light of future hope, for a new dawn where their species might still continue its journey. Firstly though, they must witness a show of the strength and brutality of nature.

Since its formation, the planet had seen spectacles such as this on quite a number of occasions. Rogue masses of rock from the open cosmos had embedded their autographs within the world's geology, as a reminder that this jewel of a sphere, no matter how precious, was no more shielded than any other world, from the traffic of space. However, this invader was unique. It was incredulous in mass, and had been propelled, at lightning speed, into a singular point on the planet's surface which was particularly vulnerable and unstable. It would leave more than an autograph, for the future.

No beast could hope to reach safety from this intrusion, even at considerable distance from the point of collision. Ground was now being torn-up at increasing distances from the impact, in all directions and at alarming speeds. All that had already befallen, was merely a commencement of unimaginable reverberations to follow. Great chunks of land were raised and tipped on end. Sure-footed beasts stumbled about, upon them, or rolled hopelessly back through sporadic concentrations of less agile creatures, now unable to progress in any direction, and clinging to ever-steepening slopes, upon which their last perseverance would surely be fulfilled. Tall rainforest trees disappeared into fissures. Every horizon was buckled with jagged edges, slithering creatures and toppling foliage, all shaking with stupendous vigour and destructive might. Now fire burst through. The mighty engine of the planet's molten mantle had been triggered.

All was aflame; even the long-trusted ground beneath. Living cores of established, time-honoured trees, perished quickly above infernos and quaking earth, that had long been a support for their networks of roots. For any temporarily, surviving creature, there could be nowhere to scurry. Now, the deepest energy ever transmitted from forces above, transferred its astral power into gigantic waves that raced through the ground, tearing all things up, rendering an already distressed landscape, even further askew. After that came peace, but a bizarre one. That mighty quake, which passed through all, had very speedily moved on. Now there was an uncanny silence like an eerie calm within the eye of a great storm. Augmenting the stillness, was clarity. For the first time in a great while, even preceding these dramatic events, dusts settled, and steam dispelled, seemingly somehow, sucked away mysteriously, into the ethers. Finally, a golden light from the Great Star, not seen for so long, bathed everything in glorious colour and energy. It was like the comfort of an old companion, restoring a harmony and tranquillity, that had existed in the world for so long before these foul and aggressive interruptions. Yet it was ironic, in the current scheme of progression, and very short-lived.

The mammoth slice of rock from depths of darker heaven, that plunged deep, into the planet's outer layer at exorbitant velocity, had scoured a vast crater, profoundly deeper, even, than the Great Canyon of the Ss'iyn. Now its displaced contents rocketed upwards, at astronomical speeds, on all sides of the impact, as a trillion, fine, white streamers, towards the stratosphere, into an expanding cloud of volatile dust. It was a slowly-exploding, supernatural bomb of unlikely dimension and character, that evolved, menacingly, so far above the heights of other natural clouds, already present. So high in the heavens, dust and debris that had been jetted vertically, at such acute velocities, now appeared to move only slightly, at such distance, but expanded, almost imperceptibly, across the sky. Its, almost silent, ghostly presence was, by no means, all that would now jeopardise what had already been victimised, upon the surface of an ill-fated world. Even now, unbelievably, there were worse nightmares to come.

No sooner had the most significant quaking and shuddering ceased, and determined beasts been extinguished in such malicious fashion, than an impossible and awe-inspiring apparition had materialised, along the entire, visible expanse of the same horizon from which all other recent assaults had sprung upon their unfortunate prey. The view of a lot of this was, at first, partially impeded by innumerable, freshly-formed protuberances of tormented landscape; no longer by elegant, lofty trees which once competed for light, above an ancient forest canopy. A sullen wasteland extended beyond all horizons, now imbalanced and unstable, above fires that raged beneath its chaos. Now, further repercussions of recent, cosmic dynamics, had reached the edge of the picture.

In reality, it travelled at great speed, though, like the immense, creamy cloud above it, swelling outwards in all directions, hugely high in the atmosphere, it appeared to stand almost still. It was an improbable sight; never witnessed in such a way before, upon that world. At first glance, with its unlikely stature and distance through much steam and haze, it might well have been mistaken for a massif of distant mountains. Yet it advanced initially, in barely imperceptible increments, and did so with an accompaniment of muted, but disturbing thunder. For some time now, all gas, dust and steam, both from fires below and the shredding of forest, had been progressing in the direction of a rising monster that was now beginning to provide the ground with another reason to tremble. All airborne fragments, but also anything freely resting on the ground's jagged surface, which was now, itself, undergoing increasing tensions, was being sucked in the direction of an exceptionally unlikely wave, which towered so magnificently high that it seemed as though the entire ocean was aloft in the firmament. Soon it was a terrifying wall of water in mid-distance that even the worst of Ss'iyn nightmares could surely not have envisaged. Thankfully, their dwelling place was some sizable distance from this death zone of deceased rainforest, and

and all that it had once so recently sheltered, though, the planet's reactions to this invader from distant recesses of the darker cosmos, had barely begun, and wider-reaching threats might well yet surface.

After a very short period, in which all was progressively colder and increasingly moist, the mountain of ocean was all but upon the tortured land. A downdraft, from the momentous wave, sucked-out all that was rich in breathable qualities from the air; small blessing there was now no life to breathe it. Then, the most astonishing instances of drama, that planet had ever experienced, unfolded, within a few, brief moments of time.

With no-one and nothing to spectate, and little but carcasses and inanimate debris within approximation, that could be lashed about or thrown upwards, by further forces of nature's malice, the impending skyful of oceanous torrent raged with unsettling swiftness across a last, defenceless divide, until it was an incomprehensible tower of water, more vast than anything upon that world could possibly generate. Deceased creatures and broken trees emerged from crushes of rock and dust, then were sucked, evermore steeply upwards, onto the wave's surface, until they ascended its shiny, arcing surface at great speeds, towards impossible heights; soon, out of view. They would become a part of a constant rain of debris falling from the wave's crown, as it broke apart at its summit, in aggressive sprays of lethal froth, laced with mud and fragments of rock.

For a short while, this part of the world would be a part of the greater sea. All that once thrived and evolved, within that vibrant mélange of life, was now extinct. Its annihilation was executed in such a brief instance, compared to the ageless flow of evolution. Relentless destruction in the blinking of an eye, yet no eyes to witness. As the great wave proceeded, mercilessly onwards, inland, a transitory and uncertain world of water had been created, out, behind its advancing, which would now await a fearsome, receding tide. Fires below would not yet be doused, as the structure of the planet's shell had been compromised. It would remain aggravated and imbalanced for some time to come. A new, but impermanent coastline, now appeared, some way down the shoreline, through steam and ashes, where higher ground had provided resistance. Above its ravaged, rocky cliffs, stood soaking, yet still ashen forest, silently smouldering above a tormented ocean.

Such a momentous surge could not, so easily, be absorbed. All land was deluged for huge expanses within low-lying zones. The stupendous wave, finally met its match amongst inland hills, within the land mass. Its stature had become tremendously augmented, as it bore an unremitting line of attack, through clefts and gorges. At last, it could swell no more and, finally, rose no further. Then a diminishing of the greatest tide, that planet had ever experienced, deposited carcasses of beasts, which had been rendered extinct, huge distances hence, far and wide, across hillsides and valleys and amongst debris of shrubbery, from a once vivacious jungle, entirely stripped of its luscious riches. All were swathed in grey sludge, soil and sand from a far-away seabed. This outer-worldly invader had eliminated vast areas, all about its zone of impact, via fire, flood and physical destruction. Its astonishing power reverberated all about the globe, even obliterating life through its legacy alone, on the opposing surface of the planet. After all that had transpired here, how could this still not be an end? Yet there was some more to endure.

Multitudinous strands of liquefied ground that were sent, rocketing skywards, displaced by the meteor, had found their altitude as a blanketing cloud, which had spread-out rapidly and would soon cloak the entire planet. Out of this enveloping accumulation, came fireballs of molten hail, that now began to rain fire, especially over lands closer to the collision. A devastating rain of lava pellets, that would kill any living beast upon impact, wasted its fire-power upon a plain of death. A storm, never witnessed in the past, nor likely the future, left fiery craters to burn themselves out in an atmosphere deprived of those gases that would keep them alive.

The world fell still, sizzling and simmering. Nothing moved, yet far from blasts and deluges, there was some persistence. Life was resilient, on this world, even against improbable forces. Closer to the blast, some slighter life forms or amphibians, that had sought refuge in crevices and cracks, or deep beneath the surface of sheltering ocean, had survived the holocaust, thus far. Those exceedingly fortunate to have slipped through the fingers of this profound string of attacks, or else be far away from more severe destruction, might be fortunate enough to carry their species into a new dawn. Yet still, they would have to endure great darkness, drought and famine. To have defied such implausible odds, thus far, might still not be enough.

All was growing darker. Dense ash was now, all the sky. The Great Star had long since disappeared, even some time before its usual, nightly passage beneath its planet. A lugubrious, murky twilight, replaced what should have been afternoon. The air was stifling, tainted with poisons from subterranean vents and newly-created fissures. The world throbbed, in a stunned silence. It was the commencement of a long and unsettling night.

A little further inland, from where the great wave had finally met its match, a group of forlorn-looking reptilian beings stood, collectively surveying a dark and starless horizon, from where events of the shortest, but also most vigorous day, ever observed on their planet, had unfolded. The Ss'iyn had been somewhat caught-out whilst observing the cataclysm unfolding from their canyon's edge, yet it somehow seemed to matter little. Now they stood, in solidarity, defying molten showers, that ensued in patches around them. They were highly spiritual creatures, who cared little for their physical demise, but now, in many ways, they had given up. Where was that purpose they had striven for, throughout their historically-distended existence? Their labyrinth was polluted, no longer offering refuge. Nothing was edible. Their waters were poisoned. Far more importantly, from their angle of reason, the source of that energy they had always craved, was unattainable. There was little wellbeing to be gained and diminutive prospect of attaining that internal, communal sanctuary which yielded precious emotion, powerful reasoning or even fresh ideas that had given them such direction, and, though it was of least importance to them, intellectual supremacy over all other species on their planet. They stood in withering darkness, inhaling bitter air, with wilted posture and grief-stricken expressions. They were waiting for a sunrise that would never materialize. They were waiting to die.

CHAPTER 10

The girl who wasn't Celia

Summer, or at least a more favourable duration of it, was doing its best to create warmth and light for students, emerging from their lectures, into sunlit grounds. Most would merely walk through them before disappearing into the local town, beyond, to hunt for snacks in café's, takeaways and shops. It was perhaps startling how many broke away alone to achieve this, tracing crooked paths towards suburbia, whilst glued to phones. A handful of students would generally remain, usually possessing food of their own, thus extending their break, by eliminating a need to walk anywhere. The mass exodus of so many into town, also meant that they had some very attractive and spacious gardens to enjoy, by themselves. However, most of those students did not tend to congregate, either, enjoying solace and private picnics. Hannah was one such individual. Today, as usual, she made a beeline for a part of the extensive grounds, she had not yet visited, heading for a large patch of shrubs on the far side of a great lawn. It was always her will to encounter something undiscovered.

Hannah was content, when controlling her own destiny. Mixing with others was done, when preferable to do so. She was not antisocial but preferred to manage her own company, whenever possible. She listened well, but thought for herself, tending to draw individual conclusions. She was aware of fashions and conventions, but dressed individually and comfortably, often in a fairly punky way, with radically, coloured hair and lots of black, but some fluorescence in a tee shirt or perhaps an array of badges, expressing political or musical taste. Bling was *always* essential.

Hannah had been weaned on rock by her parents, but had also found much solace in other genres, including music from cultures, around the world. Just as she had trained herself to appreciate foods she didn't care for, as a growing child, she had taught herself to listen to and appreciate sound worlds far from that rock with which she'd been brought-up. Even more distant styles, such as funk and disco, could now become appealing. Unlike so many other students around her, who often downloaded tracks and albums, simply because everyone else was listening to them, Hannah would research and discover whatever tracks she really wanted to hear. Her most cherished possession was probably a device she used to download and listen to her music. Any time or place, she could search a world of sound, and access virtually anything that could be streamed through her headset. However, despite a will to discover musical diversity, she was fairly hard to please, in terms of taste. Much of her listening was purely educational, or else an effort to provide a suitable atmosphere for something else she was doing.

On a regular day at Greenbank, apart from her music player, lunch box, latest novel and college work, there would be little else in Hannah's bag. She placed value in things that weren't material, such as walking, discovering or reading. This made her quite different to most students at her college.

Hannah was her *own* person and had always made decisions independently, apart from one. She was studying to be a banker because her parents had cajoled her into doing so. This had seemed a good idea at first, but lately she had been asking herself questions about how well she was fitting-in with all those other people who were studying the same thing. The very essence of her individuality had certainly set her apart from her peers, in many ways. In terms of a banking career, she might be loathed to water herself down, wearing *acceptable* suits and *professional* hair. She shuddered at the thought of behaving in an office-like manner, day in, day out, until her zest fizzled down like a campfire on a damp night. In a job like that, her soul would surely be captured by the material world, until she became a dreary creature, negotiating watered-down aspirations, amidst some sort of repetitive rat race. However, there was still a reservation in her outlook. Her parents were both bank clerks. They were also pretty adventurous, travelling the world and trying out new things. The house she'd grown-up in was interesting; full of artefacts from holidays, colourful hangings, contemporary paintings and photographs. Hannah had been forced to conclude that working in finance did not necessarily destroy a person's spirit. Could it be though, that her mother and father were somehow unique in their resistance to conventionality, or perhaps it was not just them, rather their entire generation? She was aware, possibly because they always told her, that a lot of water had passed under the bridge between their generation and hers. Not so long ago, in human history, communication had been far more restricted. Before mobile devices and computers, which linked the world in many ways, people had been largely confined to detached, isolated communities of culture, which were much more individual, expressing themselves through clearly definable, regional accents, using different terminologies, practicing separate methods to achieve things, holding their own beliefs, adorning themselves uniquely and practicing personal customs with inimitable ceremonies, music, literature and dance. From those days until now, there seemed to have been a gradual increase in the ability of people to share their lives, even at great distances. People had now learned to speak in similar ways, express themselves with more universal terminology, go about tasks in a standard way and so forth. So much of humanity, now watched the same sort of TV or were inspired by similar online media. They spoke with comparable vocal expression and inflection, to people who lived great distances from them, who had perhaps been inspired by the same influences. It seemed to Hannah that her parents had sprung from slightly more individual times, when jazz and folk music could still arrive at number one in the charts. Those had been times, when it was necessary to visit a lot of different shops instead of just a single supermarket, thus forcing people to interact with a slightly greater number of people. In their day, the internet was young and phones were merely for speaking with. People were not continuously sharing details and ideas about themselves via technology and perhaps maintained their identities more strongly. It appeared that Hannah's parents had planted in her something of what they were, themselves. She had been allowed to develop freely and individually. In truth, her parents had found a career in banking most fruitful and reliable and had given their daughter what they thought was a solid start in life through advice and encouragement. In their eyes, banking was just a job, and a key to being able to enjoy such things as travel, arts or entertainment. It was a stepping-block to greater life choices. Hannah had managed to view things from their perspective. She appreciated their love and help and had been adequately moved to opt for Greenbank.

Hannah took an interest in the world around her. She was always genned-up with news, weather or anything of note, that was taking place on her planet. She did possess a computer and a phone, which could grab her attention for some moments, but far and away her greatest interest was a combination of listening to music, whilst reading an exhilarating novel. Though some people might be distracted from one by the other, it was not the case with Hannah. For her, if care was taken, the two disciplines could complement one other. To ensure this marriage was successful, she would usually attempt to link her book with a playlist, in some way by genre, culture, historical period or geographical relevance. Her musical choice might be anything from the plainsong of monks to grunge or grime. It was this effort to add a musical dimension to her reading, which had probably rendered her rather diverse and holistic with respect to musical appreciation. It also tended to carry her attentions away from some more dreary aspects of, as she had come to label it, 'Grimbank College'.

Hannah loved her musical-reading diversion so much, that escaping from lectures was always done with utter efficiency. Once installed inside whatever hidey-hole she had recently discovered, it would be fiendishly tricky to locate her. Hannah's tendency to hide at break times was in no way a reflection of her confidence. If she desired to mingle, she would approach with confidence and contribute as she wished or needed. Her hiding simply guaranteed that she would not be disturbed, but often also, added yet another dimension to her reading. Once, for instance, she had become absorbed in a piece of fiction entitled, 'The Hollow Heart of Heatherbridge Hall'. This was a period piece, set in rural England, at some point in the eighteenth century. For this, she had chosen to reside, temporarily, partly inside a small enclave amidst gorse bushes on the edge of a slight hill, just over Greenbank's southern garden wall. From here, the elevation of a small rise, offered grand views across broad tracts of pastoral Lincolnshire. From there she could make out, beyond herds of cows and sheep, what looked something like an abandoned windmill, numerous smallholdings, cottages and even a large estate with a reasonably grand stately home. This panorama, coupled with a choice of light, Baroque chamber music, had augmented that particular read, indescribably.

Only a week remained of summer semester. The sun was making itself known somewhat, up to a point of things becoming close to intolerable, away from any shade. Hannah had situated herself in perhaps her most intriguing sanctuary to date. Through a gap in a large outcrop of meticulously-topiarised rhododendrons, hidden by its proximity to a college wall in the midst of a lawn, unlinked by paths, was a narrow passage. Hannah had squeezed through the gap into a thin but seemingly deliberately, carved corridor through shrubs, terminating at a small, circular clearing. She gasped in soft delight at her secret find. Its shade was beautifully cool. She basked in a thick fragrance emerging from vivid pink flowers, mainly outside the outcrop. A scent of sweet and spicy cloves pervaded throughout the deep-green foliage. Hannah giggled with a slight wave of euphoria at her stirring discovery.

There was nowhere to sit within her new-found enclosure, but seeing as Hannah had been perched, all morning, on a hard, plastic seat, her young joints told her it was a relief to stand. Thankfully, the springy growth behind her back, returned her gravity a bit like a trampoline, as she leaned against it. The scene was set. She was some way through a fantasy novel, which seemed fairly suited to her location. One might have imagined mythical creatures such as fairies, flying around the clearing. A playlist of tracks from fantasy fiction films made the dimensions of her experience, multi-faceted.

Hannah sank back comfortably. Flora behind her, accommodated. The angle of her head made it easy to glance occasionally, with ease, into an energised wash of azure-cyan above the bushes. Contented clouds of whipped-up cotton, drifted by, below fluorescent cirrus on the edges of space. There was great dynamism here, yet consuming peace. Hannah read on, through magical description and fabled legend. Her psyche had been transported some distance beyond a paranormal horizon, zillions of miles from *Grimbank*. It may have been something of a cliché, as far as more adult fairy stories go, but it was well dressed-up within a fresh context, and gripping enough for Hannah. The combination of her new situation and chosen sound world, amplified the literary experience and assisted her escape from the real world. She was presently rooting for a particular dashing prince, in her book, who might wield his powers and free a stricken kingdom from some grave enchantment.

Hannah's little bubble was burst fairly abruptly, by a most unexpected invasion. A youth, sleek and healthy-looking; his sporty shirt, graded in tone, from dark blue on the shoulders to white at the waist, hanging-out over his light-blue drainpipe jeans, sprang lightly and efficiently into the clearing's mouth. He halted abruptly in his tracks, causing his rucksack to slither swiftly and uncontrollably to the ground, somewhat accentuating the shock. He remained quite motionless for just a moment until a calm smile lit up his countenance. Hannah had certainly not expected to be discovered within her new location, yet a subtle air of surprise on the young man's face suggested that he was just as astonished as she, to find another soul in such a secluded den as this. Within that seemingly motionless capsule of time, whilst her face rose up to greet his, an unstoppable deluge of thoughts flooded her mind…

"I reckon you're an adventurous type. You certainly don't seem like the rest of the students around here. I'm guessing, by this little visit, that you explore this college, like me searching for hiding places. Why haven't I seen you before? Do you have different timings to your day, or something? I never saw you in my classes. I'm somehow not worried that you're going to take advantage of this situation! You seem pretty nice. You're not the same, dashing prince I'm reading about, but you might just come a close second!"

No sooner had this jumble of thoughts invaded her mind, virtually all at once, than he turned around and stole away. Hannah rested the golden storybook on her knees for a moment whilst gathering her senses. For just a few moments, there had been other things, from her point of view, even *more* interesting than reading.

She could have avoided him, when she discovered him, not exactly by chance, at lunch break the next day, but somehow couldn't stop herself from approaching. He seemed harmless and pretty interesting, looking out with obvious intelligence towards the world, from his bench, with tilts of the head and expressions belonging to someone who might be sizing-up elements of a scene. Clutching her pink, plastic lunchbox, she calmly instigated a dialogue...

"Nice day. Nice view too! Mind if I join you?"

Jed was somewhat startled, especially as he'd been talking to himself again, only a few moments ago. He prayed that she hadn't been there too long. He was also, awesomely thankful and surprised she'd turned-up at all, having been somewhat riveted at first sight the day before. Inside him was a cocktail of excitement and shock, with a dash of fear. Today she was dressed in a glowing-yellow vest top, denim shorts and unmissable, almost leg-length, black and yellow, striped socks. It was a thrilling honour for Jed to have such a class-looking girl perch herself next to him on a seat he had chosen quite independently and so far away. He had a pretty good idea she must have been looking for him.

"A good choice of location!"

...he offered, doing rather well, under electrifying circumstances to remain cool...

"Help yourself".

He waved a blind, right arm, ushering her, with airs and graces, from times long-gone which he'd continually witnessed from his father, when fooling about. She settled down, with little commotion, upon the left-hand extremity of Jed's fairly, newly-found bench and began to wrench open her lunchbox. His was already breached. Clearly, he had a crap set of sandwiches and little else. Hannah, on the other hand, was about to take pleasure from a meticulously, engineered tasting plate of morsels, ranging from houmous, carrot batons, cress and rye bread, to grapes, pomegranate seeds and a random kiwi. She sniggered as Jed described his stingy, daily offerings.

"My folks are tight-fisted bankers. This packed lunch is just one way they save money"

...groaned Jed, almost sounding sorry for himself.

"My parents are bankers too"

...offered Hannah

"How do you manage an array of food like that then?"

...queried Jed, with some surprise.

"Simple..."

... came the reply...

"I make it myself!"

Jed was somewhat embarrassed and became slightly hot under the collar. All he'd ever done was moan about his mother's lunches. He'd never even considered relieving her of the job to perhaps improve his dining experience. In typical Jed fashion, however, he maintained an air of calmness, mustered-up a polite smile and retorted...

"You do have a point. I'll never complain again and might even sort my own nosh out in future. Mind you, there'll be none of that fancy stuff you've got there, where I live!"

A spot of sarcasm ensued...

"There's these things called shops. You know, those buildings you go into with money, get stuff and come out with less of it?"

"Aren't we the queen of humour?"

added Jed before explaining that he lived miles from any shop and didn't drive. After a short silence, while he attacked a sandwich that was mainly bread, Hannah, giggling further as he did so, took the conversation forwards...

"It's Queen *Hannah*, by the way".

It was something of a disappointment for Jed to be wrong, having sworn blind she was definitely a 'Celia'. He responded quickly, as seemed to be the need, after she had introduced herself...

"...ed"

...added Jed with half a loaf on its way down.

"Ok...!"

pondered Hannah, beginning the alphabet.

"That could just be 'Ed' or..."

She paused, grinning, sifting through the alphabet...

"Jed..."

He nodded frantically before she arrived at Ned or Ted, but aware that not too many people would even have thought of the name, 'Jed', on their way to all the others. A few moments later, he apologised for not answering too clearly, to which Hannah replied...

"No worries, Jed..."

He was sneakily happy to hear her use his name...

"This was your bench. You didn't ask me to come and sit here."

Jed was ready to reply this time...

"The honour's all mine! You could have parked yourself on your throne instead."

Hannah smiled discerningly, sucking blueberry juice through a straw.

"Even a queen has to relocate herself from time to time".

She went on to ask why it was they'd never met before. Jed conjectured that it would have been difficult for him not to notice her, and then found himself having to explain carefully why that was a compliment. It was a bright effort. He managed not to refer to her so much as the other students who generally looked like photocopies of each other and merged in well with all the brown. He added...

"You seem a bit different to all the rest. Can't imagine you as a banker, though. I'd guess you have a bit more imagination".

Hannah's reflexes prevented her from withholding an obvious reply...

"So do you..."

She paused, wondering what to add and simply stated...

"But here we still are."

Lunchtime always went like a shot. At least, by the end of it, they had discovered that all of their lectures were delivered in separate parts of the building. They had also been using different entrances and exits. Hannah escaped at lunchtimes a few moments earlier than Jed and was always, purposefully and quickly, out of sight. As they stirred themselves to depart for more drudgery, in their respective afternoon sessions, Jed inquired...

"So will there be someone with a bit more spark around to chat with tomorrow?"

"You'll have to find me first."

...came the reply, almost in a whisper, throwing a little fun into the mix.

"That should add another dimension to your lunch break!"

"Great! I really do love a challenge."

...replied Jed, as Hannah set-off, in a direct line, towards her preferred college entrance. He shouted across to her...

"Just so you know, and I manage to get some sleep tonight, there won't be any surprises with my food, just yet. It'll take a bit of sorting!"

She raised her voice, some distance away by now, without turning around...

"Try to put at least *something* inside those sandwiches!"

Both suffered minor concentration difficulties, that afternoon. Warm feelings were far too attractive, not to beat economics to the forefront of the mind.

Next day, with three left before summer break, Jed set off to find Hannah, looking in the most obvious places first, such as their rhododendron cave, as well as some of the more obscure corners of the gardens. To his dismay, and Hannah's, they did not manage an encounter. After some time, hiding inside a copse of trees, Hannah had spent the rest of her lunch break, seeking-out Jed. It seemed to her, that afternoon, in lectures with an affected heart, that two individuals, trying to locate one another, could often be the prime reason for not being able to do so. She made new plans.

The following day, with that particular stretch of summer weather still persisting, her thoughts diverged from normal lines of reasoning, focussing upon herself instead of her location. Today, there would be no hiding place. She arrived at college with different hair, wearing plain, brown and grey clothes and positioned herself on a fairly obvious bench, close to Jed's usual point of emergence, amongst quite a few other students. It was not a common sight to see so many students who normally deserted their campus at lunchtime in these parts, at this time, just that some of them seemed to have been tempted to remain in the college's fine gardens, during exceptionally fine weather. He sauntered out, seemingly with tunnel vision, noticing nothing from one side to the other. Hannah could not have known that this was rather unusual for Jed, who was generally very observant, preferring to know what was all about him. A small wave of disappointment descended through her, like a downdraft before a warm and pleasant day is spoiled by rain. If he went off into the college outback he'd be there until the commencement of afternoon lectures. Her heart had made itself known, just a little, when he appeared from the building. For a moment she considered calling out to him, but something ensued which caught her attention. Jed began to drift slightly in an unusual way. He seemed to be making progress sideways yet facing outwards to the gardens. Hannah wondered if he was doing some sort of experiment. This bizarre behaviour continued to occur. Was there something wrong with him? Perhaps there were other, more profound reasons, why Jed spent a lot of time detached from his college peers!? After a lengthy and convoluted passage, around the lawn, appearing to suffer some extreme form of OCD, he began to near Hannah's bench. Soon, he was just a breath away from her and was easing down, onto the bench. Not once had he looked back. She was somewhat relieved in a couple of ways. After such a performance, it was good to discover that he possibly wasn't out of his mind. She was also pleased that he had managed to arrive at her location, today, when it had seemed, earlier, that he might have marched on into oblivion instead.

"For a moment there, I thought you'd lost it!"

...she smirked, and continued...

"Quite how you did that I'm not sure..."

...then she stuttered to make a hasty point...

"Oh by the way, this isn't me!"

Jed retorted with conviction...

"It's got to be 'you' whoever you are. Anyway, I assure you, you *are* you!"

"Err...I was referring to these clothes".

Jed moved-on quickly and addressed that point instead...

"Good ploy and disguise!"

...he replied, subtly admiring her outfit.

What Jed didn't explain was that he'd nipped outside, from Hannah's usual exit, instead of one of his more regular escape routes, and identified her, with quite some difficulty, without being seen. He had, of course, found most exits and entrances in the building, previously, whilst attempting his usual stealth missions, to discover fresh parts of the environs. After spotting Hannah, Jed had then nipped back inside and resurfaced, via his own, usual exit, acting as though he had noticed nothing and nobody. He was also able to use his selfie app, now and again, when walking backwards, so as not to give the game away, and somehow see behind him. It felt good to have one of his cunning operations, seem to succeed.

"Do you like my boring outfit?"

...inquired Hannah. Jed answered with safe objectivity...

"Often people who dress to blend, can be unhappy with their appearance, but look great."

He then nodded at her, without doing a dodgy wink, to indicate that he was probably referring to *her*. Then, with creative kindness, he added that she made the most common college colours look cool. She grinned, happily absorbing the compliment and resumed today's lunch. In truth, she wasn't too unhappy with her attire but, here and now, this was not as important as Jed saying the right kind of things to her.

It wasn't long before the topic of food was addressed and truths were revealed. Jed unclipped his lunch container, leaving the lid closed for a moment.

"And today…"

…he began in a sort of radio or entertainer voice-over style

"…drum roll…I *have*… further drum roll…"

"Well?"

…interrupted Hannah, impatiently… The lid came off…

"Exactly the same!"

"Well, that's truly a disappointment"

…proclaimed Hannah, smirking.

"I promise…"

She cut-in…

"You promised yesterday!"

"It was out of my hands, unfortunately…"

…he continued

"…She'd made it all before I got back home…"

Hannah interrupted again…

"Are you referring to your mother?"

It was obvious that Hannah knew full well who Jed was talking about, but also evident that she was enjoying being humorously bossy and picky.

Jed continued with his excuses…

"I had a word with my *mother*…"

He turned to confirm the identity…

"…and she's consented to let me create my own meals in future. Apparently though, we can't afford all that *fancy* stuff, as she put it, so I'll have to improvise with what we *do* have. I'm not exactly loaded but I'm pretty sure they are. It's just they save-up and put everything in pots, investment and so on. You know what bankers are like. They're miserly and possessive. I doubt I'll find anything interesting in our kitchen. They don't do interest"

Hannah watched with a fine degree of empathy. It was obvious that things were rather different, in the Carvey household, to her home. She had also deduced that Jed did not drive, through previous discussions of buses. Perhaps he seldom visited shops, either. Indeed it was true that Jed's parents had always masterminded shopping, themselves, for obvious reasons. Hannah decided to compare the spoils...

"My parents are nothing like that! Look what I get."

She sported a fresh new range of goodies which she'd compiled herself, but were evidence of the sort of shopping done by her family. Jed took over quickly, determined to mention something before it was too late again...

"I told mum I'd met someone..."

He hesitated, briefly

"...well, someone worth talking to"

"Aww... that's really sweet!"

was Hannah's affected reply. He continued...

"She told me to invite you to come round so they could meet you. I guess that might be a bit soon..."

He paused again, realising he had just implied they might be embarking upon a relationship...

"I mean... we hardly know each other."

"That's fine... so fine."

She beamed broadly whilst he continued and the plot thickened...

"It might be a bit remote and far-off, but would you mind visiting our local, one evening? My folks and brother will probably all be there too."

"No problem. That'd be just so cool"

"Great... I thought I'd ask as it's nearly summer and I'll soon be sinking back into the land of nowhere"

"I'll come and visit you"

...promised Hannah.

"I have several ways of getting to you."

"Horseback?"

inquired Jed, smirking,

"Actually, that could be arranged."

"Never ridden a horse."

"That's a date then."

Their conversation relaxed into everyday mundanity, now a deal had been struck, until it was time to endure more statistics, cost benefits, market structures and other enchantments. Hannah deliberated over one particular stat, at the commencement of her afternoon session, awarding Jed an overall, creditable eight out of ten so far. Few had been so esteemed. Most importantly,

Jed had been the first to win her attention as a friend. They seemed to share a special warmth, already. He also possessed something essential, in her book... a sense of humour. After pondering her judgements for a very brief moment, she upped it to a nine. He *was* rather good looking.

For the two of them, summer that year, was a brilliant ray of golden sunshine, buoyed with precious feelings and yearnings. They constantly commuted between each other's residences. Hannah had recently learned to drive, and ferried Jed around until an intensive course, perhaps surprisingly agreed by his parents, yielded him wheels, too. Their friendship seemed to blossom as corn ripened and wild flowers bloomed outside Carvey's Cottage. It was as though, for both of them, a missing piece they had not even been aware of, had been discovered. Jed analogised that they had become something like a covalent bond, sharing parts of each other, they didn't have before. Hannah joked that it was better he talked about one of those kinds of bond than a premium or savings one. In sincerity or humour, philosophising or casual conversation, and so many other ways, it seemed that they were a rare but comfortable match and soon more than good friends.

CHAPTER 11

Before a new dawn

A trickle of Ss'iyn remained; those who had the gift. Their special abilities had evolved soon enough for this annihilating event, though it was too late now for their kin. Those with nature's timely endowments, might have considered themselves blessed yet unfortunate concurrently, as they meandered silently and disconsolately, amongst inert ruins.

Inside aching twilight, a Ss'iyn changeling struggled to coordinate his movements. It was clear he could, at any time, make certain alterations to his physical structure in order to adapt to new and precarious conditions, yet he stubbornly held on to that reptilian physiology, which had always been the vessel of his greatest comforts. With forlorn bearing, he found a course through savaged landscape and bitter, polluted atmosphere, until he came to a large pool, that once flourished with rich water greens and miniature life forms. Now it was contaminated with an out-spill of angry discharge and relentless rains of ash. With almost no effort he would be able to achieve a sustainable state within its contaminated waters, yet held his favoured form for just a while longer. He mused, recalling what it had always felt like to be a Ss'iyn; the kindness of a breeze, soothing warmth from their great star, and joyful nature which had prevailed everywhere about him. Most of all, he calmed himself with deep thoughts and feelings of uplifting well-being, projected and communicated to him from his own kind. He had carried such spiritual treasures inside him, wherever he had subsisted, for countless cycles. He pondered for a while, scanning bright memories, then resigned himself. In an instant he was transformed, seemingly as swiftly as he had willed the change. With little more than the chance of a fleeting glimpse, he was a broad, dark mass beneath a tainted, oily surface. For a very great time he dwelt inside what would become, for him, a pool of dreams, as he settled into a state resembling sleep, though through a cloudy consciousness, he kept a half-watch on a throbbing world of darkness.

By now, silence was complete. Not since the world's dawn had there been such stillness. So much life had been smothered. The sky was impossibly dark and heavy, and yielded a continuous dusting of ash. A stench of incinerated chemicals mingled with rotting flesh. That was now all there was to breathe. For so long the world would be suffocated. For a great time to come, in his half-state, that Ss'iyn changeling would dwell, submerged in the depths of his mind, exploring labyrinths where his kind had once lived, soaking-up energies from rainbow spray and glinting sunlight, pouring from a canyon ridge, far above the great river. Such harmony. Such seamless stability. Such unblemished accord. So many eons residing at one with the world. That this would never come again was too hateful to bear. He quietened his losses with calm and incessant, motionless rest. He would maintain himself in freeze-frame until poisons expired and glimmers of life returned. That might be an unspeakable distance in time. By then, his world would be a very different place.

A hefty tree now stood, squat and thick, adapted to dark shade and long periods of drought. A shrub so indestructible, it might even survive a lava flow or cataclysmic storm. The tree's soul was a Ss'iyn. She sensed the world as an ocean of light but with no feeling, yet her memories, within her heart, of prior senses, was a candle to warm the soul. These jewels of recollection, were the sole reason she had chosen to use her gifts to survive. She was a plant but she was not. Her command of nature had transferred her consciousness into the core of this gargantuan shrub. An irony of juxtaposition. A sensitive, sentient soul amongst the armoury of a monstrous tree. She would wait here inside her living shelter, gently tweaking her course of growth, musing the treasures of her psyche, until such a moment, perhaps in deep distance, when an affable energy, so long missing, would finally caress her outer skin and awake her sleeping soul. Then, as though stirring from a long enchantment, she would transmute into a tenderly, swelling half-light and breathe again as a mobile form.

Ash fell upon ash, and lava over lava. Rivers of fire converged on plains, pouring over canyon sides in terrifying torrents. Another Ss'iyn, who had remained long after his kin perished, had become trapped. Although surrounded by converging flows of molten magma, he was calm, weighing his own existence in a balance. Everything he valued was gone, even that which he required to sustain his present body. Why should he not simply wait and watch over what remained of his home until nature saw fit to take it, and himself, away? Yet a tiny spark inside, made him focus elsewhere. Light appeared in his mind like a beacon of hope. All he had ever known was gone, yet something fresh was born inside. An ability to transform might be his saving, yet beyond that, and far greater, was a thought that he might still not be alone. In his heart and mind, the collective conscience of his kind, was dim but not extinguished. Perhaps it was possible they still existed, on another plane of spirit, and could find him somehow. The citadel of their memories was hazy but somehow still apparent and buoyant. A sense of things that had no tangible reason, nor proof, hinted within him that others of his species, with whom he had lost touch, during chaotic events, might yet have survived with him. Perhaps this had been via their own means. Those instincts of nature, found in all living sentient beings, somehow told him that they were either somewhere far away or else closer but inside something which might shield their souls from this angry world.

And so, the last of the Ss'iyn left the canyon and labyrinths that had been his existence from ancient times. It was with very heavy sorrow that he departed his beloved home. With little notion of what lay ahead, he embraced a courageous, new existence. Momentarily, he gazed long at the smouldering ruins of his community and breathed will towards the place from which most of them had departed, wishing them preservation and new wellbeing on another plane. There was no route, from which to depart, as things might have stood, yet he knew, from recent blessings, that unexpected means might still be summoned. Raging rivers of fire, surged close around him. In front, all ground had disappeared into depths below, where all was boiling fire. Without even a picture in his mind or a method in his reasoning, he gave himself up to gravity at the ravine's newly foreshortened edge. In a single, impromptu thought and vision he was airborne with vast, white, featherless wings. Like a giant bird of peace in a scarred and blazing netherworld, he glided higher towards safety and prospect. Amongst his deep sadness was a powerful spirit and a will to survive those monsters that had claimed his brethren. With great might, he forged through volatile billows of angry flames and venomous fumes. There was no brightness to head for. He navigated with his heart, beating back the singeing flares that lunged towards his leathery flesh, then climbed to a quieter elevation beneath nightmare ground and heavy, laden sky.

For so long he soared with modest exertion towards his focus, following a compass of instinct, over a wall of dusty mountains he had lived against for so many successions. Now in an altered composition, he felt new ability and yearning. Despite the rendering of his former life to destruction, he now experienced an increasing urge to journey. A fresh passion was driving him from his bewilderment. Throughout his existence, a universe had lain inside him, without a will to venture from the karma of Ss'iyn. Now, as a creature of flight, he would embrace an ability to investigate his planet, which had always been open to explore, whilst forever enjoying the richness of a network of memories and traditions given to him by his collective. Somehow his family would always travel with him.

An ancient forest spread to the very edge of the coast. Once it had been vibrant with life. However, its stunning beauty and zest was home to great danger, for most inhabitants. Survival of carnage was life's code. As things had stood, all prey but *one*, were food for another. That single exception had been feared by all but the Ss'iyn, who had never suffered the dire misfortune of encountering it, whilst secure within their canyon dwelling. Now there was little to fear, within an eerie, unnatural peace, all was free from peril, but perhaps worse, free from life. From high above, the forest might somehow, have resembled a giant, prickly moss that reached the limits of land, at the ocean's rim. Once it had stood atop impossibly high cliffs that cast a far-reaching shade upon the surf. Now the waters, returning from a great backwash, following the recession of a giant wave, were almost upon it. Each tree had been an environment of its own, supporting multiple species of fauna and flora within its sheltering foliage. Now all foliage stood like dark, grey ghosts adorned with thick coats of ash that drizzled upon them ceaselessly like an ironic snowfall. A rugged singularity of rock stood amongst them, some distance still from the coast. He landed with grace upon it, lording over a stark and empty world, massively high above distant waves, like a god on his throne. Now he faced another great choice, over another lofty precipice, once more with sickness behind him, and eternity in front. For another infinity, the soul of the giant bird contemplated his future. Discovery was a prospect in all directions. What form to take was an immeasurable range of choices. He was bound by decision and tethered by possibility. Twilight became consuming night. Blackness was impenetrable and air, stifling. He spread his broad, heavy wings across uneven rocks and descended into deep slumber. Caresses of silent, empty shadows, softened his desolation.

A cheerless half-light now eclipsed the world. The great bird roused to memories of everything he had left behind. Amidst an equation of reason, was the knowledge that his former life could never return but, somehow, this powerful, winged vessel had created a new urge to discover, as never before. He once again sensed within, that the souls of those who had, like him, moved on somehow, in pliable forms, would also be close by wherever he ventured. He honed their connections and felt them close. They would commute in their common mind as they always had, and forever to come.

Once more, the great beast climbed into the skies and circled as though bidding farewell to that ground from which he had been raised. Soon he was a speck amongst oblivion, out above the ocean, never to be seen again by his own kind.

And so, a smattering of an order of beings, who had progressed as one with their planet for countless cycles, would survive via their own, unreservedly, unique means. Those forces of nature that yielded them such implausible reactions, might continue to assist them in instantaneously adapting to harmful circumstance. Those few who remained, to continue the spirit of their kin, were left with both blessings and sanctions. To their advantage was an ability to adapt, in many ways, shapes and forms, to most eventualities, as long as, that was, those situations weren't too quick to measure. A Ss'iyn, bearing these newly-endowed gifts, might subsist in many forms and situations, for countless ages, as long as attention was paid to local surroundings and forces of nature. Should they be taken by surprise, innate instinct might not be so swift, such that their chances of adapting could possibly be compromised. This was a sanction they would carry into an uncertain, darkly-tainted and perilous world. Nothing, upon their planet, had ever threatened to be immortal. Neither, on the account of this, could they ever hope to cheat eternity either, despite such gifts.

Until such a time when rampant energies, beneath the land, subsided, and that poisonous obscurity of the ethers, fizzled once more, leaving deep and lucid shades of sapphire, no worldly rebirth could commence.

This newly, adaptable race would feed upon compounds and structures that were once inedible. They would inhale mixtures of gases that were, previously, un-breathable. They would extract moisture from chemicals, and tolerate extremes of cold or heat. Now, these future life forms of Ss'iyn descent, would be able to depart the land, taking to sky or ocean. They would cross great divides, scale impossible walls, negotiate complex surfaces, blend with their surroundings for safety, subsist without rest, and even disguise themselves amongst other species, taking on their like forms. Their aptitudes for physical variation, via mind power, might surrender untold ability. If one can transmute their own mass with a single thought, might one then, also possess some measure of mental control over their physical surroundings? If one can affect an ecosystem, in such a way, with impulses from their brain, why should it not also be possible to develop a capacity to discern thoughts or emotions of others of any species, or to affect objects, situations or consciousnesses within their personal environment? On the strength of a rather abrupt spike of evolution, these could be beings of great power, with much time to develop. Now also, they were no longer rooted to a single and simple ecosystem which had, despite sizable Ss'iyn intellect, somewhat stunted their knowledge of the geography and science of their planet. A truer picture of their world could now be discovered through life and travel. This was no longer a species, relying upon a very specific environment. These new Ss'iyn would be nomadic, with a passion to discover. They would conquer those horizons that had once provided only conjecture. They would also carry inside themselves, their communal witnessing of a former world in which life had progressed according to a hierarchy of physical strength and hunting prowess. Through luscious jungles, searing deserts, ice-flanked mountain terrains and life-yielding oceans, the recipe had always been the same. It was the sturdiest life-form which had endured, within any conflict. The meaning-of-life had simply been survival through any means possible. There had been no aspiration to improve, nor develop; only to overpower or dominate. Now a species with a complex and empathetic mind, had been released amongst that world. Life had granted them a route forwards. In one way or another, nature had gifted them this freedom, despite their unique contentment to remain within solitude, only communicating via the mind, which would never offer a physical way forward for their species, nor the environment of their planet. Perhaps, somehow, that ever-present intelligence of nature had seen enough of a barbaric progression, gone before, and, as may have happened all about the cosmos, as long as time might ever have advanced, put a stop to a dead-end continuum that promised so little, in such a jewel of a world. Some life had survived those deadly events that had rendered deadly monsters extinct. Still, creatures would prey upon one another as before, needing to eat to survive, though now, there was a promise of civilised thinking and a fresh way forward.

At this juncture, during the evolution of a particularly unique and stunning planet, it may have appeared that nature, which had continuously yielded miracles of creation, had decided to respect and reward a race who had always yielded as much, in return for her gifts, as they had been provided with, throughout a significant expanse of time. Perhaps, within a greater universal level, an all-integrated, cosmic intelligence, had perceived that these preliminary offspring, of meritable understanding and forward perception, could continue their favourable growth into further tracts of future, perhaps until other evolving life forms built from their experience. Adorned with gifts of adaptation, which now relieved any need to procreate, for the continuation of their species, who could predict just how much of their planet's story these fascinating creatures might witness?

CHAPTER 12

Summit Aspirations

Joaquin headed swiftly across dark, volcanic cinders and dusky-looking sand, towards a sizable pine log cabin, proudly decorated and adorned with a variety of building bling, perhaps the most notable of which, was a spectrum of world flags, wrapped around the hut's midriff. Above the front entrance was a large, rectangular sign of eye-catching orange and yellow, with dominating, black cactus, flying condor silhouettes, and a name in capitals in eloquent font... 'ASPERACIONES CUMBRE' or 'Summit Aspirations'. In his haste, Joaquin slid slightly sideways, scuffing himself against a prickly desert shrub. Oddly, he had almost come to love this sensation, which kept him aware that he was still alive, and working in a hugely inspiring and diverse setting, with a backdrop of rugged, rocky summits and loftier, distant snow-flecked peaks. There was also a generous quantity of cheery, uplifting sunlight, nearly always brightening proceedings and making training and briefing sessions more positive, energising and uplifting. He whistled as he negotiated his way around espino, polylepis, cacti and tall, thick clumps of grass, expeditiously accomplishing his new, recently chosen, alternative thread through shrubs, towards dramatically reduced lighting inside the cabin.

It was the company's mission to entice those from around the globe, with an enterprising spirit, to visit Chile and, with their physical and mental support, 'aspire to ascend'. This was their motto, Although a physical summit might be regarded as a mountain, the general word 'summit' could be taken to mean anything one can accomplish with a bit of effort, skill and teamwork.

For some, usually specially tailored expeditions, a summit might simply be a physical accomplishment around local desert, or else a hike out to a lake and back. All who visited Asperaciones Cumbre, had their own mountains in mind. As far as this business was concerned, a summit was any pinnacle of success that could be dreamed-up by someone wishing to broaden their life experience, strengthen their will power, produce an accomplishment with some effort, notch-up their own personal record of achievement, find friends, or simply have fun. This was a thriving business. People would pay handsomely to be guided through an experience during which they would be putting most of the effort in themselves and often be having to travel great distances to reach them. It was a 'parties only' business. Individual treks were uneconomical. However, a greater reason for accepting only group bookings was that clusters of people brought camaraderie, mutual support and a shared experience which people would relate to together for years to come. An experience shared is often a more enjoyable one and one from which an individual may emerge taller and happier.

There was a variety of recommended outings, which ranged from hikes through Patagonian wilderness to desert survival, forests, lakes and glacier treks. Often, summits really were the High Andes. From a location like this, they had it all. Perhaps, from the standpoint of most individuals, the trek that stood out, literally *above* all others, would probably be a two or three-week return trip to the summit of Ojos del Salado, the world's highest volcano and second highest summit in South America. As its highest point punctures the sky seven kilometres above sea level, it would be necessary for all groups of aspiring mountaineers to acclimatise for some time before attempting its highest point. This trip was only offered between December and March when weather was often more suitable, during friendlier, summer months in the Southern Hemisphere. The toughest commodity, however, would often be winds, which could blow so strongly that progress might be virtually impossible. At more than seven kilometres up in the air, there would usually be fiercely, biting temperatures, requiring of high-quality mountain protection. To add to all this, extremely rarefied air could make a person feel light-headed, drunk, dizzy or worse. From the viewpoint of Asperacione Cumbre, it would also be those huge loads of equipment, required to sustain a group for so long, in such tough conditions, that would require profound planning.

The name 'Ojos del Salado' translates as 'salty eyes'. Local Indians once believed that two particularly large white spots close to the summit ridge were eyes belonging to one of their deities looking down on them. Occasionally, when their gods observed human movements that perturbed them, they would rain down fire, ash and mud to demonstrate their disapproval. In truth, these gargantuan eyes were no more than a couple of large salt deposits within mountain glaciers. Any anger being expressed was nothing more than volcanic venting from deep inside the Earth. However, all this being explained, there had still been continuing, homegrown rumours of an all-seeing presence living upon the mountain. It certainly added a talking point during a long expedition, and although nothing more than light ash had been ejected from the main crater in recent times, any tales of volcanic displays would always add an attractive element of danger to those venturing so far from safer refuges.

There was more! New hazards could present themselves at any time. Mountain climates are unpredictable and localised. This trip could throw anything at anybody who trespassed here, out from their comfort zone. Gulps of air might often be in short supply. Add to that, profound fatigue being suffered by many during the latter stages of an ascent. Also add noxious clouds of overwhelming, pungent gas drifting across your trail, now and again, from fumaroles, plus sporadic patches of hard-frozen snow, frequently caked like chunks of icing, that stretched across summit sections of routes, even in mid-summer. Most expeditions, from this centre, were a test for experienced wayfarers. Asperaciones Cumbre had a lot to think about. There was an array of weather forecasts to interpret, and local advice to listen to. They had a lot to learn and provide for, regarding each individual group they hosted, and a huge responsibility in order to make their dreams come true, whilst keeping them safe. On the plus side, if all went well, with excursions such as the one to the summit of Ojos del Salado, it would be no more than a very long walk and scramble to an almighty high place with an exceptionally grand view.

Joaquin arrived prickled and scathed, at the equipment room, as one often does when one applies more haste than speed. His task was to grab a fresh harness within a negligible quantity of time, before a hapless customer, whose attachments had been faulty, evolved any thoughts or feelings about being forgotten. This was a precious time when first experiences sewed the seeds of that most memorable journey anyone might ever have embarked upon. Thanks to Joaquin's untidy haste, that unfortunate individual, with the faulty harness, would now be awarded a fighting chance of fitting it, in time to keep up with the rest of their party, who were about to abseil down a partly natural, thirty-metre wall, built into a craggy slope beneath the hut. The diminutive and remote complex of Asperaciones Cumbre, stood close to the edge of what was, effectively, a small canyon. There was much to climb up or scale down, and enough to test nerves, without ascending greater heights.

This particular group of young, enthusiastic urban Argentineans, had breezed in from Buenos Aires, via hired jeeps on a recent afternoon, aspiring to wander with the guidance of experience, deep into a wilderness in the midst of which, stood an isolated and seldom-attempted peak. There would not be too many problems with altitude and, on the home front, less time would be taken from money-making in their large and competitive city. On the other hand, they would be requiring basic climbing skills and something of a head for heights. They were now in the throws of their primary training, which would be intensive and merciless. They must all exhibit a satisfactory level of performance or else risk five days, grounded at the complex, whilst their friends achieved personal dreams, without them. To be accepted on such trips, required fitness and adequate ability. If training went well and individuals proved themselves, they could look forward to sharing an adventure with unique, breath-taking scenery, nights under the stars, firelight, food, tales and discussions about the meaning of life, games, and music, strummed quietly in the background from the charango of a guide named Miguel. This was a small Andean lute which he packed amongst comprehensive climbing equipment with as equal esteem as the rest of it. After all, it was paramount and an essential part of the mission that these excursions were not just safe and successful but also entertaining, inspiring and memorable.

The Equipment Room atmosphere was a cocktail of cleaning smells, ranging from a polish, regularly used to keep pine wood gleaming, to fluids used for sanitizing gear between rentals. There was also a forest air freshener, which another guide called Isabella was in love with, particularly when a bulk dump of sweaty, dusty outfits and smouldering climbing socks had been thrown in, proceeding a trip. Finally, there was always a minty scent originating from a tiny snowman air freshener, which stood at the edge of a business desk, where finances and the timing of equipment hire was coordinated.

Momentarily, there was a bright green flash, as Joaquin, garbed in a fluorescent yellow mountain outfit, shot through the door and immediately out again just as hurriedly, rendering the cabin minus one more harness. At the centre of business, sat Miguel, a rugged-looking but athletic Chilean, clad in a state-of-the-art, custom-designed, zip-up fleece which bore the

125

letters 'A.C.', next to the cactus-condor logo of his business. He clutched an Asperaciones Cumbre pen in one hand and an empty, brown, plastic coffee cup in the other, which he seemed to be using as a stress ball, if his squashing and unsquashing of it was anything to go by. Before he could assimilate that or even resume his dull and arduous bookkeeping, the telephone rang, destroying all silence and his nerves with it.

"Another booking!?"

… he contemplated, attempting to regain his composure, whilst speedily lifting the old-fashioned receiver. It was an old friend. Instantly he snapped into another mode and his slick, South American Spanish, speaking voice, mutated into an enthused but awkward and stuttering English one.

"Fr. Murphy!"

he exclaimed...

"We thought we'd never see you again!"

"You haven't!"

sparked a muted Irish voice from half way around the world...

"But you might"

He paused briefly, then accelerated...

"If this plan works, you'll be seeing a lot more of me than you might have thought!"

He faded-off a bit, momentarily, muttering only half-formed and apologetic words; the most decipherable one being 'sorry'. A suffocated smile crept across Miguel's countenance. He and Fr Murphy went back a lot of years. In that time, they had traded favours as close friends. This instigation of a phone call had 'favour' written all over it.

"Spit it out, Padre"

...chuckled Miguel. Despite a threat of upcoming, extra organisation, it was truly great to hear Fr. Murphy's voice, once more. It had been some while.

"What, no preamble? I don't ask for anything without warming-up first"

"I know this. I'll have to suffer a sermon if I don't interrupt. Come on father, spill those beans!"

"I don't have any beans but I do have a bit of a favour"

...retorted Father Murphy, sheepishly.

"You surprise me!"

...was the dry, sarcastic rebound, dressed-up with a tint of anticipation.

There was a sharp intake of breath and a sickening crack of knuckles, whilst the man, who had faced such profound adversity in his life, warmed himself up just to curry a large but simple favour. After muttering and stuttering a few points of praise for Miguel and his fine business, he was primed for begging. His recipient was silently paralyzed with laughter at his discomfort, though he meant no disrespect and kept it to himself. In truth, Father Murphy was highly uncomfortable seeking weighty assistance such as this, despite the fact that he had needed to rely upon peoples' good faith throughout his career. He attempted to console himself with the fact that he was trying to help someone else.

"OK. Here's the deal…"

He swallowed again. His obvious discomfort was hilarious to Miguel who continued to crease himself; struggling in painful silence. He would maintain respect for Father Murphy at all costs. Many years ago, he had been taken into his mission in Santiago as an orphan, when his parents were killed in a very tragic bus crash outside the city. Miguel would do anything for Father Murphy. How could he ever repay someone who had saved him, fed him, clothed him, educated him and loved him unreservedly for the entirety of his youth? He continued his tittering but prepared to say 'yes'.

"There's this young man in my Parish, here in England, who needs shaking-up…"

…continued Father Murphy.

"He's never seen the world. He has skinflint parents…"

"What is skinflint?"

…interrupted Miguel.

"Tight, mean, miserly… Do you need any more synonyms?"

…asked Father Murphy.

"What is synonym?"

Father Murphy abandoned that part of the explanation and attempted to keep things simple.

"This young man I'm telling you about has hardly been anywhere. He lives in a remote area and doesn't know anything about the rest of the world. He and his brother are good friends of mine. I want to help him by shaking him up and taking him out of his comfort zone. I…"

"You want me to provide a challenge?"

"YES PLEASE!!!"

…retorted Father Murphy, with such implausible promptness that he startled even himself and followed it with a small profanity.

"There's no need for blasphemy"

…chuckled Miguel before inquiring…

"What sort of a challenge did you have in mind?"

"The *BIG* one"

There was a pause but not for effect. Father Murphy was referring to the summit trek of Ojos del Salado. In short, a trip of about two weeks, requiring vast amounts of food and water, serious equipment and precious time away from his business. This was a favour which could dent Summit Aspirations by a fair degree. To strain matters further, it was a policy that only sizable groups were accepted on such excursions as small parties were financially unprofitable. This would be a physical test for Father Murphy and his friends, but an economic one for Miguel.

No sooner had a bubble been created than it was burst. A dagger of panic was quickly replaced with peace and enlightenment as Father Murphy divulged that he would be paying in full for this expedition, via funds from a series of sponsored parish events. There was another pause whilst Father Murphy waited for what he assumed would be a favourable response, but was met instead by a heavy exhalation of relief. The reason Father Murphy had been embarrassed to ask for this expedition to be organised was twofold. Firstly, he knew that trips for just a few people would be uneconomical and somewhat unfavoured by Miguel's business. Secondly, he knew that such an outing was supposed to be booked much further in advance and was hoping Miguel might slot them in a bit sooner. After making a request for this, he went on to explain that Jed and Jo would represent their church in what Father Murphy would refer to before his congregation as a 'spiritual challenge'. Just as a spire reaches the heights, so would they aspire to do the same, pushing back a flow of adversity and willing themselves onwards and upwards. He was somewhat moved as he pondered on this and almost burst into tears. However, it was for precisely for this reason that only 'The Big One' would be good enough for Father Murphy. There would be no talk of having scaled an Andean also-ran. Only the very highest volcano would do for such an impassioned test of strength, or as an example for his parish.

Thus, the seeds were sown, and a dialogue initiated for dates and preparation. Such a venture would be an unimagined minefield of organisation. Aside from all those obvious items of packing, equipment and briefing, there would be risks of assessment, terms to write-up, read and agree to, insurances, personal fitness, medical aptitudes, such as response to severe altitude, and a swarm of other things; some that people may never have dreamed might be attached to such a trip. In some ways, their preparation might be at least as much a trial as the final assault itself. Despite Father Murphy's wishes to will events into reality as soon as possible, it would be some months before the way could, realistically, be made clear. By then, Father Murphy and the boys would already have become substantially different people. They would have educated themselves regarding such ventures and be savvy, at least in theory, about trials and tribulations of mountain exploration. They would be fitter and stronger, after an intense program of training and endurance, though they would have to simulate it themselves. If Father Murphy succeeded, they would have knowledge of the language and culture of the place they were going. He had always felt somewhat ashamed of tourists from his own country who had often rarely attempted to gain a basic grasp of useful phrases and thoroughly lacked the ability to understand or communicate when they ventured abroad, often demanding from their resort, all those things they were used to at home. Father Murphy intended that all within his modest party would visit the country of Chile with a reasonable perspective of what they were looking at, who they were interacting with and where they actually were. Their challenge had already begun.

There would of course, be some things that could not be simulated in the months prior to their trip. Father Murphy's parish and the Carvey's cottage stood amongst vast tracts of flat, Eastern-English farmland. There were no hills to practice on, nor any such commodity as altitude unless one ascended a staircase or climbed a tree. There was also no gym nor a suitable training centre for many miles, for any of his party. Father Murphy would devise his own methods to improve their fitness and terrify them into a strict program of regular and intensive training. There would also be weekly visits to a climbing centre some thirty-five miles away, to assist with any eventualities of difficult ascents, although their Andean expedition did promise to be little more than a very long walk, with the odd scramble. Father Murphy imagined he may take on something of the role of an army general, gesturing towards plans on a screen in order to brief his young compatriots, and draw-up a detailed, achievable, time-related action plan of specific targets for the trip. In reality, however, the bulk of organisation would be sorted over a huge amount of beer at the local pub, although, during their final quest, this would be a strictly, banned commodity.

Until now, Jed and Jo had been shamelessly content to reside within their isolated bubble, in the middle of a human desert. If one is content, why move or change anything. In truth, however, this had been something of an apathy, which only Father Murphy had identified. There was certainly a naivety of geographical awareness between them. This sluggish contentment had disturbed him, endlessly, for the simple fact that he believed he saw something special in Jed, which would never develop within such quarantined existence. Hannah was quite the reverse. For her, this would be one of many great excursions she had been blessed to experience throughout her life, with parents who were most anxious to explore their home planet. Although they were also bankers, they had never viewed holidays abroad, unlike Jed and Jo's family, as a short period of frivolity, which would drain the finances. Instead, they regarded their weekly jobs as a means of purchasing tickets to see the world, and that they had done, setting Hannah up with a healthy perspective of Planet Earth. She might have felt lucky to have parents who saw value above price, and price as a means of enriching a life. Money was born of tenacity and personal exertion and, as such, could be regarded as a mark of spirit more than a level of status, if accrued in this way. Sometimes the very rich are penalised and taxed for their extra wealth, when they have possibly struggled harder than most to acquire it. Hannah was living proof that her parents' wealth had been put to good use. Her decisions and choices often reflected an upbringing which had taught her to recognise value; those things in life that were attained by exertion and aspiration.

Hannah would surely jump at a chance to visit South America and climb the High Andes. This new expedition would provide another magnificent memory for her to recall and recount to others, alongside exploring the Great Barrier Reef, trekking into Himalayan foothills and walking a section of the Great Wall of China. She would face this challenge with enthusiasm born of a carefully cultivated, optimistic attitude over years of embarking on similar outings. She would therefore, also be a useful and educated influence for Jed and Joe. Her approach to this jaunt might well be an inspiration to all of them.

In Father Murphy's case, it was his work as a missionary, which had taken him all around the globe. He had encountered a broad spectrum of cultural diversity from Africa to the Philippines, to Poland and other parts of Eastern Europe, and several parts of Latin America. This had been his life, not a vacation. He had lived and worked with communities local to these areas, learned much of their languages, traditions, diets and attitudes. He had gained his experiences as one of them, playing his part inside their communities. To Father Murphy, this unique and precious education, combined with challenges he had faced and overcome whist receiving it, were his most precious asset. By the very nature of his work, he was unselfish; even empathetic. Looking after needy individuals within missions had nurtured a lot of this strength. Now he had discovered a passion to share his inner wealth with younger parishioners. This trip should be a start; a taster to wet their appetite for travel. He hoped it would not do the reverse, although he did realise that the boys might take some coaxing to stray so far from their sheltered norms. It would also take some explaining and inspiring as to the purpose of actually scaling a very lofty volcano. Perhaps Jo in particular would fail to see the reasoning behind such a quest, that involved travelling half way around the world just to suffer discomfort for a whole fortnight. He would have to plan his opening speech well and tempt them with beer, which would be lined-up in the pub when they arrived. As a priest, he sometimes felt that he was emulating the Devil more than his master upstairs, but why not use material things to draw people into bigger, more spiritual affairs? He had learned that sometimes, just a little of a poison can be used to kill a bigger one, and create healthier entities.

Father Murphy would bully all into accepting a contract for this trip and its training, regardless of their attitude. He would buy his way in first, then crank up the guilt factor. After that he would introduce crafty plans, in a fashion that no one could easily refuse, without feeling either regretful or else puny. He began to meditate upon his approach in the local. These visits were very regular. Time would be scarce.

CHAPTER 13

A less frivolous visit to The White Rabbit

S calloped, terracotta tiles seemed to resist gravity on an exceptionally steep roof. Its centrepiece was a colossal, square, grey, stone chimney, decorated over ages with a bright yellow lichen which had attractively presented the top of it with what looked more like a splash of bright-yellow paint. Hanging baskets, in as many places as possible, courtesy of Jeff and Linda, hung amongst climbing wall plants and tubs of variegated flowers. Most bricks were a dark, dusty red-brown, contrasting with light, sandy-coloured plaster. A few were brighter in shade, and interspersed with small areas of exposed stone from the building's original core, giving something of a rustic effect, overall. Surely, not many wayfarers, driving past, could resist an encounter with such an exceedingly handsome tavern, all dressed-up so charmingly, with luscious flora and obvious history. Those who ventured inside, however, might experience something of a paradox. The White Rabbit's interior had been gutted. All that was historic had been replaced with pseudo furniture and adornments, in an effort to create an appealing, family inn. However, according to Fr Murphy's previously shared opinion, following what he considered an architectural violation, it was comfortable but cheap.

It was September. Hannah was honouring her turn to drive, transporting herself, Jed and his brother to their usual hostelry. All passed up an opportunity to sit outside, amidst glorious sunshine, upon perfectly positioned picnic benches. Instead, they crossed the threshold, as instructed in a telephone text, sent from the phone of a certain gentleman who was already indoors. Fr Murphy had been inside for some time now, setting the scene, for what he considered to be quite an important meeting. He had already irritated Jeff, the landlord, by moving his furniture. Three tables had been slammed together with screeching and straining noises, then his carefully-positioned, prized, comfy chairs had been snatched and arranged around a new set-up. If Fr Murphy had been any less than clergy, he might have suffered a flurry of relative impoliteness from Jeff, who was quietly simmering, with steam coming from his ears. Having put him through all of that, Fr Murphy then had the audacity to ask him if he'd pour three pints of beer plus a driver's consolation mocktail, and space them around his three tables, ready for his young compatriots when they arrived. In fairness, although Fr Murphy could be fairly uncomfortable asking for favours, he had not really seen this hijacking of The White Rabbit, in the same light, nor noticed the barman's discomfort. In they came, unsuspecting of Fr Murphy's scheming and settled quickly into individual activities. One perused the sports pages of a tabloid, nicked from a corner of the bar, where Jeff stood, even more exasperated than before. It's funny how what someone else is reading can become more interesting to an onlooker than if, perhaps they had control of it themselves. Ordinarily, Fr Murphy might have read the same paper over Jed's shoulder but it was a cheap and tacky publication with seedy content. He preferred broadsheets or any other paper which was accurate, objective and impartial.

It had been Fr Murphy's intent that Jed, Hannah and Joe, would first relax when they arrived. Hopefully the beer would calm them a little and transform them into better listeners. However, in Fr Murphy's mind, social gatherings were meant for communal interaction, not personal roosting. What had happened these days for young people to arrive at a pub together, yet then sit and do their own thing? Hannah was reading a book whilst listening to music through large, furry headphones. The other muted male was uselessly honing his ability to bat wads of drink mats, which he'd pillaged from surrounding tables, to the further enragement of Jeff. Joe was attempting to flick his pile of mats, into a coordinated summersault, above the table, before theoretically catching them in his right hand. However, he had exceeded at least twenty attempts to catch a pile of eight mats, during which they had visited the floor and Jed's newspaper. Hannah had even worn one. Fr Murphy studied them with alternating head movements, much like someone spectating a tennis match. He was filled with distaste.

"Has it come to this?"

…he pleaded.

"Have we engineered these routes through our lives just for…"

He hesitated, lost for words, before anti-climaxing the end of his question with…

"…that!?"

He continued to pray for at least a glimmer of a reaction. There was none. All were too ensconced in singular activities, to notice.

It was time to pounce. Fr Murphy sprang in and began to broadcast that he had something very important to share. However, first came a lengthy preamble. Perhaps it is fair to state that sometimes, just to 'come-out-and-say-it' does not fully prepare a potential market to commit. They might need some inspiration, some reassurance and some home truths to help them assess one's offer. Fr Murphy had all of this in mind. He'd even rehearsed it. He was well aware that Jed and Joe could be quite awkward at times and throw-up negative questions. Hopefully he was prepared for anything and ready to rouse them. An experienced and intelligent priest is often one of the greatest showmen. He began with a stirring hook to wet their appetites and set them thinking…

"Some of you have never seen the world!"

He paused to allow his opening comment to gather impact. It was destroyed instantly by Joe…

"I see it every day!"

Fr Murphy peered over the top of his ancient, half-moon spectacles, perhaps resembling an old-fashioned headmaster. In truth, he was not at all surprised by this interruption. He continued as though no-one had spoken, clutching some notes he'd drafted. These were to ensure he remembered all of his points, but also to look more official, and be taken seriously. He didn't even plan his sermons this much; such was the importance of this particular meeting, as far as he was concerned. He began again…

"You're all tough, fit and tenacious individuals…"

He was cut dead by Jed, this time.

"Take away the tough, fit and tenacious bits, and you've just about nailed it!"

Fr Murphy had been ready for this. They would settle as he found his stride. Hannah sat quietly and attentively. Somehow, he suspected that she would not throw-up a challenge. He was aware by now that she had travelled a bit and had a fairly robust knowledge of the wider world. She would likely welcome his plan and maybe even help him to convince the other two. His speech was mainly aimed at the boys, but at Jed in particular. He persevered further…

"If you truly believe you are lacking in those qualities then it's time to venture into something that'll help you build them up. Living and working with bankers and enduring that same local, summer holiday every year isn't going to round you as an individual. You need stretching…"

"Sounds painful!"

…retorted Joe, not even being able to resist the most obvious pun. Fr Murphy kept going, determined to deliver his speech without being side-tracked, again…

"You need to be tested to your limits, again and again, to increase your strength, fitness, stamina, mental staying-power…"

Once again he was interrupted by Jed…

"I run to the chip shop sometimes!"

Fr Murphy turned to Hannah, for her own reassurance more than his own…

"These two often make me feel embarrassed to be male."

Once more he continued to pave the way for a moment when he could unleash his grand proposition. He discussed human qualities, strengths and weaknesses. There was also a diversion into religion. He recognised that Hannah was not strictly one of his flock and had been careful not to pressure her in any way by discussing the possibility of her becoming an official member of his congregation via a baptism. However, he had seen that she was comfortable with conversations about spirit and positive actions. She was highly motivated in the kind of behaviours he recommended in his preaching; she just didn't word anything in a religious way. Also, she and her family were most receptive to religion in general. Hannah had often considered that there might be more to her world than visible material. Father Murphy comfortably discussed the concepts of self-improvement without any particular dogma. They all understood what he meant. As he had expected, they soon settled down and absorbed his spiel. He continued to reiterate that some of the company before him might benefit greatly from a regime of exercise. They might also benefit greatly from expanding their horizons and seeing more of the wider world. Finally, after quite a homily, he reached the moment they all wished he'd reached about fifteen minutes previously.

"OK, here's the deal…"

…he began…

"What if someone paid for you to fly to the other side of the world where you'd spend a fortnight s-l-o-w-l-y (he expressed that particular word *very* carefully, with space and time, painting the term with his hands and body language) ascending the world's loftiest volcano? You'd all gobble-up that chance right away. Am I correct?"

There was a deafening silence, accompanied by shocked expressions.

"Are you really serious?"

...inquired Joe with obvious surprise...

"Where even is the highest volcano in the world?"

Jed hovered, attentively, with bated breath, remembering his excursion, some time ago, to Lincoln Library. Perhaps an answer to his question was on its way. He suspected that Fr Murphy had been attempting to organise this trip in response to the dream, Jed had told him about. One way or another, this seemed like an effort to show him something that might illuminate his life.

"It's called Ojos del Salado and it's in Chile"

...replied Fr Murphy. There was a further silence, before he attempted to affirm their reactions...

"Well? Does that idea crumble anyone's cookie?"

...he asked.

"I get it"

...began Jed...

"You've warmed us up by indicating we'd get some sort of training for this. You've also picked on that dream I told you about with the volcano. Why that one in particular?"

Fr Murphy didn't exactly seem to answer his question.

"It's someone I've known for many years who lives there, pretty much next to it. I can arrange all of it, if people really want. All you have to do is say 'yes'."

During yet another silence, they looked at one another for clues as to personal reactions. Hannah was the first to offer her thoughts, out loud...

"Count me in, depending on a few things"

"Fire away"

retorted Fr Murphy...

"Money and timings"

...replied Hannah.

"Well..."

...he breathed in a little sharply, with a slight expression of regret...

136

"The mission would really have to begin some time in the winter months, say February. You'd have to miss a bit of college or your postal work, Joe."

"Never mind that…"

…began Jed

"Winter on a high volcano!!??"

"It'll be summer in the southern hemisphere."

…replied Fr Murphy, sweeping-in quickly, to avoid any moment of demotivation.

"That's why it *has* to be then."

It was Joe's turn to make his feelings known…

"Nice idea, Father, but how am I supposed to afford a trip like that on a postman's wage? I'm guessing it's a bit further than Thetford Forest?"

"South America!"

…chipped-in Hannah.

"That's the satisfying bit, and part of the spirit-building…"

…expressed Fr Murphy, going on to explain his favourite link in life to Hannah, about church 'spires' representing 'aspiring' to good and greater spirit. Jed yawned rudely as he'd heard that quite a few times…

"I'm guessing the plan is to raise money somehow?"

…he asked.

"That's correct…"

came the affirmation…

"…but I'll do most of the donkey work."

…promised Fr Murphy.

"The aim will be to pay for the whole trip via our church and community. We'll also be hoping to raise a bit more towards some missions out there. The chap I know, in Chile, has an outward-bound centre, up in the Andes, geared to help less fortunate people get a trip of some sort. All kinds of people use his business, though. Rich people from the city get together on his trips. He makes the money. All profits assist him with his vocation in life, helping those less fortunate, to enjoy the beauty he shows them. We'll have church collections for the missions, sell flags in town, organise a few coffee mornings and a bit more. All I ask is each of you helps with it all."

Their reactions were unpredictably, favourable. Perhaps Joe's was the most astonishing, however. It had to be acknowledged that he was largely something of a couch potato, yet today he was the first to nod, fairly agreeably. His nodding seemed to spread until all were expressing vigorous affirmation, simultaneously. He was somewhat startled by his own reaction, too. It felt surprisingly good to have been so positive in the face of something so challenging, but the thought of travelling somewhere really impressive and achieving something so extraordinary had almost pulled him into action by itself.

Fr Murphy grinned…

"That's the spirit!"

…he exclaimed, fairly calmly, using that word again.

"Let's get this show on the road. Meet me for a briefing tomorrow night, here at the same time, seventeen-hundred-hours. There's a bit to plan and a spot of exercise to get used to."

He left them to relax and discuss the idea, which of course, they did.

Fr Murphy's exit was fairly abrupt. For him it was 'job done', though it was only the first one on his list. He returned home to juggle a parish and plan a regime of fitness, Spanish classes, climbing centre sessions, equipment training, safety instruction and so on. There would be five months to achieve this. Flights would have to be booked immediately as would accommodation, within Miguel's complex, out in the Chilean wilderness. There was much to be achieved, now he had received a green light.

Conversational energy exploded, as Fr Murphy exited the building. There was genuine excitement amongst the three of them. Finally, for the boys, here was something significant to work towards and achieve. Life had literally just accelerated into action. Before now there had been little to generate any exhilaration. However, Hannah diluted their energies somewhat, by sharing an experience. There was no Fr Murphy to dispel any myths.

"Someone in our street got a job in Santiago, a few years back…"

…she began.

"The capital of Chile… anyway…"

she had a speedy swig of alcohol-free cocktail…

"He went to work one day and got shot!"

The boys eyeballed one another, with alarmed expressions.

"That's great!"

…retorted Jed, cynically…

"I'm looking forward to this trip even more, now!"

Hannah felt the consequences of her haphazard remark and sought to console them…

"I'm sure we'll all be fine. We'll be a long way from any city and in good hands. I've travelled all over the world. There's a lot of friendly people out there!"

Hannah could not resist sharing a proud list of places she'd been in her relatively short existence, so far. These included Brazil, Mexico, a few states of the USA, numerous archipelagos of islands in the Indian and Pacific oceans and a few more places. She had been only five or six when visiting Brazil, miles from Chile but on the same continent, and remembered little. It seemed, even for her, this would be a pretty new experience. Her parents did not tend to walk very far and didn't really climb things unless absolutely necessary. The physical aspects of this trip would certainly be ground-breaking for her. From the boys' point of view, 'ground-breaking' didn't even begin to say it. This would be more like a journey to another planet.

The next five months were packed with action, discipline and self-denial. Fr Murphy had constructed a rota of exercise and training. He had also consulted with Jed and Joe's parents regarding their diet. Within a relatively short stretch of time, they were clearly improving with their fitness. They had learned some basics of climbing, although this particular expedition would probably be more of a very long hike, than an actual climb with hands and feet. They had also developed a knowledge of equipment and safety procedures; even mastered a little Spanish. Fr Murphy was most adamant that, unlike so many British tourists abroad, his compatriots would not be ignorant or illiterate. He taught them himself.

As winter gripped the flatlands and darkness shortened their days, it was time for the team to fly south, back into summer. Everything was in place. Their test was about to begin.

CHAPTER 14

Arriving in the Atacama Desert

A grey grimness washed out most of the runway view. Hazy shapes of monstrous jets loomed through late February mist and rain, with small vehicles, barely visible, scudding between them; their faded, flashing lights distracting slightly through the airport windows. A similar gloominess emanated inside the terminal building, too. There seemed to be more of an all-pervading, library atmosphere, unusual perhaps, when considering that so many were about to embark upon a holiday. In truth, few passengers who stood, queuing at this gate, had slept adequately, having needed to drag themselves out of bed at outrageous hours in order to catch a flight due to depart shortly after five o'clock in the morning. This would surely make a fifteen-hour flight from Birmingham Airport to Santiago in Chile, a fairly uncomfortable experience for many.

Neither Jed or Joe had flown before. Hannah and Fr Murphy had described their experiences somewhat on their drive down and consoled them with some safety facts too. Despite pep-talks, Joe was still a little concerned that any flight with himself aboard, might be attempting to take-off in such adverse weather conditions, with near-zero visibility, yet now they boarded. After a fairly tedious palaver involving extensive queuing and a showing of passports and boarding passes, four amigos, progressed through fairly makeshift tunnels towards their aircraft. During this brief transitory period, Fr Murphy quickly dropped-in an observation...

"See… this is a first for you. Never mind the Atacama Desert or the Andes. Even sunny Birmingham is new territory for you two. We'll soon have you both globalised"

"That almost sounds painful"

… quipped Jed, fairly euphoric and excited at this point. He had almost arrived at the point in life he had been dreaming about a great deal in recent times.

After a warm greeting by their hosts at the plane entrance, they installed themselves in an allotted centre section of four seats. Jed was the most disappointed that he would not be able to see out of a window, especially, considering they would be flying over The Andes, but then he found a special cam app which was part of quite a complex set-up of media and controls, available in everybody's place. There were several cameras he could keep an eye on from beneath, behind and in front of the plane. This was a great blessing to Jed, who did not want to miss a trick during what promised to be a dramatic experience. Their personal, in-flight entertainment turned out to be comprehensive and lots of fun. There seemed to be just about every genre on TV including films, game shows, documentaries and so on. There were also some fairly addictive games. Even Fr Murphy indulged and quickly became dependent upon 'Hendom', which involved catching escaped chickens within different situations and levels of difficulty…

"Can't wait for the flight back"

… he had proclaimed, whilst ditching his console for the first meal of the day. That was fairly soon after he had been heard by several on the plane expressing himself with…

"Got you, you bastard".

During the outward flight, Jed quietly perused a documentary about global warming, before trying and failing to sleep, then attempting to calculate how far along the horizon it would be possible to see from the summit of Ojos del Salado at a height of six thousand, eight-hundred & ninety-three meters above the Earth's surface. Joe tripled his screen time, detaching himself from the rest of his party, only making sounds in relation to his successes or failures during gaming. Hannah read for a huge amount of the time, getting up now and again, to shake arms and legs, and perform stretching exercises in the only viable area, by the toilets. Even for Fr Murphy, this seemed to be a long episode, more suitable for the amusement of one's self. In fairness, nobody felt, particularly like socialising. They had all been rendered too weary to feel expressive, and a little anxious, regarding their emerging period of travel. As one might expect, with a single non-stop flight of this duration, things became increasingly uncomfortable for all of them, until they had been aboard the aircraft for so long, that their minds and bodies almost forgot the discomfort of sitting and waiting forever. Through a camera, looking down from the belly of the aircraft, Jed could see that, although it would now have been dark in England, for several hours, it was bright and sunny in this part of the world. By now, vast tracts of what seemed to have been endless rainforest, had become somewhat broken-up. A short time later, the ground seemed to be rising-up to meet them. Patches of snow and ice appeared. Fr Murphy, who was now admiring Jed's camera view became intrigued. This was certainly more inspiring, even, than reading a broadsheet newspaper over someone else's shoulder. He was moved to comment, somewhat emotionally...

"Bless my soul. This is the Andean Mountains. So impressive, even from up here!"

Jed was keen to share the route they had taken, which he'd been keeping an eye upon. He showed Fr Murphy an approximate flightpath which he'd attempted to sketch upon a tatty page in his notebook. It demonstrated that they had emerged over The Atlantic, from the south west of England, covering several thousand miles of ocean, before entering the north of Brazil and much interior forest wilderness, then crossing parts of Bolivia, Paraguay and Argentina. Only in the very last moments did they traverse a border into their very thin but extremely long country of destination, Chile.

"Cabin Crew... seats for landing"

...came an announcement via a speaker. As they descended rapidly, all being belted into their seats, with organs seeming to be still catching-up with the rest of their bodies, the plane banked. Now the sun shone brilliantly into their cabin on one side, seemingly facing upwards towards the sky. On the other side, was a vast suburban sprawl, everywhere beneath them, comprising of endless, similar buildings within a grid, that stretched out most of the way towards some pale but lofty, distant mountains. Details soon became closer and more perceptible, until they could all see, around those passengers at the sides of the aircraft who were hogging portholes, individual vehicles and people moving about within streets below. This was certainly a very unique world to observe. All but Fr Murphy, who had resided in Chile for quite a slice of his earlier life, were somewhat nervous about what they might encounter but kept their moods silent as they meditated upon it all.

As the plane touched-down on alien tarmac, with quite a thump, accompanied by a generous ripple of applause that resounded throughout the cabin, Joe stirred himself, at last, to communicate with those around him…

"Sorry to blaspheme, Father, but thank God we're down!"

The calmly measured response was…

"That's gratitude, not blasphemy, son, but save it for when we've landed the next time"

Indeed, there would now be a second, though much shorter, internal flight of ninety or so minutes to Copiapo in Northern Chile, some four or five hundred miles away, where Miguel would receive them and transport them to his complex, amidst Andean foothills, several miles above the Pacific. His climbing centre would also be their accommodation for some time before an expedition commenced. Any period of acclimatisation would also be required to assist them in recovering from such a long journey. Indeed, Jed had already made a suggestion…

"Perhaps, after all this, a day of sleep will be in order?"

However, he had realised that this was something of a rhetorical question, as the others looked at him silently. The climbing centre would, no doubt, be a place of discipline. Fr Murphy pointed out, within a separate conversation inside the departure lounge of Santiago Airport, that such a long journey followed by a gigantic passage of sleep might actually destroy a lot of the fitness they'd worked so hard to attain.

"We'll be gradually acclimatising, I'm sure"

… he proffered in a business-like tone.

"I'm certain, in a day or two, we'll all have landed properly in this country, and our spirits will catch up with our bodies."

Before touching-down in body, however, there was the question of that final journey north. Thankfully, there was not long to wait. They were soon aboard a much smaller aircraft, with a slightly more rustic interior. In reality, their flight was not too turbulent, nor was the plane falling apart. They had all heard stories of minor, internal flights during which passengers had wondered if some rattling and creaking they were experiencing, might be the beginnings of a disaster. Such dodgy flights seemed to be allowed to operate in remote or exotic places, where standards were perhaps more relaxed, and usually involved transport which had exceeded its sell-by date. However, despite a short passage of turbulence, their flight, to the north of Chile, was relatively smooth, although at one point, they had somewhat tactlessly, been informed by a local passenger, who might not have thought through all the ramifications of passing-on certain knowledge, that only a few weeks ago, an aircraft flying from Santiago to Copiapo had lost an engine during take-off. Undeniably, this had spooked them during their flight and there was relief when, once again, they were reunited with Mother Earth. Joe accentuated the matter by dropping to his knees and kissing the ground. Jed vocalised the melody of 'Morning' from 'Peer Ghynt', which seemed to be synonymous with incidences of extreme relief, such as finally managing to find a toilet or perhaps getting out of something one was dreading. Fr Murphy ordered that they pull themselves together, reminding that this trip and travel in general were all about risk, and that they should learn to handle their emotions less audibly and visually, whilst attempting to address any thoughts of danger with deep breaths, positive philosophy and plans of action. After this they walked, fairly silently, towards the arrivals entrance, gobsmacked by dramatic bad-land formations and dusty peaks, that surrounded large expanses of flat and empty desert.

After locating a hundredweight of luggage from a carousel, they made for the arrivals exit, at which several people stood, behind a moveable barrier, with banners or message boards, bearing their essential identifying features. Miguel was the exception. He was known by one of his arriving party. Fr Murphy immediately steered towards him. A beard had appeared since they had last met, a few years previously. As usual he was also adorned with one of his 'Asperaciones Cumbres' fleeces, but now also, a peaked cap, exhibiting his A.C. logo. His greeting was a grand, beaming smile, after which he turned, prior to them reaching him, and led them to his vehicle, very close by. After dealing with baggage and seat belts, they were hurtled-off, sharply, in a direction leading straight through the desert.

Dry, scabby dirt, tarnished the undersides of a well-tested, honey-yellow jeep, coolly rooting its robust and macho modernity with Mother Earth as it sped over a dramatically, parched Atacama landscape. They coursed through salt and cinder, amidst badlands, lava flows and alien moulds of earth and stone. It was an intriguingly evolving arena of climatic torture. Through rhythms of temperature, unique to this most consistently parched environment, everything around was ceaselessly incinerated by day, and dry-chilled by night. The toughest of formations had yielded to an overwhelming and repetitive alternation of relentless radiation burning followed by dark, shivering starlight. Cracking, crumbling and melting, oozing bands of colour across sand and lava slopes, were a manifestation of this brutalisation, yet forces beneath the ground, had also remained a sculptor for as long as this backdrop had prevailed. There were fleeting glimpses of terrains thrown apart, undermined with crevices, broken inclines and buckled, illogical configurations. The dumbfounding, geological story of this domain, was skated over somewhat in a rushed bid to reach a goal some distance away, inside a rapidly rolling and bouncing desert wagon, in which one had to manage their vertical movements for reasons of safety and horizontal leanings for imperatives of social correctness. Once or twice there may have been unintentional bonding between its occupants, as it scudded powerfully across rubble and powder, eventually joining a main road. Now the off-roading was complete and a corner cut, the occupants of Miguel's jolly jeep, as Joe described it, began to enjoy relative comfort, without bumping and banging. At this point, Miguel was able to say hello properly. He greeted them with geographical facts…

"Welcome to the driest place on Earth!"

He expressed, shouting at his driving mirror, above roaring engine sounds…

"Some parts of this place haven't seen a drop of rain in five hundred years"

There was a pause, then long after seven seconds of acceptability for a jocular response, Joe returned his attempt at wit…

"I drought it!"

Heads went down or turned in shame. Hannah felt that Miguel's welcome and impressive facts deserved better and added…

"Does anything actually live here? I can't imagine anything could survive."

"We have a few rodents, some flamingos and lots of lizards."

…Miguel retorted, still shouting a little louder than was perhaps necessary…

"We have plants that drink the water from the air or the mist on the mountains. Our animals survive, because they've learned to drink water from the salt lakes."

Hannah was glad she'd asked, as were the others. This was obviously a very interesting and unique ecosystem and the scenery unfolding in front of them was truly awesome.

A flash of Hispanic honey zoomed over the cusp of a fairly sharp summit, on a right-hand bend. At this point, Jed was crushed by everyone else, as the flanks of their cross-country vehicle made a fairly forceful, transient flirt with the dusty roadside. He lived to fight a lot more rises and dips, along the course of a nightmarish road that zig-zagged steeply upwards, away from coastal lowlands. Now and again he would get his own back, on a left hand bend, and rejoice as Hannah squealed, suffering a similar fate on the other side of the car.

This was another world for Jed, Joe and even Hannah, despite her wealth of travel. It could not have contrasted with the landscapes they were used to at home, much more. Each bend provided a new panorama of mountain wilderness. All were continually riveted by what they experienced, though nothing could be savoured for too long, as Miguel kept his foot firmly on the gas. As they whisked through ever increasingly, imposing territory, the road became more and more dusty until it resembled a track. In a momentary burst, at the top of a pass, they witnessed an unparalleled outlook over a hugely extensive plain of dry salt beds, and glistening, golden sand. As they raced down towards it, there were regimented rock formations that looked as though they'd been designed by an architect, aligned in rows above a dry river course. In all directions, there were innumerable cinder cones, in random locations, from countless historical eruptions, and cracks in the earth caused by frying heat. All was peppered by hardy desert shrubs and occasionally, cacti. Beyond this vast field of primeval volcanic devastation stood a wall of distant, faded, volcanic peaks, shimmering behind swathes of searing heat, rising from the desert floor. So vast and distant were they, that it was difficult to consider them as part of the same valley. To Jed, who's greatest experience up until then, of mountains, had been 'The Yorkshire Dales', where he had spent most of his visit, drenched in a soggy and forgettable experience, they were the feature of a fairy story. These masses of astounding stature, were also visible testament to an aggressive volcanic past. Every slope above the immensely broad valley floor in every direction and aspect, carried scars from flows of ice and mud, or flying debris from millennia of eruptions. Jed mused to himself that the contrasting, patchy regions he could see, though somewhat weakened with distance, were like different types of dessert. Cinder-toffee cones topped with cream, flanked by a variety of flavours, including caramel and butterscotch, spread about the lower slopes of approaching titan highlands. Burnt sugar and liquorice, buckled and folded below fumaroles, where Earth had vented deadly gases for many epochs. For great periods, after night-fall, with no eyes to witness the show, these slopes, whilst blackened in darkness, would sometimes have been streaked with fiery specks and twisted, woven streams of luminous liquid, as rocks were melted and fused in nature's foundry.

"There she blows?"

...exclaimed Fr Murphy, assuming he was now looking at the world's highest volcano.

"What is blowing?"

...asked Miguel, unfamiliar with the phrase. He was rudely ignored by all.

"Is *that* our mountain?"

continued Fr Murphy, pointing with a fairly enthused grin.

"It is for sure."

confirmed Miguel.

"See there at the back. More far away than it looks. Big!"

He chuckled, becoming more animated...

"VERY BIG!"

Jed, whose spikey hairstyle, flirted with the ceiling, bobbed down low, from his back seat, to view their distant goal through the windscreen, around Miguel's Hispanic hippy locks. Somebody generated a low whistle. For a moment or two, they were reduced to silence. Then the jeep, almost on two wheels, with Jed and Fr Murphy hanging on to their most extensive wits, negotiated a hairpin right, and descended, for some time, in a fresh direction.

It was rather late in the afternoon. Mountains cast their shadows in the valley bottom.

"It will be very cold here tonight"

... announced Miguel coming into his own within his favourite type of outback...

"All the heat will disappear into the sky".

For this he made a little sound... *'voom'*... then fell back into silence for a few moments. There was no reaction from anyone. A few minutes passed without conversation whilst each of the passengers pondered about where they might be hanging-out that night or whether their sleeping bags were armed with enough *degrees above zero* to cancel-out the ones below. Then, for a fairly understandable reason, Jed mentioned another commodity which was, at this present juncture, still uncertain... food. He had just experienced, as does occasionally occur in life, a transitory glimpse of a particular type of sustenance, for which he was now longing.

"Sausages!"

...he exclaimed, leaving the others in a sort of mystified surprise, though he had definitely, somehow, been reminded of them, for reasons unknown. This odd type of humour attempt, was certainly an influence from his father.

"Well that was rather random for anyone?"

…responded Fr Murphy, struggling to squint back through the jeep, via his new varifocals. He had been studying a plan of the valley and trail in some detail and was trying to focus on that, and things in the distance, such as Jed in the back of the car. Somehow he had not quite got the hang of his new spectacles and kept raising and lowering his head un-necessarily, whilst continually looking through the wrong part of the lenses, to peruse alternately between close and far objects.

"What's all that white stuff over there?"

…inquired Hannah, removing herself, suddenly, from a dismayed grimace towards Jed, after his arbitrary sausage comment, and gesturing towards a broad area, resembling a large patch of snow. It was Fr Murphy who obliged before Miguel could respond…

"Salt!"

…he exclaimed…

"Pure salt!"

He went on…

"Everything is so dry here. These mountains take all the rain, then water and snow-melt run down their slopes, onto the plains with all those minerals they collect on their way. Then the water evaporates in the heat and leaves what was dissolved minerals or salts behind. This keeps happening. More and more salts arrive until there's a thick layer of salt left. Sometimes there's so much water coming down from above that it can't all evaporate, so a lake forms over the salt. We'll be seeing a few salt lakes on our travels"

Miguel's head turned slowly sideways until his eyes met Fr Murphy's, briefly before they darted back towards some tricky driving…

"Hey… not bad for a clergyman!"

"Ah, sure…"

… beamed Fr Murphy.

"I've read a lot more than just The Bible".

Joe stretched and yawned with the gaping aperture of a roaring lion…

"I need some of those sausages my brother was talking about. When does food happen?"

"Not too long now."

…was the reassuring reply from Miguel.

"Asperaciones Cumbre complex is just around the side of that hill".

He indicated towards some distant rocks at the base of a very large mountain slope, which spilled onto flat sands, in front of them…

"We'll be there in ten minutes, then find our staying places. After that, food, for sure. No sausages though. I hope you guys don't mind chilli."

He tittered, momentarily...

"We have quite a lot of that out here".

They looked at one another, mostly with fairly neutral expressions, shrugging and raising an eyebrow or two. Jed vocalised for all of them...

"Chilli sounds good to us!"

There were vague nods of agreement. Miguel's tone brightened. He resumed his unnecessary shouting...

"That's quite a relief for me, for sure, and good for all of you"

During the final moments before reaching the complex at which they would be staying a few days before heading out, on their expedition, Fr Murphy turned to philosophy and reflection...

"Whatever happens here and on the climb, remember you've still enjoyed one hell of a trip all the way round to the other side of the world. Compare all this to those cold, damp, misty flatlands of Lincolnshire. This has saved you a few of those awkward bus journeys, Jed. Feel good!"

Jed smiled warmly in acknowledgement. Greenbank College seemed so far away in every sense. This was truly a life-changing experience for him. It was Hannah, however, who responded verbally...

"Well I've been lucky to travel quite a bit, but this place is like nothing I've ever seen. Climbing a mountain in the Andes is going to be a world's first for me!"

"That's good to know too, Hannah, but you know, it's the same for me. I might have been in this country before but this trip is good from my point of view too, as I'm reaching a point in life where I'm beginning to get excited about what happened in the past"

Joe looked quizzical. For the first time in a long time, he was not playing games on his phone. He was, however, noticing both the grand panorama around him and the flow of conversation in the car. Jed bailed him out...

"He means he's not getting any younger"

"I knew that!"

insisted Joe. Everyone else knew he didn't.

The jeep ported sharply, left, around a rocky outcrop they had seen earlier from a distance. The rocks were far bigger than they had appeared. Some of them had ropes dangling off them, or coloured pegs sticking out. Miguel braked sharply with little grace, outside the largest building of the complex. Fr Murphy exclaimed that it was just as well he hadn't been tucking

149

into some food as he'd have ended-up wearing it. This larger structure was a recreation and dining area where they would meet away from their accommodation in one of the smaller, satellite buildings. Everything was bright, modern and well-kempt. Most buildings were wooden, similarly styled with corrugated, terracotta roofs. There was horizontal timber-boarding, stained to look like redwood, also blue-tinted windows, and verandas with ornate, wooden fences. Each individual accommodation lodge had a picnic table and shade, a very large, wide hammock and an attractive surround of desert shrubs, palms and flowers. First, Miguel led them into a recreation and dining area, without their bags.

"We can unpack in some more minutes."

...he said, almost mastering the English language.

"Here, inside, is the place we meet and sit or plan or eat or talk. Come back here when you unpack and there'll be your first chilli in Chile".

A smirk crossed his countenance. This was one of his favourite, stock phrases which he used on those customers, he knew were new to his country. Upon entering, via a solid, dark-wood door, reminiscent of those on buildings associated with Spanish colonialism, they found a small hall, filled with polished-pine picnic tables. The floor was rustic wooden boarding. The ceiling was adorned with beams, which were actually thin tree stalks. In between them were multitudes of sticks, lashed together like extra-thick straw. On walls, between plain, square windows, were large works of Chilean Folklore art. There were devils and witches, ancient faces constructed with darkly-outlined areas of bold, block colours. There was a hefty painting at the end of the hall, taking centre stage, surrounded by a bulky-looking gold frame, bearing mountains of fire, being lorded-over by angry gods. Distinctly smaller, ordinary mortals suffered beneath it all, half-buried in pools of mud with fire licking all about them. There was a distinct aroma of pine wood, mixed with appetizing cooking smells. They were led through an arch-shaped aperture, into a cosy-looking area of soft chairs and drinks tables. Both floor and ceiling were the same as before but there were fewer windows. A large, stone fireplace was filled with logs, a ring of stones and some ancient, iron implements and bellows. There were also wicker buckets of pine cones, which could be burned to create a rainbow of flame colours and a pleasant smell. There was no fire burning today due to excessive summer heat, though it might be necessary at night when most warmth escaped through cloudless skies leaving temperatures plummeting. In front of the fire was a round mat, with bold, earthy, contrasting colours and shapes, reminiscent of Aztec designs. In front of that, in the midst of the room was an enormous, brown, leather sofa…

"That'll be our place to sit on an evening…"

…announced Fr Murphy, quietly stunned by its stupendous stature, and turning to Miguel to make an observation…

"…even if there's no coffee table to put my feet on!?"

After being shown around, they were guided to their staying-rooms. These were basic inside but comfortable, with beds, wardrobes, a small bathroom and a soft chair or two. Hannah and Jed might have been hoping to share a room, by now but, in the presence of a Catholic Priest, they did the honourable thing. Jed and Joe shared a twin cabin, whilst Fr Murphy and Hannah enjoyed their own, private accommodation. They all visited each other's rooms as they were instructed where to unpack and establish themselves. Two particular observations were made, within the process. One was Fr Murphy, pointing-out that there was no TV or mini-bar… to which Miguel asked the question…

"Why does anyone come to a wilderness place of great beauty, to watch a television?"

The second observation was from Joe who asked why it was so quiet. Apparently it was a total coincidence that no-one else was staying at the complex. Miguel explained that business was great. For two months everything was fully-booked and would be again when they left.

"Sounds like a meant-to-be thing"

…said Hannah

"For sure! Now you'll get more from me"

Miguel's work colleagues had taken a break together, under his instruction, during this short lull. They had driven out to the ocean, where there was a small lodge, also owned by Asperaciones Cumbre and would be in touch via radio, should Miguel require their assistance.

Upon returning to the dining area, they were served with traditional Chilean food. The chilli was really a cazuela stew, containing beef, potatoes, vegetables and some chilli for good measure. Miguel also provided them with rice and potato breads called 'chapalele'.

"This is our last alcohol until we come down from the big peak"

…he insisted, pouring them all, a large glass of Chilean Merlot. We must be sound in mind and body. The acclimatising starts here. Now, though, enjoy!"

He raised a glass.

"I'm not sure I can promise to be sound in either mind or body"

...proclaimed Fr Murphy, with his glass just about raised above his midriff.

"The mind's gone a bit quiet but the body makes lots of sound these days. Anyway, good health to you all and good luck in the days to come."

They all chipped in with...

"Good health!"

...and clinked glasses. No-one wished to jinx their luck by abstaining from a toast. Miguel's stew was delicious and was followed by freshly baked churros with walnut ice cream.

"It's all downhill after this"

...exclaimed Fr Murphy, referring to the fact that it would be hard for things to get any better after such a great meal. He was quickly corrected with typical Joe-like triteness...

"Err... no... we're all going *uphill*... very soon!"

Before anyone could think about going uphill, there was a lot of work to do. All slept like the dead on their first night, in the silence of the desert.

Beyond that, it was action-stations. First, they were subjected to a rigorous sequence of exercises, involving jumping, squatting, stretching and running. After that, they were made to climb giant boulders and walls. Then they hiked up awkward, slithery slopes, with large, cumbersome, heavy packs on their backs. Finally, they were made to suffer a long lecture about safety and equipment. Some things were a little different to what they had been shown back at home, but their lessons at the climbing centre had been useful.

The day's final exercise was probably most memorable. Miguel had them all lashed together with a rope, on a slope above a vertical drop of about three metres. At the base of the three-metre wall was a pile of crash mats. The wall was lined somewhat with a protective sponge to prevent injury. The aim was for the group to line themselves up, one behind the other, as if they were climbing up a slope. The rear climber had to jump off the wall and hope that their fall was stopped by those in front, rather than the grimmer option of everybody collapsing backwards and following them off the edge. The exercise was only done once. Joe drew the short straw. It was such a memorable exercise as, even though it was a success and Joe was stopped, left hanging for a while, then pulled back up to safety, things could have turned out somewhat differently. None of them could imagine why Miguel had allowed them to undergo such a procedure with the possibility existing that there could have been four flailing bodies, cascading onto a pile of crashmats simultaneously. That could have been, potentially, fatal. He merely responded with…

"Life is a risk. Climbing is an even bigger one. You must be trained for all risks in this discipline. Next time, you'll have no warning when someone slips or falls, and they might not be the person at the back of the group."

…and he hammered home…

"*Always* be ready!"

This was to be the last night at Asperaciones Cumbre. The first part of their trial would not be the actual ascent of Ojos del Salado. It would consist mainly of acclimatisation blended with a little training at higher altitude, in a location some distance away. Thus their introduction to this challenge would simply be a drive through yet more splendid scenery. Much of their familiarisation with altitude would consist of time spent relaxing, conversing, reflecting on life, resting and planning. Their aim would be simply to get used to breathing in a part of the atmosphere that yielded less oxygen than at ground level. Following that, it would be necessary to undergo a certain measure of exercising, to determine how they might cope, under the strain of ascent. They would have to ease into this climb, carefully and coolly. It would be a sort of calm before the storm.

CHAPTER 15

Base Camp

"Gobbledygook"
...mused Hannah, listening to a song with that particular hook, on her headset at seven o'clock in the morning...

"What a great word!"

Her latest novel was a science fantasy, entitled 'Ahriman of the desert'. Her chosen collection of music tracks, to complement the experience, was part of a concept album on the theme of witchcraft, which seemed, combined with highly appropriate and motivating scenery, to provide her with yet another riveting and multidimensional reading experience. She had perched herself on a downward slope of salty sand, looking out over a wide lagoon. Occasional, early-morning cooking smells arrived in waves from a hut inside which Miguel was slaving for them, a small distance away, once again, in preparation for their breakfast.

Fr Murphy was providing company for Miguel, whilst acting as his galley slave. He had already brewed some tea and washed a few pots and was now standing over Miguel, quizzing him about a few unrevealed details of the up-and-coming trek, whilst he created omelettes that seemed to be, pretty much, carbon copies of one another.

Jed and Joe were now enjoying separate sleeping arrangements. All four trekkers had private tents which were pitched several metres apart in fairly close proximity to the hut. According to Miguel, it was extremely unusual that they were not sharing the site with other wayfarers at this time of year, but it was nice to have the privacy and space for their small, select group.

There was an intense, uplifting brilliance, born of altitude and extra-penetrating sunshine. Miguel had pointed out that, although it seemed that they had set up camp, down in a valley, with mountains towering above it, they were actually higher than four thousand meters above sea level. Jed had equated that to two-and-a-half English miles. At this height, there was not much atmosphere to absorb the sun's radiation. The air was crystal clear. Being high-up also seemed to explain why it was not so warm despite such perfect weather. All were steeped in sun cream, which would always be needed to protect them from harmful ultra violet rays.

The mountain hut was built over natural hot springs which were like an eternally warm bath. At some point, they would all be communing within it. This would be something to relish after a few hours of training or else perhaps, proceeding a chilly night like the one they had all just awoken from. As they ate, by the lakeside, they were warned of some sobering truths about things to come.

"What's the coldest temperature you guys ever get in your country?"

...inquired Miguel.

"I read minus thirteen in my van, once"

...responded Joe, quickly, obviously geed-up by his memory. He was not, immediately met with any competition, until Miguel continued...

"Are you ready for this, everyone? Mountains are unpredictable, including Ojos del Salado. But unlike your Great Britain mountains, this one is nearly seven thousand metres up in the sky. We've got to expect anything up there. At the worst, it could be minus thirty degrees Centigrade with eighty kilometre an hour winds. This will probably happen at one point. Be ready."

Everyone looked gob-smacked and was.

"How do we get on if it becomes that cold?"

...asked Jed. It seemed a fair question.

"*When* it gets that cold, not *if.*"

...urged Miguel...

"We dress well and don't hang around. For the summit itself we get on with it all"

Miguel's accent was thick and his grammar not quite perfect, but they knew what he meant.

"Also, talking about the summit, there's some permanent ice to cross and a small climb near the top, but we'll be OK if we work as a team and look out for each other."

Suddenly this assault was looking a good deal tougher.

155

"I thought you said this would be like a walk in the park?"

...added Fr Murphy...

"Now it looks like the park's an arctic one with ice cliffs in the middle of it!"

"Rest easy, my friend."

...came Miguel's fairly reassuring reply...

"None of it is so hard and we'll camp in shelter. Maybe only minus ten degrees at night"

"Oh... why didn't you say?"

...mocked Fr Murphy...

"Quite warm then?"

After a brief silence, during which some of them might have wished for something to drown-out their eating sounds, Jed chipped-in regarding the food...

"Nice grub!"

...he proclaimed, turning to Miguel.

"What grub?"

puzzled Miguel, looking for something nasty.

Fr Murphy quickly interjected...

"He means food. Grub is another word for food"

"Tortilla Chilena!"

... added Miguel...

"To you, *omelette*"

Hannah joined in, positively as always...

"I'm looking forward to this trip even just for the food!"

"Great... thank you"

... chirped Miguel...

"I hope to serve you all well and not kill you with my food."

"No chance of that!"

...assured Jed.

"If it was me cooking, we might not make it up the mountain."

"Yeah... he even murders baked beans!"

...confirmed Hannah.

"No murdered beans from me"

...promised Miguel, smiling brightly into his cup...

"Fine tea, Padre"

...he added, turning to Fr Murphy.

"Ah that's dockyard tea"

…informed Fr Murphy…

"The number of tea bags heavily outweighs the number of cups. Thus a brutal strength of tea that strips the skin off the roof of your mouth. Perfect for an early get-up though."

"Suits me"

…added Joe…

"Is there any more?"

It was a timeless day. They had arrived at their base camp on the previous evening, contrary to original plans, and endured their first night in tents. Because of this they were already in situ, enjoying early morning peace, nowhere less spectacular than the High Andes. Miguel had referred to their present location as 'base camp'. However, it was quite some distance from the base of their mountain, and merely referred to, by that name, as it was a starting point for other peaks in the area, and a place to adapt to altitude. Their initial aim, here at base camp, was simply to become familiar with life at a significant elevation. Learning to cope with exercise would begin tomorrow. Today would be without particular structure or activity. How long a day can seem, with nothing to distract the mind.

"Funny how you never get used to this"

… declared Miguel, as they sat, fed and watered, unfettered, relaxed, and detached from the chaos of their own distant world, still looking out over the great salt lake. No-one uttered a response, but remained with their heads locked-on to the enchantment before them.

"It's so quiet"

…whispered Hannah, feeling, somewhat, as though she were bound by the same rules as a library. This gift of perfect peace and energy almost demanded extra respect. In truth, there was little out there to make a noise. Tiny ripples lapped the shore below the rocks on which they were poised and mild, fresh wafts of breeze, occasionally fluttered in their ears.

Father Murphy gazed upwards, enjoying the silence being honoured by his respectful companions. That alone was truly invigorating, for him. There was huge, natural power in this place. The clear blue, above, was unusually dark at such an elevation. For a moment, he mused about the thin divide that separates humans from a boundless universe beyond. This trip might deliver him closer to the stars than he'd ever been. Surely there would be little to mask the cosmos at night.

Distant, rugged, snow-dusted peaks, visible from base camp, were further away and even larger than they looked, yet still close enough to be perfectly mirrored in the placid, turquoise lake, which almost resembled painted glass.

"What happened to all those flamingos, I've seen on pictures of places like this?"

...inquired Jed, remembering one or two pictures from a library, many miles away.

"You won't see them here."

...assured Miguel...

"Too much poison in the water. You might see them in other cleaner lakes that have their food floating about. This area was even used to prepare people to land on Mars, some day in the future. It can be all hostile to life and toxic. People come here to do their extreme survival."

A buzz of interest ensued, but Fr Murphy diffused it by declaring that this had put paid to his morning swim.

An extra brilliance made one screw-up their eyelids to focus. It was an extreme radiance that those who'd barely ever travelled out of Lincolnshire could possibly have imagined, as they sat upon a land which was close to the sky, yet still had little to separate it from raging fires beneath the ground. It was also a place of great space, despite the size of its mountains. From the Carvey's cottage in England, there was incessant flatness in every direction which might have given an impression of lots of room. Here, however, it was probably the emptiness of the place, that enhanced the effect. They were, seemingly, alone in a desert devoid even of shrubs. From one horizon to the next, there was little but mountain desert.

Jed began to perform his usual trick, involving shutting his eyes, which was quite relaxing in such extreme brightness. Sounds and smells took over. There wasn't much to smell, either. Just a thin scent of the only vegetation visible, a small shrub, some metres away, and a suggestion of salt where a gentle lapping of water touched the lakeshore. Apart from that, it was the aftermath of food, left on plates and waves of sun cream. The air was dry and clean. Jed mused that base camp might just be a great place to rescue ones health, free of pollution and chaos.

"So, what's the plan?"

...he inquired

Miguel's single-word reply, gesturing towards everything around him, was...

"This."

Some puzzled reactions followed. Surely there would be some form of organised action. Miguel expanded his answer...

"We learn to live here and empty our minds, stay in one place, be content to be where we are, reflect, talk, eat, drink and rest. We ground ourselves."

In some ways this was a relief. In others it wasn't. All four of Miguel's guests were *doers*. Even Joe, who tended to loaf around a bit more than the rest of them, was always doing something, even if it was a game on a computer or phone. There were signs that all of them, apart from perhaps Jed, were losing their ability, in life, to stay in one place or simply meditate. Fr Murphy could relate to this particularly from flying experiences, where he'd been delayed for more than just a few hours. At first, one could be angry at the inefficiency and inconvenience of being held, perhaps far from one's destination, scuppering plans and aspirations, often in a situation of discomfort at some airport. Eventually, he had found that, after six or seven hours, he had settled and was relatively accepting of a situation. In simple terms, these long delays had trained him, temporarily, to stay in one place and calm down. He looked forward to achieving this again, without being at an airport. It might also be easier now that nobody's phones had a signal and they had only each other to communicate with.

Jed aired an observation...

"I think I like the fact that I could walk anywhere here without trespassing on someone's land."

"Not many places near us like that!"

...added Joe.

They were both swiftly corrected by Miguel...

"Actually, you guys don't know. You can't just walk up there, I'm afraid. I had to organise permits from Copiapo before I met you at the airport."

"Why"

...asked Joe?

"How could you be trespassing up there, in the middle of nowhere?"

"It's not about that"

...said Miguel...

"It's all safety. They need to know who's putting themselves at risk and when. It's really a good thing, for sure. You can get away without a pass on the Argentina side but they still like you to tell them if your going ip a mountain. That way, though, is much longer for sure. It could take three weeks"

Joe was staggered by that...

"This thing really *is* big, isn't it? It doesn't *look* that big"

"I know!"

...exclaimed Hannah...

"It looks like you could just walk round the lake, nip up that slope on the left, shin-up that steepish, valley thing, hit that high bit and be down for an evening meal!?"

No-one grinned except for Miguel whose mouth nearly met his ears...

"I guess that's why you guys all need this experience, no?"

...he spoke with a gentle sigh...

"You'll find out."

The day passed exceptionally slowly. For much of it, each went their separate ways. Miguel had suggested that they all wander off alone, without going too far away, to fully appreciate the beauty and silence of such awesome desolation. For Hannah, this was a simple, chilled experience, doing what she often did anyway; glue herself to a special spot with a book and a suitable music playlist. Her favoured location seemed to be a couple of squarish-looking rocks which formed a sort of chair and gifted her an idyllic panorama across the lake, with that to-die-for reflection in the centre of her vision. She was remarkably quick at reading, seeming to absorb vast tracts of information in large batches. Her previous novel, 'Ahriman of the Desert' was already done and dusted. Now she was racing through a fantasy thriller involving some lost Inca treasure. She had armed herself, purposefully, before the trip, with Andean Mountain music, performed upon indigenous instruments such as pan pipes, charango, flutes and drums. It would take just a couple of things to distract her from this particular utopia; Jed or food. Here, there was neither.

Jed had marched-off hoping to discover as much as possible and make the most of this vast opportunity in a unique setting, on the other side of his planet. His first discovery, however, was that it appeared to take a heck of a long time before he felt he'd gone anywhere at all. The landscape was seemingly stretched out, as though each part of it had been extended over lots more ground than one might have calculated when attempting to walk somewhere. Everything was definitely much bigger than it seemed. Jed reasoned that his poor judgement of distance here, was simply a result of his inexperience of such extensive landscapes. He took care not to amble too far, in case he caused a rescue to be launched before his party had even set off. Within a couple of hours or so, he was back at base camp, having found that the locale was much of a muchness. A more substantial journey in the jeep might have yielded a bit more variety. However, his mind was rich and creative. During his sojourn, he had burbled to himself, continually and passionately with concepts, theories and imaginary scenarios about his planet and all that existed beyond it. There had been no distractions to his thinking and no-one to have to share it with. His mind had run wild

Fr Murphy was used to solitude, as indeed were many from his neck of the woods. He networked and socialised within his work, but lived alone. Such isolation was often very useful for one who regularly needed to chat to 'The Man Upstairs'. He had spent much of his acclimatisation, doing the same. He asked that they might all be looked after on their quest. He also partially planned a sermon, inspired by this experience, that might bring some of it to his congregation. To reinforce matters, he had also snapped many a sight with his camera, for the creation of a photo gallery, which he'd be placing in his church hall, for all those kind folk, who had sponsored this event, to see the fruits of their generosity.

Joe was suffering an absence of technology. No-one had a network here. Anyway, his phone charger was on the blink. Only Fr Murphy had thought to bring a UK-to-Chile plug adaptor. He might have thought to remind the rest of them, but had not, perhaps by design. He had certainly harboured sneaky thoughts regarding the pleasant scenarios that might ensue if no-one could access personal entertainment, and gobble-up social possibilities. Joe was also being subject to less food than he'd been used to before training started in England. There was no more 'casual grazing' on junk food, as his father (who was just as guilty as him) had put it. Joe was already beginning to realise that when the belly shrinks, hunger urges dwindle too. Joe was actually pretty comfortable here. He sunbathed on the shore, played skimmers, walked around a bit and read through a collection of fun, though fairly adult, comic books. Acclimatisation had been almost cool!

They reconvened for their next meal. This was a fairly simple affair involving fish and pasta. This time, they ate, propped-up against the cabin, on a thin wooden bench. It was the same sort of bench, that's often found in school gyms, but probably a lot dustier. After they had shared a few details of their completely unplanned individual experiences, Miguel asked them how they were all feeling. More than one of the admitted to being concerned that they had achieved nothing. Miguel assured them that their minds and bodies would disagree, now they were more relaxed and rested. Joe admitted to feeling extra-chilled but he could tell there was less oxygen than usual. Hannah pointed out that she'd hardly moved all day and was quite tired. Miguel suggested that inactivity can cause more tiredness than exercise. It could make one sluggish. The bright sun might also have strained her eyes somewhat and given her that slight headiness she was experiencing. Fr Murphy confessed to feeling a little light-headed at times. It was just a sensation now and again, when he'd felt as though his brain might have switched-off.

"Yeah, that's the thinner air"

... assured Miguel, but stabbed Fr Murphy in the back with his next comment...

"It's also your age, my friend!"

Fr Murphy ignored this and turned to Jed...

"You have an exceptional radiance about you, dear boy. Did you find a massage parlour somewhere?"

"Not out here"

...sniggered Miguel.

"Actually, I feel great... larger than life. It's quite weird. I didn't sleep very well last night. It's almost as though I didn't need it"

"Ah, the bliss of youth"

...added Fr Murphy, sounding un-deliberately jealous.

"That's enough. You've had your turn"

...prompted Miguel...

"Maybe you can talk to your friend up there..."

...he gestured towards the sky...

"...and ask for some magic?"

"It doesn't work like that, I'm afraid..."

...smiled Fr Murphy...

"Thought I taught you that all those years ago. Long as we all get through this in five pieces, I'm a happy man"

"It'll all start to show, tomorrow when we try to walk up hills with weighted backpacks..."

...began Miguel...

"We'll find out then if we're okay to go up high. The wind and cold are another thing though. No-one wants to give anyone false hope, here. We need to be realistic. We'll take things one little bit by another little bit, no?"

"Little-by-little"

...mouthed Jed without making a sound.

"And now..."

continued Miguel...

"There's only one thing left to do tonight, which is to get inside the springs."

This might have sounded a bit misleading. He was, of course, referring to the pool inside the hut, made perpetually warm by heat from the Earth's crust. Having not been warned about this (there were several things Miguel might have warned them about, before this trip), no-one had brought a swimming costume so it was shorts and tee-shirt, then allow the intensely parching climate to dry them out overnight.

Everyone but Miguel lowered themselves down into the pool with some trepidation, having seen or read horror stories connected with natural phenomena like this, they needed some reassurance that it was totally safe and they would not be blanched. Miguel's sarcastic humour attempts were not what some of them needed...

"We've boiled peas and carrots in here. Don't worry, you'll get used to it."

By the time he had released this foolish report, he was safely submerged, thus nullifying its credence. One or two faces exhibited bewilderment, but their owners continued to lower themselves into the water. Regardless of this, Miguel maintained his vegetable theme...

"The world of vegetables has a lot to teach us; they never stop trying to survive, even under torture"

Whilst it might be accurate to express that the plant kingdom does continue to survive against many odds, Miguel's statement did not survive for very long at all.

"That's even more random than when I try my best to find something unrelated to anything at all!"

...insisted Jed.

"It's true though!"

...prompted Fr Murphy, almost experiencing a wave of pity for his old compatriot.

"I'll be thinking again, next time I steam sugar snap peas"

There was a lull. Some of them might have thought that Miguel would have a themed conversation, a game or a song or two, lined-up for this occasion. More silence ensued, with just the rippling of warm water and people's breathing sounds, especially Fr Murphy whose exhalations were sometimes punctuated with slight vocal expression. Finally, Miguel dissected the calm...

"Some people are uncomfortable with no noise. I think you guys might be a bit more the same in your country, until after today's solitude. Maybe you're all more comfortable now?"

"He's not wrong"

...admitted Jed...

"Look at my brother!"

It was true. Joe spent most of his homelife trying to empty spaces in his life. He would normally be playing a game, reading a paper or something less intense or else fidgeting or pacing about. He grinned calmly at his brother...

"I'm so chilled, I might cool down this water"

Another period of hush followed. It was so relaxing and inspiring to dispense with all that chat, people seem unable to do without. There was no pressure to talk. All were simply content with each other's company. In the midst of them arose a small flurry of bubbles...

"That wasn't me"

...assured Fr Murphy. Miguel was quick to reassure...

"Sometimes the gases escape from underground. We usually blame it on someone."

Amongst the frivolity and peace, Miguel offered a wisdom...

"This is how to spend a day, no? No-one knows what will happen tomorrow. Make the most of it all. Each day is like a life. It's as if you're born in the morning, then again the next day. Live each one as if there were no more days."

Nobody responded but all nodded or affirmed in some way. Although Miguel had simply dressed-up the old adage... 'live every day as if it's your last', it was perhaps the sort of motto that people might appreciate and even aim to take on, as a New Year's resolution, if only they could keep to it. Right now, in the timeless peace of this wilderness it was as though a mist had cleared, leaving them a richer view of the world and themselves. The application of Miguel's philosophies did not seem so awkward to a mind and body, calm and focussed. Hannah had pointed out that she seemed to be thinking more plainly and even reading more quickly without her usual distractions. Fr Murphy had never planned a sermon so fast; even at home. Jed and Joe had enjoyed similar experiences, but Miguel had warned them, with his thick but therapeutic Chilean accent and grammar-in-progress, of that rarefied air up on the mountains...

"Even in the most tiring parts of this climb, you must keep the calm from here. Remember how you are in these peaceful moments to help you think up in the sky. Also remember if it's tough at the start of a day, it'll probably be going to get better. Most of the best days you ever had could have started a lot badly. Most of *my* best days happened after I was afraid of something big. I'd build myself up to what I thought would be a great challenge so I was armed, for sure, with more caution and strategy than usual and might succeed because of that. Either way I might be really happy to come through all that and look on that day as a good one. I think this challenge might be something like that for you. A healthy fear is sometimes a friend, that prepares you for a trial."

It was pretty clear where he had gone with all this. It had been a suitable time to plant such seeds in their minds, immersed in a relaxing, healing bath. It had not been so difficult to listen to, with sharper attention skills, honed by harmony and hush during the day. Now perhaps they would live each one as their last and enjoy this experience. They might also remember to stay calm throughout their trip, quietly respecting what might be a tough but, hopefully, conquerable summit. Each of them began to see that this had been an essential time of mental preparation. Perhaps they had achieved more than they thought.

Some time was spent warming their bones, which would certainly be feeling the pinch, at high altitude. Then, at the onset of night, they prised themselves free, with reluctance, from what had been a very desirable, little situation. Fr Murphy refused to leave...

"It's like being back in the womb."

"You remember that?"

...joked Joe, mindful though, of the fact that some people actually do.

"Don't make me have to get out!"

...implored Fr Murphy

"Just as long as you don't cry like a baby does when *it* comes out!"

...chuckled Miguel. He paused, looked at his excessively large and robust, sporty watch and announced...

"Now, there are two things you must experience. You've all seen one of them but maybe not fully experienced it properly"

They looked at one another, puzzling as to what these two things might be. Jed deduced the more obvious of them correctly...

"I'm guessing one of those things is the night sky? It was like being out in space last night"

"Good scholar!"

...chirped Miguel...

"Right here, we have some of the best views of the stars in the world. No light pollution, clear skies at high altitude, less interference... and..."

He was attempting to multitask, and cut himself off in his own tracks.

A little time was spent drying-off and adorning with blankets, to preserve personal warmth, in a night where much heat had escaped for a variety of geographical reasons. Miguel began to move towards the door, gesturing them to follow him, but avoid looking upwards. He dimmed his lamp until there was a negligible degree of light. They pursued him with flailing arms and movements exaggerated by extreme caution, in virtual darkness, willing their pupils to dilate sooner. Miguel cut the gas from his lamp, completely, and calmly reassured them, virtually whispering, as though waiting to give someone a surprise party...

"Our eyes will soon adjust to the night and the sky will sharpen-up even more."

He closed the cabin door. They walked out, almost in the absence of moonlight, or anything else that could have assisted their navigation, towards his extremely vague silhouette. Intense darkness and a lack of any breeze made the vast space, inside which they were walking, feel almost like an enclosed room.

"No-one light a torch or we'll spoil this effect."

...cautioned Miguel, settling on what felt like a sandy surface, five or ten metres beyond their tents. It was hard to manoeuvre without looking upwards, from time to time. Miguel asked them to close their eyes and lay on the ground. They did so in relative calm, obeying his orders, scuffling their trainers and flipflops in gritty dust. His final instruction was...

"Now look upwards."

There was a minimalised but deeply, emotive response, resembling 'wow' from both Joe and Hannah. Everyone trained their upward gaze immediately, in response to orders. It certainly looked as though they were beginning to act as a team, after so much recent, military-style training!

Although they had all experienced something of the Chilean night sky, on previous evenings, the effect was now greater. It was not just the fact that they were now at a significantly higher altitude. This time, they had not lacerated the darkness with flashlights, nor been stressed about camping in such un-familiar circumstances. Any radiance from their hut was also, now extinguished. The heavens emerged sharp and vibrant. In the last few days, some of them had experienced truly awesome landscapes. Now they observed

Chile's flip-side... its scenery up above! Fr Murphy was blown away at the sight of The Milky Way...

"Heavens!"

...he exclaimed with a completely accidental pun...

"Up, in our country, you have to point-out the Milky Way. Down here, it's in your face!"

He paused, trying to remember, from his time in that country, if he'd ever seen such a cosmic display. In truth, he'd been rooted to a spot, most of his time, in and around a missionary, on the Pacific Coast. Four thousand meters above the ocean, was clearly making a huge difference.

"You do all realise we're looking out into space, from a distant spiral arm, right into the centre of our galaxy?"

...with a quiet aside he acknowledged...

"I know you know about that, Jed."

Jed emitted a soft and subtle 'hmm' in affirmation. He was in space.

Massively bright stars, which could now, more easily, be recognised as distant suns, hung with commanding presence, over a slightly more faded universe. Each of these closer neighbours, radiated its singular tint. One was distinctly blue. Some shone with fiery gold. Others were vaguely red or crimson. Some of the southern constellations, which were new to these particular observers, formed decisive, and recognisable, angular shapes, much like those they had seen from England. Beyond these obvious foreground beacons, were more distant specks, like particles of glitter on dark velvet. Underneath them, was a milky glaze, comprising trillions of virtually imperceptible light sources and hazy areas which resembled faint, luminous clouds.

A telescope might have been a good idea, but then there was so much that could easily be identified with the naked eye. Miguel was also most informative. He directed them towards various objects, including a couple of galaxies, which appeared as faint patches, somewhat larger than the stars around them. They were enormous, containing billions of stars, just so distant that they were barely perceptible. They also saw nebulae and patches of murky dust. He told them of the Incas who had related to dark shapes between the stars, such as the head of a snake beneath the Southern Cross, the curving tail of a serpent, passing through the Milky Way, and a mother llama, holding her baby, with two eyes formed by a pair of stars. Fr Murphy and Jed could not help interjecting occasionally with some of their own ideas. Jed was most keen to point out that, as they perused the skies, they were looking back in time. Some of the objects they perceived were being seen as they had been, thousands or even millions of years ago. There were other profound observations and explanations such as to why stars appear to twinkle. They also learned about dates when meteor showers and comets were visible. All was deeply thoughtful, intellectual and riveting, until Joe interjected with a laughable but serious question...

"Do you believe in aliens?"

"Oh God... off we go!"

...protested Jed.

"Someone had to ask that."

...assured Miguel...

"Sure! There's got to be some life somewhere, even if it's only basic or like some vegetable. With a billion, trillion stars, there's got to be big amounts of planets, for sure, and some life. It can't just be us?"

...he shrugged and cast his gaze towards the hut...

"Now we have to have that bit of small fun before our trip to the mountain itself. You guys know how to light a campfire don't you? See how fast you can do it!"

Miguel disappeared into some shadows, near the hut, seemingly upon some small mission. His team remained, for a moment, upon their backs, mentally glued to the sky. A few reluctant moments later, Fr Murphy began to scuffle awkwardly, into a recovery position, before attempting to assume any sort of vertical posture. His comrades followed upon his efforts, before beginning to search for something to burn. Amongst such intense darkness, there would be little opportunity to forage. In fairness, there were miniscule quantities of fire fuel around, anyway. Of course though, there *was* a supply inside the hut for this particular eventuality. As Miguel well knew, everything required had always been stored within a circular, makeshift cupboard, comprising of foraged fuel. It yielded a bucket of lump-wood, scavenged from hardy desert shrubs, some firelighters and a box of matches. Jed was inwardly disappointed that he and his team would not be having to face the challenge of starting a fire from first principles, after all of their previous home training. This had been a stimulating part of their preparation; a trial they had all enthusiastically accomplished in those backwoods of Lincolnshire. Jed's expression betrayed something of his disenchantment. It was obvious enough for Miguel to deduce his thoughts...

"Guess you're going to have to cheat, huh?"

...he grinned.

"I suppose so. A bit dark now, for a wood-quest, maybe?"

...reasoned Jed, mustering-up just about enough energy to return Miguel's smirk.

The night was young but very dark, with negligible light pollution. No human establishments bordered any horizon. A little light from a gas lamp assisted their movements. Within minutes, they had sparked-up a compact, glowing fire. Although it was not profoundly late, there would be a severe breach of comfort tomorrow, even before dawn, as they embarked upon the beginnings of their long-awaited mountain assault. Whatever happened next would be their final comfort before gruelling days ahead.

Despite simple efforts to create flames, the group sat somewhat proudly around their eagerly blazing bonfire. In truth, things were so dry in this part of the world, that this may never have been such a difficult accomplishment, to begin with. However, it had provided them with some confidence and a little warmth inside the cooling night.

Miguel emerged, juggling lots of sticks and something else, balanced upon a tray...

"No-one should ever forget toasted marshmallows and Navegado, at times like this one."

Their faces lit up, within the deep shadows of Atacama night. Soon they were holding marshmallows on skewers, over flames they had created, and sipping what was now apparently, some sort of Chilean mulled wine.

"Just like the wild west!"

...stated Joe, with a very spirited but poor attempt to impersonate a cowboy, and sounding more Australian, though not even that. He proceeded to torture his first marshmallow within the deepest heart of the fire.

"Try not to incinerate the bloody thing!"

...exclaimed his brother, whilst Hannah sampled one which was barely warm.

"Mmm... good call!"

...she assured with slightly too much passion, having the time of her life. Although she had visited much of the world already, this was no ordinary outing. There were elements of exhilaration and risk she had never experienced before. There was no safe hotel, no beach, no gift shops, no traces of tourism nor even a choice of cuisine. They were far from any such thing, within a desert, seemingly on the edge of space, with volcanic peaks towering above them behind all-consuming blackness. A great uncertainty lay ahead. With that came a fair degree of anxiety. However, Miguel promised hope and warmth with his confidence, camaraderie, and culinary contributions. The comfort provided by a hot drink, toasted marshmallows and a bonfire under the stars, instilled a golden-lined eagerness that dulled any inevitable fear surrounding the anticipation of an immense, impending, physical undertaking. These were special moments. Hannah further reinforced her delight…

"Could I just press 'pause' on this bit of the trip? I'm having so much fun, here."

Miguel smiled across, glad his efforts were being appreciated; always pleased to use his skills for a satisfying effect. The only thing resembling a spanner-in-the-works, at that juncture, was Fr Murphy, who had to enquire…

"At what sort of temperature did this particular drink emerge from the heat?"

"Oh, don't worry…"

…assured Miguel…

"I burnt-off all the alcohol before serving. We can't have people with hangovers at the bottom of a big mountain!"

Fr Murphy's single-word reply was…

"Shame!"

This might have been his last chance of a decent drink for some time to come.

At that moment, all harmony and concord exploded, as unexpected music polluted their peace. What had been deep silence and reverence, had suddenly become something between homophony and cacophony. Miguel's rendition of a Chilean dance, known as 'The Zamacueca', was raucous and vulgar, as he bawled, brashly above aggressively strummed charango chords, out into a night that offered nothing back. His music persisted for some time, disrupting all airwaves. His team looked on, somewhat bemused, but lapping up an unanticipated slice of Chilean culture. There was no attempt to join in, as every lyric was of Miguel's native tongue. His audience applauded lightly and politely. When all was done, night was restored, in its calm completeness. Miguel's charango disappeared into his coat, as quickly as it had been whipped-out. All retired shortly after, into individual shelters, under the threat of a very early start.

The following morning was certainly the assault they had been promised. Miguel rose at first light. The rest of them awoke to bangings and clangings, created with a metal spoon inside an empty kettle. It was game-on immediately. All washing and eating was regimented Soon, they were all standing together in a military line, packed with heavy gear. On their backs and about their persons, was all that might be required to keep themselves and their quest alive, inclusive of climbing rocks, walking across ice or keeping themselves dry and warm during extreme weather. They stood, awaiting instructions.

Their day consisted of gruelling, mock-ascents, dressed in full gear, carrying all but the kitchen sink. During this process, they were bullied onwards and upwards, through awkward or uneven terrain. Their progress as individuals and as a team, was carefully monitored by Miguel. A couple of individuals displayed clear discomfort at various points during the test, though one was known for his propensity to wear his heart on his sleeve. The other was simply just a little older than the rest. One of the other two either suffered in silence or was managing fairly well in adapting to the conditions. However, the fourth individual appeared to be unusually, even strangely energised and exuberant. On the previous day, it had been made clear that they would be constantly scrutinized throughout their ascent. Conditions would become gradually more severe and bodies increasingly fatigued. However, they still had much climbing to achieve, so the full effects of altitude could not yet be measured and a running assessment would have to take place as they battled-on. The way ahead may have been aptly described as a very long and arduous walk with a bit of scrambling, yet this was a hike which would take them almost seven thousand metres above sea level. Reaching such crazy heights was not something which could be accurately predicted. One way or another, however, they were deemed *good to go*, with an understanding that the plug could be pulled at any time, if it was observed that any single climber was exhibiting reasons that might prevent them succeeding safely in their quest. Should any one of them become a cause for concern, it may affect the possibility of anyone at all, finishing the ascent. They would have to stick together. For now, Miguel had given them a green light. They had been cleared to attempt an offensive of the world's loftiest volcano.

CHAPTER 16

Up towards the heavens

An *early start* didn't even begin to say it.
"It's still the bloody night"
...groaned Jed.
"What time actually is it?"
...croaked Hannah, in disbelief, peeping through a tent flap.
"Four-thirty."
...informed Miguel...
"Nearly time to go. We'll have our first meal when we get there."
In truth, they had enjoyed quite a lengthy time-out, retiring to their tents at about eight o'clock. After such an arduous day and in profound blackness, that had seemed quite late. Now they were able to arise at an unearthly hour, still relatively refreshed with adequate rest, and use every second of daylight, when it arrived. There would be a substantial drive followed by a climb of reasonably punishing difficulty to fit into that expanse of daytime. Miguel rounded them up like sheep. Their equipment was strictly organised, too. Everything had its place. He had taught them, by now, the quickest and most efficient ways to stow it all. Soon it was with them inside the jeep, or else above them, on the roof, in crates. Miguel hit the gas without delay and, with the usual, vicious jolt, they were rocketing off to somewhere else they had never seen before, across a sleeping desert.

The journey yielded little but an occasional reflection of their own faces, looking back at them through darkness. There was much rattling and rolling, as Miguel steered off-road, from time to time. This was another of his well-rehearsed routes, designed to cut-off corners or else gain altitude more quickly. Constant racket and engine vibration, coupled with an inability to communicate without shouting, and therefore incur longer periods of silence, with nothing much to see through the windows, caused all but the driver to fall asleep. They arrived, muted and sedated, at Atacama Camp, about two hours later. Upon being awoken, with little sensitivity, by Miguel, Hannah admitted, with a gaping yawn, that she had not been expecting to drive so far, all the time. Jed added to the moaning by confronting his brother, who was still in the position in which he had maxed-out...

"What's the deal, falling asleep on my fiancé?"

Joe was mortified and shot-up into a vertical position so fast that he banged Fr Murphy onto a door handle.

"Good job it wasn't me!"

...he jested, completely ignoring the physical assault, then added in a purely practical and dry voice...

"Although it's a generous size, I suggest this is the last time we all share the back seat."

Fr Murphy went on to explain to Hannah something about the fact that they were on a large continent, unlike their little island containing England. Everything was bigger. Fr Murphy was the only soul amongst the tourists, who had much of a notion about the scale of this place and the stature of its mountain and desertscapes. His young compatriots had little idea, until now, that they would be travelling such extensive safaris, in between the stages of their pursuit.

Miguel had been sole witness to the dawn, less than halfway through the drive. It had commenced as a barely perceptible fluorescence, low on the western horizon. As it gradually vivified, like sluggish mood-lighting and melted away all blackness, a watery, rippling disc had begun to edge its way upwards; large and milky, inside a stubborn cloud-bank which glued itself down to the distance. As the intensifying sun, quite quickly rose above the clouds, emerging more clearly circular and stable, like a bright, vermillion light bulb, the tops of the high Andes were spectacularly reborn, bathed in a soft, warm blanket of misty-pink, above a dark, hazy, blue band where Earth was not quite yet awake. Miguel's lonely countenance brightened, never too blasé to enjoy this riveting display of his world awakening, yet he let his passengers sleep. They would need all the energy they could generate for their athletics ahead.

Another meal emerged before they had carried out their instructions. Some of their gear was to go with them to another camp, higher up the mountain. The rest would remain for them to collect and transport back up, when they returned back down! This had sounded like a contradiction to them all, at first, but was well-explained by Miguel as they made light work of his chilli-bean and ground-beef stew, with crusty bread. This was their first meal of the day, though they had all stolen oranges and bananas from a tub standing outside the vehicle before they set-off. Miguel had hinted they may need a little extra sustenance before reaching the next port-of-call.

"Food certainly tastes better, out in the fresh air"

...assured Fr Murphy.

"Out in the wilderness I remember the world is nearly all about food."

..added Miguel, almost keeping to the point.

"Well..."

...piped-up Jed

"...whatever we take away from this trip, I'll remember these great dishes you keep brewing-up"

...he said, turning with a cheerful expression to Miguel.

"I don't know how you conjure-up such great food so fast."

"That's most kind of you, Jed"

...beamed Miguel

"It's pretty basic, really, for sure"

"Not to him"

...added Hannah.

"His parents are pretty mean with food. You can't get much more basic than the things they give him and Joe. To Jed, everything you've given us is 'haut cuisine'."

She mustered-up a high, shrill and perhaps slightly over-enthusiastic laugh, like a jackal on helium. The others generated efforts to support her humour, ranging between grins and grimaces.

"Well, I'll remember this great nosh too."

...bellowed Joe, slapping-down his empty plastic plate and standing-up to stretch and walk around. Miguel looked up at him and around at the others, conveying a wish...

"All I can say is I hope this trip gives you all something you were looking for or else something maybe you find that you didn't know about before you came here."

Jed was prompted to admit what had so far shaken him the most...

"It's given me energy! I don't know why I have so much of it. It could be the air here or the altitude, or even your amazing food, but I feel like I've never felt before."

He paused and looked above. noticing Earth's little friend, still hanging around in the day-time blue…

"Like I could jump over the moon…"

He got no further before Joe brought him back to the ground…

"Aw… how sweet! You mean like the cow in 'Hey-diddle-diddle?'"

Fr Murphy dived-in quickly to avert a fraternal fracas, but also did so, as he had a contribution of his own…

"This trip is good for me too as I've reached the point in my life where I'm beginning to get excited about what happened in the past."

He was immediately comforted by consoling words from Hannah and Miguel and told that he still had an awful lot of future left to be excited about. Jed then seconded Miguel's notion that this trip would definitely be a good reason to look back in life, in the years to come. Fr Murphy was suitably warmed-up, and soon the meal was duly and quickly wrapped-up.

After washing dishes via a large flagon of water in the jeep, they were ushered, hastily, to an area on the other side of the camp. There was a smattering of tents but few people around. Apparently this was very rare. This was a very popular mountain and was, more often than not, infested with ant-like trails of adventurers, who arrived here from all over the globe.

"It's possible they're all up on the mountain, but they could be other places too. I've got to say this is unusual. We should be here, for sure, with lots of people. I can't explain."

…informed Miguel, as they sauntered, somewhat slothfully, through the dusty-looking camp, towards a preferred spot on its far side. Miguel noticed how laboured one or two of them seemed to be, and pointed out…

"You may feel heavy and slow now, with all this weight on your back, for sure, but you get used to this as we keep going. Remember to enjoy all this, despite the hardship! You might never come back here. Have fun today. Each day is a life."

"Good job each life isn't just a day!"

…muttered Jed into his boots, sensing his humour might not meet the mark.

They arrived at a random spot next to the commencement of the trail, leading upwards towards the next refuge and eventually the peak itself. All was dust, gravel and rubble, as far as the eye could see. In Hannah's words, it was like a sort of giant slag heap. All framed rucksacks were ditched immediately. Their shoulders breathed a sigh of relief. Automatically, a line was formed in the same order as they had been briefed, a few days previously in training, with Fr Murphy ready to lead. This was to ensure that they would be able to walk at the same rate as the slowest member of their party, keeping him constantly in sight. With some nerves inside all of them, born from the unknown ahead and their abilities to face it all, they stood, awaiting further directions, like lambs to the slaughter.

"Let the ascent commence!"

... bellowed Father Murphy, in a sort of stage voice, sounding like someone launching an army into battle. He was met with sluggishness, unwilling body-language and an unusual flurry of belches. Seeing Miguel was not quite with them yet, they sat down, to savour the last few moments of rest they might enjoy for some time to come. A rapidly approaching Miguel, grimaced from a distance, supressing emotions connected with questions he had regarding their ability to achieve this grand and distant goal. If such an uninspired beginning was anything to go by, fitness and attitude were both in question, particularly regarding a couple of members of his party. Essentially, they had all satisfied minimum requirements back at the Summit Aspirations complex, but in Miguel's bible, fitness was also a state of mind. In order to employ one's physical strength efficiently, a positive personal drive would always be essential. Some of the roots of this concept had evolved from examples of his greatest ever mentor, Father Murphy, who had definitely infused passion into him from an early age, at his mission. Thus Miguel's company policy was all about inspiring achievement. 'Summit Aspirations' was a name but also a mantra. They practiced what they preached in order to become what their title suggested and inspire others. This group was looking a little reticent. Perhaps it was time to address them with a pep-talk.

"Can't we acclimatise for one more day?"

...whined Joe, pulling himself up from the floor with his harness and a waistline of metallic adornments, a bit like climbers' bling, jangling about as he rose. He had lately lost a significant amount of his former bulk, which had established itself via a constant surfeit of mini-feasts, whilst grazing between unhealthy meals and family-pack crisp frenzies, mostly inside his postal van, which was perpetually littered with various forms of such evidence and eternally in need of a valet. Until recently, for Joe, a spirited effort could only have been associated with the sort of stunt driving he did between deliveries, which he employed in order to reach an oasis in time, whereupon these material delights could be enjoyed. Now, standing here in thinning air, with dwindling temperatures, in the Andean outback, things felt very different to those notions they had all projected, back home, of what things might be like, here. Despite Joe's new, slimline stature and experience of recent exertions never sustained before, his spirit was harder to find. In fairness, this was a very early start with little but hardship ahead. Beyond all of this however, Miguel sensed a bit more apprehension amongst his party, than he was typically used to observing amongst other parties, and wasted no more time in launching his speech…

"Have we travelled around the world just to feel intimidated by this great prize?"

He began, perhaps slightly over the top, with a stirring tone and an unusually powerful, command of English (this was because he'd read it in a book!). He paused to study facial expressions as they awkwardly raised themselves and their large, state-of-the-art burdens, into vertical positions. They were like overloaded donkeys, waiting to be led.

"This is the real deal, now!"

He continued…

"From here on, it gets windier, colder, icier and a bit steeper. The further up this trail we climb…"

… he gestured with a fairly aggressive, repeated, pointing action upwards, towards the gods of the mountain, then performed a one-eighty to signal downwards, into the milky distance of lower Earth …

"…the further we separate ourselves from the world below and the human race, for sure. This is a giant mother of a mountain. Sometimes she gets angry."

There were faint suggestions of quizzical expressions on Jed and Joe's faces…

"She can shake things up at any time, for sure, and catch us all out. Remember what we shared back at the base? On a mountain, the weather can turn in a second, for sure."

Not one of them didn't wonder why he kept saying 'for sure'. They seldom heard anyone say that in England. Of course, no-one would think about interrupting such an important briefing with such trivia, nor would they wish to seem rather personal and judgemental. He continued…

"If we get unlucky and do get caught in a sudden, freak storm, what do we do then? What is there to do to help us survive?"

"Common sense?"

...offered Jed, looking quite a bit more awake than the rest of them.

"For sure... Good!"

...acknowledged Miguel, with a few too many nods of the head for an individual such as Jed, who rarely required so much praise and affirmation.

"What else?"

Fr. Murphy sensed something of a brick wall and began randomly pointing at the people to his right and left, until the penny dropped for Hannah and she muttered, in a rather 'it's too early in the morning' timbre...

"Each other?"

"Right!"

...chirped Miguel, so gratified that someone had actually produced the answer he was searching for, despite the fact that he was not so sure himself that it *had* been that obvious!

"A team can look out for each other. We keep all our eyes open together. We hear the wind..."

"There'll be plenty of that!"

...Joe was thinking, whilst catching Jed's eye. After all, they'd been subject to a heck of a lot of frijoles and chilli, whilst acclimatising. From now on it seemed obvious that dinner would mostly come in a can, and contain those ingredients. Miguel continued, blissfully unaware. His gaze and body language gestured outwards and upwards in the direction they were headed, and, right on cue, as though by magic, a disturbing flurry of cooler air gusted through them like a disquieting wave...

"See the spirits of this mountain are telling us, right now, we shouldn't go up, but with each other, we can beat them."

No-one bought this, although they were brought down to Earth, somewhat, by the erratic movements of the atmosphere. He was, rather over-obviously, attempting to hit them with dressed-up drama by latching onto a spur of the moment squall, in order to stir them into a greater awareness...

"We watch the approaching clouds. We continue to check our bearings and know of the route ahead."

His voice was becoming a little melodramatic and tremulous. Hannah could not prevent a smirk from momentarily appearing, mercifully away from Miguel's gaze. It was perhaps a good job that acting was not his day job, although he was certainly generating an appropriate energy for the purpose of motivation. Father Murphy mused that Miguel might try to watch a film of Henry V or something to get a better idea. There was more to Miguel's dialogue...

"If there's something wrong in here..."

He gestured towards his head, paused, then towards his stomach...

"...or in here..."

They had been briefed by him already regarding the symptoms of altitude sickness, which should be identified and communicated as early as possible, and could easily manifest in any of their team...

"...or anywhere else!?"

He paused again to take a well-deserved breath...

"If all of us always observe *all* of these little things, we'll stay ahead of the game and defeat *her*!"

He gestured hugely strongly towards the mountain. The way he referred it, one might have though it had done him an injustice or two...

"But first, we concentrate on maintaining our bodies and minds on the route and travel at the rate of the slowest in our party."

"Yep... that'll be me!"

...interjected Fr. Murphy.

"...and we think good, strong thoughts about succeeding. We're all ready for this. We've done all the work down there."

... Now he gestured wildly again, below, towards the Atacama Camp at two-thousand metres, from which they had begun to acclimatise...

"Yes... we all know where it is!"

...thought Jed, quietly.

"We use the higher levels of energy we've attained, carefully. We move calm and steady, and conserve energy."

The speech was over. A slow ripple of applause spread reluctantly through the team who had been blasted now, by both the wind and also Miguel's words of motivational instruction.

"Are we ready?"

...he yelled, doing all he could to jostle them, neglecting only to raise a sword into the air. They nodded, weakly in approval, somewhat daunted by great weights upon their shoulders and that recent show of elemental force by Mother Nature. They were also bemused by Miguel's ever-so-slightly, unconvincing delivery, which was supposed to have enthused them, though failed somewhat, due to awkward, morning moods. Once again, he missed a few of their furtive expressions as he continued towards them, holding out a fist for all to pump. They gravitated slowly and silently towards him. After a scrabble of heavy boots on volcanic rubble and a clink of climbers' percussion, in the form of harness buckles and belays, they formed a brief wheel of five spokes, and connected fists. Miguel continued to speak during those moments of bonding...

"In less than a week, we drink to this! Until then, we look after ourselves and make this mountain top safely, for sure, so we can definitely do that."

They understood him, through a slight misplacement of his words and the thickness of his handsome Chilean accent, and were, rather miraculously, somewhat more positively focussed.

"Let's do this!"

...piped-up Joe, as pumped as any of them had seen him, forever.

This outing had been specifically designed with Jed in mind. Fr. Murphy had somehow sensed in him, a potential that was not being tapped, within his present circumstance. A wisdom, somewhere inside him, had made him feel compelled, on Jed's behalf, to gift him this opportunity, far away from any experience he had ever enjoyed or endured. Whilst he did not believe that dreams had any particular meaning, he had felt, somehow, that one involving someone atop a volcano, might have represented some sort of unconscious, instinctual message, from their psyche, that was urging them to do something a bit more bold and outward-bound. Oddly perhaps, despite these fairly compulsive concerns about Jed's direction in life, Fr Murphy still wasn't completely sure why he'd organised such a trip. It had seemed like more of a calling. Something in his nature; a fairly sketchy inkling, had urged him to do it. He was, of course, attempting to kick-start Jed's life in a way that an over-safe life, both at college and home, would probably never do. He hoped he might ignite a passion to explore. It might increase Jed's global perspective and lead him away from being fairly insular. One way or another, Fr. Murphy was convinced that Jed had far more to offer than the career into which he was being directed. His manner, his expression, his ability to logicise, his creative wit; everything about him had told Fr. Murphy that he was not only talented, but wasted.

Right now, Jed seemed to be magnificently energised. Perhaps it was the freshness of the atmosphere, or all that resting by the lake. One way or another, he was more than ready to begin his quest. First though, there would be even more to endure in the way of instructions. Miguel was certainly making them a little restless with his lectures, though such comprehensive preaching was quite obligatory, before such a profound undertaking. He began by reinforcing details of their itinerary. He reminded them that they had spent several days training at the centre, also some time driving and walking through the Atacama Desert, and finally some days acclimatising and familiarising themselves with new surroundings, bathing in hot springs and preparing minds. Now they would spend several days climbing the mountain, but perhaps not quite in the fashion they might have expected. They were to leave their jeep behind for three days. They would most likely have to be back before then to avoid some severe weather, that had been hinted at in a local forecast. Their plan was to walk up with half of their equipment, mainly that which would be needed for a final summit climb. This would include crampons, ice axes and so on. They would take all this to Tejos Hut at five-thousand-eight-hundred metres, then walk back down to Atacama Hut, where they already were, to stay one night. This would be a climb of just 600 metres in altitude, but a reasonable distance to walk, particularly with weight on their backs. The main reason for this would be to ensure they could operate safely at an even higher altitude. It would be foolish to walk so far from safety into an environment so low in oxygen, before realising that one was suffering symptoms of altitude sickness. Even beyond this point, their progress would be scrutinised by Miguel. Any question of struggling would mean they would all turn back. However, even after this was made clear and agreed upon, Joe, who was certainly keen to achieve the summit, still found a reason to moan…

"What kind of a downer will that be when we reach the next stage and then have to undo all our work?"

"It's my insurance, Joe!"

…affirmed Miguel.

"What kind of a downer would it be if you suffered severe altitude sickness and had to descend in a stretcher or worse?"

Nothing more was said. Miguel raised a thumb, intending to wish them all good luck, then a hand, waving them forwards. They were off!

Fr Murphy was somewhat internally dissatisfied at being in a constant pole position, but carried his feelings silently, as was his job description. He was never sure if he was holding everybody up and was unable to read anyone's body language. He had often joked about human beings needing wing mirrors. Now, he thought, might have been a good time to evolve them. The way was tough for a man of his age. Miguel had raised a few questions about his fitness. One thing was organising such a trip for three young and relatively fit people. Another was insisting on bringing yourself with them. Having recently surpassed a milestone birthday, his energy was somewhat dwindling and his life-speed slowing. However, his performance had been deemed adequate during aptitude training. It was clear that he was a man of great experience who might be useful in adverse situations. Meanwhile, Fr Murphy could feel everyone's silent scrutiny as he steadied his efforts onwards and upwards. He was attempting to set a pace that was hopefully maintainable for himself. This was not fully appreciated by some of the members of his party who might have liked to move along a little more briskly. However, they were all feeling somewhat compromised by rarefied air and a strengthening breeze blowing downwards into their faces, hindering progress, and making communication a little more difficult, as it buffeted their ears via powerful, sporadic bursts. After a very short while, they ceased to converse sociably, concentrating on personal self-maintenance. As each of them fell into individual silences, a serious mood seemed to descend upon them. Their real test had begun.

A wide, gritty trail led them slowly upwards in twists and turns. The summit of their peak lay a great distance away, beyond the tops of some enormous hills, which they could see from where they were, rising from beyond their next camp. These were, in truth, all part of the same mountain. As often happens when climbing, there would be false summits. These would be tops which obscured higher peaks behind them. It might have been a blessing that they didn't yet fully realise the true position of their final goal.

For some hours they struggled upwards into unknown territory, pausing occasionally to relieve themselves of their hefty loads, and take on fluids. After one of many long silences, Fr Murphy turned around to the others and declared...

"None of it's getting any nearer, is it!?"

In truth, the scale of this climb was so great that it would take a considerable amount of time and effort to encourage the scenery to alter itself. Once again, Miguel jumped-in with some reassurance...

"I can't deny it takes a lot of time until that mountain gets any nearer, but you'll see that suddenly it does. It's a long way from Atacama to the top of it, but then you reach a bit where it all gets close much faster!"

They vaguely understood his point and put their trust in him, although the conversation which ensued, on a brief pause for water, indicated that a few of them were gasping as they talked.

"Do we all feel OK?"

...inquired Miguel. Nods happened and conversation progressed. He posed another question but answered it himself...

"Can you see that sandy-coloured hill up there? The hut is just behind it. Maybe less than an hour from here. Then we eat before coming back down with less gear than we took up."

Whilst there was still, obviously, a lot of work to do, this was quite a comfort. Soon they were back on the trail, eating into that final part, leading to the refuge.

The Sun's energy was strong here at a more godly altitude. This was now an unpitying summer's day. Joe struggled to maintain a covering of sun lotion as his own perspiration left his face and neck dry and salty and him beginning to feel like the victim of a large-scale barbeque. Armed with an old grey towel and a bright orange container of total sun-block, he continually renewed his defences until he had to settle for the towel upon his head, like a poor man's emulation of Lawrence of Arabia. After some hours of dusty, arduous and silent ascending, along a scorched and barren rocky trail, they turned around together to sample their progress and survey a distant desert-scape, now significantly lower than themselves. As they enjoyed a momentary respite, in soothing silence, on the rim of a precipice of knotted, black volcanic rock, they could each hear their own hearts thumping. However, such a physical demise could not prevent them from being awestruck at the immensity of those views beneath and around them. Here they were, far from home. This was another world, utterly different to theirs. It was a dissimilar silence too, to the sort they were all used to, when they returned home, from work or college, to cottages, out in Lincolnshire's sleepy farmlands. Here there seemed to be an invisible, magic vigour in the atmosphere around them, born of intense sunlight and clear, cleansing air. Clouds of dust from their boots had now settled on parched earth, and that breeze which had earlier tried to push them back, had abated as though it had been somehow switched off. All was completely still. No-one spoke. The energy was overpowering. Miguel, who had visited this spot many times, grinned to himself. It was partly moments like this that gave purpose to his work. In some ways, it was always like seeing it for the first time through someone else's eyes. He could absorb the reactions of those newcomers who had made their way here for the first time. Huge waves of warmth permeated them as they perched on large igneous boulders, looking out over the western deserts of South America. It was a combination of perfect climate, breath-taking views, from three and a half miles up in the sky, and that momentary relief when sitting down to rest without their packs, after a tough slog, that uplifted them so much. Finally Fr Murphy broke the silence with a respectful, sensitive tone to proclaim...

"Well, this'll certainly be one of those moments I cherish when I look back from the future".

The others smiled and nodded in complete agreement.

"If this had been all we came here for, it'd have been worth it"

…added Hannah, still transfixed by broad swathes of coloured rock and sand that stretched so far away, they blended into the horizon.

Miguel added nothing, for once, but rose with a radiant smile. They followed suit with no resistance. It was as though their spirits had now incarnated properly. They had walked-themselves-in and found rhythm. It was true to say, however, that their packs did not seem to be getting any lighter. They took their strains once more and followed in Miguel's tracks. Fr Murphy sidled around him, fairly uncomfortably and untidily, to resume his lead.

It had been a *very* long slog, as Fr Murphy had put it, but now they were there, almost like magic. They ascended a small ridge, over the top of which was a slightly more level plain. In the midst it, was a fairly large, red hut, sitting at the bottom of the part of the route they would not be attempting for a night or two.

"There she blows!"

…said Miguel, coining an English phrase he had recently learned.

"About time!"

…moaned Joe…

"We still have to go all the way back down!"

"That'll be a lot easier."

…assured Miguel…

"You'll be carrying less and also walking downhill. At the end, we have a campfire and good food."

"Can't help wishing we could do all that here. I do get this acclimatising lark, but I'm sure I'm fine."

…whined Jed, somewhat uncharacteristically. Miguel responded, having deduced that the word 'lark' was not likely to be referring to a bird.

"Never forget that we are more than just yourself here. There are some amongst us who might not realise, for sure, how much they need to acclimatise, right now".

"Sorry!"

…offered Jed, with a virtual tail between his legs. He was not generally a complainer, unlike his brother, but still exercised his right to do so. Upon immediate reflection, he was a little embarrassed about expressing his feelings in such a way, perhaps seeming to be a little selfish. In truth, however, he was presently undergoing some mysterious issues regarding his own personal performance. Ever since training at base camp, he had felt like an angel with a glorified body. It appeared that now he could run for prolonged periods, in pleasing comfort. He'd seldom done this before Fr Murphy's recent training regime. He also seemed to be able to manipulate tricky surfaces better than anything he could remember on his walks back in Lincolnshire; even climb with confidence and calmness. It seemed to Jed that there was little holding him back, and limited reasons why he should return to base, using up another day. His dilemma, as they headed steeply upwards towards the bright, red hut, still some height above them, was that he even felt he could accomplish the entire climb in one go. Earlier, Hannah had branded him a 'mountain goat', as he had continually insisted on making un-necessary diversions over boulders, up onto the banks at the trail-side, or else anywhere more interesting than their straightforward route. Miguel, who had also noticed this, as Jed manoeuvred himself continually around the group, supervising their movements, had commented...

"You look born for this, Jed. Maybe go for the Himalayas next?"

Jed was, at least, content that his performance had been exceeding expectations, but was now, at a loss to comprehend where his energy was coming from. Earlier his reply to Miguel had been...

"Either I've been operated on by aliens or it's all that chilli you've been feeding us!?"

Joe had attempted to convince him that the first option had probably happened years ago. Now, as they walked towards the door of the refuge, Jed felt a little sorry for his sibling, who had just exerted himself far more than at any other time in his previous history, to arrive at where he was. He turned to Joe and offered some consolation...

"OK bro, I guess we've both just proved we're supermen for different reasons. I suppose we have to do the right thing for everyone here, now. You and me both."

He paused his movements and offered his fist for pumping purposes. Joe flashed his eyebrows with a smile somewhere around the corner, shuffled awkwardly towards him, with loose gear, belts and buckles, swinging around on his giant backpack, and met his brother's fist. Fr Murphy was warmed to witness such a bridge of understanding between siblings, and added his affirmation...

"That's the spirit, boys. Now we've completed the *getting here alive* bit."

Beams appeared on faces. One way or another, they *had* all arrived at this higher stage, in those five pieces Fr Murphy had hoped for. They now stood outside a refuge which would not be offering them any accommodation, on that particular night. As they entered the rusty-coloured building, which seemed to be more of a large shed, but looked suspiciously more like a couple of containers, fused together, their eyes struggled to adjust to the shade of its interior, which was quite some contrast to the extreme brilliance outside.

Inside Tejos Refuge, there seemed to be a bit more space than one might have predicted, when observing it externally. There was also a vaguely stale scent of long-finished meals, damp clothes, sweat and perhaps even a distant memory of polish. Miguel led them into a small, off-white, and slightly dusty closet. Such a building could not have been easy to maintain, whilst standing nearly four miles up in the sky. The closet was close to a dormitory and cooking area, which they would be using, at this rate, by themselves, upon returning. Miguel was somewhat upbeat about how quiet things were...

"It's a good job there are so fewer people than normal here today. Now we have a good place to put the equipment!"

There were no questions asked about whether it would all get pinched or not. Sense told them that most people who ventured to places like this would probably be good, honest and spirited people. Miguel had earlier pointed out that he had experienced such parallels with those who ventured into the wilderness. Also, it was easy to reason that not many people would want to climb all the way up here *without* their own equipment, nor would they want to *add* to that equipment and increase their burden. They stashed quite a lot of gear, intended for more precarious parts of the climb ahead, and made for the exit, having only been indoors for a few minutes.

"Now we sit, talk, eat a snack, hydrate ourselves and look at the views for a while."

...informed Miguel, heading to the edge of a relatively level area on which the hut was standing.

Their return journey to Atacama Camp was a breeze for all but Fr Murphy, who was, in his own words, 'a bit past his sell-by date'. Miguel had some reasons to be concerned about him and spent some time, on the descent, quizzing him about his fitness. However, the possibility of him remaining at Atacama Camp was ruled out after he managed to assure Miguel that he had merely been 'walking-himself-in'. His performance had now been tweaked and his driving forces primed, but he promised to be *up front* about his physical condition, as they progressed. He would communicate any uncomfortable feelings or problems, should they arise. This being settled, he was granted permission to continue.

At the same time that Fr Murphy was being grilled by Miguel, Jed was proving to be a concern of the opposite type. His off-piste meanderings were getting out of hand. Miguel had been concerned that he would burn himself out before they recommenced the ascent, in the morning. This had come to a head when Miguel had been forced to shout over a substantial distance to Jed, as he scree-hopped down a slope of small cinder-like stones, some way from the descending track, sending voluminous clouds of ash into the air behind him. He had tried to reassure Jed that he was *not* that mountain goat, which Hannah had likened him to, and would later suffer consequences of such extraneous behaviour. From that moment, Jed had re-joined the party and done his best to conform and contain himself, although it had been a major effort. He really did possess an unearthly amount of energy.

Upon returning to the trail's base, Atacama Hut was full. There were also quite a lot of tents nestling around its complex.

"That's more like it!"

…commented Miguel…

"This is how many people we usually have here."

They pitched their tents and cooked an early meal, but there was no rush. Tomorrow would require less effort than they'd required today, to arrive at Tejos. There would be leisure time and lots of rest before their official ascent commenced. Now the way ahead was no mystery, their moods reflected that they were more relaxed. The weather was also fine, for now. After a day of much exertion, not one of them had any difficulty sleeping, but whilst they slumbered, some awkward changes were beginning to occur.

CHAPTER 17

Unexpected twists

They awoke to their tents being shaken vigorously. Quite a severe breeze had developed through the night. For the first time, they experienced a taste of real mountain weather. It took a fair amount of effort and volume to communicate with on another from their tents, through a howling wind. There was also a sporadic mist, occasionally obscuring everything, then subsiding to allow the sun to shine, from time to time. Miguel was talking through some sort of radio, in his jeep. It seemed that the weather might be changing, though there were uncertainties as to how severe it might be, or how long it might last. They had all been briefed as to how quickly things could change upon a mountain. He signalled to them to join him in, but was forced to warn them, through an open window, that they would have to be very careful opening doors as it was quite common for extreme gusts to blow them off.

For a moment there was chaos as they scrambled to get in via a variety of techniques, ranging from body-blocking their doors and slithering round them, carefully, to opening them quickly and hoping for the best. Suddenly it was calm. Miguel began in a clinical tone…

"As I said, for sure, the weather up here can turn just like that. We're maybe going to get a blizzard, soon, too. We hoped we wouldn't see this for a few days. So we help each other get the tents down, soon, and sit here and see what Mother Nature's going to do."

"That could take hours!"

…grumbled Joe.

"No worries…"

…continued Miguel…

"If it's going to take that long, we'll be leaving! We can take a bit of bad weather, but we don't want to be high in the sky if it gets bad for a longer time."

They understood him and appreciated his reasoning. Despite possible disappointment, there was still some residual comfort within a thought that they might not have to tackle this beast, after all.

"Well… if there's nothing else to do…"

…began Fr Murphy before starting to tackle a crossword.

"No time for that, Padre."

…resumed Miguel…

"We have to get these tents down. Better to pack them dry, while we can. We just have to try not to blow away ourselves!"

Not blowing away was really rather tricky. In the end, they had to put tents on the back seat of the jeep, so they could roll them up properly. All packs were filled, with the assumption that they would still be climbing a volcano at some point on that day. It was then, that unbelievably, the moment they had re-seated themselves inside the vehicle, with all tents and backpacks safe and dry, that a biblical blizzard began. Within virtually no time at all, there was nothing to see but whiteness. Miguel started the engine. Its windshield wipers scraped out something of a view.

"We were lucky, no?"

…he said as powerful blasts of snow and wind buffeted the car, shaking them all about a bit.

"We could have been up there, in this!"

…exclaimed Hannah, explaining something which was fairly obvious, then continuing with a question…

"What would happen if we *had* been caught in it?"

Miguel returned some reassurance, as usual.

"We'd keep going, to get out of it quicker. Sure, we often get caught in this sort of thing. Just it's better we avoid it if we get the choice."

"I'll second that!"

…agreed Jed, now incarcerated with the rest of them inside an icy tomb.

It wasn't a long wait, though. Within fifteen minutes, they were able to emerge into what was now a very different landscape. Within a very short time, the environment had been altered from desert to alpine. Their route of ascent was hard to pinpoint and might have just become a bit more challenging than on the previous day.

"This is not so bad!"

...assured Miguel...

"See the weather is moving away, over there. Where it came from is clear. Better to have this now and the sun melt it, than at night when it's cold and everything ices over. We're lucky. Sometimes these mountains attract a storm for longer. Now we should be able to go."

"I suppose that's quite reassuring"

...expressed Fr Murphy...

"This is summer, though, right?"

"Yes..."

...began Miguel...

"...but *everything* happens up here."

He paused...

"Now, we go for it with crampons from the start."

They kitted up in regimental fashion and with fairly impressive speed. Soon they were on their way upwards, far earlier than they might have guessed only a short time ago. The crampons gave them substantial grip and confidence, even if there was mostly only soft snowfall, rather than ice. In fact, as Joe suggested, it was actually easier walking with them on a covering of snow than it had been in walking boots, on the slightly unstable grit and dust of the trail, now beneath it.

They trudged onwards and upwards, creating satisfying crunching sounds, as they turned over newly-fallen snow. Wind continued to gust, fairly aggressively, from time to time, blowing fine particles of ice into their faces and depositing drifts and mounds on the trail's sides. Fr Murphy led the way, with his usual plodding style and pedestrian pace. The track was reasonably clear, despite its wintry covering. They continued in silence, as on the previous day, slowly taking the strain, each with their own thoughts and feelings. Hannah spent some time, at the start of the climb, thinking about home. It had been some time since they'd been in the East of England and she'd not really given it much of a thought. A wave of home-sickness almost brought out some emotion, until she reasoned that she would soon be wishing herself back somewhere like this again. Inside her was a strong will to succeed. It would be difficult to have to tell everyone who asked about her mountaineering, that she'd failed to reach the summit. Of course, this feeling was shared by all of them.

Jed had been attempting more mental maths. He had tried to calculate how far it would be possible to see from the top, towards the Pacific ocean. He had given up when it became necessary to multiply five-figure numbers, then thought about food, much of the time after that.

Joe was also had food on his mind, a lot. It was often sausages that provoked his thoughts. They were possibly his favourite foodstuff, yet he'd not been fortunate enough to sample any for some time. Musing about food was not a random thought-process for Joe. It was something he thought about constantly. However, in recent months he had thought about it a lot more than he'd eaten it. He had also deliberated about how he was not actually missing playing games on his phone. In fact he was beginning to realise what an addiction it had seemed to be for him. He wondered about other things he might now be able to do within those periods when he'd normally have been gaming. Everything he had done recently, seemed to be making him more spirited. For the first time in his life, he was finding himself wanting to achieve greater things. This was a mission at which he was willing to succeed.

Miguel had no need to reach the summit for his own purposes. He had climbed this and other mountains many times before. However, it meant a great deal for him to deliver his present party to its summit, for their sakes. Their achievements were his success. Right now, however, a few of his thoughts were with his colleagues and friends, who were currently spending some time by the ocean. It was highly extraordinary not to have bookings at this time, and unlikely that any of them should be basking, as they no doubt would be, in the Pacific or barbecuing something, on a wild beach. However, he was comforted by the fact that, before these few weeks when Fr Murphy had made it preferable for him to remain in the mountains, they had enjoyed many bookings, as in fact they would be doing again in not so many days' time. All seemed okay with finance, yet Miguel could not help wondering what was going on. It was likely that most of the crowds they had seen at Atacama Hut were still acclimatising, there. However, since then, they had seen no-one enroute to the next stage, or even descending the mountain. This was quite bizarre. Both, his lull in business, and the fact that the mountain had seemed greatly less busy, at the moment, was causing him to wonder if there was some great world event taking place, that he knew nothing about. What else could explain such a hole in commerce at this stage of the summer season. How attractive that break with his friends seemed, now though, with freezing conditions around him and all those pressures that come with a responsibility of shepherding groups of people into situations of potential risk.

Fr Murphy was feeling a little light-headed. They were now about an hour and a half, at his pace, above Atacama Camp. Perhaps it was a combination of yesterday's fairly extreme exertions mixed with today's thinner, colder air, that had made him feel like this. He had decided that he would request a stop for a few moments, in a little while. Apart from some questions he still possessed, regarding his physical ability to perform the rest of what he had just started, his thoughts were mostly on success. However, for him, it was more important that his friends achieved the accomplishment they had worked so hard for, during the last few months. Having said that, he would walk on for as long as his body allowed, as long as he was in no-one's way. Miguel had coached them about altitude sickness symptoms. It might be anyone, not necessarily the eldest or weakest of them, who could suffer it. Their ascent, however, was to take them to such significantly high altitudes, that it was more likely everyone would feel at least its minor effects at some point.

Five fluorescent figures, in reds, yellows and oranges, eased across a monochrome snowscape. Higher up the trail, spiteful squalls blew about so much icy powder, that visibility was compromised. Snow depth seemed to increase as they climbed, at least on the trail's less steep parts. Temperatures had dropped, noticeably. Wind-chill made matters even less bearable. It was hard to believe they had walked this way only the previous day in such brilliant conditions. In truth, it was just the ever-deepening snow and wind-strength that rendered conditions hazardous. Miguel was aware that the antics of Mother Nature would probably be confined to these mountain slopes, which often attracted such weather. From a distance, the blizzards they had encountered, would possibly just resemble a small band of cloud hanging from the side of a section of slope. There would probably be pure and unblemished sky, somewhere not far above them. Meanwhile, it was those slopes he'd have to address. One of Miguel's current tasks was to continually evaluate the nature of their descent, should they require one sooner.

Several hours later, winds had dropped, considerably. However, the snow had begun to freeze, and as they graduated to steeper slopes, out came ice axes in readiness for that particular eventuality when someone lost their footing and started to slide rapidly downhill. One violent blow of the implement into the ground, would most likely stem a fall. In Miguel's mind now, this was a lesser problem. During their last two pauses for breath, Fr

Murphy had confided in him his developing nausea and continuing dizziness. The antidote to this might not necessarily be to abort the ascent. Perhaps a longer rest or two would suffice. Certainly, they were not too far from their second encounter with Tejos Refuge. Once installed there, they could assess health and prospects, over a lengthy rest. It would be some battle, however to erect their tents if the hut was jam-packed. Weather like this had often rendered that, the case. However, so far they had encountered no other mountaineers, passing in either direction, and there had been no other tracks in the snow, which was now verging on becoming ice. That did not mean there was no-one else at this height on the mountain. There may have been any amount of people at a higher altitude than them, at any time so far. Other parties may have ascended before the blizzard arrived, leaving no trace of themselves. Yet there was no-one attempting to descend, or they would surely have witnessed it. Miguel continued to puzzle over the strange calm on this popular peak. He wondered if it was pure chance or else some other factor, he had failed to pick-up on. In no way did he believe it was just about today's conditions.

The grand panorama they had savoured on the previous day, was gone. Gale-force gusts had returned, hurling further swarms of miniscule ice crystals at what small parts of their faces were left uncovered, behind sunglasses. They'd worn these to defend themselves from continual snow-glare, rather than from intense sunlight, as in previous days. Incessant whiteness strained the eyes and could, otherwise, cause temporary damage. Those exposed parts of their faces, outside glasses and fur-lined hoods, were beginning to smart. No-one would have wanted to stop for a view anyway, at this very moment. They pressed-on, making a beeline for Tejos Refuge. The sooner they ascended, the quicker they'd find that shelter. However, the higher they climbed, the colder things seemed to get, despite heavy exertions. Things were warm; even too hot, under thick clothing, but face were bitterly cold. They would be bright red at the day's end.

It was some skirmish, attempting to reach that level ground on which the refuge stood. Powerful gusts battered them head-on, with steepening gradients already persecuting them. Fr Murphy was clearly struggling and would certainly become a question mark in reckonings to come. At one point, Jed actually assisted him by pushing him uphill. He was quickly policed away from it, by Miguel, telling him he should save his own energy, but also avoid that greater chance of slipping which occurs when exerting extra pressure in order to push someone else up a slope. He rounded-off his warnings with one more important observation...

"The Padre will have to make it on his own. We need to see that he can, with as many stops as we realise he needs".

Although Jed was understanding of the reasoning behind this latest reprimand, it seemed there was still a question hanging in there. What if they gave him plenty of stops and he still couldn't make it? Going back down was a heck of a long way, now, but ascending to the hut on fairly icy slopes could be even worse. There were several long pauses, during which Miguel was keen to get going and reduce the distance. Also, he needed to keep his party warm, by not standing around, for too long. At these junctures, Fr Murphy apologised profusely and repeatedly, in one form or another, promising he would wait for them at the hut, so as not to spoil their achievements. Miguel had cleared-up matters, after several of these heartfelt outbursts, saying...

"No-ones promising anything yet. There's a lot to think of tonight, about different things. You did the right thing in your country, sleeping in low-oxygen tents to try to get used to this air, but there's nothing like the real thing, when you get here. You did what you could, but you weren't climbing all day then, either."

Hannah seemed to be feeling alright, under intense circumstances. Joe also looked like his usual self, if not a bit battered, soaking wet and colourful in the countenance. Spirits were beginning to rise as they all knew they were close, now.

For a few moments, the wind backed-down. Within seconds there was warmth and peace. Miguel stopped the party, released his hood and beamed at them...

"You know it's all just around the corner, right? Enjoy this moment for a second before we fight to get in the hut. There's another squall around it, now."

...Fr Murphy explained to them, in a very breathless voice, that this was an independent wave of wind, which sailors would look for on the surface of a lake, via its effects on the water, in order to catch the wind. One could also become visible via clouds of drifting snow; the sort of clouds that had battered them for the last few hours. As they looked above the banks on the sides of their trail, towards where the hut would be, there was a deep, severe-looking greyness, obscuring all beneath and beyond it. Above it was pure, blue sky. It was almost like looking through the eye of a hurricane. Miguel gestured towards the phenomenon...

"That is very strong winds, blowing down the gully across us…"

…he informed, sternly.

"That's a sort of small valley."

…whispered Fr Murphy, somewhat euphoric in the welcoming hush and calm.

"I'll tell you what though…"

…interrupted Hannah, completely changing the subject and chuckling somewhat as she spoke…

"The same journey today was like a totally different one to yesterday! Not sure we've walked to the same place."

No-one retorted. It didn't seem right to make small-talk at this present moment.

"Prepare for a bit of roughness, now…"

…warned Miguel, re-hooding himself and starting to advance.

"…You might want to say a prayer that we can get into this refuge. The tents will definitely be second best option tonight"

Fr Murphy did just that, crossing himself once or twice.

They rounded a bend, into open space. The deluge was immediate. It was as though someone had just switched on a giant, industrial fan. This very localised wind, however, also came with a deep chill and more of those ice crystals which had battered them throughout their ascent. So powerful was the squall, which powered across them, that they struggled even to stand upright. Fr Murphy was the first to sink to the ground, hauling himself inelegantly forwards, on hands and knees. It was every person for themself, employing their own, individual techniques to manage progress towards the hut, which was not so far away. Joe sidled forwards, with his head turning partly away from the air attack of pins and needles. Jed and Hannah linked arms and progressed gradually, leaning right over into the wind, which was more than adequate to hold their weight. Miguel spread his feet and bent his knees, lowering his centre of gravity and looking somewhat like a gorilla. Before long, after some fairly ingratiating displays of unique movement, they arrived at the hut. It took two of them to wrestle the door open, after which, they were pretty much blown inside. The metal door slammed shut, behind them.

For a moment or two, they stood, looking at one another, basking in warmth. Someone had seen fit to transport a couple of storage heaters in there. This was bliss. Frozen faces throbbed and dripped. Hearts pounded. Ghostly moaning sounds exaggerated a roaring of wind, through breaches in the building. Miguel began to assess their situation, browsing the small amount of space available in there…

"It looks like there's a few people coming down from the peak to stay here tonight, but plenty of room for us. Sometimes it gets like a can of sardines in here. Not this time. We can have this space."

He gestured around a spot on which he was standing…

"We have sleeping bags and mats. That's all we need. No tents."

They all breathed a sigh of relief. Fr Murphy perched himself on a wooden crate, masquerading as a chair, and sighed even more.

"You don't look a million dollars, my friend."

…sympathized Miguel.

"How are you feeling?"

"Like I just *lost* a million dollars"

…quipped Fr Murphy, feeling quite a bit worse than his response might have suggested.

The others stood by him, sympathetically smiling or projecting a friendly air of concern. He continued…

"A splitting headache and the urge to vomit. Thought I'd get that out before it gets too close to tea-time"

It was clear to all of them that these were fairly obvious symptoms of altitude sickness. It also didn't take much to deduce that he probably wouldn't be coming with them to the summit, tomorrow. After all he had done for them, this would be a gloomy prospect. He sensed their pity immediately, putting on a brave smile and a warm tone…

"Hell, don't worry about me. I'm already three times higher-up than on any other mountains I've climbed in the past. My head and body keep telling me my next great achievement will be to sleep for a hundred years."

"We can probably grab you a few of those hours, Padre."

…smiled Miguel, reaching for some pain killers and water.

"*All* of us…"

…he insisted…

"…need to keep on with this stuff. It can help a lot to keep hydration."

He held up the mug of water, he'd just poured-out for Fr Murphy.

"It could be any of us, any time, with these indications of altitude illness."

Miguel began to set-up some sleeping arrangements for his party. This was now a priority due to Fr Murphy's delicate condition. As he started to do so, the door burst open, rendering them open, once more, to freezing Armageddon. As an added extra, bodies started to fly in through the same aperture. These were three climbers who had lashed themselves together with a rope, made it as far as the refuge, then fallen in through the door in a clump, propelled by extreme gusts, behind them.

"Good job that wasn't a stage entrance!"

… muttered Jed. One of the three men attempted to close the door, behind them, from a virtually horizontal position. Joe rushed over to give him a hand.

"Muchas gracias!"

…uttered the man, obviously a bit breathless.

"De nada."

…beamed Joe, using some of the basic 'traveller's Spanish', instilled in him by Fr Murphy. Miguel shouted over to them, the Chilean equivalent of…

"Good afternoon. Are you all OK? Have you come down from the top?"

As they untethered themselves from each other and found more dignified spaces, with their connecting ropes removed, one of them responded, with obvious vocal stress patterns. Following Miguel's translation, it became apparent that they were fairly inexperienced mountaineers, from Eastern Argentina, who had managed to get permits and convince authorities that they should be allowed to climb to the summit of Ojos Del Salado, from the Chilean side. Miguel had previously explained that things were a bit less demanding on their present route, compared with an ascent from Argentina, especially in terms of distance. However, current conditions seemed to make experience more than preferable. A tall, dark-haired man with a carefully topiarised ring of hair, around his mouth, had explained that they had been forced to abandon their ascent, due to severe weather. It had been the intensely belligerent breeze that had continually forced them back and made them think again, about the dangers of being caught by a sudden gust, when balanced upon precarious terrain. They had made their decision to return to the hut, before attempting to cross a steep ice field, not too far from the summit. The mountain had beaten them today, but they still had a little time in which to wait for better weather, if they wished to try again. Their reports might have seemed like fairly bad news to those who had hopes for the summit. However, Miguel remained upbeat about the elements, which had always provided as much promise as surprise. Right now, there were other matters on his mind.

Apart from a trio of opportunist volcano-baggers, it seemed that Miguel's party would be the only ones residing in the hut tonight. Most unusually, they could now enjoy comforting space, in which to spread.

"Make the most of it!"

... insisted Miguel, still puzzled himself...

"It is very uncommon here."

The three men retired to a satellite wing of the hut, walking as though they'd just landed on the moon. Fr Murphy retired to his sleeping bag, hoping to reverse some symptoms and charge his personal batteries. Miguel set about cooking an evening meal. Hannah, Jed and Joe shed their sodden, outer layers, crampons, boots and thick socks, yielding fairly unwanted scents, and collapsed in three horizontal heaps on the rug-covered, metallic floor. Winds continued to wail and shriek with apocalyptic amplification, all about them. One might have suspected this would be a restless night.

Such had been the endeavours of everyone today that, excluding Miguel, all fell separately into different planes of consciousness. There was puffing and blowing; even snoring from around the corner, where the three inexperienced pioneers had assumed residence. Miguel found himself having to revive everyone before he could feed them. They dined on the floor, with backs propped against walls. Faces were molten red and swollen, from eternal altercations with snow flurries. The weather had tried its best to erode them, like everything else. They had begun to see how brutal conditions could be, high-up in such an elevated mountain chain. How amazing food tasted though, after all that. Simple meat and macaroni from a can, was the tastiest and most satisfying of all experiences ever. Steaming tea was more than a drink, it was also a sauna for the head. Brains began to thaw, and extremities such as toes and fingers, gradually wiggled back to life.

As spirits were warmed, simply by relief, rest and sustenance, conversation seemed to return. Jed rather dominated the airwaves, for a while, with specialised knowledge and technical jargon. He had attempted to explain some of the geology of the region, using terms he had picked-up in Spalding library, such as 'stratovolcano', 'fumaroles' and 'saline deposits'. His mind-numbing facts were even noticed and suffered by Fr Murphy, who was still lying face-down on his pillow, having never joined them for the meal. His singular, muffled comment to Jed was...

"Is there a chance someone might quit that decadent showing-off? It's hard to endure in these strained circumstances."

Jed was a little deflated. He had been saving this stuff for such an occasion. He apologised to Fr Murphy, but still had to add one more fact about where vulcanologists went to the toilet. After announcing his answer, 'to the lava-tree', he was booed by his un-welcoming friends and forced to wash the dishes.

Not too much later, Miguel appeared, looking fresh, if not red-faced and with somewhat affected body-language, as though he was attempting to divine something from the air. In actual fact, he was trying to train his ears beyond the din, some of them were making, with their card game. They paused for a moment, looking quizzically at him.

"Have you noticed?..."

...he began, paused, then tilted his head, as though listening intensely, attempting to encourage them to do the same. They fell silent. Hannah was the first to speak...

"The winds have stopped!"

This might have seemed fairly humdrum, seeing as they were all now installed in a fairly cosy shelter, safe from most elements that could rampage at such an extreme altitude. However, Miguel's tidings bore quite a lot of salience regarding possibilities for the next day, and all they had travailed for in recent times. One glance at the drifted snow outside would surely trigger some sort of urge for somebody. It had certainly occurred to more than one of them, that a snow-fight could be on the cards here. Miguel didn't hesitate to add...

"All of us know what you want to do!"

Fr Murphy, looking a pitiful sight, but appearing to be resting in good hands, now face-down on his pillow, had also discerned the situation and further added, in a strained voice...

"Does that mean we'll get some peace?"

An empathetic Hannah, bent over him and whispered, sympathetically...

"So sorry, Fr Murphy. I apologise if we've been a bit noisy when you're not well. We'll try and go away from the hut a bit."

"That's great, Miss!"

...retorted Fr Murphy

"Throw a few at Jed for me, won't you?"

"I'll make sure I do, Fr."

...said Hannah, sniggering and raising an eyebrow, at both brothers. Miguel, acting as a parent, added...

"And make sure you all come back in one piece, if you want to achieve what you came here for."

He beamed, having reasoned that this might be a good time to bring a bit of fun to their itinerary. It was true that, earlier, he had cautioned Jed for being ostentatious in movements that might have put him at risk. However, he could also reason that this whole trip, on a dangerous mountain, was enough risk in itself, and this may just be the time to let one's hair down. After all, how many young people get to enjoy a snow-fight, four miles up in the sky? The snow, here, was thick enough to cushion a fall. Miguel smiled in approval and let them get on with it. As if fate could be tempted?

There was a rush for hats, extra layers and gloves, then the door. With only an unconscious awareness of magic sky, eerie lighting and a mighty view, they coursed through powdery snow, atop harder ice, to a point some distance from the refuge and began to assault one another in random fashion. The definition of a 'snow-fight' does not necessarily imply that only snowballs are hurled amongst a party of temporary enemies. In this particular case, vast amounts of snow were tipped inside jackets, or sprayed into faces, via boots or hands on the ground. In a very short time, there were three drenched and hysterical individuals. Then, during the heat of battle, came an awkward and uncomfortable silence.

Joe lay awkwardly, on his back, with one leg, somewhat unnaturally twisted over his body. It was immediately clear that there was no play-acting going on. He lay quite still, grimacing upwards, in freeze-frame. Both Hannah and Jed had observed his demise, as he slid uncontrollably and awkwardly sidewards, due to an unexpected change of direction. They had easily deduced that this could *not* be good.

Joe was in a lot of pain. His body and right knee had just travelled in opposing directions. He was in a state of shock and quite afraid to move or be moved. His motionlessness was a coping-strategy. Partly, he was assimilating his condition and coming to terms with unknown damage. Also he was, to some extent, hiding his head in the sand. It was as though, if he lay still, this all might even go away. On top of his physical distress was the knowledge that he would now, no longer, be able to reach his grand goal tomorrow. That was truly a blow to his aspirations. It created a surge of emotion, similar to that often realised by a small child, making them burst into tears after a fall or shock. Joe was stronger than that but welled inside. Expressions of compassion in his friends' countenances, as they leaned over him in concern, almost brought it all out.

"What are you feeling?"

...whispered Jed, fairly empathetically. There was a bit of a pause. Joe slowly pivoted his head towards his brother, then up towards the darkening sky, in a restful position. One or two stars were already awake. A gut reaction was to describe the sickening pain in his right knee. Instead, he bravely managed an uncharacteristic apology...

"Like I've just ruined everything."

Hannah immediately stooped down and laid a reassuring hand on his head. Jed took off his coat to use as a pillow underneath it.

"Don't you worry about that, bro. you're far more important than a mountain. You're going to be fine!"

In truth, he and Hannah were more than concerned, regarding Joe's physical status. It had been a very disturbing fall.

Quite by chance, Miguel appeared, like a bolt from the blue. He had detected that all the screaming and shouting had subsided and had been hoping to catch some of the action on camera, for the sake of future memories. Quickly he absorbed that this was, no longer, a time for photography. As he approached, Hannah & Jed moved sensitively out of the way. He began by pacifying his patient...

"Everything's OK, Joe. Try to breath calmly and relax.

"He's done a pretty good job of that, already!"

...offered Hannah, with some admiration. Miguel carefully explored the leg in question, whilst keeping Joe still and comfortable. There was no need to inquire as to what had happened. The problem and cause were fairly clear.

"Good move with the pillow!"

...acknowledged Miguel, eyeballing the coat underneath Joe's head. Joe's all-weather trousers had zips at the bottom of each leg. Miguel, quite easily, exposed the injured knee without any sideways movement. He began to test the leg with very slight motions in different directions. There was no need to keep asking whether it hurt or not. Joe's reactions told him everything he needed to know. Eventually, after a small sigh, born of the fact that his latest summit aspiration had obviously just come to a sticky end, he announced...

"OK... I don't think anything is broken, but this is a sprain, for sure. Things are going to swell a bit. We have to get you inside, keep the knee up, level, and use some of this snow to get the swelling minimum."

Hannah and Jed were visibly relieved it was not what might have been anticipated; just a sprain and not a break...

"Crikey!"

...exclaimed Jed...

"You must have elastic ligaments!"

Miguel was aware that a sprain could sometimes be worse than a break, but there was a lot more than just this on his mind, now.

They dragged Joe, backwards on Jed's coat, keeping him relatively still. A few unpreventable gasps and groans proceeded, as he was raised a small amount, in order to get him through the door. Walking was completely out of the question. No-one even suggested it. Between them, they organised quite a decent bed for him, with a state-of-the-art, inflatable pillow, belonging to Hannah. Joe lay there, panting and wincing as they encircled him, watching Miguel applying a snow-filled, plastic bag to his knee, whilst attempting to reassure his stricken comrade, that everything would be OK and that he'd be making a descent without even having to stand up. The unexpected, weary and sickened voice of Fr Murphy, piped-up from the corner…

"You chose a great place to do this, Joe. Honestly, you couldn't have chosen better. Twenty thousand feet up a mountain peak, just before nightfall, in arctic conditions. Well done, lad! That's some achievement, maybe even more than climbing the peak itself?"

"It's my fault."

…insisted Miguel.

"I'm the one with the experience. I guessed you'd all probably be OK, having some fun."

There was an immediate flurry of efforts, attempting to relieve him of any guilt. Miguel praised his party for their camaraderie and conceded that, though they had met with unfortunate circumstances, which had certainly created a huge question mark on the trip, they were one of the best groups of people he'd ever accompanied on an expedition. He was moved to make a suggestion…

"Maybe we can do this again together without the fun part!"

He was, of course, referring to the ill-fated snow-fight. Despite the fact that their recent experiences had shown them how tough such a climb could be, this seemed an attractive prospect, given that it was now obvious that they would not be ascending any further, this time. Jed had tried to disguise disappointment, whilst busying himself with sympathy and understanding for his troubled colleagues, but his expressions were visibly forlorn. With two members of the party requiring medical assistance; even transport, there could only be a further ascent, with one guide to lead it and another to escort others off the mountain. It was now that Miguel began to wish he hadn't taken a decision to allow his entire team, a long break. Situations like this had occurred before on a few occasions, but always with more than one mountain leader. He was now absolutely clear about the next course of action, and explained himself to his party over a hot drink. Whilst addressing them, his body language was hesitant and apologetic, almost as though he was doing a confession with Fr Murphy. He wound into it slowly, with clenched hands and slightly bowed head...

"We... err... you know, we can't go on tomorrow, for sure."

They looked back at him, not so much in disappointed silence, but in a way that said 'tell us something we didn't know'. Not one of them, however, did not feel a little sorry for him. He was clearly a man who was disheartened not to succeed, if not for the sake of other people. Their careless merriment, which they began to express further regret for, had cost them some proud and striking memories of a very impressive climbing achievement. It would also mean a return to family, friends and a church parish, which had so kindly raised their expenses, having no ultimate success story to relay. Fr Murphy's muffled comment, from a continued horizontal position, some yards away, about there being 'no failure, whenever trying', was not really strength-enough for any of them, true though it might have been. Their fun in the sun had cost them a lot. However, they started to realise how much of a set-back this was going to be for Miguel. It was not only, that he could have been absorbing fun and sun with his friends, on desert shores by the Pacific. Now he would have to organise 'Plan B'. This would not be easy. First he would be forced to involve a few of his friends, via his radio, to arrange a helicopter rescue for all of them. This would profoundly disturb their break. Then there would be political questions asked as to how one member of his party had managed to render himself temporarily lame, at such a dangerous altitude, and also, how another individual in his group, had suffered quite profound altitude sickness after what was supposed to have been thorough training and acclimatisation. There would be questions, regarding risk assessments and safeguarding. However, those who worked for him, were not the Spanish Inquisition, nor even a modern day Chilean version. They would be professional and courteous, as they had been coached to become, by Miguel himself, and no doubt console him in his difficulties. They would certainly be mindful of the fact that he had been good enough to fill-in for all of them in this rather unusual and exclusive expedition, engineered especially for the sake of friends. Miguel had agreed to this, for the sake of his greatest mentor and friend, Fr Murphy. Now he was conscious of the fact that he might have let him down; even misled him a bit, regarding the realistic possibilities of such an inexperienced group of climbers reaching high Andean summits. His interrupted announcements finally continued following a great deal of sincerity and reassurance from his party...

"One of us is sick and shouldn't go higher. In fact he does not seem to be improving and should go down soon."

Fr Murphy's silence was succeeded by a gentle snore. It was some relief that he could rest from the pains in his head and unenviable nausea. Miguel adopted a whisper...

"We also have someone who cannot go up *or* down, and must be airlifted off this mountain. I will have to radio my friends and organise a helicopter to arrive from Copiapo, quite soon after first light. This will be a *big* helicopter..."

He gestured 'big', fairly unnecessarily...

"...that will fly all of us down to Atacama Camp, where we can get the jeep, while these two fly on to Copiapo, with one or two of my friends, and we meet them a few days later, for sure. It's a good job I have these friends, as sometimes, these rescues are costing people many thousands of dollars and pounds."

A thunderous hush was the reaction to this statement. Although the facts about returning to base without a pinnacle of success had already been understood, they still had not been truly felt, until that moment. Now it was set in stone. Their disappointment was resounding and touched Miguel, somewhat.

"I am really sorry for all of you."

...he whispered, with some obvious emotion, promising to make checks on Fr Murphy and Joe in the night. He would set his watch to come and tend to them. His sleep would be interrupted. The night would be broken with disturbance for all of them. It might not be easy anyway, for one of them, so energized and aspiring, to sleep, facing the disappointments of his comrades, alongside personal thoughts of failure. All that being said, there was a lot of snoring going on that night; not just from those gentlemen who had fallen-in from the cold some hours earlier, around the corner. Miguel's troops had all striven hard to achieve this altitude, via some extremely demanding circumstances. Refugio Tejos was largely still and silent, except for all that snoring. Deep shadows enveloped their slumbering souls. Little could have pulled them back from such depths.

CHAPTER 18

The summit of everything and more

Unlike his friends, including a slightly dishevelled Miguel, Jed could not actually sleep. He felt, and *was*, ridiculously alive. His brain didn't seem to be capable of shutting down. How stupid could that be, after what they had all endured that day, and previously? He writhed and wriggled in his camp bed of foam mat, sleeping bag, mountain blanket, fleeces and coats. He considered that the vague smell of unavoidable sweat, all around, from previous hordes of climbers, was partially triggering endorphins, activated from recent, intensive training in places where people perspired a lot, but this seemed like more than just a vague, physical inspiration, triggering endless energy. Both body and mind continued to insist that he could still reach the summit. He felt utterly compelled to ascend that long-savoured, final part of his personal conquest, despite all common sense, barking at him to ignore any contrary signs. It was a yearning he had *never* felt before. It seemed there were few things in his life he'd wanted with so much desire. Somewhere inside was an almighty, instinctual force, stirring him into action.

Jed lay for some hours, looking up into the shadows of the refuge, trying to talk himself out of doing something extremely foolish. He reasoned that these thunderous impulses inside him, were not just about disappointment arising from failure. It seemed, to him, as though an internal voice was telling him that this was something he absolutely *had* to do. Finally, a moment arrived when he could stand it no longer. He mused that there could be little wrong with getting up and going outside to look at the stars. He could always say that he couldn't sleep and didn't want to miss a final opportunity to gaze at the heavens from high altitude.

Jed arose with surreptitiousness, carefully avoiding any rustling. He pulled-on some thick clothes and sneaked quietly through the door, leading outside. This time, with complete calm outside, it provided no resistance. As he peered at a crystal cosmos, unfettered by artificial light, and up the slopes towards what had been their goal, he was filled with overwhelming emotion and unbearable longing. His walking gear had been close to where he was sleeping. He re-entered the hut, collected, silently what he required, aided by industrial-level snoring from Joe and Fr Murphy, and kitted himself up outside.

"I must be an idiot!"

...he muttered to himself.

"Somehow I don't feel like one, though."

Jed actually wondered if he could even get up and down before anybody noticed. There was a helicopter due in the morning, though he was not quite sure when it was scheduled to arrive. He applied his crampons and armed himself with an axe. With his watch reading one-fifteen in the morning, he set off, without looking back. In his mind was the thought that, to quickly examine the refuge might tempt fate and cause someone to come out after him.

There had been little consideration of routes. Recent snow had covered any tracks, but there seemed to be a logical-looking course, up to his right. He would follow instinct. He tried to block out any thoughts of danger, or mull over any of the possible consequences of his actions. It was true, he could easily injure himself. No-one would know where he was, or even that he was out there. There was also the deep anxiety he would no doubt provide for his friends, who would probably also be extremely angry with him. Jed was not normally so thoughtless and reckless. Right now, he was single-minded and blinkered. However, nothing about his current situation felt at all normal.

The Moon lit Jed's way, and interfered only minimally with his view of the heavens. It was impossible to ignore the sky, tonight. To one side of him was a very prominent cluster of stars, called The Jewel Box. He had also noted a constellation like a large cross, called The False Cross. At this altitude and clarity, The Milky Way was easily distinguishable as a galaxy, rather than just a blurred, creamy trail, across the sky, as he'd often seen it. He really would not have been lying to the others, at least, regarding stealing an opportunity to savour the closest he'd ever been to being an astronaut.

206

Jed ploughed-on through crunching snow; his icy breath illuminated in the glare of Earth's little sibling. He struggled tenderly forwards amongst jagged rocks and glassy crevices towards a fairly distant summit, which was just about visible. Ascending it, would probably be requiring of further awkward passages of scrambling. He deliberated that this summit, too, would probably be just another of those false ones. Overall, the exact nature of this giant beast of a hill was unknown to him. Jed's mind defaulted to a notion that this would be exceedingly testing for him. However, his prize would be conquering the world's loftiest volcano. disappeared quickly, up into the night, with inexplicable energy and confused senses. It was almost as though he was not himself.

Something pulsed gently underneath Miguel's pillow. It was an alarm he had set to wake himself for checks on Fr Murphy and Joe. As he approached them, all was quiet. Even those guilty of dynamic snoring had subsided into peacefulness for a while. Fr Murphy seemed to be awake. That explained a part of the subsiding in snoring.

"How are things with you, my friend?"

…whispered Miguel.

"Not great."

…was the very conservative reply…

"Head aches a bit; even a lot. Bit hard to breath."

In truth, Fr Murphy was suffering the effects of an unnaturally low percentage of oxygen in his breathing. To prolong his state, would not be a good thing, yet there was nothing that could be done before the arrival of their helicopter.

"You give me a shout if this gets any worse, OK Father?"

…demanded Miguel.

"I'll do that. Thanks."

…was the continued feng shui of Fr Murphy's current conversational potential. He remained motionless, trying to endure his condition.

Joe was fast asleep. That was good enough for Miguel. A quick glance towards Hannah and Jed was all that was needed. He returned to his sleeping arrangement at the other side of the room. Fortunately or unfortunately, Jed had thought to perform the old trick of padding-out his sleeping bag with a framed rucksack and a few spare items of clothing, providing the illusion that he was still amongst them. Miguel was hoodwinked. Should it ever be necessary, Jed's rescue would now be delayed even further. On the other hand, in actuality, the helicopter would not be arriving as soon as some might have preferred. It would have a long flight and possibly face difficult conditions at high altitude. This would give Jed some leeway, though he had seriously underestimated the typical time taken to complete a return trip to the summit. Yet there was something about his bewildering energy and speed, that might have made his conquest seem more plausible, despite his unusual disregard for common sense and safety.

There was a nonchalance in the way Jed ascended; appearing to progress as stealthily as anyone should be allowed. Although there were no visible footprints, from previous parties, the trail's approximate, well-trodden shape, beneath the snow, was quite apparent. Jed ascended in a steady direction, to the right of where he had started, following a vague, shallow ditch. Both generous moonlight and icy brilliance, made his visual judgements more certain. After pursuing that direction for some time, he came to an abrupt halt, staring down a steep slope into shadowy oblivion. He leaned, tentatively over the edge, searching for a continuation of his route, but could see only smooth sheets of snow, racing quickly downwards, to darker ground in the depths below. He paused, wondering if his breakaway expedition was about to come to a premature close. Without the continual scuffling and crackling sounds of his boots, added to fairly heavy breathing, there was utter silence. Jed reasoned that this was probably the most intense stillness he had ever experienced, completely alone, so high above his world; no creatures, no human activity or roads within a great distance. This hush was greatly moving and inspiring. It was something few people ever encountered, aboard this busy planet. Some might even have found it frightening. For Jed, it was a reminder of how isolated he really was. He would remember the impact of these stirring moments forever.

Turning back seemed the only option, but as Jed revolved to glance backwards at the way he'd come, another possibility presented itself. It seemed that he had been supposed to make a sharp turn to his left, not far from where he was now standing. He could just about make out a route, which tacked from left to right, gradually ascending the slopes above him, which were about as steep as the one he'd just looked down. Wending his way, on a new, snaking trail, Jed was reminded of some sailing he'd once enjoyed, on a small lake somewhere west of his home, when he'd had to manoeuvre a dinghy into an oncoming breeze. It seemed that progress up a steep gradient or into a wind were both made more possible by tacking. He progressed, workmanlike and quickly, rounding the turns as though he were in some sort of race. He swooped around each corner, uttering 'ready about' before and 'lee ho' as he had been taught to do, when turning a boat's steering wheel hard towards the wind. Ironically, as he began to do this, a weak but steady wind, stirred-up, buffeting him a little as he ascended. It would surely have been quite a bizarre sight, to see a young man, seemingly hurtling along like a child in a playground, in such a place, on such demanding slopes with only rarefied air to breathe, shouting out, playfully, on each turn. Perhaps it was actually the rarefied air that had rendered him like this. One way or another, Jed was soon turning to his right, at the top of what was normally, when the whole mountain wasn't covered in snow, a sheet of permanent ice. At this point, the track's gradient slackened-off a bit, although the slope to the side of it was exceedingly steep. Anyone stepping off it would probably slither down, at great speed and considerable acceleration, to a sticky end. Jed stood motionless for a while, mulling over those he'd left behind. Atypically, for him, there was understanding but little emotion, even when he considered, the thoughts and feelings of his girlfriend, brother, Fr Murphy and Miguel. All senses seemed to be telling him that he was doing a respectable thing, he would be alright and would see them all again. He was unsure, however, how easily he would be forgiven.

Things became a little less straightforward after that point. At times, Jed found himself scrambling over loose rubble and crumbling rocks. There was even a point which might have been better described as climbing. A very strong wind hit him in the face as he ported, sharp left, onto the final part of what seemed to be, a summit ridge, physically knocking him backwards. Temperatures seemed to plummet, fairly suddenly, with a new change of direction. He gasped, fairly breathless. In some ways, it was good to realise he was still human. As fit as he might have proved to be recently, powerful gusts, arriving in fits and starts, often caught him out. Breathing became increasingly problematic with such minimal levels of oxygen, and violent blasts of air deluging his lungs. Jed arched himself, counter-balancing in different directions, to combat those now increasing monster-squalls that negated his spirited efforts. Ascending the summit ridge may have been comparable in distance to part one of his climb, but might possibly have taken up to three times as long to complete, thanks to severe conditions. Finally and fairly suddenly, he found the crater's edge. One part of it was much higher than the rest. He observed a vague trail which seemed to meander towards one of its walls and began to follow it.

First light was already beaming between distant eastern clouds, though it was still very early. Despite extreme altitudes, this part of the mountain was fairly well sheltered from winds. Jed was able to think a bit more clearly. It was slightly warmer here, too. Now underfoot was smoother, sandier ash, covered only with a light peppering of snow. Much of the wintry covering, here, had been blown away by incredibly fierce winds and stacked into rocky cliffs on the crater's edge. Right now, all had fallen fairly silent. To Jed, this alien-looking landscape, in some ways, resembled The Moon's surface. For a moment, he assumed slow-motion, and coined his best American drawl…

"One small step for a man. One giant leap for mankind!"

Immediately he thought of his brother, Joe, who had always insisted that he sucked at accents. Jed wasn't totally devoid of compassion, despite his present compulsive behaviour. He at last found some empathy for his brother's injuries and Fr Murphy's ailing condition. He regretted leaving the girl of his dreams, who would no doubt be upset and worrying about him. He was already mindful of the fact that he might have jeopardised Miguel's position, as questions would be asked regarding such an incident, especially if he failed to return, yet he had continued as far as this, against even his own comprehension. He started to accelerate, in order to reach the summit as soon as possible, hoping to return before anyone could worry for too long.

There was some scaling of rocks to be done, before an ultimate height was attained. However, nothing too technical stood in Jed's way. Within a few moments, he was standing, gobsmacked, at the top of a seven-kilometre-tall volcano, whilst once more being battered about by gales, some way above the relative shelter he had enjoyed below the crater wall. Having ascended from the north, he was now treated to a completely fresh view, south, along the Andean cordillera. Rugged mountain peaks rose-up from brightly-coloured desert, as far as the eye could see; impossibly high. Each was coated in ice, above what seemed to be a general snowline. So lofty were these giants that they caused their own manifestations of winter during what was actually summer. Some were volcanoes. Some were just mountains, caused by immense faulting and folding within The Earth's crust. Jed assumed that he could probably see landscapes which were over a hundred miles distant. Certainly these high Andes were so tall that they were easily visible, beyond the curvature of Earth. However, eventually, in all directions, everything seemed to disappear into a haze. For that reason, Jed could never tell whether or not it was the Pacific Ocean he was looking at, to the west, or else just more distant land. All was faded. It was strange too how the horizon, far beneath him, actually looked as though it was up in the air. By an illusion of perspective, it appeared to be even higher than he was. Jed savoured everything as much as was possible whilst being knocked-about by winds of huge strength and enduring freezing temperatures. He had no camera, due to special, unforeseen circumstances. He would have to take an extremely powerful, mental picture to help carry these special moments into the future.

There was only so long Jed could stand, admiring the view, in such Antarctic conditions. He was also somewhat delirious, due to low concentrations of oxygen in his system, and ran a continual commentary, out loud, almost believing at times, that he was addressing his absent friends. After a final, longing look at the panorama which could have resembled an alien planet, he began to descend, continuing to talk to Fr Murphy and the others as he moved. Back in the crater's shelter, he paused for a moment to examine a fumarole, out of which was seeping a smelly, sulphurous gas. Daylight was quickly growing. Atmospheric conditions never ceased to amaze up here, almost upon the edge of space. The sky alone was once again an immense spectacle of dazzling fluorescence and colour. Jed treated himself to a little more gawping in the comfort of calmer air and temporarily zoned-out of whatever was close to his normal consciousness. There was plenty to kidnap his thoughts, on the wings of a new dawn.

It had perhaps taken a while, but then again he was not quite himself, in those moments. At last he once again recalled that dream he had experienced, some time ago now. He had long-since discarded any notion of extra meaning or significance attached to it, deciding that it must just have been a very powerful but random reverie, concocted by his own mind. Now however, witnessing in reality, a strikingly similar setting atop a mountain, in spectacular morning lighting, that realisation seemed to drive itself home with a disturbing awareness. He checked himself, seeking reassurance that he wasn't still somehow wrapped-up in the same dream. In his recollection however, the events within his sleep one distant night in the past, had seemed a lot like reality! Now, added to the matching view, were the same dramatic, icy, atmospheric conditions; even similar feelings and slight exhaustion he recalled suffering from, at the time. Jed had experienced déjà vu before and felt he could explain the phenomenon, though this didn't appear the same. Somehow it did not seem like either a coincidence or an accident. Before he could recall the next bit, it had begun.

Jed was no longer alone, even within his own mind. Someone or something was in his head, alongside him, amongst his brainwaves. Whatever intelligence this was, had somehow discerned his discomfort and magically begun to soothe him from within. He felt paralysed yet beautifully calm.

Then, just as in his dream or premonition, an overwhelming torrent of emotions, memories that weren't his, concepts, ideas, principles and theories, began to swamp his brain, infiltrating circuits, loading memory banks, creating connections and accessing parts of his mind, he had never used. He felt great pressure, as though his head might explode, yet no discomfort. Mysteriously, what might have seemed like a mental assault, was feeling more like the honorary receiving of an unimaginable gift. Waves of adrenaline coursed through his system as swathes of unencountered emotions, attached to bright reminiscence, took their place within compartments of his mind. There was indescribable joy, as Jed was united with precious recollections of life-forms, he had previously been totally unaware of. Quickly he was beginning to relate to their ways of being, their mannerisms, their ethics, likes and dislikes; even individual characteristics. He even saw faces and expressions. He was beginning to know these beings, almost as though he was one of them.

Jed stood, trembling slightly, having more than likely, endured the greatest download in history. Whilst it seemed it was now all over, fairly abruptly, he still sensed a presence, close by. After all he had just experienced, there was no fear inside him, only a longing to meet whoever had just implanted all that was now a part of him. Jed revolved on the spot, scanning the horizon, but detected only a dark blur, seemingly fairly close by, which had possibly been behind him for some time. To say that it suddenly spoke may not be to deliver the truth as it really was. Rather than a speech with words, there was a mysterious sort of dialogue, generated somehow directly into Jed's understanding. Things progressed as follows …

"It is not that you have found me. It is I who sought you out."

Jed battled to focus on the presence, but could not find a face, or anything tangible upon which to concentrate. It was virtually translucent, with a vague, dusky form, somewhat like Jed's idea of a soul, without a complete, physical manifestation. Powerful memories came to him, like an overwhelming tide, sweeping him away in an involuntary direction. There had been a journey, he remembered, completely alone, yet somehow still in touch with others. The world had been dark, yielding rage and fire. He was a bird, but he was not. Now he was submerged with an oily skin, yet he was someone else. He was even inside the trunk of a thunderous tree. Somehow it all made sense and he knew the lifeforms who had maintained these states. The being before him had even populated his mind with its own memories. With this knowledge, Jed was able to see, what he now realised, was an ancient creature, in himself, and himself within it. A focus was achieved. He listened with a newly-born concentration and undiminishing curiosity.

"It is not many of you who have the right mind to take all I have just given. It is a matter of physical compatibility. Over much time, more than you could ever imagine, I have learned to listen to our world. Yours is a mind that longs to know so much. Now you know more than you might have dreamed of. Yours is a brain which can carry what I have born, without faltering. Now it carries all I have ever known. You have youth on your side and a good heart. You like to live amongst the energy of our world; not behind walls and false technology. You live in such ways via choices but don't fully understand why you make them. You have connected yourself with nature and possess intelligences which cannot be measured on human scales. I called you across the world to show you new life and to give you these gifts. This is where I have resided from times before your species arrived in this world. I am older than some of these rocks. I live well in this clarity, on the roof of our planet. There is peace and solitude from your dominating species, yet I am connected. There are intrusions from those who venture here but I have learned to be indiscernible. There is a lack of warmth and air here, for your kind but I need neither. I have harmony, but require more…"

He was stopped in his tracks by Jed, who had realised he too could communicate without physical noise…

"I know."

…he said

"I mean, I know *now*! I see your kind as though they are my own. They need to be remembered."

"More than that."

…continued the ancient creature…

"Once there was a great ball of rock and fire that came from the stars. It brought a bitter darkness that killed most of my kind and much of the life upon our world, but all that we had been, lived on in the minds of a few of us who had learned to adapt and nurture the treasure of our legacy within our connected minds. Although we learned to counter threatening circumstances and survive, we are not immortal. Unforeseen occurrences can claim our existence before we can respond. I am the last of my kind. Once we lived in serenity, together in the Canyon of the Great Rainbow. There was peace and light. We maintained our harmony for countless cycles of the Great Star. It was a haven, concealed within a dangerous world, where terrible monsters preyed upon the weak, and ruled with might and strength. We learned to hide our kind and live at one with the Universe. Our civilization was not one like yours, with material wealth and status. We had few possessions but placed value in the things we could aspire to, to improve our wellbeing or understanding of the life around us. As we shared our thoughts and ideas, there was never a need for jealousy and nothing to steal from one another; only much to give. We learned that to build one another up with warmth, meant that each of us would always receive it ourselves. We learned great reason and exercised our knowledge amongst each other. You use so little of your potential. Now you know how much can be stored in a mind and what can be done with it. We maintained ourselves, barely expanding our numbers, for many eons, unlike your kind, who now threaten extinction by their numbers alone. As we developed, in time, our mutual empathy was honed until we heard each other without speech. As we remained in such balance for so many cycles, our physical forms saw little change, but the world around us has an intelligence of its own. Our planet is an organism in itself. Just as some creatures are blessed with camouflage to protect them from danger, it seemed that the courses of nature had gifted some of our kind with similar but more profound abilities. These are now in you. You will discover yourself, as you progress through this life, and you will discover us. It is not just that you show your kind who we were, but that you inspire them to make the changes that might save our world."

Jed stood flabbergasted. The young man of a few moments ago was still very much himself, just overwhelmingly older in experience and spirit. These revelations were more than astounding, and far more than just gratefully received. However, he was disturbed by the implications of carrying this responsibility. The ancient creature had sensed this and continued to calm him.

"It is a task I have given you, that will place you in great attention, yet inside you is an ability to calm yourself, even amidst scrutiny and fame. Your kind may not listen without miracles. Now you will show them what fruits can emerge from those who live an existence, listening to nature. They must be inspired by your abilities and take notice of what is shown to them. Choose your way forward, carefully. Seek audience with those in high authority who can be trusted. You have much to do, but calm yourself and measure these moments. This wisdom is now within you. Encourage those of your kind to begin a new way forward."

Though calmed a little by reassurances and empathy from the ancient creature, Jed was still somewhat awash with confused feeling. His life had changed out of sight within just a few moments. Yet, as he thought upon his task, he was pacified by new abilities and began to control his own feelings independently. The way forward would somehow become clear, but there was still a significant question in his mind.

"Why have you not shown the human race yourself. Why me?"

"It is true..."

...said the creature...

"...I could have appeared amongst your kind, but these gifts and knowledge have to be planted into the mind of a human for an understanding to begin. It is more likely that humans would care to believe I am from another world. Far more a miracle when one of their own kind has special gifts but is believable. I have waited longer than you can possibly imagine, for you to come."

The creature could not have created such a channel into another mind without exposing his feelings. Jed sensed a great sadness but also something else that was harder to identify; perhaps a knowledge that the ancient being himself had reached some sort of threshold. The creature continued...

"Now you have the sum of my soul and those of my kind, it is time for me to join with them, once more. We have believed that leaving this world would be no more than a transition. I do not sense them in my mind, but feel them in my heart. Although it is piteous to depart the planet I have known and loved for more cycles than anyone could have experienced, I am weary of a long and lonesome existence. I have glided along ocean floors, sailed through skies on the edge of space, explored deep forests and painted deserts; even the cities of men. I have witnessed numerous splendours in this precious world and enjoyed a rich life, longer than entire species. It is within me to terminate my existence here. In you is our legacy. In me is a will to move on. We were the first truly conscious offspring of this world, before we were annihilated in the great suffocation. I have told you that I am the last of my kind. I have held on to everything that was ours. Inside your human mind is the record of an entire race. Make sure we are not forgotten."

There was no time to interject; no time to say goodbye. Intent was obvious. Jed could only watch as the faded mass began to dwindle. For a moment, a small, viridescent, reptilian creature, stood before him. Splashes of turquoise seemed to varnish its body, where dazzling, morning sunlight broke over its slender frame. It appeared to examine the horizons, for a brief instant, with a single and supple revolution of its scaly head. Then, much like a mirage, its form began to dwindle. Jed perceived the equivalent of a smile, in his direction, but sensed it more, inwardly. Then there was nothing. He stood alone in the crater; also within his mind. The oldest living thing in his world had left it, forever. He revolved, slowly, examining everywhere round about. The results qualified his solitude. He stared, longingly, towards the darker west where night seemed to persist a bit longer, towards a distant ocean, and bade the departed creature farewell. It was as though a part of himself had just died. He yearned for it not to find obscurity, as he gazed into a dying night, wondering what his own departure might be like, one day. For a moment, it was as though he was connected to all time; great depths of the past, from whence the creature came, and the uncertain future that lay before him, like a blurred trail. He uttered some words, softly, with deep, welling emotion…

"Farewell, my dear, old friend. Your life will count for something here. I promise."

Just then, quite randomly, but born of the type of confusion which might ensue when one receives a gigantic flood of other beings' memories, mixed with those of one's own, a flashback from his former life came back to soothe him. It was a fond memory of some visit to a dinosaur museum in a sleepy village, where rain hammered down, outside an old school building, and he and his family, were witness to some proud exhibits pinned to the theme of dinosaurs. Now, it crossed his mind that somewhere, he actually owned authentic memories of them, to perhaps describe to people like those who wrote with such passion on that subject. As he pondered this, he was rewarded with unlikely but chillingly, realistic images of great beasts, descending quickly, with legs flailing, as they plunged in front of him, from above, where they had stampeded over the edge of a canyon. It seemed to Jed that, with brain connections having been so comprehensively honed, he could now view his memories almost visually. This new mind would surely yield many spectacular moments.

It might have been reasonably understandable, under recent circumstances, that Jed had not spared a single thought for his compatriots, some distance below him. They would surely be waking up by now, in readiness for the arrival of a rescue helicopter, which Miguel had promised. At this point, Jed's priorities changed somewhat and he turned to descend, quickly reapplying crampons and hitching a small rucksack back onto his shoulders.

Below the crater rim, the trail, via which Jed had ascended, seemed to disappear into a lake of mist, hanging silently below him. It was remarkable how weather changed, high in the sky. One minute there were dramatic gusts and wintry showers; the next, total calm. After a short passage of awkward negotiation, through more ice and mist, Jed emerged into intense sunshine. Much of the trail's snow-cover, beneath him now, was balding and slushy. He halted for a few moments to dispense with crampons and thicker layers of clothing, which included unzipping the lower legs from his weatherproof trousers, converting them to shorts. Although temperatures were closer to freezing, his efforts made him warm. Climate-wise, It was as though he had instantaneously graduated into another season, where all was tranquil and bright. With all these changes, he might make better progress, now.

Free of heavier, restrictive clothing and spikes on his feet, Jed broke into a trot. Thanks to some newfound mental aptitudes, he was able to manage any anxiety, about getting to the others speedily, with cool mindfulness and efficient action. Whilst negotiating tricky terrain, he began to ponder upon exactly what he might say to them. He felt light and uplifted. If anything, those remarkable reserves of energy he had enjoyed, throughout the ascent, seemed even more plentiful, now. It was quite clear to him that the ancient creature had given him such fitness, upon arriving in Chile, to ensure he arrived at the mountain's summit. Without conscious thought, his speed increased, until he was virtually flying down inclines, seeming to contact the earth, only when essential. There was no question of exhaustion, nor thinking about where to put his feet. It seemed that he was now easily capable of assuming a state of autopilot during complicated negotiation. Jed was at one with his mind and motion, but more was to come. It was like one of those fun dreams he could remember, where he was skiing through stunning scenery or flying by simply beating his arms. In the midst of plummeting downwards, like a lightning bolt, he grinned and nonchalantly surveyed the views out to left and right, attempting to milk this experience for all of its worth. At that moment, he hit a patch of tougher, glassy ice. In an instant, he was sliding, face up, on his back, like a kamikaze skeleton competitor at some Winter Olympics, away from the path onto steeper slants. There was no plan but strangely no panic. Should he encounter a rocky outcrop, he might be skinned alive. Should there be something larger, he would crash into it at impossible speed. Somehow Jed managed to remain peaceful within his thoughts, without even comprehending how he was able to muster-up such a strong and directed rational constitution, at such a moment. He had remembered advice from training in the months leading up to the expedition, where someone said…

"Just see it succeeding. Visualise the correct outcome and it will happen."

All was in a flash, without time for deliberation or scheming. Jed simply imagined a possible scenario, which might turn out alright. An initial sensation was unusual tightening. His shirt didn't seem to fit properly. His boots felt awkward. To add to this, was a bizarre feeling that something was going on within his muscles and organs. It was a fairly awkward but numbing experience, as though, for a very short time, he was not totally conscious, whilst at the mercy of some process unravelling within him. During this latest revelation, he had closed his eyes for a moment. There was a powerful rushing of air over his face, and scratching, scraping sounds as he hurtled across ice. Within split seconds, any discomfort was over. There was a pleasant lightness and lift. All thuds, grating and grinding had ceased. Jed opened his eyes, still expecting to wake up. Not many people could have arisen to a day like this! Each side of his body was a large, thin, dark, rubbery membrane, rounded at the periphery by slender, curved limbs, of great extension. His feet had transformed into similar sails of significantly shorter stature. He was not sure about his head, but his nose seemed to be darker than usual. Jed willed a right turn. His flipper-like feet made arrangements. He scudded gradually around, using alternate angles with his larger, upper membranes and hovered with control in an arc, until virtually traversing the slope. The trail he should have been descending upon, crossed his path, quickly. Jed made manoeuvres to port left and loosely follow it.

Whilst this had been unimaginable entertainment, a reasonable question had entered Jed's mind, from the outset...

"How the hell do I get out of this?"

He remained in glide-mode for a short while, before a second question eclipsed the first...

"What on Earth, else am I capable of?"

Another brainwave raised his personal sails, more vertically, like air brakes. He came to rest on safe, gritty ground, close to the trail. It must have been habit, such as the need to stand on one's feet after getting out of a car, which immediately produced another metamorphosis, back to his old self. Jed shook himself about like a dog, drying-off; grinning even more than before, whilst screaming to an imaginary world, about how cool it all was. Here was an ability to transmute, in ways which could be either useful or fun. He must learn to control it. He must find a way not to do this too much by accident. As Jed began to walk towards the trail, as his default self, he cogitated that he might be able to avoid all sorts of hardship; even danger. However, surely he could still fall foul of an accident, if he was unaware of its approach. He must remain careful. Perhaps, he wondered, that was one reason why the ancient creature had lived away from the world of men.

Once a Ss'iyn had flown, as a great bird, through the skies, away from his kind, on a mission of planetary discovery. Now a human being was walking back, towards his own species, with the task of rediscovering it. Jed was, however, a somewhat dishevelled one. After such a sudden and fairly violent adaptation from person to living glider, his shirt was in tatters and footwear, destroyed. He paused for a moment to bind his feet with what was left of his socks; now just a couple of fairly shredded tubes. There would need to be some thought, in future, regarding such items of clothing. Infinite possibilities might ensue. Perhaps someone, somewhere had invented a super-stretchy fabric, for eventualities like those that now seemed inevitable.

"Wakey, wakey!"

Chirped Hannah, closely and quietly, so as not to stir three men sleeping around the corner, with a bell-like tone, towards a rounded mass beneath Jed's covers, in the shades of the refuge. His outline remained motionless, clearly slumbering extremely deeply.

"Oy! I'm talking to you!"

…she verified, in a strangled whisper, hovering for a moment, awaiting some kind of reaction, and beginning to wonder if Jed was dead. Surely he should have awakened by now? He must be bluffing. He was well known for his practical jokes.

"What a lump! How rude and ignorant!"

…she grinned, beginning to lose the will to play along. After a further silence, she aimed a pillow at his head. The penny dropped before she could think about peeling-back the covers. He wasn't there.

"Where the hell have you gone?"

…she battled, internally, fighting for an explanation.

"I'll bet he couldn't sleep and went outside."

This seemed a fairly logical assumption, if his recent excess of energy was anything to go by.

Things were still a little chilly but no longer like the Antarctic. Although it was fairly early, the sun was already quite high and easing temperatures. Jed was nowhere to be seen. Hannah made a circuit of the refuge, scanning each horizon as she progressed. Where was he? Perhaps he was hiding inside the lodge after all. This had to be the only rational explanation left.

Behind the heavy, external door, Miguel, who had heard some of the whispers, was already on his feet, having already checked all remaining spaces, indoors. He emerged from the hut, propping open the door, to access the attention of those inside and out…

"He's not hiding in here."

He was met with grave silence. Hannah's heart sank. This was serious. Jed had never walked in his sleep. He was usually sensible and rational. Nothing made any sense. Miguel checked-out the other men who were all snoring simultaneously; one like an industrial vacuum cleaner. All cupboards and corners were investigated. All possibilities were explored or assessed. Eventually, he conceded what they had all been thinking, in a low, dry whisper…

"I believe Jed has gone to climb this mountain".

Joe, who had slept heavily, all night, and awoken to find that he couldn't walk, and was now the unfortunate owner of a brightly coloured and swollen ankle, jetted-out a huge sigh.

"As if things could get much worse!?"

They shushed him with separate measures of compassion. Fr Murphy, who's health was still a concern, directed some heavily enunciated, whispered consonants at him…

"Stay positive. Certainly, Jed has common sense and regard for others. He wouldn't want to trouble us, and he can look after himself. There'll be an explanation that none of us have thought of. He'll be alright."

Hannah began to erupt. Before she could raise her voice, Miguel whispered firmly…

"Let's take this outside, so we don't wake the gentlemen."

They all arrived in the sunshine, using a variety of means. Fr Murphy rolled from his back into recovery position, found his feet and sauntered slowly, like a zombie. Hannah stormed out like a perplexed schoolgirl. Miguel stood, attempting to encourage silence amongst them, with careful body language and expressions, whilst Joe slithered across the floor, dragging his tightly-bandaged ankle, behind him.

Outside the door, Miguel took control of proceedings.

"OK what we do know is that Jed is not here. What we don't know is exactly which way he went, but the odds say he has climbed the mountain. What reasons would he have to go downwards on his own? We have a helicopter in about an hour. With that, we will be able to look for him. He has bright colours on him, which will be visible, for sure. Let's all try to…"

He was interrupted rather abruptly by Hannah who was impetuous with her emotions…

"Why would he do this?"

Fr Murphy stepped-in, struggling to breathe between sentences and wincing with head pains…

"Understanding feelings, intellectually, is one thing, but we don't really appreciate anyone's actions until we fully comprehend their emotional state. Sure Jed might have thought a bit more before he did this, but it's important to understand rather more, how he was feeling before he set-off."

"What about *our* feelings?"

…complained Hannah.

"Yeah…"

…seconded Joe.

"…He can't have understood *us* all that well if he's swanned-off like that."

Fr Murphy continued…

"We must be careful how we treat him when he returns and not let anger cloud our judgements. I know you're worried and a bit angry…"

He too was cut-off, mid-sentence, as Hannah, who could still not contain herself, nor find any patience to listen to philosophy, burst-in with…

"Angry?"

…she snarled…

"I'm absolutely bloody livid! How stupid and thoughtless can a person be? I'm sorry, but I can't just sit here talking about it."

This time it was Miguel who interrupted.

"And what will you do? You go one way and he's probably gone the other. We *have* to wait. We have to wait for the copter and try to be calm. In an hour, we'll be able to look *with* it."

There seemed to be nothing else to say. There was not much that could be done, either. Joe pivoted on his rear end, attempting to pull open the door from ground level.

"Here… let me get that."

…said Fr Murphy, assisting him.

Inside, Miguel began to prepare some food. As he did so, he thought of Jed, who probably would not have eaten for some time. It had been something of a façade, which Miguel had employed, to instil calm. Internally, he was wildly concerned. He had been forced to summon an air rescue for a sufferer of altitude sickness, who perhaps should not have been allowed to climb so high. He had also allowed a snow fight to proceed, which had caused an individual to crack their ankle. As if two serious issues were not enough, he now had a third. As most people would probably have done, he reasoned as to how things so often happen in triplicate. Jed's departure from the group was now, by far, the most serious of his problems. Fr Murphy arrived to console him and make a hot drink.

"Don't you worry, Padre. You need rest."

…advised Miguel, doing his best to maintain a whisper, although the levels of snoring going on, next door, would surely even mask-out even canon-fire. Fr Murphy was having none of Miguel's suggestion and began to make coffee.

"Don't you take all the blame, Miguel. A lot of it rests with me. It's my influence that's got us up here in a bit of a rush. If I hadn't been so insistent, you might have been able to plan things a bit better. For instance, I probably wouldn't be here… likely none of the rest of it would have happened, either."

Miguel looked unmoved.

"It's not blame that worries me, Father. It's the facts. I have a missing person and two casualties."

Fr Murphy continued to console.

"Well look at me, things aren't perfect here, but I'm still on my feet. Count me as just half of one."

"You need to get off this mountain soon."

…came a dry reply. Fr Murphy finished the coffee, patted Miguel on the shoulder and cleared-off, realising that the only solution would be to have everybody rescued and Miguel to be able to deal with what had happened.

Food took little time to cook and even less time to demolish, after which, there was not much to do. Any form of entertainment was out of the question and beyond anyone's interest. The atmosphere became like a doctor's waiting room, punctuated by constant snoring. It was a wonder how their neighbours slept so deeply, given the disturbances they had provided. At one point, Joe felt compelled to ask if they'd ever been to bed before.

Extra to sitting and looking at one another, continual visits ensued, checking horizons for any sign of Jed. There were far more gazes up the hill than down. It seemed obvious that he must have attempted to tame the beast on his own. Finally, Miguel's radio burst into life. Their helicopter was about twenty-five minutes away.

"Oh, come on Jed!"

…implored Hannah, in an exasperated tone, on her way outside, in an attempt to will him back before another rescue had to be made. As she leaned, with her back against the lodge's cold, metallic walls, having calmed-down a little, tender feelings and memories flooded her heart. Even despite negative circumstances, this seemed a suitable time to reflect on her connection with Jed. Something told her that she couldn't have reasoned about everything, just yet. Fr Murphy might have been correct in what he was saying. She had known Jed for long enough to see that he was generally a caring, rational and communicative individual. Surely there was something here that she'd missed. He may have been a fool, but that alone might not be enough to destroy everything they had built together. A sense of yearning seemed to triumph over all other emotions. She stood, fixated upon the slopes above her, pleading for him to return.

Jed had plenty of time to contemplate his re-entry into a world of people. The first part of it had surely got to be awkward. However, he had reasoned, at some time during his life, that it was often better simply to endure the fury of those one had upset. Perhaps he should allow them to vent most of their ire first, before embarking upon any sort of explanation. In this case, his clarification of events would certainly be even more awkward than the apologies. However, this was not the same Jed who had ascended the mountain. It seemed that he now possessed a superior abilities, with which to calm himself and prepare for such circumstances. He would reunite himself with his friends silently and bear the strain of any rage. Only after they had bared their feelings and concerns would he attempt to explain that he had been called from the other side of the world, by a creature which had lived for millions of years, and received memories of an intelligent species, which had dwelt upon Planet Earth, long before humans. After the dust from that had settled, if it ever did, he would have to convince them to help him use his gifts to change the world. He was fairly confident that he would be able to convince them about this improbable truth, but not so convinced that they would still be there to persuade. Miguel would have to ensure his injured team members were taken to safety, as soon as possible. Still assuming they would be at the hut, he had chosen to rendezvous with them, as the Jed they would recognise. He had no wish to frighten them, via any other form. He moved quickly. Beyond the brow of a hill, the refuge was visible, some distance below him; it's crimson walls, glinting in the sunlight. His encounter would be soon.

Hannah heard Jed before she saw him. Above the silence and stillness, a sound of distant, clattering rockfalls, pinpointed his tiny figure, high above her. A broad smile lit-up her face. He seemed to be moving unusually quickly. It would not be long before he reached her. For a brief while, her tensions eased. Her worries were over. Then, gradually, as she tracked him with her gaze, descending to safety, her thoughts slithered back to realisations of what he'd had actually done. Irritation returned.

Jed was relieved to glimpse Hannah, waiting for him. He was not too late, but as he approached, it was clear by her body language of folded arms and head, slightly tilted, that his reception might be anything approaching hostile.

"That doesn't look good!"

...he mumbled to himself.

As Hannah registered his shredded shirt and bootless feet, she mumbled to herself...

"What the hell's happened to him?"

His poor appearance seemed to add to her annoyance. She prepared an intimidating expression for him, intending to make him work for any mercy she might show. There were no plans to concede any. Jed arrived and stood some distance away from her, awaiting her reactions. He looked down at his dusty, dishevelled socks and dilapidated top half, feeling more like a child, in lots of trouble. Before he could raise his head again, Hannah commenced her firework display. It was almost a relief to be getting it over with.

"Don't imagine you're a hero or anything. I doubt there's any explanation you can give me or *them...*"

She gestured towards the hut, behind her...

"...that'll be good enough for anyone!"

She raised her pitch, melodramatically...

"What were you doing, Jed? What on Earth were you thinking of?"

She stormed inside, floundering with the tricky doorhandle; spoiling her drama somewhat. Jed was gifted no time to answer. He hung back, expecting a cohort to emerge from the hut, at any moment. Sooner than that, they had assembled before him, as though about to watch a play. Joe performed his usual trick of adding to the severity of things...

"You are in *so* much trouble, bro."

Hannah fixed him with a terrifying expression, that scorched his ego. Fr Murphy took the opposite road and welcomed him back...

"Good to see you, still in one piece, Jed. Can't say the same for your clothes, though!"

Miguel took an uncharacteristically, firm stance...

"Why did you do this Jed? You put us all in a very difficult position. It's not the most clever thing you ever did. Good you're OK, for sure, but you'd better see how things could have been different."

There was a painful pause. Jed felt an unusually, powerful empathy for his friends. He had caused them all to worry, and placed Miguel in a particularly unenviable position. Joe and Fr Murphy had suffered enough, even without his mysterious disappearance. It took a lot to make Hannah angry. Now he had dented what had been so special. After all these people had done to help him over the last few months, they had been forced to endure a difficult end to all they had aspired for, themselves. He felt pity for them. Then he pinched himself. In truth, it was not actually his fault. He was coerced by unique forces, which had pulled him across a planet, compelling him to ascend a mountain. Now he understood the context of it all. This was the needs of the many over the few. Jed knew that there was no reason for him to bear any guilt.

Fr Murphy broke the lull with quiet diplomacy…

"I suspect, Jed, that *now* might be a suitable time for you to attempt some sort of explanation."

He began cautiously, paving himself something of a way forward…

"This is *not* going to be easy…"

He was immediately interrupted by his brother…

"That's because *you've* made it difficult for yourself! It's simple for us. We *know* where you went and we're pretty sure you weren't thinking of anyone else when you did it!"

His voice increased in pitch as he spoke, relieving himself of some recent stress. Today was certainly a day of amateur dramatics. Jed continued, unpredictably calmly…

"Maybe you're right. Maybe I didn't try to stop myself. Maybe I couldn't?"

Hannah added some crossfire…

"Couldn't stop yourself climbing the High Andes in the middle of the night, leaving your stricken friends sleeping in their beds while you swanned-off just to add to your own personal bucket list? Really, Jed… do we mean that little to you?"

Jed carried on with his preamble, expecting and even embracing the fierce interjections that continually punctuated it. His colleagues were providing him with a perspective as to where he stood with them…

"Of course you mean a lot to me…"

He looked at all of them in turn.

"…but you're all going to have to dig deep here. None of this is easy to say. You know me better than this. I don't just do things without sparing a thought for other people around me. It's just, you won't believe what I have to tell you…"

"No we probably won't!"

…heckled Joe. Fr Murphy, whose mind was always open, butted-in. He was genuinely looking forward to this particular explanation, which still hadn't managed to get off the ground.

"Can we let the boy speak?"

Hannah was determined to put in a final word…

"Go on then. Try us!"

She folded her arms again, eye-balling him intensely, attempting to make life as difficult as possible."

"Okay. Here it is. Don't say I didn't warn you."

He cleared his throat and began an unenviable elucidation…

"I was called across the world for this. You might think this was all Fr Murphy's doing, but it was more than that. I was summoned here by a superior being who resided at the top of this mountain."

Hannah and Joe turned to look at one another. A few moments passed. Hannah gasped, with a tear in her eye. Was it possible that Jed might be struggling somehow with his mental health?

"Oh Jed."

…whimpered Hannah…

"Please tell us this is one of your sad little jokes. I think I'd rather be facing that than anything else".

She slumped, fairly heavily, against the walls of the hut, sniffing and just about staving-off weeping. Jed was resolute…

"It's not a joke. It's all completely real."

Joe gasped…

"Jed. Steady on. Think about all this. It's OK. We'll forgive you. Just think about what you're telling us. No-one wants to see this. Bruv… come back to us!"

Jed modelled a reassuring smile and pointed to his own head…

"Have no fear. We're all okay in here."

Referring to himself in the plural, might not have been the best idea, given the context. He prepared to continue enlightening them, but then noticed that Joe was squeezing some sort of rubber ball. He had encountered students at his former school doing this to relieve stress or assist concentration and tended to carry it with him, wherever he went, for the same purposes. Jed's account was going nowhere. He decided to change tack…

"Throw me that ball, bro.

Joe was puzzled, but neither reasoned nor questioned. His aim was never great; certainly not on this occasion. Things were awkward, with a gammy leg. It was also tricky to direct a projectile from a sitting position. The ball hurtled upwards at a steep angle, jetting well above Jed's reach. Before he could think, he had reacted, although that part of it *was* expected. In an instant, he had sprouted an extensive, slender arm, with a hand as large as a baseball glove. He clasped the ball immediately, before rapidly dragging it back down to earth. All of this, with a single, sudden impulse from his will.

"Talk about needing a demonstration!"

...grinned Jed, nonchalantly.

"Do we need to see more?"

Heads shook from side to side in confused silence. Not one of them didn't wonder if there hadn't been something strong in their coffee. Tables had turned so quickly. Now it was them questioning their sanity. It was for this reason that Joe asked for another trick...

"It's not that I don't believe you, bruv, but could you produce another trick just so I can be sure it's not me who's seeing things, after all that?"

Jed was anxious to explain his feelings and the status of things...

"I think these gifts are meant to be used when they're needed and convince people of stuff they might not believe without a bit of magic. Just so you know, I'm not a freak or a circus animal. I'm one of you; just carrying something very unique and precious."

Hannah's expressions had warmed, considerably, though they were mostly still blended with bewilderment. How on Earth could any of this possibly be reality, yet it seemed clear to her that Jed was telling the truth. Why would he not have unleashed something as stunning as this before, if he was able? The main thing that concerned her was their future. These new truths had huge implications. These gifts would definitely attract mass public attention. Jed had already suggested that he would need to use them, perhaps, to persuade people about change. What might that mean for her? Some people could be cruel. She stood silently watching the young man she thought she had known, wondering what would become of them both. Although most people might be fairly keen to see what else he was capable of, she had reasoned that there would be a lot more time to witness his tricks in the future, and reassured him...

"I won't need to see any more, Jed. I'm sorry we couldn't believe you before. I guess we all feel the same."

Jed nodded with a beam and thanked her. Miguel added his own respect…

"I'm sorry too, Jed. I guess it was hard to believe, for sure. I guess we've all learned something big about the world we live in."

"As I said…"

Began Fr Murphy…

"Always keep the back door open!"

Miguel turned around, inspecting the refuge door. He had to be prompted as to what sort of door Fr Murphy was actually discussing and what was a metaphor. Fr Murphy was keen to hear as much as he could about Jed's experiences, the ancient creature and everything else. Everything about this was a few horizons beyond fascinating. After Jed had explained all he could about his dream, his excessive energy, his climb, the receiving of memories and gifts from an entire species and the use of them on his descent, some pieces of the puzzle became clear. Fr Murphy was somewhat excited to think that the Ss'iyn had influenced himself somehow, to bring them all to the correct part of South America. In truth it had been the recounting of Jed's dream, which had sparked the idea of climbing a faraway volcano, but obviously no coincidence that they had ended-up in exactly the right place. It was as though the Ss'iyn had always known about him and his links with Miguel. He found great excitement in the thought that an incredible, primeval being, had actually been listening to his mind and guiding his movements.

Jed left them for a moment. They assumed he was spending a penny or something. At the same moment, three travellers emerged from the hut, on their way back down the mountain. They had decided that their collective energy was lacking a little. Their exertions during the storm had sapped them considerably. Silent, physical exchanges were made between the parties as they tramped, slowly downwards, northwards, back towards the desert, having no idea what they had just missed, outside. A mystified lull ensued, as Joe, Hannah, Miguel and Fr Murphy looked at one another, somewhat blown-away by what they had just witnessed. It seemed that they had so much to learn about their own world and life itself. However, all were still pinching themselves to check if there was a possibility they might still wake up. There wasn't much time to stand, being bewildered. In just a few moments, the heavy door began to reopen. An extraordinary-looking creature, emerged. It stood before them; essentially a humanoid in profile, but scaly and mottled with variants of turquoise and green. Its glossy, marble-like eyes were large, in proportion to other features, and very expressive. Its head tilted back and forth, seeming to communicate in complex signals, with blinks and hand movements. So much could be expressed, without the use of sound. Then came, perhaps, the most profound part. Despite the fact that no words were formed, each of them heard it inside their heads.

"Don't be alarmed. It's only me! I have become the ancient creature, so you can see and understand."

Even if they had not noticed Jed disappearing inside the refuge, they would certainly have known it was him. His essence was now right there, inside each of them. The Ss'iyn had found a way, not only to communicate internally, but even to create connections inside each other's minds. Jed was able to make this real for them in some small part, though it seemed, as far as the ancient creature had been concerned, that quite some evolving would have to ensue amongst the human race for others to be suitable for receiving such gifts as he had. He began to build for them, an understanding of life as it had existed, deep in the past, on their own planet, though he could not possibly impart to them what he had, himself. The ancient creature had waited long to find him. Jed's communication was fluid, bypassing any awkwardness of words or physical distraction. He chose to speak *as* the Ss'iyn, delivering his communication from rich recollections of theirs…

"We were an ancient race, long before the marker you call an extinction event…"

All of them were familiar with the great asteroid that savaged the planet, extinguished huge amounts of life and altered the balance of all things, some sixty-five million years, previously. Even if they had not, somehow they were gifted with memories of great fires in the sky and a dark and tortured world. They felt it and understood it.

"Before this event, we resided in the Canyon of the Great Rainbow, at peace with our world. For eons we lived to build our energies and ideas. Each other's contentment was our own. We found our happiness in the provision of well-being for each other. Our race was compact but stable. We were few in number, with no significant need to procreate. This we did at pivotal moments in our history, often when loved-ones departed. We maintained ourselves, not multiplied, with no threat to our environment, safe from the beasts that devoured one another and diminutive prey, such as ourselves.

Our pursuits were spiritual. We sought a harmony which graces a life, completely at one with the world around it. We had no material worth nor aspirations to harness it. All we needed was with us and inside one another. In time we had nurtured a living network of memory, knowledge, ability and conjecture. Our excitement was born of building our collective ideas and abilities. All we had ever been, remained and grew into the future of our species. Towards the close of our race's existence, a few of us developed special gifts. It was as though nature had rewarded us for our continuous accord, whilst so much else was about to be destroyed. It seems that to dwell in calmness and care for so long is to hone an existence that can yield new charms and a greater connection with the universe.

Then came the Great Cataclysm. We had tracked a light, on the horizon of the heavens, from the rim of our canyon, for much time, before it arrived. Over many cycles it grew, until darkening the firmament. When it came, it was terrible for all. Our skies were alight with flame. All life ran uselessly, together, from its path, only to be extinguished. That which survived, perished amongst the poisoned darkness that followed. We sat and mourned, for our history was complete. Our world was sick and tainted with death. But some of us possessed a gift. Those who did not, could still rejoice that our legacy would continue, and so it has. Now we are alive inside your race.

You are creatures of great potential. You have learned to cross the skies and even the heavens beyond, but you have not discovered the extents of the cosmos within your own intellect. You have spent so much time looking outwards, and conforming to what you see in others, that you forget who you really are, yourselves. You do not know what you are truly capable of and stand alone in your singular minds. Because you are so keen to procreate, you have multiplied and now threaten this world, which will soon not support you. You have worked hard to preserve your species, up to a point where it is now a threat. Once the legacy of our kind was saved by our gifts. Now it is time to use them again for the same reason."

Jed disappeared, once more, inside, and resurfaced as himself. This was necessary for a purpose they might just have reasoned, had he transmuted back to himself in front of them. This way he had clothes on!

"That was truly awesome!"

...bellowed Joe...

"For some reason, I can now remember dinosaurs, recall the great meteor we read about at that museum place, on holiday, and see things happening in the Mesozoic Era."

"Cool, isn't it?"

...grinned Jed.

"Plenty more memories to hand-out, here. What I didn't tell you all was that the creature departed its life in this world after he gave them all to me. He had lived so long and believed he would be with his friends again, somehow, on another plane of existence."

There was so much to debate, here and so much to take-in, but surely their minds would now be far more open to possibilities they had formerly refused to entertain. That alone might expand their capacities to think, in future. Miguel stepped forward to converse with Jed.

"I get it all now. Makes me feel good that it wasn't all my fault. You guys had to come here, somehow. Now I know why you climbed a mountain in the middle of the night, and something tells me when you get famous, I'll be able to talk my way out of the trouble I might've been in."

"All's well that ends well?"

...nodded Jed, warmly, communicating a lot more compassion and gratitude than the words, with his expressions, but coining a bit of a cliché.

"So your energy, Jed..."

...inquired Miguel

"...when you were running up hills and all around us, was it this ancient creature that gave you the power, somehow?"

Fr Murphy had arrived, still looking, and feeling, pretty terrible.

"It gave him his energy, so he could get up the hill to visit him. Is that right, Jed?"

Jed nodded. Miguel continued further...

"If that's right, why can't you give some of that energy to Fr Murphy, here?"

Jed responded apologetically...

"I'm afraid it doesn't seem to work like that. I can alter things about myself and transform to get me out of a mess. I can empathise with people and even communicate inside their minds, but I can't give them what I have. Sorry!"

"If you ask me..."

...began Fr Murphy...

"...the creature you showed us, knows it would be bad to interfere with our evolution too much; just in small doses, maybe. In my profession, you have to believe that we're all here for a reason, to prove something. If you start handing out gifts like that to everyone, it's like saying 'here's heaven everyone! Don't worry about all those things you were supposed to achieve in this life, to earn it'. I think he was doing the right moral thing."

"Sounds good..."

Conceded Jed...

231

"Or maybe he only had the ability to transfer his gifts to just one lifeform?"

"No need to flatten the ethical debate!"

...retorted Fr Murphy. After this, he put on his *serious* hat.

"We have a lot to do, now, Jed. And I mean *we*. I believe I was called to help you. You'll not be alone in this. I have a friend or two who can get us an audience with local councils, then maybe we can take it from there. Meanwhile I suggest we all take an oath to keep this secret. Who knows what might happen if rumours start circulating in public. You could be inundated..."

"Say no more."

...assured Jed.

"I get the picture. You're so useful, Fr. You have a lot of useful friends too."

He directed this comment at Miguel, who beamed at him warmly.

There was a short conflab between them, regarding confidentiality. Fr Murphy explained very well, some important reasons for such secrecy. It would be necessary for Jed to disclose his knowledge and power, only through correct, official channels. They were all sworn to a pledge, but it would be particularly difficult for Miguel to explain things to his colleagues whilst concealing certain truths. For a while, he would have to shoulder blame and bear criticism, until a time when the world's eyes were opened to those revelations he had witnessed. On that day, when implausible reports appeared on Chilean news, for his colleagues to observe, he would be able to say...

"That's why we had an ancient priest come all the way to us, across the world, with a special young man, his brother and girlfriend, to climb the world's highest volcano, rendezvous with a creature as old as the dinosaurs, then attempt to change history."

For now, even if Miguel wasn't sworn to silence, it seemed highly unlikely that anyone could possibly accept any excuse, including such facts. He would surely have to face some awkward procedures, upon his return.

A muted, throbbing drone, eased-into their general soundscape, until consciously perceptible, then recognisable as the rotor blades of a helicopter. At that point, Miguel's radio burst into life again, with distorted, Hispanic voices, haling an approach. Miguel gave immediate instructions to fetch all gear, quickly, warning...

"The copter will have to make a landing. Air is a bit thin up here for its fuel mix. It won't hover and they won't want to stay long. We should be ready".

In fairness, he'd already made them collect and organise the heavier parts of their gear to make these moments efficient. Despite certain members of the group requiring careful assistance, they were in and out of the refuge reasonably speedily, whilst the helicopter blasted it with fine powder, on its way down to earth. In double-quick time, a couple of brightly-dressed individuals burst out and jumped to the ground with a stretcher. Joe was swiftly helped into it. After some brief exchanges of dialogue, Fr Murphy was handed an oxygen mask and helped into it by Miguel. Within a very short period of military-style precision, they were 'good to go'. Their copter eased-up, once again spraying clouds of ice, across the landscape, before blasting forwards, away from the mountain. Amidst clanking and intense vibration, Jed perceived, what seemed to be, hordes of people in large parties, on the slopes below, wending their way upwards towards the hut. It was as though all things, everywhere, had suddenly sprung back into life.

"Yeah… that's the way it should be up here!"

…yelled Miguel, leaning over his shoulder, raising his dynamic to compete with intense engine noise. It had not taken much for Jed to reason why this might be. It seemed that someone might have been keeping things quiet for a good reason. Even with special gifts bestowed upon himself, however, it was tough to understand how that particular, single creature had possessed so much influence, even across such significant distance. He projected thoughtful feelings towards the sky, in a vain attempt to wish the Ss'iyn an eternally serene existence, with long-lost friends. He marvelled at the enormity of his own recent encounter and its significance regarding the future of himself and the planet. He mulled upon what he might become and how long his life might now endure, within a world where he knew of no other lifeforms that might enjoy such longevity. Wave upon wave of revelations hit him, hard, as he descended, rapidly towards the Atacama Desert. Could it be that he might just outlive Hannah by so much time? He looked long and hard at her, across the aircraft, willing circumstances to keep them together, somehow. He needed her to want the same, and willed the time forward when they would be able to talk and console one other. Somewhere inside his heart, he felt that there would be a way to make things work.

It seemed obvious to Jed that he was now destined to achieve some level of renown. He pined for those quiet times he had enjoyed in peaceful, eastern flatlands, but simultaneously welcomed a chance to do something hugely significant for the rest of his kind and their remarkable world. Although his predicament was daunting, it might yet have been the best thing ever to happen to him or anybody else. It seemed that the moment he was presently passing through, was also a good one in which to say goodbye to his former life. From now on, his existence would have to be more about others than himself. He searched deep within and bathed himself in the code of the Ss'iyn, who's entire existence seemed to have been about reaching out to one another and their environs. Surely rescuing the planet would have to include such obvious things as conserving natural environments, planting trees, recycling waste and so on, but so many people seemed to be either already doing this or else completely ignoring advice. One way or another, the planet was already suffering a crisis, thanks to obvious historical neglect and abuse. Jed mused that part of a program for improving the world significantly should also encompass helping one another find wellbeing, as the ancient creature had described. If people could learn to think of one another first, perhaps something special might happen, such as a sharp increase in general happiness. People who feel loved and accepted can often approach their community and environment with a more positive attitude. How hard might it be to instigate things like these? World peace and communal happiness had always seemed like a distant dream. Notable figures and world leaders had been trying for millennia. People were stuck in ways and routines. Perhaps, however, as the ancient creature had implied, if Jed was to demonstrate unusual powers and also show them what the Ss'iyn had achieved, their attentions would be awoken. If they also found out that such gifts of metamorphosis and telepathy had once been awarded by nature to those who had practised such positive and empathetic ways of living, they might even be motivated into addressing their own lifestyles. All this aside, Jed was already aware of a more pressing issue that would need to be addressed. It had been a fascination of his for some time. He recalled a statistic, that modern humanoids had resided on his planet for a fifth of a million years, yet their population had suddenly almost quadrupled to nearly eight billion since nineteen-twenty-eight. This kind of growth of a species that acts so furiously with its environment, was surely the greatest risk of all, yet how little it seemed to have been addressed. So much advice on green issues but so little evidence of anything advising how much the human race was obviously procreating. There was much to find out from those in the world who possessed answers, and those who had the power, authority and regard for life and health, who could execute a plan, in which Jed might be the central inspiration. The time ahead was an ocean of questions. Great powers within him were a ray of hope, but for now he would practise his newfound abilities simply to stay calm and focussed, and find a way.

CHAPTER 19

Deep in a future

A truly gargantuan edifice, known as 'The Memorial Building of the First Children', dominated a busy metropolis, with elegance and splendour. It was a cathedral of nature, mastered by humans who had long-since learned how to reside in tune with their surroundings and use its forces to guide their actions and creations. It was a living shrine, dedicated to those who, epochs previously, had embraced their natural stance in a similar way. High in the sky atop the edifice, was a special garden. Consorts of magical florae burst, like iridescent flame, amongst twisting, glossy shoots and darkly shaded crevices, out of which sprang dragon-like roots and fireflies. Within a blanket of spray and steam, hung a vibrant rainbow, adorning a bubbling pool, fed by a smooth, creamy cascade that poured from an overhang above dark, dampened rocks. A disturbingly large lizard was poised, motionless, somewhat resembling a rugged rock. It bathed in intense rays of sunshine, pouring through gaps in vegetation.

By the pool, a youthful-looking man, sat brooding on daily matters, whilst feasting on spectacular views of a thickly forested city, far below him in distant haze. The prodigious shrine, from which he enjoyed such a panorama, marked the centre of all suburbia roundabout. The metropolis itself had been constructed in concentric circles, each separated by natural woodland, through which local fauna wandered at will, largely undisturbed by any hustle or bustle, that might take place inside or beneath the city's buildings. Below ground was a complex network of mobile pavements, linking each part, even each dwelling, and connecting with other settlements around the

235

globe. These automated pathways were propelled at speeds appropriate to their connections. Those which led towards other places, beyond city fringes, could attain significant velocities, with such silent, effortless ease, that one could travel great distances with barely a notion of personal displacement. Each subterranean route was encased with walls that offered virtual views of whatever was currently above the surface, relayed by multiple visual devices and intelligent technology which circled the planet, on the edges of space. Those using the grid, could request a route which would guide them anywhere around it, for commerce or pleasure; even simply to join with others and share ideas, via a form of travel that yielded no contaminating fumes. All was pure and clean. The surface of the world had long, since begun to regenerate. Food could be perfectly synthesized, as could many other commodities. Industry was minimal and muted.

In a world of such favourable balance, there was a freshness that had once been absent. The ether of Earth was rich and oxygenated, fed by exhalations of expansive forests across its surface. Its waters were untainted crystal. The ground itself yielded flora as diverse as the beasts that walked and fed upon it. Humans seemed to have found their equilibrium, working their movements and technologies in harmony with their planet. Nature's essence was perceptible on the breath of the wind, in the warming rays of the sun, and in the unruffled stability of all elements in peaceful accord. Once more, Earth was a jewel.

The young man eased himself up from a large, smooth boulder, which had supported him throughout his meditation. His expression conveyed a radiance of wellbeing. His heart pulsed calmly with a rhythm of serenity. He had every reason to be happy. All was well. His work had proven fruitful. His world had listened and engineered ways forward, heeding his unignorable examples. Now there was space in peoples' lives to converse and deliberate, or else simply sit and soak-up an untarnished environment. There was time to focus on life's direction and determine a way forward. There was also time to dwell in open air, amongst cosmic energy, away from the containment of buildings and virtual technology.

In the young man's head were thoughts and feelings of others, to whom he could listen, more easily, from the calm of a lofty roof garden. Cherished above all, were those of family and friends he had known and loved, in ages gone by. They had touched his spirit somehow, when he had learned to focus more deeply on worldly echoes. He felt their contentment, then it was his, too. Within his own mind, he was never alone. He strode intently forwards, to the tower's edge. A strong breeze rushed upwards from suburbia, far beneath, to greet him. A contented smile, spread across his countenance. He jumped. Forces of Earth pulled him quickly downwards. Turbulent airstreams embraced his sinking mass. Then, with a singular will, he was airborne.

Great forests spread all ways, before him. Beyond city limits, for considerable distances, lay unchallenged wilderness. He sailed for a great time outwards, on colossal but graceful wings, gliding effortlessly through dwindling light, towards a glittering, western ocean. This would be the way forward now. He would travel far and wide, listening eternally, to the voices of his planet. He would remain endlessly attentive to universal energies. Always, he would carry within him, the spirits of his friends.

Once, a great bird battled bravely, navigating with her heart through bitter blackness, towards faded prospects of safety and deliverance. Now, another soared gracefully through boundless light and warmth, towards prospect and hope.

POSTSCRIPT

Your spirit is like a bird
Soaring in an ocean of feeling
Sometimes the rain
Sometimes the shine
All but one thing is certain
It'll triumph over time.
When your soul finds its end
And your time here is done
The colours of your life
Will rise in the dawn

Martin Power 1992

Printed and bound by CPI Group (UK) Ltd, Croydon, CR0 4YY